The Deathless

Also by Peter Newman

The Vagrant
The Malice
The Seven

Short Stories
The Hammer and the Goat
The Vagrant and the City

PETER NEWMAN

The Deathless

HARPER
Voyager

Harper*Voyager*
An imprint of HarperCollins*Publishers* Ltd
1 London Bridge Street
London SE1 9GF

www.harpercollins.co.uk

First published by HarperCollins*Publishers* 2018
1

A catalogue record for this book is available from the British Library

ISBN: 978-0-00-822898-9 (HB)
ISBN: 978-0-00-822899-6 (TPB)

Typeset in Sabon LT Std by Palimpsest Book Production Limited,
Falkirk, Stirlingshire

Printed and bound in the UK by CPI Group (UK) Ltd, Croydon CR0 4YY

MIX
Paper from
responsible sources
FSC
www.fsc.org
FSC® C007454

This book is produced from independently certified FSC™ paper to ensure
responsible forest management.

For more information visit: www.harpercollins.co.uk/green

For my friends,
who I really should see more often!

CHAPTER ONE

Vasin Sapphire had risen long before the three suns, unable to sleep nor act, waiting, like the rest of the castle, for the drums of the hunt to begin.

He wished it were otherwise, that experience had taught him how to be calm, allowed him to conserve his strength, but it was always the same, his nerves as much a part of the ritual as everything else. How many times had he participated in the hunt? How many lifetimes? To his surprise, he was hazy on the exact number.

But his body knew. An instinct made him tense, the muscles bunching as he held his breath. And sure enough, on the next beat of his heart, the first drum was played, a single, thunderous strike. Housed at the very centre of the sprawling castle, its reverberations were felt at every corner, through the stone and in the guts, echoing throughout as the note faded to make way for the next. This was the deepest drum of the set, and its beat would steadily quicken as time passed, signalling all to prepare for the hunt.

1

Vasin exhaled. Some of the tension he had been holding in his limbs released. He kept looking out of the window. The darkness remained, starless and black, a greater emptiness that echoed the one inside.

Clearly he should be getting ready now, but the motivation simply wasn't there. It was all he could do to resist lighting some Tack and inhaling its aroma of sweet oblivion. He'd been eking out his dwindling supply over the last year, taking just enough to bury his troubles.

But for all of his lack of motivation he didn't dare. The honour of House Sapphire was in his hands, and no matter his misery, no matter how far he had fallen, he was a Sapphire, blood, bones, and soul.

The deep drum sounded a second time. Servants would be flowing down corridors, their measured steps at odds with their excited faces.

Hunting was at the heart of everything. The road-born supplied the castles of the Deathless, and the Deathless kept them safe from the demons of the Wild. If the hunt failed, then all Vasin's people would suffer, the road-born from attack and the sky-born from starvation.

Though only he and his hunters would take flight, the whole castle would be present: the quality of the send off, it was believed, affected the hunt's chances of success. Everyone had their part to play, especially Vasin.

But am I ready? It was a question he asked each time he led a hunt, but rarely with such uncertainty. A memory of his first life arose, *him in another body, younger, nervous, his mother coming to his rooms to—*

He dismissed it with a growl. He would not think of his mother. Not now and especially not today.

One set of feet stopped outside his open door and a man's voice began singing for permission to enter. Without turning from the window, Vasin waved him in.

'May I, my lord?'

'Yes,' replied Vasin.

A moment later, he felt the teeth of a brush in his hair. It started low, at the small of his back, banishing tangles from the tips, and worked up, each pull of the brush growing longer. There was a symmetry between the brush strokes and the drum beats that pleased Vasin.

'I didn't send for you,' he mused aloud, and the brush hesitated halfway down his back. 'Continue. I'm not displeased. Who sent you?' he asked, curious. Who would know he had not requested assistance, and come to the conclusion that he needed some?

'Your brother, my lord. Lord Gada bade me aid your preparations and tell you that he is on his way.'

It was unusual to meet before a hunt. Whatever was bringing him here it was unlikely to be good. They'd barely spoken in the last year, but clearly his brother was still keeping an eye on him, enough to know that he wasn't grooming himself as he used to anyway. Vasin wondered what else Gada had seen and felt a twinge of shame as he regarded his room. The knowledge that a member of his family was arriving shortly threw the state of his quarters, and himself, into stark relief.

Vasin groaned, his brother always thought he knew best. 'How long do I have?'

The servant, who looked familiar in a way that suggested Vasin had seen him before, and if not him, some ancestor who looked similar, chose his words carefully.

'Lord Gada did not share that information with me, my lord.' The servant made an apologetic face. 'But if I were to guess, I would say he has already left his quarters.'

'In that case we had best get to work. There is no time to bathe, but I must be scented and dressed before Gada arrives, and all of this clutter must be gone.'

The servant looked about the room, dismayed. 'My lord.'

In the end it took the two of them to get everything straight, and Vasin had to spray the scented water over himself, then bind silk around his own chest, arms, and thighs, which was difficult, but by the time Gada entered, the illusion of serenity and cleanliness was established, betrayed only by the glistening sweat on the servant's brow.

The body his brother had taken in this incarnation was classic Gada. Tall, thin, lightly muscled, as if exercise was something to be sampled but not indulged in. The thick eyebrows and beard, both neatly trimmed, suited, adding weight to an otherwise ephemeral appearance.

Like all Deathless, Lord Gada Sapphire held his own castle and looked after his own settlements. Despite this, he had become a regular fixture of Vasin's life since their mother's exile. Gada was still playing the game, fighting to keep them both in High Lord Sapphire's favour. It was a fight he seemed destined to lose.

A slight flick of Gada's finger dismissed the servant. They were alone.

Gada's smile of greeting lacked sincerity, but then, it always had. It was why few trusted him and fewer warmed to him. If blood didn't tie them, Vasin doubted he'd be very fond of the other man either. It wasn't fair, because Gada had always looked after him, had taken his duties as elder brother seriously. Perhaps that was the problem. He'd always felt more like a duty to Gada than a loved one.

Vasin stood there, his habitual social ease failing him after years of disuse. Gada seemed afflicted by the same problem and so the brothers simply stared at one another, Gada's smile looking like it could flee the scene at any moment.

Meanwhile, adding to the tension, the space between each beat of the great drum grew steadily shorter. Soon, the second drummer would begin, and Vasin would have to leave.

'You look well,' said Gada.

'No I don't.'

Gada's smile faded away. 'No.'

'If you have something to say . . . '

'Yes.' He contradicted himself by pausing and Vasin felt frustration well up. His brother's surprise visit was stirring up feelings he'd worked hard to bury. Grief stirred within him like a beast coming out of hibernation. He'd isolated himself on purpose, hiding behind his walls, refusing to see people. And when that hadn't been enough, he'd used Tack, smoking himself into oblivion. Bad enough that he had to face the outside world today, but must he face the past as well? Why couldn't his brother just say whatever it was and leave?

Gada closed the space between them, casting a nervous glance over his shoulder as he did so. 'I was surprised to hear you had volunteered to lead the hunt.'

'And you weren't sure I was up to it?'

'This has to go well, Vasin.' His words were hushed,

conspiratorial. 'It's bigger than you or me. All eyes are on us now, from below and without, and across the other houses . . . After the last hunt failed, we—'

He'd heard about the failed hunt, the hunt that failed even to happen. Sorn, one of the Sapphire holdings belonging to Lord Rochant, had called for help against the Wild. Lord Rochant had been between lives at the time, and so it had fallen to Yadavendra, High Lord of the Sapphire, to oversee Sorn's protection. They'd made the proper sacrifice, followed tradition, but, for the first time in House Sapphire's history, the call had gone unanswered. Not only had the High Lord turned his back on them, he had forbidden the other Sapphire Deathless to get involved. Since then, nothing had been heard from Sorn, and a feeling of unrest had settled over the rest of the Sapphire provinces. Sagan had been the first settlement to call for aid since, and though Yadavendra hadn't responded personally, his silence allowed the others to take action.

'If it's so important,' said Vasin acidly, 'why doesn't High Lord Sapphire lead the hunt himself?'

Gada's expression was pained. 'He's still too disturbed by grief.'

'What?'

'Please don't, Vasin.'

'*He's* disturbed by grief? *He* is! What about us? What about our grief? She was our mother—'

The sound of the second drum cut off Vasin mid shout. Two beats, close together, following on the heels of the first drum. Gada spoke into the quiet that followed.

'Hunt well and thorough, brother.'

Vasin forced his fists to unclench. It wouldn't do to part

like this. He pulled Gada close, feeling the man stiffen before settling into an awkward embrace. 'I'm sorry,' he began, but his voice cracked and his throat tightened, swallowing the rest of the sentence.

'Sssh,' Gada said. 'Deal with the hunt today. I can wait till tomorrow, the court for a while after that. One thing at a time.' He peeled himself out of Vasin's grip as another beat of the drums reverberated through the castle. '*Hunt well and thorough.*'

Unable to speak, Vasin nodded and left the room. His eyes were blurry with tears but it didn't matter, he knew the way well enough, the hallways and rooms mapped over many lives.

With effort, he could push aside thoughts of the Sapphire High Lord and his brother, but the rage sat there, burning, like a hot coal in his chest.

It had been a glimpse, nothing more. The bottom half of a tunic and a pair of boots ascending a stairwell. One of the night guards doing the rounds.

Honoured Mother Chandni wandered to the bottom of the stairs, a frown spoiling her features. She knew all of the guards by sight and yet this one had seemed like a stranger. She also knew the routines of the castle as well as she knew the habits of the babe in her arms, and there were no change-overs due for at least an hour.

Still frowning, she continued up the stairs and stepped out onto the ramparts. It was still dark, the three suns some hours from rising, but Satyendra showed no signs of sleepiness. She felt the same. There was simply too much going on for her mind to rest.

A guard saluted her as she came into view. His name was Ji, one of the older ones. Ji was not the one she'd seen on the steps, they had moved too quickly, their stride that of a much younger man.

'Did another guard come this way?' she asked.

'No, Honoured Mother. It's just me and the cold out tonight.'

'You're sure?'

He nodded. 'Even the castle is quiet.'

'It's holding its breath. We all are.' It was Lord Rochant Sapphire's rebirth ceremony in the morning and they all wanted him back dearly. The halls had seemed empty since he'd gone between lives.

'When do you think he'll come back to us?' asked Ji.

'When he's ready. It's not for you to question the time or place.'

'Sorry, I just miss him.'

Chandni allowed herself a polite smile. 'We all do.'

It's time to replace Ji, she thought. *The man's losing his focus. I'll keep him on long enough for Lord Rochant to see him in uniform one more time, and then retire him.*

She made a slow circuit of the walls. Had she really seen that guard? It was dark and she was tired, perhaps she had imagined it? Chandni didn't believe that though. There was something in the air, a tension that she hoped was connected to Lord Rochant's return. But it wasn't hope she felt in her stomach. Satyendra stirred in her arms, uncharacteristically restless.

'You feel it too don't you?' she said softly. 'You're not alone. I doubt any of us will sleep easily tonight.'

Satyendra regarded her with dark eyes. He had always

been a quiet baby but there was something alert in his manner, a watchfulness that suggested a wise head rather than a vacant one.

'Somewhere over there,' she continued, pointing into the night, 'is another castle just like this, floating high in the sky. It belongs to Lord Vasin Sapphire. At dawn, he'll be hunting for demons in a place called Sagan. Normally your grandfather, Lord Rochant, would do it, but his soul is somewhere else, somewhere far, far away.'

All along the battlements were sapphire lanterns that took the sunslight of the day and turned it into a series of little blue halos. Chandni loved the constancy of their light almost as much as she loved the order of their placement, each painstakingly positioned the exact same distance from its neighbours, a visible testament to the perfection of House Sapphire. She found it much more impressive than the stars, strewn messily across the sky.

Only the greatest minds can create such order.

And Lord Rochant's castle was a beacon of order. Strong walls, symmetrical, smooth, polished so that the stone and sapphires shone. She had lived here her whole adult life and never felt safer or happier.

Her imagination re-conjured those feet on the stairs, unfamiliar, moving quickly, and she looked down into the courtyard, then across to the opposite wall, then either side of the ramparts.

Nothing.

The castle was as it always was. A fortress hanging impossibly in the sky, held aloft by ethereal currents and forgotten arts.

Safe and dependable and beyond the reach of demons.

The thought made her look in the other direction, out, over the edge of the battlements, away from safety.

Below, she could see miles and miles of unconquered woodland spreading in every direction: the Wild. Strange. Threatening. The very sight of it chilled her, and in the dark it was all too easy to imagine it growing, reaching out to engulf the road-born who dwelled on its perimeter.

She couldn't imagine living so close to death. *How do they sleep down there?* she wondered. *How do they bear it?*

Her eyes moved to the silver-blue ribbon sparkling in defiance of the dark: the Godroad. There were many paths through the Wild but the only safe ones were the Godroads. Relics from the Unbroken Age, each was built straight and true, cutting clean lines of glittering crystal through the trees, dividing the great forest into sections.

Chaos and order. The Wild and the Godroad. The demons and the Deathless.

She let the thoughts roll around in her mind, seeing the way one connected to the other. Like a set of dance steps repeated over and over, endless.

The road-born scavenged the forest, in part to provide for themselves, and in part to provide for people like Chandni.

Inevitably, their activities would catch the attention of the demons and a stalking would begin. After a while, a farm animal would vanish, or a child that had not listened to the warnings of their elders. When this happened, a village would call to their crystal lords for aid and the hunters would come, sending whatever it was back into darkness one way or another.

So it is with the people of Sagan. A cycle. Demons, sacrifice and then the hunt. Soon there will be order again.

But then, should it not also have been that way for the people of Sorn? Chandni shook her head sadly. High Lord Yadavendra had left Sorn to the mercy of the Wild. It was Lord Vasin, not Yadavendra, that was coming to Sagan's aid.

Things are not as they should be, she thought. *We need Lord Rochant back now more than ever.*

Satyendra shifted in her arms and she realized she'd been ignoring him for too long. She lifted him up so that he could see over the top of the battlements.

'Somewhere down there, the elders of Sagan will be choosing their tributes and sending them into the forest. Tributes are very brave, they draw out the demons so the hunters can get them.

'If you look closely, you might even see their lights. Each one carries a torch to guide the hunters to them.' Each one would also bear a fresh cut to lure the demons with their blood, but she didn't mention that.

There were complicated rules about the choosing of a tribute. Some villages would pick their best in the hope that they would survive, bringing honour to all involved. Others would pick their worst, as the hunt was the neatest way to deal with undesirables. For a pariah, such an outcome could be a second chance. More than once, Chandni had heard tales of criminals volunteering to become a tribute in an effort to be forgiven for past crimes.

'Though the Wild is cruel, my Satyendra, our world is fair. The road-born can rise all the way up here, if they are able enough. Lord Rochant proved that when he became Deathless.

And even the Deathless can fall if they betray us. The traitor, Nidra Un-Sapphire, and the previous High Lord, Samarku Un-Sapphire, proved that when they made deals with the Wild. So you have to be perfect in all that you do and never bend, for when crystal bends, it shatters.'

Satyendra's eyes attended her as she spoke. *He is such a bright little thing.* Chandni knew he could not understand her yet, but she liked talking to him and believed that, on some level, the spirit of her words was sinking in.

'Our thoughts are with Lord Vasin and his hunters tonight. *May they hunt well and thorough.*'

When Satyendra gave a soft gurgle, she took it as agreement and planted a kiss on his forehead.

The rest of her walk passed peacefully, and soon she was back where she'd begun, at the stairwell.

Satyendra yawned and, a moment later, she found herself stifling one of her own. If she went back to her chambers now, she might have time for a few hours of sleep before the rebirth ceremony.

She turned to give Ji a goodnight wave before going inside. He was not the man he used to be, but he had served loyally and she was fond of him.

Halfway through the gesture her hand stopped, confused. Ji was nowhere to be seen. His post empty.

Though she knew in her heart that things were bad, Chadni took the time to check Ji had not simply slipped away to relieve himself or take refuge from the cold. He had not. She checked again. Then she ran.

The Chrysalis Chamber was glass on three sides, letting sunlight pour into the space. Even on a dawn like this one, when only the weakest of the suns, Wrath's Tear, was peeking over the horizon, the heat was palpable, like a wall that Vasin had to press through.

Normally, sapphires adorned the back of the chamber, slowly spreading in pools of milky liquid, but on hunting days all was cleared away save for a single stand of armour and the two Gardener-smiths ready to help him change.

Each life that Vasin lived demanded a new set of armour, the crystals picked and grown by the Gardener-smiths the day his newest vessel was chosen, taking years and a great deal of skill on the part of the smiths to form it to the individual and establish a firm bond to the body. Though he preferred to be reborn as an adult, Vasin had gone through several childhoods and could recall little more tedious than the long modelling sessions.

Luckily, his last rebirth avoided the whole mess, his descendant having reached maturity before the soul was replaced with Vasin's. This meant, thankfully, that it was his descendant, rather than him, that had spent several hours a day wearing each piece of crystal as it was grown and cut to fit.

It resulted in armour that fit so close and so naturally it was like skin.

More than that though, each set was grown from crystals harvested from the set before, and over time, they developed a personality of their own. For Vasin, putting the armour on was like reconnecting with the best part of himself. It was like coming home.

He raised his arms, assuming the ritual stance, and the Gardener-smiths took a little blood from his palms, daubing each piece with it, waking the crystal to his presence.

As the drum beats continued, nearing the point where the third and fourth drummers would join, the Gardener-smiths helped him into his Sky-legs, a pair of boots ending in long curving blades that would allow him to land safely, or bound easily into the air. Once mounted, he stood several feet higher than them. This was one of the things Vasin enjoyed most when hunting, the feeling of becoming something greater. Once, in better times, he'd talked about the feeling with his mother, and she'd told him it was the closest they came to being like the gods they were descended from.

The rest of the armour was then attached. He shivered as the crystal greaves were locked into place. At first he could feel them, cool against his calves, and then it was as if they had melted and become part of him.

Plates were attached to his thighs and groin, to his chest and shoulders, arms and hands. He turned his head from left to right, catching a glimpse of crystal wings, feather carved, curved and blade thin, sprouting from his back. Unlike those of birds, his were rigid.

At last a helm was placed on his head. Open-topped to let his hair spill out like a waterfall down his back, the crystal was thinned to give only the slightest tint of blue to his vision, and grown to leave breathing space at his nose and mouth.

Into his outstretched hands they placed a long silver-handled spear with a sapphire tip. His fingers moved naturally to the trigger set halfway down the shaft.

'Hunt well and thorough, my lord,' said the Gardener-smiths together, bowing low.

Vasin saluted them, pleased with their workmanship, and

made his way to the edge of the Chrysalis Chamber, being careful to take small steps so as not to engage his Sky-legs too early.

As he approached, the Gardener-smiths backed away and the glass went with them, sliding aside to allow him onto a balcony overlooking the central courtyard of the palace.

People had gathered below, their adoring faces peering up at him. A block of hunters stood in the centre, their spears and wings glinting proudly in the sunslight. They were armoured in leather, not crystal as he was, and their Sky-legs and wings were lesser, the most their limited skills could handle. It was not their fault, there was simply only so much that could be achieved in a single lifetime. Vasin did not judge his mortal followers for it as some did. In fact, it made him proud how far his people managed to get within so few years. According to his mother, Gada had taken two lifecycles to reach their standard.

About the hunters were their families, and about them a greater crowd of staff and visitors, traders and children. All were dressed in their finest, a shimmering display of silks and crystal, sparkling, joyous.

Vasin raised his spear, and the third and fourth drummers joined in, one deep like the first, and one lighter like the second. The resonance was growing, the faster beats beginning to build, forcing him to lean forward as his wings were pulled back by each wave of sound.

It would not be long now.

'Who has made the call?' he said, and it took all of his skill to project his voice high enough and far enough to be heard below.

'The people of Sagan!' came the choral reply. Sagan, a

sister settlement of Sorn. He wondered if the plight of one had become the plight of the other.

'And who has answered the call?'

'We have!' bellowed the hunters.

'Then there will be a hunt. And who will lead the hunt?'

'Vasin,' replied the crowd as one, 'Lord Vasin, Lord Vasin of the Sapphire Everlasting, it is he who leads the hunt.'

'And what will carry him through the Wild places?'

'We will!'

'And with what will you carry him?'

'With song and heart and blade and blood.'

'Prove it!'

And with that he leaped from the balcony.

The drums paused for the slightest part of a second, long enough for the crowd to take breath, and for Vasin to plunge down. He held his arms out, straight and still, and closed his eyes.

Wind whistled by, hurling back his hair.

Then the drums played again, all seven this time, a frenetic blast of sound, with the higher ones dancing over the lower, and the crowd's cheer blasting over that.

Each of the sounds came together to form a net, swelling beneath his wings.

There was a moment of utter weightlessness in the gasp that came between falling and soaring, like the moment between one life and the next, and then Vasin was skimming over the heads of the crowd, spear thrust in front, calling for the hunters to join him.

And they did, each step a sailing bound, bobbing beneath him as they raced towards the outer wall. When they reached it, the hunters threw themselves over the edge, trusting to their wings and the essence that rose up from far, far below. For directly beneath them was a great split in the rock, a chasm that led into fathomless depths. The sides of the chasm were grey and so smooth they were almost soft to touch, like stone worked by years of sand and sea. From it, currents of essence rose, oddly coloured wisps of purple and yellow that slowly bled transparent as they mixed with the air. It was these currents that held the castle in the sky, like a giant cork riding gentle, invisible waves.

As the hunters passed over the lip of the wall, the ethereal currents swept them upwards, allowing them to glide in Vasin's wake.

This was one of his favourite parts of the hunt, before the dive, where the world was spread out below. The floating castle was picked out by the rising red light of Wrath's Tear, its chain bridge a flopping tongue that reached down to Mount Ragged and the deep path gouged into its side. But the base of the mountain was mist-shrouded, hidden beneath trees that carpeted everything as far as the eye could see and beyond: the Wild. Monsters and nightmares, tricksters and demons lurked beneath that twisted canopy; all desperate to get their hooks into the unwary.

He could feel the lift starting to fade from his wings and banked to the right, making a slow circle on the edge of the castle's essence currents. The hunters followed his lead, all eyes alert for the signal.

A cry went up from Vasin's right and he saw Mia, a young hunter, pointing. Following the angle of her arm, he was able to see the glimmer of light winking from the trees far below. It irritated him that the first spot was not his but he let it go. There would be more than enough glory to go round by the time this was done.

He raised his spear high, then let the point fall forward as he started his dive.

Away from the chasm, the essence currents were weaker and harder to manage. Enough to glide down but not enough to give lift. The Wild itself was a web of invisible essence but only the most skilled gliders could navigate it for long. The trick of the hunt was to drive the quarry towards the edge of a Godroad before putting down, otherwise the hunters could easily find themselves lost and overwhelmed.

As they descended on the first tribute, they could see the light was moving quickly through the trees, bouncing and flickering as it flitted under the canopy: something was making them run. This was to be expected, as each tribute was cut before they set off, the combination of blood and light designed to lure any demons from their hiding places as quickly as possible.

Another cry went out from the hunters. The second tribute had been spotted. Vasin frowned as he located them. They had become separated from the first and were moving deeper, their light flickering off to his left. The second tribute was not going as fast as the first, suggesting they were not under immediate threat, but Vasin was sure that would soon change.

He considered his options. The sensible thing to do would be to lead the hunters after the first tribute. They would surely lose the second but would maximize their chance of saving the first and killing the beast that pursued them cleanly.

However, this hunt did not need just to be successful, it

needed to be perfect. The second tribute was nearly beyond the reach of his hunters but he could still get to them if he went immediately.

The thought made his wings nudge that way, as if the part of him that had seeped into the armour over the years, the better, bolder part, already knew what had to be done and was just waiting for him to catch up.

'Mia,' he called out. Hoping that his voice would carry over the winds. 'You have the hunt.' He pointed to the light of the first tribute and the dark shape glimpsed behind it. 'Go!'

Whether or not she heard his words, she saw the way his spear pointed and read his intent, leading the hunters down in a sharp dive.

As they sped away, he banked left, doing everything he could to maintain his height. Still, it was not long before the greens and browns of the trees were racing only a few feet from his chest.

The canopy was thick here and he lost sight of the second tribute's light, but it did not trouble him. In his mind he could still picture it, his imagination mapping its progress where his eyes could not.

This deep into the Wild, the gaps between the trees were few and far between, and it was a delicate choice to decide when to drop to ground level. Too soon and he would have to chase the tribute on foot, too long and he would crash into the branches.

One gap passed him, and through it, he was rewarded with a glimpse of a torch, another, and he could just see the outline of the one holding it. To his surprise, they'd stopped moving.

He dived into the next gap without thinking, submerging himself in the dark of the woods. The sudden stealing of the light left him blind for a second but he twisted and turned with the wind, instincts guiding him between the trunks as lesser branches clawed at his armour.

Three times his Sky-legs touched the ground, absorbing momentum until he could skid to a halt on the fourth.

Without the roar of the winds, the silence was abrupt, shocking. Vasin turned on the spot in the direction of the tribute's torch, to find it was coming slowly towards him. An outline of a cloak, and a hood. Vasin's eyes were still adjusting but he could tell the tribute was an adult.

A little of the red sunslight fingered its way through the trees above, coming in slender shafts in the space between them.

'You have called and we have answered,' he said. 'Fear not, for you are under the protection of the Sapphire Everlasting.'

The figure stopped to laugh, a bitter and oddly familiar sound. The torch went out and the tribute threw it to land, smoking, at his feet, the damp grass hissing in protest against its heat.

Vasin raised his spear in readiness, glancing about for signs of others. He could see no one else, though in that moment he wasn't sure who this favoured.

'Who are you?'

The figure moved closer and Vasin's throat tightened, his body knowing and reacting to the truth before his mind could grasp it.

'Oh my sweet one, do I pass so quickly from memory?'

She pulled back the hood. Her dark skin had paled a little,

and there was a scar on her cheek he did not recognize. Sorrow had marked her eyes and put new lines around her mouth but there was no doubt who she was.

Ashamed, Vasin lowered the spear and cast his helmet aside. 'Mother?'

'Always,' she replied, stepping into the space where his spearpoint had just been.

CHAPTER TWO

It was quiet as Chandni hurried along the castle halls and she hated it. Most of the inhabitants were in their beds, asleep or fretting for the future, and Captain Dil had pulled the guards back to the Rebirthing Chamber. It made the place seem deserted. Normally the castle moved to a beat she knew, everything and everyone in its right place. On special days, like those of a hunt, the beat changed, but it was still one that was known. This was the first rebirth to take place in her lifetime, and the strangeness of it put her on edge.

By now her summons would have reached Captain Dil and she imagined he'd be unhappily making his way to her room. She was determined to get there before he did.

Chandni only paused by Honoured Vessel Kareem's door. The room was empty now and would never be filled by his presence again. The young man had already been taken away for the rebirthing ceremony. Either he would prove to be worthy for Lord Rochant Sapphire's soul, or something else would come through and make an abomination. Kareem would die in the morning, that was certain. Only the manner of his death remained to be decided.

She'd miss the man's quiet confidence, and the dash of humour lurking behind his studious nature. Chandni's thoughts went to Kareem's Honoured Mother. How must she feel right now? Such a strange thing to balance the joy of a son being chosen as an Honoured Vessel against the grief of losing him.

An impulse made her hug Satyendra close. Of course, if the house ever needed her to give up Satyendra, she would. *But I hope it never comes to that. Kareem must succeed, he must. And Lord Rochant must have a long and prosperous lifecycle, and my Satyendra must live a full life. One that stretches far beyond my own.*

Not just for herself, but for the house, she hoped Kareem would succeed. He was a good match for Lord Rochant, disciplined, intelligent and well educated. If Kareem failed then the honour would pass through his other living descendants: Mohit was next in line, then Dhruti, and then her Satyendra.

However, any vessel other than Kareem would be a disaster for the house. Mohit, for all his sweetness, was a bad match. He was hard working but dogged, lacking the brilliance that so characterized Lord Rochant's actions. And while Dhruti and Satyendra were more promising, both were too young, which would mean more years of waiting.

Chandni prayed it would not come to that.

We need you now, my lord.

She rested her hand on Kareem's door for a moment, a silent goodbye, then walked the short distance to her own chamber.

Satyendra seemed sleepy but not quite ready to settle. She

carried him over to the Wall of Glory. A single slab of grey amid the brickwork, the Wall of Glory recorded those of importance. Names were engraved deep, then painted in gold. Lines of blue displayed family links and unions. Each of House Sapphire's Deathless was inscribed there, and she had positioned Satyendra's cot so that it would be the first thing he would see in the morning and the last thing at night. She pointed to the highest and boldest name, and tried to sound sincere when she said: 'This is High Lord Yadavendra, greatest of all.'

Her finger paused in the air over a blank piece of stone. Once it had held the name of Nidra, Yadavendra's sister, but since her exile those details had been removed, leaving the stone a paler shade than those around it. Somehow it made the absence more glaring, harder to forget. The sight of it always brought on a sadness in Chandni. Normally, if one of the Deathless lost their status, they would be replaced, just as Lord Rochant had replaced Samarku Un-Sapphire. But not this time.

Since the end of the Unbroken Age, seven Deathless Sapphire had stood watch over the land. In his grief, Yadavendra had made them six, destroying not only his sister but the seat of her immortality as well. There was a hole in House Sapphire and no good would come of it.

Not wanting Satyendra to see her unhappy before bed, she pointed at the name below the empty space. 'Look here,' she pointed at some golden letters, 'the name of the one leading the hunt in Sagan this night. Yadavendra's nephew, Lord Vasin, who is always happiest in the sky.'

And may the sky restore him. May this night restore all of us.

'You see,' she continued, 'all of the Sapphire Deathless are related by blood, save one.' She held Satyendra up so that he could paw at the one name separate from the others in their nest of blue lines. 'Your grandfather, Lord Rochant, started life as a road-born but he was so brave and so clever that High Lord Yadavendra brought him to his castle to serve as a hunter, and later, an adviser. When Rochant gave his life to save the house against Samarku Un-Sapphire, High Lord Sapphire made him into a Deathless. Your grandfather is wise and perfect, the very essence of what it means to be a Sapphire.'

She heard a voice sing for permission to enter and granted it, recognizing Captain Dil's voice immediately.

The captain wore his best uniform, and had put a little wax in his beard to make it look fuller. Nerves made him seem younger than usual. *It is his first time protecting a rebirth too, I must remember that.*

'Honoured Mother, I hear there's a problem?'

'I saw someone in the castle, a stranger wearing a guard's uniform. I didn't like the way he was creeping about.'

Dil nodded to himself. 'I should have guessed it would be something like that. There's nothing to worry about, you just saw some of the extra protection I've brought in for tonight. I'm sorry, Honoured Mother, I should have informed you.'

'I see.'

'Is that all?'

She didn't like his tone, it made her feel as if she was being unreasonable rather than thorough. 'No, that is not all. I spoke to Ji earlier tonight on the ramparts. When I finished my walk, I saw that he was no longer at his post. Nobody was.'

'All of the guards are checking in with me at regular intervals. As a matter of fact, I've just spoken to Ji.'

'He left his post without replacement? That makes no sense. Why was a section of the castle unguarded on this night of all nights?'

Dil bristled. 'No attack is going to come over the wall, Honoured Mother. We live in the sky. That is why Ji is on duty there, it's the safest posting I could find for him. The bridge is secure, the Rebirthing Chamber is secure. They are the places that matter and they are protected at all times by several of our best. I have it all in hand.'

'My apologies, captain, I'm sure you do.'

He took a step towards the corridor. 'Can I ask you to keep to your room from now on, it makes it easier if I know where everyone is.'

She looked down at Satyendra who had gone very still in her arms. 'I don't think that will be a problem. Is all well with you?'

'Yes.'

'Forgive me, captain, but you don't seem yourself.'

Dil paused to fuss with his uniform. 'The Bringers have arrived. They make me nervous.'

Few people got to meet the Bringers of Endless Order. They were the ones who carried out the rebirth ceremony, and dealt in matters of the soul. Nobody even knew what they looked like under their masks and heavy robes. 'Has it started?'

'Not yet. Soon though. I should be going.'

He left quickly, leaving Chandni with a sense of foreboding. *He's worried. Good. We should be worried, it will keep us focused.*

As if giving the lie to that, Satyendra fell asleep. She placed him in his cot with a faint smile and settled down, knowing she would not be able to relax until the ceremony was over.

Few were allowed to bear witness to a rebirthing ceremony, the honour reserved for Crystal High Lords and the Bringers of Endless Order.

Pari Tanzanite was neither.

The tunnel she'd used to breach the inner castle was secret, winding, hidden by glittering architecture and sumptuous art carved in ancient crystal, smoothed by the touch of admiring hands. Behind hard faces of blue gemstone it went, through spaces between the castle's floors, bending around stairwells and pillars, allowing one to spy on the great halls of House Sapphire, or gain entry to a select number of bedchambers.

It was said that in the ancient days, when the gods still walked the earth, unbroken, that there were those who could look into the face of another and know their secrets. Pari had spent many of her lifetimes trying to rediscover that art with only partial success. She could not read thoughts or summon specific knowledge from the minds of her enemies. Nor could she overwrite their thoughts with her own, such powers remained the province of the shattered gods and the things that lurked in the Wild below.

However, her efforts had borne some fruit. Sometimes, Pari would know that a lie had been spoken, or have a sudden insight into where a person was going, or who they might harbour secret affections for. As if all of her observations were gathered in a wordless part of her mind and joined together, the resulting sequences given back to her as feelings or hunches.

These insights were only sometimes useful and always impossible to prove, but she had learned to trust them, to grasp and follow them before they slipped away. It had led to her having a reputation of being flighty and chaotic when the truth was very much the opposite.

So when an anonymous message had arrived four days ago, slipped under her dinner plate, she had known at once that she was reading truth:

Things are not well in the home of your lover. Loyal friends are posted elsewhere. Strangers walk the halls, sharpening knives while they wait for his return. He needs help. He needs you. Come now. Come carefully.

Without hesitation, she had made a show of throwing up and had then retreated to her room, leaving strict instructions that she was not to be disturbed. An hour later, she was on the road, hidden in the back of a wagon, and en route to the castle of Lord Rochant Sapphire.

He was in danger, of this she was certain, and that was enough to have her enter, uninvited and unlawfully. Discovery would mean disgrace and the possible loss of her immortal status. But not to act, to allow whatever was coming for Rochant to take his life unopposed, was unthinkable.

She had been twenty years younger the last time she used the tunnel. Though it was unchanged, her age lengthened the journey, doubling the effort required for each drag of the knee, tripling it where walls and ceiling narrowed and she was forced onto her chest, worm-like.

For Rochant, it would feel like no time at all, the space between death and life but a moment for him, while she had felt keenly every second they had been apart. And she had lived those seconds, time taking its toll on her body. Would he still be drawn to her? Would he still recognize her? *Of course he will*, she chided herself, *our attraction is stronger than common sense, or family taboos, or time.* She tried to picture his surprise at seeing her, and his joy. The picture in her mind found a mirror on her face, infused by the growing sense of excitement that, at last, they would be reunited. And while the feeling did little to remove her discomfort, it made it a lot easier to ignore.

As she inched her way forward, noises of the castle wound their way up to her. The chatter of servants, hushed, preparing to retire. Snores of the drunk, rattling and regular. And softer, a groan of relief, followed by a litany of curses directed against shoes and the people that made them so tight. Nothing that suggested danger. A little doubt wormed its way into her thoughts. What if she was wrong? And what if, by being here, she put his life and reputation at risk? Perhaps the letter was a trap rather than a warning and her instincts were wrong. What a bitter irony that would be.

One by one, the noises settled, till only the snoring could be heard, and Pari came to the end of the tunnel and her lover's bedroom. In the dark, her fingers fumbled, memory not enough to guide them, until persistence brought them to the catch.

Inside the room, a painting of a surprised young man slid aside, allowing Pari to pull herself free. Able to stand upright again, each limb was stretched in turn, joints cracking like whips. Pari grimaced, knowing that she would pay for this excursion tomorrow. *Such is the price of age*, she thought.

Not so much that we have less fun, just that the cost of it keeps going up.

She allowed her hand to slide along the gem-studded wall, until there was warmth under her skin, and pressed. Solar light, captured over the day and piped where needed, spilled out, filling the room with heat and illumination, blue-tinted.

The bedroom was mostly as she remembered it. Plain walls hardly visible beneath the paintings, all of them of live subjects, and by a variety of different artists. She used to know the history of every piece but it was so long ago. The subjects were long dead and her memories were of Rochant's face rather than his words, and the way his stern features became so delightfully boyish when enthusiastic.

No dust had settled on the furniture, and the sheets on the bed were perfectly smooth until Pari sat on them. The room smelt fresh, clean, but it did not smell of him, and she was struck by the hollowness of the place.

It's waiting for you to come back. We all are, my darling.

Pari went to the door on the opposite wall and slid it back to reveal a rack of clothing. Hanging underneath Lord Rochant's cloak, hidden, was a second simpler one of Sapphire design, the kind worn by the castle staff on a cold night.

She took out the cloak and slipped it over her shoulders, pulling the hood forward till it cast her face in shadow, hiding her only concession to vanity: a pair of golden earrings that fastened to the top and bottom of each ear; a gift from him to her from their early, heady days.

There was a sad lack of mirrors but some of the paintings were protected by glass and, from the right angle, she was able to see a paler version of herself. Her reflection gave her an approving nod, before smiling.

Much better.

So far, her intrusion had been easy. The routines of the castle had not changed, and it was a small matter for her to sneak in through the servants' quarters. House Sapphire had few enemies, and Lord Rochant fewer still. With most of the guards assigned to the ceremony, she had plenty of opportunities to cross from the courtyard where visitors were taken, to the outer wall. From there, it had only been a short run to the tunnel's entrance and complete concealment all the way to Rochant's bedchamber.

The hard part was yet to come. She slipped out into the corridor and began her walk towards the Rebirthing Chamber. By her estimate, the suns would only just be starting to rise. Rochant had been born under the lesser red sun, Wrath's Tear, and so she still had a little time before the ceremony began.

In short bursts, she travelled, crouching by glazed vases bursting with yellowed leaves, then dashing forward to hide by a statue of a serious looking man in long robes: Lord Rochant Sapphire, rendered in crystal, and mounted on a plinth. It had been grown over years, sculpted meticulously to match the subject at every stage of life. If the rebirthing ceremony was successful, the statue would be moved to the ancestral hall and a new one would be put in its place. Accuracy had been given priority over flattery, every feature worked to match the original's. The artist had done an exquisite job and it was no accident that Pari's hand came to rest on the statue's bottom.

Where are the guards? she wondered. So far, she had seen no one, heard nothing.

Halfway to her next hiding place, she saw one coming

out of a bedroom, closing the door, carefully, quietly. It would only be a few moments before he looked up and saw her. Instead of diving for cover, Pari straightened, trusting to her disguise.

No longer creeping, the sudden sound of her footsteps filled the pre-dawn quiet, and the guard jumped so high the plume of his helm nearly tickled the ceiling.

Making the most of the man's surprise, Pari hurried past: the guard stayed facing the door until her back was to him. She heard him then set off quickly in the opposite direction.

She'd noted the slight shine of his cheeks and wondered about it as she turned the corner. Something in the man's manner nagged at her, slowing her steps. Embarrassed or not, the guard she had encountered was in the family wing of the castle on the night of Rochant's ceremony, and he should have challenged her.

Suddenly, all thoughts of her reunion faded away, banished by the puzzle. Not only had the guard not challenged her, she realized, he had been as keen to get away as she was. And then another thing occurred to her. When the guard had left, he was going at speed, and yet she could not remember hearing the sound of his footsteps.

Pari stopped. She didn't understand what was going on but all of her instincts were telling her to run, and so she did, away from where the ceremony would be starting and back to the door where she had first encountered the guard.

It was quiet on the other side of the door, the same kind of quiet she'd experienced in Rochant's room. With a sickening feeling, Pari turned the handle and pushed open the door.

Dim light from the corridor bled through into the dark room, painting a sleeping girl in greys, serene. Pari would guess her to be no more than fifteen, most likely one of Rochant's grandchildren.

Around her the room contained a few hints of chaos: a broken chair, a scattering of beads and a second body, a young woman in a guard's uniform, chest down, head twisted too far to the left, as if she wished one last look at the ceiling as she died. Her right hand clutched at a dagger, the tip daubed in fresh blood. *She marked him before she died. Good.*

Unable to help the unfortunate guard, Pari crossed to the bed where the girl was. Her chest neither rose nor fell, and in the soft light, she saw a thin needle protruding from the girl's throat.

Too late, Pari. She cursed herself. *Far, far, too late.*

A part of her wanted to examine the scene, another to rush to Rochant's side but the guard, *the assassin*, she corrected herself, hadn't been going towards the Rebirthing Chamber. *Either he's finished here or his next target isn't Rochant.*

Pari rushed outside and noticed a speck of blood, glinting in the gemlight of the corridor. She went in the direction the assassin had gone, finding another speck some way further down. Whatever wound he'd received was bleeding slowly, making a poor tracking aid, but it confirmed she was going the right way.

She ran, wondering where in the name of the Three Blessed Suns any of House Sapphire's guards were. Their absence now seemed glaring, ominous rather than fortunate.

A soft thud sounded from one of the rooms behind her.

She slid to a stop, backtracked three paces until she was level with the door, and went straight in.

The assassin was kneeling, bent over a baby's crib, his right hand raised and curled around something she couldn't make out through the gloom. The thud she'd heard had been his head being banged against the side of the crib by the woman on his back.

Even in the half light, Pari could tell the woman was highborn, her skinny arms sticking from her flapping night-dress like sticks from a sail.

By some miracle, the baby wasn't crying, making Pari fear she was too late a second time.

With a grunt, the assassin drove his elbow backwards into the noblewoman's gut. She bucked with the force but kept hold, knocking his head against the crib a second time. The assassin elbowed her again, then brought his fist up into the woman's face.

Pari was halfway across the room as the woman fell down.

She considered her opponent, as yet unaware of her arrival. He looked young, fast and strong. Closer now, she could just make out another of those long murderous needles in his grip.

Not someone to play games with.

Though her body was not as fast as it once was, her instincts remained sharp, and Pari let them guide her, flowing into action before her conscious mind fully understood what she was about to do.

She reached out to his raised hand and plucked the needle from it. His reaction was swift, one fist lashing out on instinct. Pari barely managed to get her arms in the way in time. The force of the blow slammed into her, bruising forearms, and she tripped on the other woman's leg, stumbling back to the far wall for support. Before she could recover her breath the assassin was leaping after her, one hand raised, index and middle fingers locked together ready to strike.

His movements suggested that his hand-to-hand training was excellent, at least as good as one could be in a single lifetime. In a younger body, she would have dealt with him easily, now most of her efforts were going into staying upright.

As if he sensed her fatigue, the assassin lunged forward but Pari, still leaning against the wall, showed him her empty hands before giving her best smile and flicking a look to his throat.

The gesture made him pause. His eyes widened as his fingers touched the side of his neck and the needle protruding from it.

He just had time to look at her in understanding before something seemed to switch off inside, and he collapsed to the floor.

Pari pushed herself upright and moved to the side of the crib, rubbing her arm. It turned out that the baby had woken after all, his eyes staring up at her, two black pools in the grey.

'Well,' she said, picking him up. 'You're a very calm fellow, aren't you?'

The baby didn't reply, watching her with intensity. The woman by Pari's feet however, was another matter. 'I know that voice . . . Pari? Lady Pari Tanzanite, is that you?' At her nod, the woman became haughty. 'I demand that you tell me what is going on this instant! Who was that man? Why was he trying to kill my Satyendra? And what are you doing here?'

Pari peered down at the woman, unflustered. Satyendra did the same. She saw a delicate face, the kind that smiles too rarely and was not built to handle tears. 'All good questions . . . ' she paused to allow the woman to introduce herself.

'Chandni.'

'Can it be? Little Chandni, all grown up and an Honoured Mother! I never would have recognized you. Who is in charge here?'

'I am,' she replied, standing up and regaining something of her dignity. 'Lord Rochant entrusted me to oversee the castle in his absence.'

'My, my, it has been too long, my dear.'

'You haven't answered my questions.'

'True,' replied Pari, 'and you haven't thanked me for saving you and your baby either.'

'I . . . thank you,' said Chandni, then again more calmly, earnest. 'Thank you.'

'Much better. As to who the man is, I'm not sure yet. But he's already killed at least twice tonight.'

Chandni took a fortifying breath. 'Who?'

'One was a girl, younger than you, the other her guardian.'

'No!' Her hands flew to her mouth. 'It must be Dhruti. But why?'

'She was a descendant of Lord Rochant.'

'She was,' Chandni's eyes widened. 'Like Satyendra!'

'Yes —' she replied, giving the baby a squeeze '— like Satyendra. How many more blood descendants are there in the castle?'

'I . . . '

'Come on, Chandni, think!'

'Well, two. There's Satyendra's father, Mohit, and Kareem. But Kareem was chosen, he's in the Rebirthing Chamber now.'

'Show me Mohit's room.'

A minute later they stood at Mohit's bedside. There had been no guard to protect him and the needle in his neck was still quivering. Like the girl beforehand, Mohit's death had been swift and, she hoped, painless.

'He's only just died. You know what this means?' Pari asked, pointing at the needle.

Chandni covered her mouth and gasped behind her hand, 'Poor Mohit. Quickly, turn Satyendra away.'

'It means there's a second killer, maybe more. The castle isn't safe.' She passed Satyendra back into Chandni's arms. 'You have to leave.'

'What?'

'Right now. Don't stop to pack, take Satyendra and go, use the tunnel.'

'What tunnel?'

'I'll show you. It'll take you to the main doors.' Pari took off one of her earrings. 'I have a man outside, his name is Varg. Give him this,' she said, and placed the earring into Chandni's hand, 'tell him I sent you. Tell him to get you as far away from here as he can.' She kissed the baby's forehead. 'Keep Satyendra close. If things go badly, he might be Rochant's last hope. I'll come for you when it's safe.'

'Wait, where are you going?'

'To the Rebirthing Chamber. Someone is trying to erase Rochant's line, and I intend to stop them.'

Vasin's mother stood before him. Wonderfully impossible. Though her body had been weathered and scarred, aged by time and sorrow, it didn't matter. She was here! As purposeful as ever. Just the sight of her made him feel safer, as if things could begin making sense again. And yet, her very presence meant that the world did not make sense, and would not again.

'They may take my title, strip me of my crystal skin, sever my link to the immortal, bury me with lies and hatred –' she reached up to his face and he could not decide whether to move forward or back '– but I will always be your mother, I will always be yours, and you mine.'

She was also a traitor, accused and found guilty of selling out their people to the Wild. Treating with demons was a terrible crime in itself, but for a Deathless it was a thousand times worse, a betrayal of their most sacred duty. Such a thing could not stand, especially not in House Sapphire where it had happened before.

But this was his mother, alive and fierce. He'd never entirely believed she was guilty. Never forgiven himself for not doing more to defend her when he'd had the chance.

'Forgive me, Mother. I'm happy to see you, thrilled. I never thought . . . I mean . . . I thought you were . . . ' He couldn't finish the sentence. There was a chance he was dreaming and if that was the case he didn't want it to end.

Nidra gestured to the looming trees. 'This is a kind of death. A slow and terrible kind.' She gave him a bitter smile. 'I intend to outrun it.'

'But how did you survive? Where have you been living?' He looked down at the smoking torch. 'How did you become one of Sagan's tributes? I don't understand.'

'I've spent lifetimes studying the Wild. I'm not afraid of it like my brother is. A hunter is more than weapons and armour. That knowledge saved me. And I have allies still, ones that serve from the shadows. We have been preparing, they and I. One will come to you soon. Treat her requests as if they were mine.'

'I will, of course I will, but I need to know, where have you been?'

'Sorn. The Wild has had its way with it and nobody else dares to go there. It's a ghost town, and I'm its ghost.'

'And now you're in Sagan?'

'No. I stole the torch so that I could signal you. I knew none of the other hunters would be able to fly this deep.'

With the Sky-legs he was so much taller than her that he had to lean down to bring his face close to hers. Her fingers touched his cheek, smearing the fresh tears there and he finally leaned into her touch, the grief and sadness he had kept bottled up these years melting away.

'I've been lost without you.'

'I know. And now you're found again.'

Her stoicism made his guilt worse. How could she be so strong when she had lost so much? 'I should have been there at the end. I'm so sorry.'

'There was nothing you could have done. I'm glad you didn't have to see. Your uncle made the whole thing a public show. My humiliation a spectacle for his amusement.' Her face hardened at the thought of it. 'They hacked at my reputation with their lies, the Story-singers making me into a monster in the minds of my people, and then the Bringers came and cut the bonds between my soul and my Godpiece. It was an agony I have no words for. It left me without dignity, an animal.' She shook her head, firm. 'No, that is not how I wanted to be remembered by my son.'

'I still should have gone to the trial. I know Gada did.'

'Yes. But Gada is not you. If you had been there, you would have done something beautiful and foolish. It was right that Gada was there then, just as it's right that you're here now. I need you, Vasin, I need you more now than I did then.'

'I don't understand.'

'It's simple, do you want me to die, finally and forever?'

'No! No. Not when I've just found you again. I'd do anything to make things the way they were, you know that.'

She removed her hand from his face. 'Good. Because I am going to need you to do things for me, things you may not like.'

Vasin frowned. Living too long in the Wild was known to bring on madness. 'But there is nothing to do. The Sapphire High Lord has given his judgement. And even if he overturned it, he's already destroyed your Godpiece. Your soul is without anchor . . . It's too late.'

Her features hardened. 'There are other Godpieces among the Sapphire that would suffice.'

He was aware of her eyes on him as he thought through what this would mean. It would be like becoming Deathless for the first time again. Her soul would need to be attuned to a new Godpiece by the Bringers of Endless Order. Though what she said was true about there being other Godpieces within the house, they were already allocated. To give one to his mother would mean destroying another member of the family, wiping out every member of their line. Rather than follow that to its unpleasant conclusion he decided to focus on a different issue. 'But only the High Lord can take or give Godpieces.'

'Then you will have to find a way to persuade the High Lord . . . or replace him with another more sympathetic to our cause. There are those that will support us. It will take a long time to achieve but things have already begun, this very night plans are in motion. I will provide the Godpiece and you will mobilize the house to see that it is used to restore me.'

'I wouldn't know how. Since your exile, I have not been myself. I turned my back on the court. I . . . left those things to Gada.'

She took a deep breath and Vasin shrank from her barely contained anger. When she spoke however, her voice was calm. 'Then you will go back to court and you will see who remembers the name of Nidra Sapphire with fondness.' She slipped a pack from her back and began unfastening the top.

'There was a time, before you were born, when I was considered the best choice for High Lord. However, the machinations of my brother and his pet, Lord Rochant, put paid to that. Your uncle was not always head of this house, nor will he reign forever, that I promise you.'

She opened the bag and held it out for him.

Vasin peered inside to see what looked like a human arm rendered in shell, with antennae sprouting from the knuckles. 'What's that?'

'A trophy. You'll take it back with you, as part of your glorious return to court.'

His eyes widened as he realized what it was. 'Wait, you killed the Scuttling Corpsema—'

She hurriedly put a finger to his lips, cutting him off. 'Not killed. Maimed.' She looked over her shoulder suddenly as if expecting to see something. Vasin tensed and did the same but there was only darkness between the trees. 'It's still out there, somewhere. We would be wise not to use its full name.'

'But how?'

'Later. You must go before questions are raised. Take my gift, take the glory. Use it well. Come to me when you have news and I'll tell you all about the Corpseman and what I've been up to in the last few years.'

'I will. I won't fail you again.'

'I know you won't.' She pulled up her hood and made to step back into the shadows, but Vasin could not bear the thought of her leaving, and dragged her into an embrace, lifting her till her toes skimmed the top of the long grass. 'I love you.'

'And I you, my sweet one. Remember that when you are in the world above the Wild and I am but a memory.'

She had to force herself out of his arms, and only when she was gone from sight did he turn back towards home. He would find a way to make this right, or he would die, a true and final death, in the attempt. Vasin swore to himself that if it came to that, he would not go alone.

CHAPTER THREE

It was as Pari feared. The majority of the castle's guard had taken up posts outside the Rebirthing Chamber, protecting the two doorways into the room. Traditionally, one was used by the Bringers of Endless Order as they escorted the vessel in, one was for the High Lord, if he or she wished to attend. There was a third way into the room but this was used only as an exit should the ritual fail.

Pari had never witnessed a ritual go wrong but she had heard rumours of bodies inhabited by infernal spirits and turned into tragic, destructive creatures. Some believed, if the proper rites were not observed, a demon could push aside the waiting soul and enter the world in its place. Pari had little time for such notions, sure that the pain and confusion of a botched rebirth would be more than enough to explain away the rage of the poor wretches.

Whether due to madness or demonic possession, the results of a failed ritual were too dangerous to be allowed to live, and the third exit was a means of dealing with them: a beautifully designed portal covering a chute that was nothing more than a glorified hole in the underside of Rochant Sapphire's floating castle. Anyone unfortunate enough to use it was ejected directly above the gaping chasm, far beneath.

Unguarded, and unknown to most of the castle's inhabitants, it was arguably the ideal route for someone trying to sneak in without being seen. However, the only way to reach it was by scaling the outer walls, and even if she'd had time, such feats were beyond her in this lifecycle.

Pari studied the faces of the three guards stood to attention outside the first entrance. The Bringers of Endless Order must have already gone inside. She didn't like what she saw. Nothing was obviously wrong but she didn't recognize any of the guards, and as her eyes swept over them, a word screamed into her mind: killers.

Quickly, she moved to the second entrance. It was similarly guarded, but one of the men was familiar.

She tried to think where she had seen him before. A wispy beard covered his chin and cheeks, but beneath it was a face she knew. Older and harder but not entirely unfriendly. The picture of a young boy came to mind, shy, with watchful eyes, who blushed at the slightest praise.

She approached him, so bold that it took them all a moment to react.

'Who are you?' he demanded, one hand going to the Sliver Pistol at his side. The man and the woman flanking him followed suit, reaching for well-worn hilts.

She ignored the impulse to run and focused on the man she knew. 'Shush now, Dil, I need you to listen.' Then she noticed the extra bands of colour around his right arm. *A captain now,* she thought. *And he was such a quiet boy.*

The man spluttered in surprise at the use of his name but something in her tone and manner disarmed him and he came forward. 'Do I know you?' He frowned. 'No! It can't be! Lady Pari Tanzanite?' Despite himself, Dil bowed.

She couldn't help but smile at his naked amazement. 'Your eyes are sharp as ever.'

And there it was, the sudden colouring of his cheeks. 'But . . . '

'There's no time to explain, Dil. Lord Rochant is in danger. Assassins are *in* the castle dressed in House Sapphire uniform. You must find them. And you must let me inside the chamber. I'll protect him.'

'What? That's . . . No.'

'No? You don't believe me?'

'I believe you.' A little sweat formed on his top lip. 'Has anyone already been killed?'

'Mohit and Dhruti.' She let it sink in. 'At least one of your people died defending them. One assassin tried for Satyendra but I managed to save him . . . '

She sighed inwardly as Dil's hand slipped from the Sliver Pistol, his frown deepening. 'Who else knows?'

'Just you, me, and Chandni.'

'Good. Where are Chandni and Satyendra now?'

'Safe.'

'Are they in their room?'

'They're safe, don't worry.'

'Tell me.'

'Later. We don't know who else might be listening.'

He turned away with a scowl. 'Of course.'

She stepped past him to find the other two guards had drawn blades and were levelling them at her chest.

'Stand down,' commanded Dil and they reluctantly sheathed their weapons. 'Open the doors.' As they complied he turned to Pari and added. 'If you do anything to disrupt the rebirthing . . . '

'I'll be quiet as a Flykin,' she replied, 'I promise.'

The Rebirthing Chamber was not much to look at, smooth stone walls that curved to make a circle, and a stone floor, equally smooth, grey, featureless. A spiral of pillars started by the first entrance and slowly wound their way towards the centre. Though the pillars were as dull to look at as the walls, each one was double her girth, giving Pari plenty of places to hide.

The soft light in the room came from the Bringers of Endless Order: stored sunlight released slow and muted through cloudy diamonds atop their wands of gold. As tradition dictated, seven Bringers were present, dressed in robes of black and white, their faces covered in plain masks divided down the middle, white on the left, black on the right.

Pari wasn't convinced that any of them were required for the rebirthing to work but she was grateful for their sing-song murmurs as they masked the sound of her tiptoeing from one pillar to another.

She could see a young man, naked, strapped down on a slab set at the centre of the room: Kareem Sapphire, living the last moments of his life before his soul made way for Rochant's to return. In typical Sapphire fashion, the young man was stoic about his fate, neither railing against it nor revelling in the honour his body was about to receive.

She took some time to appreciate the new form her lover

was to assume. Lean but not too thin, with a pleasing firmness to biceps and buttocks that she looked forward to exploring further. She was also pleased to see Kareem had cut his hair short against the fashion. Not only was this good for Rochant, who had proven himself immune to the fashions of court, it was also good for her. Long hair was fine to look at, but it tended to get in the way. Pari was already imagining what those lips might feel like against hers.

One of the Bringers took out a needle, raising it theatrically in the seven directions: up, then down, to the left and right making a cross, then three times more, across the left shoulder, then the right, and finally down at a forty five degree angle from the right hip.

The sight of the needle made the breath catch in her throat. Could one of the assassins have hidden themselves within the Bringers? But no, this needle was different to the other two she'd seen, a more elaborate tool. She watched as the Bringer switched it on, and a concealed pouch began to beat within their robes, like a second heart jutting from the small of their back. Shimmering liquid was pumped from the pouch through a tiny corkscrew tube that ran within the Bringer's sleeve, and into the back of the needle. The other six were humming but she could hear the needle humming too, like a living tongue, sharp, now tipped with golden spittle and ready for its task. The Bringer raised the needle to Kareem's unblemished flesh, and set to work.

Kareem's head was worked on first, a jagged line of gold drawn from forehead to cheek, narrowly missing the eye. At the bottom the line forked and forked again, forming a lattice that spread back towards the ear: this was to symbolize

Rochant's first death, when his head had been split open defending his lord during the Battle of Bloodied Backs.

Next, the Bringer worked on his chest, inscribing tiny rows of text across his heart. Rochant's second death had come when his body was ancient, and was caused by heart failure, which in turn was caused by the arrival of an unexpected message, the contents of which remained a mystery to Pari, much to her irritation.

Not all of his deaths would be represented, only the ones of significance. With bated breath, she watched as they added marks to his right hand and his cock. Neither of these were familiar to her and there was little of Rochant's body she had not seen. Another puzzle. If only she could examine them more closely, she might be able to discern clues as to why they'd been added but if the Bringers found her here, there would be consequences even she feared to face.

Pari took a moment to appreciate Kareem's strength of character. Though the young man gripped the edges of the slab and his body was locked rigid, he did not cry out at any time, enduring the stab-stab of the needle with barely a grunt. Even from a distance, it made Pari's eyes water.

This is why he was chosen. Not for those cheek bones, that's a common enough Sapphire feature. For his self-discipline. Rochant is a stickler for it.

Eventually, the needle went quiet, vanishing into the cavernous sleeves of the Bringer's robes. More whispering followed, the Bringers reciting history and lineage, recounting a life that skipped across generations before surfacing to influence the Sapphire line, then vanishing again.

The whispers were just loud enough to sound enticing and, for the second time, Pari wished she could get closer.

She also wished there was somewhere to sit down. Her feet were throbbing, and one of her knees was starting to tremble.

The Sapphires can have their self-discipline and suffering, she thought, *right now I'd trade all of my dignity for a cushioned seat and a footrest.*

Though she couldn't hear the words, it became clear to her that the Bringers weren't addressing Kareem, rather their masked faces were tilted towards a small box that had appeared on the upturned palm of the lead Bringer. Fine lines were brushed into the sides of the box, each movement making ghost-shapes along its surface. The lid was open. She could see the contents nestled snugly within: a platinum sphere, about the size of a human eye. From this distance it appeared flawless, but she knew in the right circumstances clever mechanisms within would rotate, cracking open to allow vapours to pass through the outer shell.

Nobody knew exactly where the soul went between rebirths but there was a good chance that it was there, right now, in the box, in the Godpiece, waiting to begin its next life.

For a rebirth to be attempted, a noble house would have to entreat the Bringers of Endless Order to attempt a ritual. This was normally a formality but one which had to be observed, and paid for.

Assuming this went well, the family would have to produce the relevant Godpiece: a relic of the immortals that once ruled the world, and the only thing capable of anchoring a soul once it had left the body.

Each Godpiece was attuned to a different member of the crystal dynasties; each one was unique, irreplaceable. Its allocation was a thing of incredible potency, and the singular right of the Crystal High Lords.

Most of the houses, her own included, had already allocated all of their Godpieces, meaning that any new immortals could only be made by removing one of the old, again a power held by the Crystal High Lords. It was also why Pari was always polite to High Lord Tanzanite, no matter how annoying she could be at times, and why Pari kept her affair with Rochant a secret.

It was one thing to break a taboo, quite another to get caught doing it.

The third requirement of the ritual was its location, ideally the correct family stronghold, though Pari and Rochant had debated whether any of the dynasties' floating castles would suffice.

The fourth was time, the Bringers scheduling the ceremony to take place at the same moment of the day, and with the same alignment of the suns, as the immortal's original birthday. This was why everyone, even the least fortunate, took careful note of the sky when a child was born.

Finally, a suitable host was required. They had to come from the immortal's line, with stronger blood ties preferable. Each house endeavoured to groom potential hosts to have skills and interests similar to the immortal, to make the rebirth easier, however this was not always possible, and some immortals had lived lives in the opposite gender, and in bodies of a variety of shapes and sizes.

For Rochant, the signs were good, better than good, and yet Pari could not help but worry as the ritual drew to a close. The thought of having to wait another generation to be with her love was painful, the thought that she might never see him again, unbearable.

Somewhere nearby, Rochant's enemies were moving,

preparing to act. Pari doubted they'd dare try anything while the Bringers were present, but as soon as they had gone, Rochant would be easy pickings for any that could get past his guard.

And if they do, they'll find me waiting, thought Pari, but the bravado sounded hollow, even in her own mind. She was tired already, and scared. *What if I'm not good enough? What then?*

One of the Bringers produced a mesh of wires and solemnly approached Kareem. Another stepped up to the side of the young man and placed their hands either side of his head. Kareem did not resist, though she thought she saw him flinch as he caught sight of the device. The lump in Kareem's throat bobbed as he swallowed, and then the young man opened his mouth.

The mesh was placed inside, flattening down Kareem's tongue and jacking open his jaws. There was a click, loud, and the device locked into place, whereupon the lead Bringer stepped forward, took the Godpiece from its box to place it carefully, ritualistically, into Kareem's mouth, into the mesh.

The others closed in, making a loose circle around Kareem, wands pointing inward, much of their light blocked from Pari. Their murmurings became louder, not quite a song, but a series of harsh lyrical whispers, ends and beginnings brushing over one another. Planes of light could only escape in the gaps where the Bringers' robes were not touching and in the space above their heads. A tableau of shadow danced on the ceiling, and to Pari, it looked at times as if the shapes were wrong, the Bringers seeming to have too many limbs, and extra protrusions defying the human form.

She looked away but the noise still reached her. The strange words, and beneath them, muffled by the mesh, Kareem, making a sound she could not name but was born of suffering.

Until now she had never really thought about the ones that gave up their lives so that she and those like her might live again. It was always spoken of as an honour, and of course, those that took that honour for her, Pari had never met. But she found herself thinking about it now, that curious part of her brain forced to consider that Kareem did not sound like a man experiencing a great honour, and to wonder what would happen to his soul once Rochant's took up residence.

Gradually, the whispers faded, each of the Bringers falling quiet in order, like waves receding from the shore. When they were done, they took a step back, widening the circle.

She risked a glance, and saw that Kareem's eyes were closed. *Or were they Rochant's now?* She had to know if he had survived the ritual and edged out from behind her pillar, sliding rather than stepping, until she managed to align herself with a gap in the ring of Bringers.

His chest. Is it moving? Yes. It moved! She felt joy that he was alive, tempered with fear. The body lived, true, but it was not yet certain what dwelled inside it.

Together, the Bringers raised their golden wands, touching them one to the other, so that the seven diamonds clinked softly.

The man on the slab groaned, then opened his eyes.

'One man is welcome here,' the lead Bringer said. 'Are you that man?'

Pari saw the muscles in his arm flex against the straps that held him fast. He worked his jaw slowly, as if testing it for damage. The motion was so considered, so calm, that her heart leapt. It was Rochant, it had to be! The Bringers may not know it yet, but she was already certain.

'I am Lord Rochant Sapphire,' he said. And again, Pari rejoiced, she knew that intonation better than her own.

'Lord Rochant Sapphire is welcome,' replied the Bringer, 'if you are he.'

'If,' hissed the others.

'If you are he,' continued the lead Bringer, 'you will prove your humanity. Examine yourself, and tell us what you find.'

This was to be the test then. Pari had undergone several herself. Each time was different, a means to be sure that the immortal had truly returned, rather than a demon.

'I feel the marks on my skull. The scars of my first life.'

The Bringers said nothing, none of them moved, though each seemed poised to act.

'I see the marks on my heart, and remember my second life.'

Again, the Bringers said nothing, and Rochant turned his attention to his hand. There was a long pause. She saw the flicker of concern on Rochant's face.

Something's wrong.

The silence was stretching too long. If Rochant didn't answer correctly, and soon, the Bringers would become suspicious. He might even fail the test.

'What is this on my hand?' Rochant asked.

The lead Bringer matched the pause, and Pari felt her heart clench. Then said ominously, 'You do not know?'

Rochant only frowned.

Perhaps this is it. What if the assassin is among the Bringers, or if the Bringers themselves want him dead. If they put a mark on him that should not be there, then he cannot identify it, and he cannot pass. They will kill him and there is nothing I can do to stop it.

Rochant licked his lips to moisten them. 'I know nothing of it.'

'It is a mark of shame.' The other Bringers made a soft chorus of the word 'shame' as the lead Bringer continued. 'When you were killed for raising your hand in disagreement with your High Lord.'

'Then, this cannot be my hand,' replied Rochant. 'For it, like me, has always been loyal.'

There was another long pause before the lead Bringer stepped in close. Pari's breath caught in her throat as she saw a sweep of the robed arm, too fast for her to intervene.

When the Bringer stepped back, the marks on Rochant's hand were gone and the straps that had held him in place hung loose on the sides of the slab.

'Lord Rochant Sapphire is welcome.'

'Welcome,' agreed the others.

Their work complete, the Bringers bowed, but before they could leave, Rochant spoke again. 'Wait, there is another mark I do not know.'

The Bringers paused, and the sense of them being poised to act, to strike, returned.

Shut up! Pari urged silently. *You've passed the test you idiot. Just let them leave.*

'The one in silver ink rather than gold –' Rochant allowed a delicate pause '– below. Can you explain it to me?'

A look passed between the Bringers. If Pari did not know better she'd have said there was some gentle humour being shared.

'It is a warning from your High Lord. Of an end for this life if you do not heed it.'

Rochant didn't reply but she saw his jaw clench and his eyes close.

He's being told to stay away from me! She consoled herself that High Lord Sapphire could only suspect. If he'd learned the truth about their relationship, Rochant's rebirth would have ended much more abruptly. *We'll have to be even more careful from now on.*

The Bringers turned from him, processing outward, single file, following the spiral of pillars towards the first doorway.

For a moment, she was sure one of them was looking at her, and she caught a glimpse of peridot eyes that seemed to glow with their own soft light.

Pari pressed herself back against the pillar and held her breath.

The tunnel was smaller than Chandni had expected it to be. *Why go to all the trouble of making a secret passage that's almost impossible to use?* she thought to herself. *What were the architects thinking?*

She hated being in this undignified position, squeezing herself and Satyendra through the tiny space between floor and ceiling. It made her feel like a stubborn lump of food stuck in the throat.

But most of all she hated Lady Pari. Bad enough that the Tanzanite had broken into her chambers, she'd started giving orders in a Sapphire castle. Even worse, she knew more about the castle's secrets than Chandni herself. It hinted at the true depths of the friendship between Pari and Lord Rochant.

She stopped.

If it is just a friendship.

No. Such a thing was unthinkable, impossible, against the rules that governed the Deathless.

She shook her head, forcing herself to carry on. It was not her place to question her lord. She was just in shock, that was all. Whatever was happening, there would be a true and proper explanation that would be given to her if it was deemed appropriate.

She still hated Pari though.

Most of the stress in Chandni's life had been the kind one could prepare for. From difficult guests from other houses who needed to be handled with care, to complicated negotiations over rights, to pregnancy. All were managed with meticulous planning and Chandni was proud of how smoothly she'd navigated through.

To the outside eye, it appeared that she never broke sweat or struggled, and that was just how she liked it. Exactly as a true Sapphire should be.

Yet again, her head knocked against the top of the tunnel, and she bit her lip to stop from crying out. Satyendra jolted in her arms but did not cry. His tiny fingers splayed in surprise, then settled again, gathering the front of her nightgown in two tight bunches.

Pride for her son's stoicism overwhelmed the throbbing on the back of her skull and she paused to kiss his forehead. He'd always been calm in spectacular circumstances, including those surrounding his birth. For Satyendra was born on the same day as the Sapphire High Lord, Yadavendra, and under the same alignment of the suns. Upon hearing this, the High Lord had come in person to inspect the baby, and was so taken with him, he decreed they should share a name of equal length, an honour normally reserved for the other heads of the Crystal Dynasties.

Beneath her, the castle was surprisingly quiet.

Surely Pari should have raised the alarm by now? But even as she thought that, Chandni knew there were many reasons for Pari to fail. Perhaps the assassins had caught her, or perhaps the real guards had arrested her. Perhaps she was still hobbling along in that ancient body. *She's probably fallen asleep!*

The image made Chandni start to giggle until she realized she was being hysterical, at which point she started to cry.

It was cold and dark in the tunnel. Her knees were raw from crawling, and she had to shuffle one-handed so that she could hold Satyendra in the other. As babies went, hers was small and light, like her, but over time that little weight seemed to increase, until it was like hefting a sweet, huggable boulder.

A tear fell onto Satyendra's head and she heard the tiniest intake of breath.

Then, summoning the inner voice of her mother, Chandni berated herself until the tears stopped falling. *This is not how a child of the Sapphire behaves! It simply will not do! Your face should be inscrutable, a puzzle for your enemies to fret over and your allies to admire. It should be held still, a weapon, only moving when it serves your purpose. It should not wobble and blush like a spanked bottom!*

Chandni nodded, shaking, but herself again. *Thank you, Mother.*

She forged on, gritting her teeth as the skin of her knees ground against the stone.

Just as she began to despair that the tunnel was endless,

her head connected with the exit, causing her to curse Pari, the assassins, the castle's architects, and her own stupidity.

A panel slid away, admitting her into the main entrance hall behind the feet of an ancient statue from a time long-forgotten. The crystal had been grown through several floors of the castle and carved in sections, so that the head emerged in the feast hall and the feet straddled the entrance. There was an old belief that the great sapphire giant held the castle together, and kept it in the sky. Chandni had always liked the statue and thought it sad they did not have a name for it. The man depicted had a kind face and was the only crystal-forged smile to be found in Lord Rochant's home.

Mohit had said the hollows where the eyes should have been were creepy, but she disagreed. She felt the dark spaces gave the statue a sense of intelligence that the others lacked.

Mohit, my poor, poor, Mohit. He had been kind, respectful. And though not the best of lovers, he had endeavoured to follow her instructions to the best of his ability. What he had lacked in initiative, he'd made up for in determination. In fact, by the end of their time together, she'd hardly been bored by him at all.

The panel closed behind her, softly, bringing her back to the present. It was a short walk from here to the main doors of the castle. Unfortunately, they were closed and barred, and from her hiding place, she could see several alert looking guards in place.

Even from a distance, she could tell they weren't her people. Chandni made it her business to know every member of staff at the castle. She didn't tell them of course, saving the knowledge for when it could be employed to maximum advantage.

These are the assassins. Not just one more as Pari believed, but a group, possibly a whole unit.

The castle kept only a small team of defenders but they were highly trained, at least she had always considered them so. It troubled her that they had been dealt with so easily.

There was no way she could leave by the main entrance, but there was more than one path in and out of the castle. Using the statue as cover and keeping out of sight of the gates as best she could, she made her way towards the kitchens.

She had almost reached the stairwell off the main corridor when she heard a woman's voice behind her. 'Hold there!' It was coming from the other end of the entrance hall. She was not surprised that the speaker was unfamiliar.

Pretending not to hear, she walked a little faster, giving Satyendra a calming smile, and making sure her body blocked him from sight.

'Hold there, I say!'

She turned into the stairwell and, as soon as she was out of view, took the steps three at a time, her feet skidding off the end of one, straight onto the other, threatening to fly out in front, as her long hair flew out behind.

Satyendra's eyes grew wide and his hold on her tightened, but the baby kept his peace, just as his mother did.

Like a thing tossed from a storm, she burst into the kitchens, her feet bruised, her nightdress filthy, her knees swollen.

'Ooooh!' crowed the old cook, who moments ago had been asleep but was now most definitely awake.

Chandni straightened, and raised an imperious finger, cutting off the questions forming on the cook's lips. She'd served the Sapphires all her long life and was talented but slow, and liked the sound of her own voice far too much for Chandni's liking. 'Open the outer door. Tell no one that I've been here. You have not seen me or Satyendra, do you understand?'

'Of course, Honoured Mother. But what—'

'—Immediately, dear Roh.'

The cook beamed at the use of her name, then went the wrong way, snatching up a bag and stuffing it with food.

Chandni channelled her mother again as she admonished the cook. 'Were you not listening? Or is this an act of deliberate insubordination?'

'But you'll be wanting something for the baby, and a cloak for your shoulders. Wouldn't do for you to be seen out there in your nightwear, I'd never forgive myself. And what about your poor feet?'

Behind her, Chandni felt rather than heard someone enter the room. She went to step away but a hand caught her arm.

She turned to find a woman dressed in House Sapphire uniform – but most definitely not House Sapphire – looking at her. The absolute lack of respect in the assassin's eyes was chilling. She was about to say something when the assassin pulled out, not a sword, but a long, thin needle coated in something that glistened in the gemlight.

Chandni made to pull away but the assassin simply stepped with her, keeping close, the needle arcing down towards Satyendra's neck.

Instinct took over, and in the next moment she felt something bite into her palm, briefly painful, and then suddenly, worryingly numb.

The point of the needle protruded from the back of

Chandni's hand, quivering inches away from her baby's skin. Blood rather than poison coated it now.

Chandni exchanged a helpless look with Satyendra, whose little eyebrows raised questioningly, as if asking if this was an appropriate time to cry.

Yes, she thought. *This is the perfect time to cry.*

If the Bringers saw Pari, they made no comment as they passed out of the chamber, keeping to their ritual path. She listened intently as their robes whispered their way to the door, paused, then came the measured sweep of the door opening and them passing through, one by one, taking the light with them. The door closed with a heavy thud, plunging them into darkness. She heard Rochant sigh.

'You can come out now.'

Pari used the pillars to navigate through the darkness, letting each one brush cool against her fingertips. 'How did you know I was here?'

His voice was tired but not without warmth. 'I didn't, I just hoped.'

She reached out for him, finding the line of his shoulder in the dark. 'Ah, there you are.'

'Yes.'

She wiggled onto the side of the slab, enjoying the feeling of his warmth against her, and leaned down so that her lips hovered just above his. 'And here I am.'

'Yes.' He lifted his head so that the word brought their mouths brushing together.

Pari longed to stay like that but neither her conscience nor her back would allow it. 'Yes,' she agreed, breathlessly. 'But we have to talk, you and yours are under threat.'

'Something's happened?'

She told him quickly of the assassins, of the recent deaths in his line and the attempt against baby Satyendra that she'd foiled. He didn't argue or interrupt until she'd finished.

'Who would do this to me?'

Pari considered. 'High Lord Sapphire could have done it, the Bringers implied he was angry with you.'

'You heard them? By the Thrice Blessed Suns, is nothing sacred?'

'No, and you should be grateful. Without me things would be much worse.'

Rochant found her hand and squeezed it. 'You're right about me but wrong about my High Lord. If he had wanted me removed it would be done publicly, as an example to others. He would never stoop to knives in the dark.'

'Perhaps that was true once but I hear rumours that High Lord Sapphire is not the man he was.'

She felt Rochant turn his head away. 'I tell you it is not his way.'

'Who then?'

'I don't know.'

'Even someone as charming as you must have enemies.'

'Whoever it is has planned well. They've taken full advantage of the disruption the ceremony causes.' She could hear the interest in his voice. Despite the threat, he was intrigued by the puzzle. 'The assassin you confronted, you said he was in Sapphire uniform?'

'Yes.'

'Did it fit?'

Pari thought for a moment. 'Yes, like it was made for him, in fact.'

'So that means either he had been working here for some time, or he'd had the uniform made specially.'

Pari shook her head, then realized Rochant wouldn't be able to see the gesture. 'Or he found a guard of similar size and stole his.'

'In any case,' Rochant continued, 'this is something that has been planned well in advance.'

'I agree but how does that help us here?'

'Motivation. Someone wants this done but is willing to wait to achieve it.'

'But why? Revenge? Ambition?'

'That's the next thing we have to understand.'

'No,' said Pari. 'The next thing we have to do is get you out of here.'

'Wait, I'm not ready to move just yet.' Though his new body was exhausted, his mind seemed agile as ever. 'There are two obvious reasons to remove my line. One, because the person or persons behind this desire my death. Two, the person or persons behind this stand to gain from my death. If I and all of my descendants were gone—'

Pari nodded, '—then High Lord Sapphire would be able to raise a new member into the Crystal Dynasties. Who would he have in mind? We need to find out . . .'

'And I need to think about the past, cases I have presided over, decrees I've made, anything that could have seeded resentment.'

'While you're doing that, I'll go and make sure Chandni is coping with Satyendra. I fear life outside the castle is going to be a bit of a shock for her.'

'Quite.'

Though she couldn't see it, she could imagine Rochant's

expression. His face rarely gave much away, but there was a whole language kept in the crinkles around his eyes. She resisted the urge to touch his face, seeking them. 'It's good to have you back.'

He took breath to reply but the second door to the chamber opened suddenly, interrupting him.

Pari slid from the slab, darting behind the nearest pillar.

She just had time to tuck herself out of sight before a pair of boots could be heard marching on the stone, and then Dil's voice, oddly cold, 'My lord.'

'Dil? Is that you?'

'Yes, my lord.'

'Ah, the mantle of adulthood suits you, captain.'

'Thank you, my lord.'

Something in Dil's manner seemed off, but it was hard to read the man by sound alone. Unable to help herself, Pari peeked round the pillar. With the second entrance wide open and light flooding the chamber, she was able to see, not just Dil, but two other guards alongside him.

But I only heard one pair of boots!

She had to hold her hands together to stop them shaking. The assassins were here, and Dil was oblivious. She prepared herself to act. Perhaps between them, they could hold off the killers long enough for help to arrive.

'Forgive me, my lord,' said Dil, 'but you are about to be attacked by an assassin sent by the Tanzanites.'

The comment was so ridiculous, so unexpected, that she nearly came out of her hiding spot to argue.

Luckily Rochant seemed happy to do it for her. 'Explain yourself, captain. The last I heard, our accords were strong with all the crystal dynasties.'

'They are, my lord. But after we've killed you, that's what we're going to tell everyone, and I suspect the accords won't matter then.'

Dil turned to the man and woman behind him. 'Find the Tanzanite.'

They immediately drew weapons and split up.

Pari retreated further into the darkness on the opposite side of the chamber. *After we've killed you! Who is this man?* Dil had served Rochant his whole life. Where was the faithful, quiet child she remembered?

'There's no one here but us, captain,' said Rochant, the epitome of calm.

'That's a lie,' replied Dil, 'but then you've always been good at lying, haven't you?'

If the sudden change of tone surprised Rochant, again he gave no sign. 'Ah. I see anger in your eyes and can only assume I am responsible. Whatever the problem is, let us solve it peaceably. You have always been reasonable, even as a boy. Negotiation is the only path, surely you can see that?'

Dil snarled and sprang across the gap.

Still weak from the ritual rebirth, Rochant was unable to defend himself and Dil clapped something over his mouth, hissing, 'I don't want to hear your voice ever again. But I want you to know that I was the one that ended your line. Me!'

Pari could see her lover struggling to breathe. Dil intended to kill him, wanted to, but something was holding him back. Perhaps he just wanted to make Rochant suffer first but that didn't fit. The man seemed impatient, even desperate, to get revenge. Whatever the reason, she would not stand idly by as her lover was murdered. She edged into position, removing her remaining earring. The pin was too short to be very effective but if she could get it into one of his eyes, she might have a chance.

But, before she could make her move, another figure appeared at the door.

'We've searched the castle. There's no sign of the baby or the mother.'

'Then search further,' snapped Dil, releasing the pressure from Rochant's face, 'and keep searching until you find them.'

Without a word, the silhouette vanished as quickly as it came.

From nearby, startling Pari, the woman spoke, 'What now?' She'd been so absorbed in what was happening to Rochant, she hadn't realized how close she'd come to being discovered.

'Have you found the Tanzanite?' Dil demanded.

'You'd know if I had.'

Dil swore under his breath, then covered Rochant's mouth again, and Pari tensed, the urge to protect her lover battling a strong instinct that she should wait, though it tore at her to stand by.

Dil maintained the pressure until Rochant stopped struggling and flopped on the slab, unconscious.

'You, grab one end,' he called out to the man, then to the woman, 'you the other. We take him with us.'

'They won't like this,' muttered the woman.

'Piss on them! We can't kill him yet and we can't leave him here. Now do what I say.'

Pari stayed silent as the two assassins carried Rochant from the room, Dil following behind. Several times he checked over his shoulder, but each time, she ducked out of sight. She was just about to give chase when the door swung shut behind them, sealing her inside.

In the dark again, Pari fumbled her way forward until her palms pressed against stone, then the door they'd left through. She tried the handle but the door was locked. Frantically, she made her way round the outside of the chamber to the first door, the one the Bringers had used, but this too was locked. She let her forehead rest against the stone, trying not to panic as she thought about what to do next. About Rochant. About Chandni and the baby.

To be of any use she had to escape, and there was only one other way out of the Rebirthing Chamber.

Pari hugged herself tight, feeling the many complaints of her tired, aching body.

Come on! she urged herself and felt her way to the third exit. It was set into the floor directly beneath the slab of stone that Rochant had recently lain on; seven hinged triangles that could be released independently or all at once. This allowed the Bringers to jettison abominations, slab and all, without needing to untie them, and ensured they would fall fast and hard. She felt the edge of one of the triangles, marvelling at the intricate designs under her fingertips that would never be seen or appreciated by anyone save the Bringers, and pushed down. Unlike the other doors, this opened easily, and a cool breeze washed across her face. Pari climbed inside, settling her legs over the edge of the chute.

The other end would eject her from a hole at the base of the floating castle. If she failed to hold on, a long drop would follow to the chasm waiting below, and then another, into the bowels of the earth and beyond.

In order to avoid thinking about what could go wrong, she thought of Rochant, and she thought of Dil, of what she would do to the traitor when she caught up with him. And she thought of the mystery demanding to be solved.

And then she jumped.

CHAPTER FOUR

Chandni blinked, at least she thought it was only a blink, but when her eyes opened she was sat in a chair, Satyendra in her lap, and a thick wad of fabric strapped around her hand and several bands wrapped painfully tight around her wrist. Underneath the padding her hand felt hot, far too hot.

On the floor at her feet the assassin was sprawled out flat, dead, her expression frozen halfway between smug and surprised.

'Nasty little fingers,' said the cook, looking at the body with disdain. 'Dirty nails. In all my years I've never seen one of good Lord Rochant's soldiers with dirty nails. You can't trust one that can't clean themselves.'

'Thank you, Roh. I won't forget this, but how did you—'

The cook waved off her questions and hooked a bag over Chandni's shoulder, plucking her own cloak from a peg. It was warm from the stove and full of pouches, many of which felt full. 'Eat from the left pockets but not the right, Honoured Mother, never the right.'

She tried to take this in as a wave of nausea hit her. 'I don't . . . I don't feel myself, there was poison . . . '

'Aye. I've drawn and treated it best I can. Have to wait and see now. Stick a pin in the wound when the suns are at their peak. If you don't feel the pin, lose the hand. Then stick a pin in your wrist, your forearm, until it hurts. Keep what hurts, Honoured Mother, lose the rest.'

Chandni nodded, too shocked to speak as the cook unbarred the outer door and pulled it open. Air, cold and fresh, rushed in, and she closed the cloak around Satyendra to protect him.

The cook helped her to her feet and propelled her towards the door. 'Do you have somewhere to go?'

'I do, a—'

The cook raised a finger, mirroring Chandni's earlier gesture with almost mocking perfection. 'Less you say, Honoured Mother, less I can say.'

'There are more enemies in the castle. They'll be angry that you helped me.'

'They won't suspect a daft old woman,' replied the cook with a wink, pushing Chandni outside.

'But what are you going to do about the body?'

The cook tapped the side of her nose and smiled to reveal a full set of yellowing teeth. 'Don't worry, Honoured Mother,' she said as she closed the door, 'they won't even find the bones.'

Chandni stumbled away from the castle. She was so tired she felt it should be dark outside, but all three suns were just visible on the horizon, the two greater ones, red and gold, Vexation and Fortune's Eye, only half visible, while the smaller third, Wrath's Tear, arced above.

Underneath her cloak, a small hand tugged at Chandni's nightdress and she realized she'd stopped moving. She'd lost focus, lost time, staring at the suns like a simpleton.

This will not do!

She staggered on, feeling the vibrations beneath her feet. For the great chunk of rock that the castle sat on was shot through with veins of crystal, and these crystals chimed and sang, rising and falling like the tides.

Though Rochant's castle floated it was not static above the chasm, it bobbed slowly up and down. Because of its size these movements were rarely noticed, like being on board a vast ship, but if one looked outside, they would see the horizon gradually moving.

An outer wall circled the perimeter of the rock, protecting Chandni from the worst of the winds but doing nothing about the cold. Soon her feet had become clumsy lumps on the end of her ankles and she feared she would fall. The drop in temperature was easing her fever however, allowing her mind to function more clearly, and the burning sensation in her hand was less distracting.

A few eager travellers had tucked their tents alongside the wall, like plush barnacles, no doubt wanting to be the first to take advantage of Rochant's return. None of them were flying Tanzanite flags but that was no surprise. Wherever Pari's man was, he'd be trying to keep a low profile.

She could not escape the feeling that she was being watched, and began to worry that more assassins had been placed outside.

It's what I would have done.

After discounting the first tent because it was too grand, and the second because it was crammed full of people,

Chandni came to one discreetly pitched next to a wagon. A five-legged Dogkin, white-furred and almost as big as the wagon itself, slept alongside.

Though the tent's occupant had not come out to meet her, she could make out his tensed silhouette against the fabric. *Here is a man ready to take action.*

She looked over her shoulder, sure that someone would be there, but the courtyard was empty, save for the slow-turning shadows of the wall.

Chandni turned back to the tent and whispered, 'Varg?'

The flap opened almost immediately and a man's face appeared, broad and bearded, with a high, weathered forehead. He took a long look at her and the baby, his lips paling as he mashed them together. One arm held open the tent flap but the other was kept out of sight and she was in no doubt that he was armed.

'My name is Honoured Mother Chandni of House Sapphire,' she said carefully, watching for any hint of malice, 'and this is my son, Satyendra. Lady Pari sent us. We need you to get us to safety, urgently.'

'Piss off,' said the man, vanishing back into the tent.

Chandni crouched down, unsteadily, and slid Pari's earring under the entrance flap.

There was a pause. Then, from within: 'Fuck.'

Seconds later he was scrambling out of the tent and throwing a pre-packed bag into the back of the wagon. 'I'm Varg,' he confirmed as he bent down to grab the edge of the tent, pulling until the under-suckers came free of the stone with a loud pop. 'Where's Pari?'

'She's not coming.'

'Fuck.'

'Varg, if we are going to travel together you will need to broaden your vocabulary.'

He was halfway through hauling the tent onto the back of the wagon when her words sunk in. 'Doesn't bother Pari, and she's a lady.'

If things weren't so desperate Chandni would have laughed. 'That's a debate for another time. What can I do to speed things up?'

'Start waking Glider. But watch out, she's a biter.'

She went straight over to the Dogkin, taking a large floppy ear and shaking it, while calling Glider's name. Satyendra leaned forward in her arms, trying in vain to make contact with the glossy coat.

Eyelids slowly lifted, revealing a dark eye, hostile, and a second lighter eye, glassy, unseeing, human. One legend had it that Dogkin were the reincarnated souls of children who had wandered so long between lives they'd forgotten what they were. Another, that Dogkin were descended from people cursed by the old gods during the Unbroken Age.

Chandni preferred the first legend as it came with the promise that if a Dogkin could remember its true nature, it would be reborn as a human child in the next life. She liked to think that there was always a way to make things better.

'It's time to get up,' said Chandni.

Glider growled meaningfully and then shut her eyes.

Refusing to be ignored by an animal, Chandni tried again. This time Glider's growl was louder and her teeth snapped in the air, coming awfully close to Satyendra's reaching hands.

Rather than intimidate, the animal's behaviour converted all of her pent up worry into anger, and Chandni slapped the Dogkin across the muzzle so hard that a lance of pain shot through her bandaged hand.

Glider looked up in surprise, before opening her mouth to snap again.

'No!' said Chandni, pitching her voice as deep as it would go, and slapping the Dogkin's mouth a second time.

Glider whined pitifully and lowered her head but Chandni resisted the sudden urge to cuddle her, and kept her expression stern.

'Better. Now get up.'

Glider stood up.

'Good.' She reached into the left hand pockets of the cook's cloak, searching, and found one that contained some dried sausage. She held it up in front of Glider. 'If you run fast and without complaint, I have more.'

Glider's mouth opened and Chandni threw the sausage in. The little chunk of meat vanished, like a coin into a well. Glider's mouth remained open however.

'No more until you've earned it.'

The Dogkin made to lick the grease from Chandni's fingers but she pulled back her hand. 'No more I said, not even a sniff.'

With another noise of disgruntlement, Glider padded over to the front of the wagon, where Varg stood staring at Chandni in astonishment.

'Well don't just stand there,' she said, 'help us up.'

She placed Satyendra within the wagon but was forced to rely heavily on Varg's strength to climb on – her own was fading fast.

'You don't look right,' he muttered. 'Are you sick?'

'No. Just tired.'

Varg didn't look like he believed her but gave no argument, fitting a harness over Glider's head and untangling the reins.

Chandni looked back to the castle. The great doors remained shut, and all appeared far too peaceful. On a normal day the early risers would already be up, preparing for business, and Chandni was always one of them. It forced the staff to match her example and made sure things started when they were supposed to.

She didn't believe that people were inherently lazy, but it was better to take away the temptation just in case.

How many of the castle's inhabitants would be rising early today? she wondered. *How many would not be rising at all?*

Varg leapt up alongside her on the seat, bumping against her as he settled into position. 'Sorry,' he muttered.

She glared, about to reprimand him, when she realized she'd naturally sat dead centre of the driver's block. He'd been forced to squeeze onto the end, one of his buttocks hanging, precarious, from the side.

Not quite willing to apologize, she made a noise that she hoped sounded sympathetic and slid away from him.

It only took one shake of the reins and Glider was off, pulling them bumping across the courtyard.

'You certainly got a way with Glider,' he said. 'She's been a stubborn one ever since she was a pup.'

'Animals know authority when they meet it,' she replied.

'Usually have to scream murder to get her arse off the mud.' He shook his head. 'Never seen her so obedient.'

'Not even for your mistress?'

'Pari?' He laughed, a short and nasty sound. 'Pari's no good with Glider. They can't stand each other.'

Chandni quickly turned her head away so that Varg wouldn't see the pleasure she took from hearing about Pari's shortcomings. She'd felt usurped by the Tanzanite in her own castle and it had awakened a petty need to score back some points. However, it wouldn't do for Varg to realize that. Sapphires were supposed to be above such things.

The wagon was soon approaching the gap in the outer wall, big enough to manage a unit of ten soldiers marching shoulder to shoulder. A short lip of rock stuck out on the other side before cutting off, abrupt, leaving a long fall to the chasm below, and then another, longer fall after that.

There was nothing to bar their exit, no gates, no guards, which was odd as there was usually someone posted at the outer wall at all times.

Chandni shook her head, feeling sleep draw her in.

As they continued forward the Bridge of Friends and Fools came into view. Made of chains and planks, it was the only way back to earth. It had to be flexible to account for the air currents that moved the castle in constant, shifting increments.

The bridge was also the main defence. Two mechanisms held it fast to the rock. If the castle came under attack, it took only one soldier to release them both and send the bridge, and any unfortunates still on it, plunging to their doom.

She remembered being terrified of the bridge as a child, and a single look down reminded her why.

Through gaps in the slats she could see the crack in the earth far below. And from those depths, plumes of mist rose, pale purple, green, and yellow, seeming to hold some shape as they first broke free before dispersing, like mouths stretched so far they tore themselves open and scattered on the wind.

It was the power of the rising mists that held Lord Rochant Sapphire's castle in the sky. Chandni did not understand how or why, but accepted it as part of life.

Meanwhile, the wagon bounced its way across the bridge. Satyendra watched for a while but it soon became too much stimulation for young eyes and he buried his head in Chandni's chest.

'Sshh,' she said, stroking his dark gossamer hair.

'Be best if you get in the back,' said Varg. 'Keep quiet and out of sight. There's a little den back there you can use.'

This was true though it was also smelly in the back of the wagon, a mixture of musty cloth and Pari's perfume. The idea of resting in a place where Pari had no doubt slept filled her with horror but she did not complain. Varg was right about the need to hide.

Her mind was full of worries, for her own health, for the safety of her son, and how this treachery and murder would impact on the family in general. She tried to process what she'd seen and make appropriate plans, but as soon as she'd arranged herself and Satyendra had settled down, the warmth of his body and the exertions of her own lulled her into a swift, dreamless sleep.

Even as she fell, and Pari's mind was questioning the sanity of her decision, her body was reacting, adrenaline overriding fatigue, lifetimes of training overriding fear.

The chute was short and steep, taking a near vertical route through the floor of Rochant's floating castle. In the seconds it took to reach the end of it, Pari cursed that she had left her climbing claws in the wagon. But in her belt she had her silk rope, and the gland of the Spiderkin that spun it. Twisting her body, she pushed her feet against one side of the chute, pressing a shoulder and one hand against the other. Warmth then pain flared against her palm, and rough stone scraped viciously across her scalp. Her descent slowed but did not stop as she gripped the rubbery gland in her free hand and raised it to her mouth.

The flesh of the organ slid under her teeth as she found purchase, then stretched out absurdly, before tearing open. One end of the rope was still joined to the gland, the other to her belt. Pari squeezed hard to force the milky ooze to the surface of the new hole before jamming it against the roof of the chute. With a sound like a wet kiss, it adhered to the stone, sticking fast.

There was just long enough for Pari to shudder at the flavour on her tongue – a muddy bitterness with a stomach-turning gritty aftertaste – and then the edge of the chute thrummed past her feet, past her fingers, and she was spinning through space.

She tumbled for only a second before the silk jerked taut at her back, stopping her fall but leaving her at the mercy of the winds. And if Pari had thought the breeze that blew up the chute was cold, it was nothing compared to being fully exposed to the elements.

As she spun there, like a child's toy dangled between the underside of the castle and the great chasm waiting below, buffeted back and forth, Pari considered her options.

In many ways the simplest thing to do would be to detach herself and allow this lifecycle to come to an end. There would be a brief moment of pain when she hit the ground but that would be tempered by the memory of the fall, an exhilaration that she would treasure for many incarnations to come. The next thing she knew, she would be rebirthing in a Tanzanite stronghold, in a younger body. Several had been prepared, raised elsewhere in preparation for her next life. From what she had heard, the primary match, Rashana, her granddaughter was perfect.

However, her family would want to wait for an auspicious day for the rebirthing ceremony, and the required alignment of the suns was months away. That would be months for Rochant's enemies to act freely. Chandni was a spirited girl, and Varg, despite his coarse edges, would be an able protector for baby Satyendra, but neither of them were Deathless, and a single life only got you so far. Pari could feel the hand of another immortal behind all of this and did not dare a long absence.

She took a long hard look at the crack in the earth below. Its dark was thick, fathomless: the combined light of the three suns did not penetrate its depths. All floating castles of the Deathless were built above similar fissures and were kept aloft by the ethereal energies they exhaled. Nobody knew how deep they went, or if they even had an end. There was a chance that if she let go, she would not die. She would simply fall, endlessly. Perhaps her soul would travel too far, beyond even the reach of the Bringers to call back. Or perhaps she would travel beyond this world, into the realm where the demons lived. Pari normally had little patience with such superstitious nonsense, but dangling there, gazing into the hole far below, her usual bravado faltered.

Taking death out of the equation, there were few roads open to her. Her recent adventures were fast catching up, and she could feel a great wave of fatigue building, heralding a sleep that even the winds and the cold would not disturb.

It was tempting to simply hang there and sleep. Scaling the underside of the castle might be possible if she were more rested.

Pari laughed at herself, knowing that such thoughts were folly. The truth was that the next time she woke would be agony, her body already preparing to punish her for all she'd put it through in this ill-considered venture. Besides, she would never wake from such a sleep. Either the cold would finish her off, or the constant swaying of the silk rope would work the Spiderkin gland loose from the chute.

Come on, she exhorted herself. *Putting this off isn't going to make it any easier.*

Gritting her teeth, Pari hauled herself upwards. Three times, she heaved, placing one hand above the other, before she had enough slack to wind the rope around her right foot, taking some, but not nearly enough, of the strain from her shoulders.

It was dizzying, the way the wind spun her, but she blocked it from her mind, narrowing her focus down to the silk, her hands, her feet, and the next stage of the climb.

Soon, she had a rhythm, and her left foot was looped too, allowing her to progress swiftly back to the mouth of the chute.

She leaned against the back of the chute, letting it and the silk share her weight. The fatigue threatening to overwhelm her, and again she pushed it away.

I can't climb any more. I can't. I daren't fall. If only I had my wings!

In her mind she could picture her armour mounted on its

stand. How she longed for its embrace, the feel of the crystal against her skin, protective, supporting. If she were wearing it now, it would be a simple matter to ride the essence currents to safety.

How strange, she thought, *that the great mass of Rochant's castle could defy gravity, while she would fall as swiftly as a common stone.*

Her eyes were drawn to a cluster of sapphire poking from the rock. Over the years the crystals had grown, giving the castle greater stability and, to her mind, beauty. As the essence currents met the base of the castle, it made the crystals vibrate and sing, soft, like the murmurings of a sleeping giant.

The crystal . . .

By leaning out and trusting her weight to the silk she could just reach a long slender lance of sapphire that cut a diagonal slash across her view of the horizon.

The crystal . . .

She tapped along its length with her nails, attending to the way it chimed, until one of the notes sounded off. She tapped that place a second time to be sure. Again, the note was dull, flat. The crystal here was flawed.

Pari pushed against it, so that she swung backwards on the silk rope. When the momentum drew her forward again, she leant with it, striking the crystal with the heel of her hand. There was a sharp crack and then a chunk broke away. Pari tried to snatch it from the sky but the crystal tumbled from her tired grasp, splintering into fragments, leaving her to watch, powerless, as it fell.

But the fall was only momentary, the next updraught catching each splinter and making them tinkle, like rain on a rooftop, as they rose once more into her waiting arms.

Once she was wedged into the chute again, Pari bound the sapphire pieces into her cloak, bundling them tight, binding the ends together, and tying each to her wrists.

She worked the gland free of the wall, paused, and sighed. *This is it.*

Too tired to jump, Pari simply released the tension in her legs, flopping out through the hole.

As soon as the bundled crystals entered the current, they began to push upwards, taking the cloak with them and snapping Pari's arms vertical. Not enough to hold her there, but enough to allow her a measured descent.

Perfect.

It was not the same as hunting. She had little control beyond being able to nudge slowly to the left or right. But she had spent many lifetimes in the air, and made the most of that skill to keep to the stronger currents, dropping in gasps and stutters.

To the east she could make out the Bridge of Friends or Fools and, despite the early hour, a cart rumbling along it. Though it was flying no house flags, she was certain it was of Sapphire design, and moreover, that Rochant was tucked away inside it.

They are taking you from me, my love. But where?

She stared after it, straining her eyes until it was swept from view and she was forced to consider her own predicament again.

Gradually, the crack in the earth below grew larger and darker, and she could make out individual wisps as they first emerged, a pluming flurry of purples, yellows and greens. Rather than be repulsed, she found herself drawn, a part of her wanting to give herself over to that place and be swallowed up. But it was a false part of her, and she repressed it with a shudder, forcing her eyes away from the hole and towards the rocky ridge that surrounded it.

The further she moved away, the weaker the currents became, turning her landing into a barely controlled fall. She hit the ground at speed, falling naturally into what would have been a graceful roll had she not become tangled in her own cloak.

Several tumbles and groans later, she came to a stop amid moss and stone. Pari allowed herself a victorious grimace before taking a tally of her injuries. No bones were broken but she had sprained muscles in her shoulders, thighs, and ankles. And the bruises! She managed to count three on her cheek and was just about to start on her arm when sleep embraced her.

CHAPTER FIVE

'Tell us the story!' said a voice from one of the far tables.

'Yes,' chorused several others. 'Tell us!'

Vasin smiled easily, casting his gaze across the feast hall. 'Again? Most of you have heard it already, several times.' He sipped at his drink, then added, 'I'd rather hear about how Mia led the other successful hunt.'

All eyes went to Mia, and she was nudged swiftly off her cushions to the applause of the assembled. Before she started her story, she bowed low to Vasin, and he saw the admiration in her eyes, and the desire.

To his surprise, he felt a flicker of lust. It had been a long time since he'd taken anyone to his bed. But then, it had been a long time since he had felt up to it. His victory over the Scuttling Corpseman had given pride back to House Sapphire, just as it had restored his own.

Even though it was not his victory.

Even though it was a lie. His mother had battled the Corpseman, the first person ever to wound it as far as anyone knew, and the second Sapphire Deathless to betray her house. What did that make him? The third?

Mia began her own story of the day, starting with a generous account of how Vasin had stirred them all, and as she told it her eyes met his, sparkling, and his smile grew that little bit wider.

He had allowed himself some Tack before the evening's festivities. Not a full dose, he needed his wits about him still, but enough to ease the tension in his jaw and shoulders. He had to appear relaxed, the very image of the champion they considered him to be. When news of Rochant's death reached the High Lord, there would be an investigation, and it was important he only draw the right kind of attention.

And so, despite the stress, he sat back and listened to Mia's voice, his thoughts made pleasantly fuzzy by the Tack.

Then he saw a figure drift by the entrance to the room, pausing just long enough to catch his attention, and the smile fell from his face faster than a wingless hunter from the sky.

To a casual observer she appeared like just another Sapphire servant but he knew better. Her loyalties were more discerning than that. There was no signal given, no communication needed to get his attention. The very fact that she had come was all the summons he needed.

It's all gone wrong! he thought, even as he forced himself to smile again and set his drink down, so that others would not see the way the liquid trembled in his cup.

Her name was Yi, and she had first come to him after his mother's judgement at the hands of the High Lord. It had been night, the castle had slept. She had presented herself to him at the zenith of his grief. She had talked and the words had meant nothing. Yi was an agent of his mother, raised and trained in secret, ready to serve in all things. To advise, to take revenge, to act where others could not.

At the time he'd had no interest in taking action, had screamed at her to leave him, and she had gone without protest. The whole incident was soon forgotten, buried under a tide of emotions and drug-fuelled emptiness. Now he remembered, however, and now he understood, and now, he would listen.

To leave in the middle of Mia's story would be an insult to her. And though any possibility of enjoying her company later had vanished, she deserved better than that. Besides, if he survived whatever Yi had come to warn him about, he would need many allies within his house.

So he waited, trying to be calm like his brother would be, while nodding and laughing at all the right places.

When he did stand to go there was a pleasing sound of disappointment from the assembled. 'Please,' he told them, 'enjoy the bounty that grateful Sagan has provided. Eat, drink, whatever else brings you pleasure.' There was a chuckle that he turned into a laugh by adding, 'Except you, Zir. You stick to the food and drink.'

They made another attempt to get him to stay. He very nearly sat back down again. Another dose of Tack and he'd be able to escape his worries until tomorrow. A single thought of his mother, exiled, alone, mortal, was enough to banish that idea. 'My friends,' he began, 'to be with you again has been the greatest of honours. I must go now, but I promise you this: keep the lights shining, keep your voices warm, and I will find you again.'

And with that, he left, the sounds of their banging on the

table and singing his name, honouring him, carrying him from the hall.

He moved swiftly, worried he would attract more servants or dignitaries hoping for a private word, working his way to the lower, less frequented sections of the castle.

A door opened on his left and he could see Yi's outline within. He turned quickly, went through and she shut the door behind him. Without a word she led him on. The light of the gemstones was waning, their stored energy almost spent, casting the walls in pale twilight. Even though it was late, the corridors were clear, and they made their way swiftly, without seeing another soul.

Vasin did not think too hard about how this was possible, there were plenty of other things to worry about. Though Yi appeared calm, the fact that she had sought him out anywhere other than his private chambers conveyed urgency, and disaster.

They descended deep into the bowels of the castle, into a tunnel that appeared on no maps, a short, angled, bumpy thing, like a piece of anatomy evolution no longer needed, forgotten, useless. Here, Yi stopped. 'You met with my lady?'

'I did, and I swore to do whatever it takes to bring her back.'

'Then you should know that we have already begun and there have been complications.'

'Well?' he demanded.

'All of Lord Rochant's descendants are dead, save two.'

A partial success or a total failure? 'Which two?'

'A baby, Satyendra. His mother managed to remove him from the castle. She had outside help.'

'Outside help?' He pressed a hand to his forehead. 'I don't understand.'

'Lady Pari Tanzanite. She knew we were coming.'

'How?'

Yi bowed deeply, apologetic.

If Pari knew then who else did? And did they know about his involvement? The deal he'd made with his mother? What she was trying to accomplish? A wave of panic rose up inside, enough to make him lean on the wall for support. From the tumult of worry a thought managed to swim free. 'Two. You said two had survived. Who was the other?'

'Lord Rochant. He survived the rebirthing ceremony but we have him.'

'Where?'

There was the slightest pause, Yi's thin lips pinching in displeasure. She pointed to the door behind her.

It was everything Vasin could do not to shout. 'Here? You brought him here?'

'On Captain Dil's order.'

And clearly that order had left a bad taste in her mouth. 'Where is Dil?'

'With the prisoner.'

Vasin levered himself upright and strode through the door. The top of a crystal had poked itself through the back wall, its gemslight weak, silhouetting the two people in the room. They had stopped mid-motion at his arrival, giving them an unreal appearance, like a painting, presented for his approval.

And he did not approve. Not in the slightest.

A pole had been driven into the ground, old enough to have held many other prisoners before this one. Now, Lord Rochant Sapphire was tied to it, his wrists bound above his head, his legs tucked underneath so that his feet could be tied to the pole also. A rough sack with a breathing hole was strapped to his head. Through it, Vasin could see bruising, fresh. He looked from that to the swelling on Dil's knuckles, and the heat in his face.

Enough, he thought.

And though his reflexes were dulled by the Tack, they were more than enough to intercept Dil's wrist. He could feel the fine bones under his fingers and, in his anger, it was tempting to break them. *How dare this man, this underling, sully the face of a Sapphire!* But Vasin could not stoop to his level, so instead, with a single shove, he ejected Dil from the room.

Rochant had been responsible for his mother's fall. He deserved to be punished, but that punishment would be just, and it would come from his or his mother's hand. Anything else demeaned their cause.

He became aware that the bag had twitched in his direction. He turned and felt Rochant's regard. It was as if the man could see through the bag, as if Vasin stood exposed before him.

And whether this was true or not, he could not bear to stay in the room a moment longer.

Once the door was closed behind him, he converted his fear to anger and turned it on Dil. This man had forgotten his place in the order of things and Vasin would ensure that he never forgot it again. 'You failed us.'

'It was that devil, Pari—'

Vasin's fingertips came to rest on the soft flesh of Dil's neck, cutting him off.

'And how did you deal with *Lady* Pari Tanzanite?'

'I trapped her in the Rebirthing Chamber. I think she's still there.'

His fingers pressed ever so gently deeper. 'You think?'

'I mean she is. She's there. She's definitely there. We sealed her in. There's no way out and . . . and her body is old. It might even be dead by now.'

Vasin glanced at Yi, who nodded.

At some point, he'd pushed hard enough that Dil had gone on tiptoes to escape the pressure. Vasin took a breath. To navigate these waters he would need to master his emotions, be more like Gada.

'And if she isn't dead?'

'I-I could denounce her!' exclaimed Dil.

Yi gave a slight shake of her head, mirroring Vasin's own. 'Your word is wind against a member of the Crystal Dynasties.' She turned to Vasin. 'For it to hold, his accusation would have to be unchallenged. We would need proof of her betrayal.'

'Her presence in our lands was secret, yes?'

'Yes,' Yi replied. 'The official word is that she has withdrawn to her castle to recuperate after a mysterious illness.'

Vasin nodded, a plan forming in his mind. 'Who else can access the Rebirthing Chamber?'

'Only the Bringers of Endless Order and High Lord Sapphire himself,' replied Dil, tilting his head up in order to speak. 'I have the only other key, my lord.'

'Then we go there, now, before the High Lord does. We must find out what she knows. And how she knew!'

'I will make her talk, my lord,' said Dil.

Vasin did not like the look in the man's eye, he turned his hand ever so slightly, snuffing out Dil's disgusting enthusiasm.

'You will do as I command, nothing more.' His lip curled as Dil capitulated.

'Trespasser or not, Lady Pari deserves our respect. I will speak with her and learn the truth behind her involvement. When I am satisfied, we will pay a visit to her home, in order to prove she is not in residence. At that point, Dil will denounce her in the name of his murdered lord. The Tanzanite will protest, naturally, and there will be an investigation, but when they find her body in the Rebirthing Chamber at Lord Rochant's castle, all further doubt will be erased. With luck she will be tried and condemned before her rebirth, privately and without disgrace.' He leaned close to Dil's face and gestured towards where Rochant was being held. 'Do not cross the threshold of that room ever again, do you understand?'

'Yes, my lord.'

He withdrew his hand. 'Prepare yourself for travel, we leave within the hour.'

Dil's eyes lingered briefly on the door, but then he straightened, saluted and left. Vasin and Yi shared a look, neither needing to express their misgivings with words.

'Look after our prisoner while I'm gone,' he instructed. 'Keep him secure, but if you can, make him . . . ' he struggled for the right word. 'Comfortable.'

Did Yi's eyebrows twitch as she bowed? No matter, unlike Dil, she could be trusted to follow his orders to the letter.

He returned to his room, so busy lamenting the fact that he could not return to the feast, that he didn't spot Gada pacing by the window until he spoke.

'Where have you been?'

His brother was in his finery, tightly bound silk on his

limbs, and a river of the same fabric flowing from his shoulders. A scent like air on a cold morning wafted from his face. His cheeks were darker than usual and the formal make-up was exaggerating his scowl.

'Well? I have been searching high and low for you.'

'What's wrong, brother?'

'The High Lord is on his way here, now. And he is most displeased.' He paused to peer at Vasin more closely. 'Are you yourself? Tell me you haven't been smoking that filth again.'

Vasin did not meet his stare. 'I'm fine.'

'You'd better be. We must be ready to weather the storm of the High Lord's anger.' Gada turned his attention to the rest of him. 'You must refresh yourself, change, and help me with the preparations. There is to be a gathering of the Sapphire.'

'Here?' replied Vasin weakly. 'With so little warning? There can't be.'

Gada's smile was weaker still. 'There can. The whole family. Here. Tomorrow.'

A rough jolt of the wagon woke Chandni up. It took her a few moments to work out where she was and how she'd come to be buried under several layers of heavy cloth.

When it all came back, what little relaxation she'd gained from sleep flowed out of her.

But we're still moving, she told herself. *So they haven't caught us. We're safe, at least for now.*

She began to consider her next move. The best thing to do would be to go to another family stronghold. There was an aunt in the north she could trust. If Chandni could find refuge with her she could request an audience with the Sapphire High Lord. An attack of this nature was surely an act of war. *What if Lord Rochant's line was only the first targeted? Or worse, what if it wasn't? What if other Sapphire lines have already fallen?*

Her lips were dry and her throat was worse. She needed a drink and something to eat. The best plans were made with a cool head and a quiet stomach.

She lifted Satyendra, still fast asleep, and saw a line of drool linking his lips to the clasp of her cloak. Chandni smiled and rested his head on her shoulder, before shuffling to the front of the wagon on her knees.

'Is it safe?' she whispered.

'We're well away,' Varg replied. 'You can come out here if you like.'

It was getting dark, the red suns Vexation and Wrath's Tear already below the horizon, with Fortune's Eye not far behind. She'd expected to find them on the Godroad, part of a network of crystal pathways that linked the Sapphire strongholds to those of the other great houses. Given a choice, everyone used the Godroads. Not only were they untarnished by the passage of time and quick to travel on, they kept the denizens of the Wild at bay.

But instead of pulsing crystal running smoothly beneath their wheels, she saw a path of broken stones, rough and overgrown.

'What kind of excuse for a road is this?'

'A quiet one,' replied Varg. 'I'm hoping they don't have eyes on it.'

'And where is it taking us?'

'Somewhere safe. Now how about you tell me what kind

of shi—' he saw her hand raise and corrected himself, 'trouble I've got myself into.'

He offered her a flask of fruit-touched water, and Chandni had a long drink before recounting events as best she could remember them. She was just coming to the part where she had to flee the castle when the words fell away.

'Something wrong?'

'How is it the suns are going down already?'

He gave a shrug of his broad shoulders. 'That's what they do.'

'But it was only just morning when we left!'

'That was a long while ago, believe me. I've been driving Glider as fast as I can, only taking short breaks. And we've made bloody good time if I do say so myself.'

'And I've been asleep all day?'

'Yep, you slept like the dead. Reckon the baby did too. Never heard a peep from either of you.'

Fresh sweat broke out on her forehead. 'Oh no,' she said. 'Oh no, no, no.'

'Something up?' he asked.

Chandni ignored him and retreated back into the wagon. She laid Satyendra down on a nest of folded cloth and sat down heavily, staring at her bandaged hand. Seconds after she'd let go, Satyendra's eyes opened and his face split in a yawn which became a stretch, whole bodied.

She ignored that too, and began to pull away the knots holding the bandage in place. Sweat stained the armpits of her nightdress and the back of her neck was slick with it. *Is this nerves? Or is it fever?*

Straps were removed and the wad of padding peeled away. A puffy red dot sat in the middle of her palm, the skin around it raised and angry. After rifling through the bag the cook had given her she found a small but very sharp knife. Slipping it from its sheath she pressed the point to her palm.

There was nothing.

She pressed harder, making sure that the point pierced the skin. The wound was sufficiently deep enough she could make blood seep out by squeezing the sides of her hand together.

Why can't I feel anything? I've left it too late. By the Thrice Blessed Suns, I've left it too late.

She moved the point of the knife further down until it sat at the thick edge where palm meets wrist. It felt clumsy using her left hand but she pressed the knife in and, when she saw rather than felt the blade, made several more cuts around the area.

Each time, her horror deepened.

How can I protect Satyendra out here with just one hand? It's not even my good one!

All of a sudden she missed the castle, and all the staff there. Several of them were her friends. She felt sure that she could manage if they were here. But she was alone, and her baby needed her to be strong.

I am more than strong, she reminded herself. *I am Sapphire.* She looked at her arm. Little streams of blood ran down it to start dripping from her elbow but she ignored them.

She directed the point of the knife above her forearm.

Please let this next one hurt. Please.

Just as she raised the blade, the flap at the front of the wagon was pulled open.

'What's going on in here?' shouted Varg.

She brought the knife down and cried out, delighted. Never before had the sensation of pain brought such relief.

She heard Varg say 'fuck' several times, then felt the wagon come to an abrupt halt as he ducked in to join her. His face grew pale behind his beard. 'What are you doing? Are you possessed?'

'No,' she gasped.

'There's blood everywhere!' He grabbed the hand that was holding the knife. 'Do you want to get us killed?'

A little indignation stirred within her. 'I am not trying to kill anyone, quite the opposite.'

'Shit and suns and fuck! They're going to smell us a mile away.' He picked up a piece of cloth, looked at her arm and then handed it to her with a look of disgust. 'Clean yourself up.'

'Aren't you going to help me?'

'I've been too close to you as it is,' he muttered, releasing her arm and backing away. 'You're going to bring half the fucking Wild on our heads!'

Chandni replaced the bandage but it took her several tries to retie the straps. Though she couldn't feel her right hand, she found she could flex the fingers. It was strange, as if the digits belonged to someone else. She forced herself to hope. Surely it was a good sign that her fingers still responded to her commands? If the poison had worked, wouldn't the hand be useless?

Satyendra made an unhappy noise, one that would be followed by a proper cry if she did not feed him.

'Ssh,' she said as she opened the cook's cloak and pulled down one side of her dress. 'I'm coming. Ssh.'

When she picked him up, Satyendra's mouth was flapping,

fishlike, so eager that he missed, head-butting her shoulder before latching on.

She stroked his head as he grunted, content.

The wagon was moving again, faster this time, with Varg's deep voice a constant companion to the creaking wheels. She found both the tone and the content objectionable.

Being careful not to disturb her son's feeding, Chandni edged to the front of the wagon. No suns were visible now but a little gold still inflamed the sky. Long grasses swept to either side of the road. Not the short, leafy clumps she was used to at the castle but thick stalks over half her height, each one covered in buds the size of her thumbnail, each bud shaped like a human ear.

As Varg muttered, the grasses rippled, the nearest stalks bent by the sound, touching their neighbour, whispering and passing it on. Like a breeze, Varg's voice was carried away across the fields.

Chandni's eyes followed the trail until they came to rest on a distant shape, an anomaly in the gloom; she couldn't tell if it were a person or animal, but whatever it was towered above the grass.

She cleared her throat and pointed. 'What is that?'

The grasses caught her words, scattering them across the fields in a flurry of frightened echoes. 'What is that, what is that, what is that . . . '

As the ripples reached the shape in the distance it began to move, unfolding long appendages. Fabric hung down from them like a pair of wings, tattered. And then it began to glide, and Chandni could not be sure if the grasses simply parted for it or if they were passing it along, one row to the other.

'That,' said Varg, 'is a Whispercage.'

Glider started to whine and Varg responded by shouting and applying a boot to the Dogkin's backside. 'Go faster you stupid lump or you'll really have something to complain about!'

'Faster, faster, faster,' said the grasses, 'you'll really have something, you'll really have something, you'll really have something.'

She had thought it big before, but as the Whispercage got closer Chandni realized she had not done the creature justice. It was nearly three times her height and twice as wide, with a long stretched skeleton, wrapped in rippling cloth.

Or is that loose skin? Chandni's gorge began to rise. *Is it wearing someone else's skin?*

'It's going to overtake us!' she cried.

'Take us,' echoed the grasses, 'take us, take us.'

'We're nearly past the fields,' shouted Varg, 'it won't touch us unless we look at it or talk to it, understand?'

'I understand,' she replied, as the grasses whispered: 'Touch us, touch us, touch us.'

'That means keep your fucking eyes down and your mouth shut.'

Chandni bit back a retort and did as she was told.

With Glider's five legs pumping for all they were worth, the wagon seemed to fly along the path, but the Whispercage was waiting for them up ahead. It leant out from the edge of the grasses, its arms – long poles of dirty bone – held high.

As they went past, the wagon rocked sideways as the Whispercage latched onto it, and Chandni felt something brush her cheek. It was surprisingly gentle, and soft as peach skin.

Don't look up, she told herself.

From the corner of her eye, she could see the edge of the fields in sight, the grasses thinning out and giving way to a wall of twisted trees.

She forced herself not to react to the movement by her ear. The Whispercage was right next to her. In her periphery, she was aware of it watching, waiting for her to turn and make eye contact. It wore a hood of sorts, and within it something moved where she'd expect to find a mouth, a tongue-petalled flower, opening.

Don't look up.

Satyendra's urgent suckling had settled into a steady guzzle, now it stopped completely. She heard his happy sigh, then felt his head turn away. Too late, she tried to turn it back.

Everything went dark as the Whispercage lunged, covering her. She flailed against it and it struck back, and all became a flurry of movement, as if she sat within a flight of furious birds.

For a terrible moment she was convinced that Satyendra had been taken, his weight had gone from her arms and she screamed in despair, but when the Whispercage was ripped away, like a sail torn from a storm-tossed ship, her baby was still there, staring up at her. The blanket that he had been wrapped in was gone, but he appeared unharmed. And yet, despite the evidence of her eyes, she could not escape the feeling that she'd lost her baby.

Varg looked across and nodded. 'Thank fuck for that.' But he didn't slow down and Glider seemed all too happy to keep running, until the last of the light faded away and only stars could be made out through the sparse canopy above.

By the time the wagon did come to a stop, they had left the grasses far behind. They were safe. Chandni breathed a long sigh and held Satyendra close.

To her surprise, he opened his mouth and began to scream.

Waking was as unpleasant as Pari expected. Muscles ached, joints locked up, stubborn, and bruises protested all over.

It was dark around her, the three suns having set some time ago. She wondered how long she had slept. *Not long enough*, replied her body.

The luminous Godroad cast a pale glow onto the night's clouds. Pari allowed it to guide her, grunting and groaning, towards it. Soon, a choice would have to be made. Much as she would like to examine the bodies of the assassins more carefully for clues, and question Lord Rochant's staff about Dil's movements, she knew she couldn't. Dil had named a Tanzanite as the one behind the attack effectively preventing her from approaching any of Rochant's loyal staff for help.

Besides, both Rochant and his last living descendant were outside the castle now, and they both needed her help.

As she slowly approached the Godroad, a feeling of unease crept over her. A prickling of skin on her arms, followed by the thudding of her heart, beating out a warning. Suddenly sure she was not alone, Pari whirled round. The castle floated high above, lights winking in its windows. Below it, hidden in the dark, was the chasm, surrounded by moss covered rock. And there was something else too. Something she could not see, staring back at her.

Something of the Wild.

Twenty feet from where she stood, two orbs, milk white, split the darkness. Big enough to be human eyes but too close together for a human face, with no discernible pupil or iris. They rose from behind some rocks to match her height, making a slow, hypnotic circle.

Pari had been on hunts before. Not as frequently as some, but she had done her duty as a Tanzanite. On those occasions she had worn her crystal skin, and been suitably armed, flanked by a dozen hunters. Here, tired, alone, with no weapon save an earring, she remembered why to most people 'Wild' was synonymous with 'fear'.

She tried to gauge if it was going to attack. Some creatures would wait for their victim to turn their back, others would strike regardless. Though she had no idea what she was facing, there were still clues in its behaviour that she could learn from, clues that might just save her life.

However, all Pari could think was: *That thing isn't a head!*

The unblinking eyes continued to move languidly, holding her attention. *A distraction, a sleight of hand. The attack will come from elsewhere.* And as she realized this, she became aware of a second, subtler movement to her right, drawing swiftly closer.

At the last moment, Pari threw herself to one side as teeth flashed into view, snapping shut in the space where her neck had just been.

She looked for the mouth but it had joined the shadows again, invisible. Every so often she thought she could make out shapes moving to flank her, one on her right, one on her left. And all the while the milky eyes continued to circle before her, placid and patient.

Opening her arms wide, Pari stepped forward and shouted as deeply as she could. The creature flinched, giving her a brief impression of its size, three blind heads attached to a flat body on sinuous necks. Her first instinct had been correct, the thing distracting her was the creature's tail. Pari did not even bother to try and count its myriad legs, instead turning and running for the safety of the Godroad.

Her feint bought her a few precious seconds and then she heard the sound of pursuit, a pattering multitude of tiny limbs scratching stone and kicking up dirt.

She wasn't nearly fast enough. There was no snapping at her heels but she could feel how close the creature was, the hairs on the back of her neck rising.

It was getting ready for a final strike. *At least it would be brief,* she thought. Another part of her had time to wonder where the creature would bite and how distasteful the Bringer's tattoo would be for the next rebirth, when something flew over her left shoulder to thud against the creature's shell.

'Keep going! You're almost there!' came a voice from the Godroad, young and female.

Pari didn't argue, focusing all her attention on the welcoming light just ahead. She put her head down as another missile flew past, and another, the sounds of impact followed by a strange lisping snarl.

The last few metres were uphill with the Godroad set a further six feet above the rock. Momentum tailed off as she forced her tired legs up it. *Just a little further,* she urged herself, *come on!*

But it was no use. She had already pushed her body well beyond its limits. Her fingertips were able to touch the curved lip of the Godroad but she lacked the strength to pull herself into its protective light.

A man watched her from the Godroad's edge, his feet either side of her hands.

'Help me,' she wheezed.

He started to lean down towards her but hesitated mid-motion. Pari could understand why. There were many stories about goodhearted travellers being lured to their doom by monsters wearing a human face. So long as he stayed on the road, he was safe.

'Quickly,' she added, 'before it gets me.'

'How'd I know you're a person, straight and true?'

'If I was of the Wild I'd talk less and look much more appealing than this.'

'Thas fair,' said the man, and leaned out, his hand open, stretching out over the lip of the road. She threw herself towards him, her hand locking onto his wrist.

There was a sound like someone vomiting behind her, and then something hard struck her between the shoulder blades, shattering like a rotten egg. Pieces of matter spattered over her shoulders and arm, a large chunk hitting the man's bicep and sticking there.

The force of the impact sent her to her knees, and the man was nearly pulled off the road to join her, but another pair of hands grabbed onto his belt, holding him precariously.

Pari could hear a hissing sound. At first she thought it was the creature, and then she realized it was the sound of her clothes burning where the spit had touched them. She glanced at the man's arm and saw steam rising from the edges of the gobbet.

She made to push him away but he was having none of it. 'Heave!' he shouted, and the two of them began to pull. Pari dearly wanted to help but there was nothing left inside. All she could do was make herself as easy to drag as possible.

As the man's upper body came back into the protection

of the Godroad, the mucus disintegrated, turning to mist then air in seconds.

The crystal light of the Godroad rippled as Pari was pulled up and she felt herself held by it as surely as the man.

Safe.

She was safe.

The three of them flopped down on the Godroad, panting.

When she turned back to see what the creature was doing, she saw nothing. No milky eyes, no noise, it was if the thing had never been there.

But it *was* still there, Pari was sure of it.

She glanced back to her saviours to catch a look passing between them. The man was younger than she'd first thought, with a familial resemblance to the girl next to him. She appeared barely into her teens, and the man only a few years on top of that.

'See?' she said. 'Not a monster. Just a very, very tired woman.'

The man pointed to a cart behind him. 'You can sleep on there if y'want. It's plenty soft.'

'Please. I'll need you to help me on.'

Though they were skinny, they were strong, and the two of them made short, if unceremonious work of putting Pari onto the cart. As soon as she was in, they went to the back and started to push.

The two youngsters wore the garb of House Sapphire servants, long blue tunics trimmed in grey, over darker trousers with blue piping, but it hung from their frames, the fabric vibrant against their dirt smudged skin. She could sense a nervousness that put her in mind of her first life, when she was still learning to deal with the excitement that accompanied being naughty. There was a story here, and a part of Pari itched to learn what it was. However it was only a small part: the majority of her was far more keen to enjoy the lulling of the cart as she rested her aching bones.

Each wheel had crystal threaded through the spokes, and these hummed merrily as they moved, infused with the power of the Godroad, not enough to lift it into the air, but enough to make the cart glide at a touch.

Such vehicles were expensive, owned only by a select few, and rarely found alone, especially not in the hands of poor teenagers.

It did not surprise her that, a few hours later, when they thought she had fallen asleep, they crept up to her with cord, and bound her wrists and ankles.

The arms that bore baby Satyendra were not his mother's. Where hers were soft, comforting, these dug into him, greedily stealing the heat from his naked flesh.

Something else was with his mother now, something that had looked at Satyendra as they'd been swapped by the Whispercage, and rippled, and taken his image.

He missed his mother and father. He missed the many smiling faces from the castle, and he was afraid. And yet he did not cry out. Fear gripped his throat, some instinct telling him that to make a noise would be to draw attention to himself. Perhaps the Whispercage would hear the sound. Perhaps it would turn its hooded face down to him again.

Satyendra did not want that.

They moved swiftly through the trees, ever deeper into the Wild. Around them, the trunks were old and crooked, their branches interlocking savagely with one another to form a tangly mesh above. Thick vines joined in the mess, energetic, their skin visibly pulsing to some alien heartbeat.

Only the odd shard of sunslight reached down to the forest floor, and even this seemed tentative, like a child dipping its toe into a hot bath. Satyendra stretched towards the glimmer of red, desperate to touch something warm, but his arms were too short, the distance too great, and soon it was behind him, gone and forgotten. Inexorably, the Whispercage spirited him onwards, into the Wild, into the gloom.

They came to a clearing where maimed roots poked from the earth, gnarled and bone-like. Three figures awaited them there. Each was vaguely man shaped in appearance but even Satyendra could see that they weren't human.

In place of hair, ropes of skin sprouted from their heads, draping over shoulders and hanging down, the ends brushing their toes to make living robes, sleeveless. They were tall, not as tall as the Whispercage, but far wider, with brawny limbs and bright red skin. Their ears were large and budded with fine antennae that stood up as Satyendra was brought towards them.

But there were differences between the three. The face of the first was featureless, save for three eyes arranged asymmetrically. The second had no eyes at all, his face dominated by a slash of mouth, vertical, that ran from forehead to chin, while the third had neither eyes nor mouth, his face a harsh triangle broken only by a single nostril.

'What this? What this?' said the one with the mouth. 'Crunch hears a Whisper. Does it bring the Red Brothers a gift?'

The Whispercage said nothing but extended its long arms forward, offering Satyendra.

'It does! It does! Do you see it, Eyesore? Is our gift promising?'

Eyesore clapped his hands.

'Good! Smell it, Pits, tell us if it's good and ripe.'

Pits stepped closer, his hands probing the air before him until they brushed against the rags of the Whispercage. Then he stopped, leaned over Satyendra, and sniffed.

All the while, Satyendra kept very, very still.

Pits sniffed a second time, long and indulgent, and then, in an echo of Eyesore, clapped his hands.

'Gift!' said Crunch, starting to clap as Pits stopped. 'Whisper brings us a gift!' He paused, then nodded to himself. 'I have first chunk.'

Eyesore shook his head, then slapped his own chest with a broad palm, prompting Pits to do the same.

'I first!' insisted Crunch.

The brothers stumbled closer until all three stood together. Then they began bumping each other's fists in a trial of strength, slowly at first, then faster, harder, until knuckles cracked and their fleshy hair swayed violently with each impact.

Each of the brothers wanted to win, and so they kept going, even after their hands began to swell with pain. But it didn't take long for the injuries to overwhelm the hunger, nor their pride. Eyesore's trio of orbs were squeezed against the pain, Pit's nostril flared, and Crunch's mouth twisted, unhappy.

When it became too much, Eyesore stepped back, followed, miserably, by Crunch. Pits punched at the space where they'd been a few times before realizing his victory.

As he clapped in delight, Eyesore guided Crunch to where

Satyendra lay, a curl of goosebumps that did not move, save to shiver. He did not cry out when Crunch took his wrist, nor did he make a sound when his arm was pulled towards the widening mouth.

But when Crunch's tongue looped around his little finger, he gasped. And when his mouth closed, snipping the digit away, he could not help but scream.

Unnoticed by the brothers, the trees around them shivered, and for a moment, the vines tightened on the branches, gripping them tightly, shocked.

The Whispercage noticed though, and it leaned down until the shadow of its hood fell across Satyendra's writhing body.

Abruptly, the baby's scream stopped, withering in his throat.

Crunch chewed slowly, working the tiny morsel in his mouth. 'Hmmmm,' he said, nodding, and, 'Mmmmmhhh,' and, 'Ooooohhhmmmm.'

Pits prodded him, impatient.

Reluctantly, Crunch spat a browny pink something into Pits' waiting palm. The mashed lump looked nothing like a finger.

Pits parted the sinewy hair that flowed over his body, revealing an expanse of red stomach. Black lines crisscrossed the skin and he picked at one of them with his free hand until he was able to slide his nails inside and peel a section open.

Through tear blurred eyes, Satyendra watched as Pits carefully inserted what remained of his finger into the hole before pressing the flap closed again.

Pits put his head to one side, thoughtful, before rubbing his stomach in delight.

'Gift good, Whisper. We like,' said Crunch.

The Whispercage made a noise somewhere between a wheeze and a sigh, and the three brothers leaned in to listen, each tilting an ear toward it. Satyendra squirmed and wriggled but could not escape the iron grip of his captor.

The three brothers nodded eagerly, as if agreeing to something, and then Crunch reached for Satyendra's leg. 'My turn.'

The Whispercage maintained its grip on his body and so, when Crunch pulled at his ankle, he was stretched painfully between the two of them. As Crunch's lips parted, Satyendra began to whimper; when the tip of his tongue darted against Satyendra's heel, he screamed.

Though the other two brothers were still waiting their turn to eat, they could not help but get involved. Pits ran his vast nostril over Satyendra's exposed back in a single extended inhalation, while Eyesore gazed longingly at the frantic kicking of his chubby leg, and flexing of the little toes.

No matter how hard he tried, Satyendra could not get his ankle free. This time, Crunch's tongue selected the big toe of his right foot, wrapping around to hold it still.

A line of drool ran across the ball of Satyendra's foot, tickling, making panic instead of laughter.

And then, all around them, the leaves rustled as one. But it was not the sound of wind playing through the woods, rather the sound of wings flapping, a beat that matched the pulse of life through the vines, a beat that sounded as if it were directly overhead.

The three brothers froze, Crunch's teeth pausing, pressing, but not breaking the skin.

Then everything was moving too fast for Satyendra to follow.

He heard a screech, angry, like that of a bird, and this too was taken up by the trees and amplified so that it came from every direction.

He heard the sound of the three brothers slapping their hands together and moving, fleeing.

He heard rags flapping and a hiss.

And then he was dropped, landing hard on the uneven ground, dead roots prodding him all over.

Directly overhead, a shape was descending, black wings an outline against the shadows, with glittering eyes and an angry demeanour.

The Birdkin screeched a second time and Satyendra screwed his eyes shut, as if that might somehow lessen the sound. When he opened them again the Whispercage had vanished, as had the brothers. There was no sign of their leaving, no tell-tale marks of their passage, they had simply gone.

Satyendra blinked in surprise, ignoring the Birdkin as it settled nearby. He looked to his left, to his right, but could not see them. The fear that had gripped him so tightly faded a little, allowing the pain in his maimed hand to fully dominate his attention.

He took a deep breath, his tiny body visibly filling with air, and began to cry in earnest. The leaves moved more softly this time, a sympathetic chorus for his suffering.

At first, the Birdkin hopped away, raising a wing as if to fend off attack, but it soon recovered enough to strut over to where he lay.

Satyendra was dimly aware of the Birdkin making a slow circuit around him. With its wings folded in, it had the appearance of a thoughtful creature, pondering a problem.

It came to a stop on Satyendra's right, where the blood from his hand stained the earth.

Satyendra turned to look up at it. The Birdkin was as big as he was, its ivory beak nearly as long as his arm. Its eyes were compound, like a fly's, and Satyendra saw himself reflected in them many, many times, tiny and pathetic.

For a few moments they regarded each other, and then the Birdkin's beak flashed down, parting, widening, so that a long proboscis could lever out from deep within its throat. It brushed quickly over the spilled blood, sucking and skimming, taking off the top layer of the puddle before it could be stolen by the soil. Then the Birdkin threw back its head and swallowed.

A shiver ran through its feathered body, and when it settled again, the creature held itself differently. 'Sa-aat!' it shrieked. 'Sa-aat!'

Its beak came down a second time, swift and precise, and Satyendra felt it pinch his wounded skin closed. There was a moment of incredible pain coupled with a burning sensation, and then he felt nothing, as if the Birdkin had nipped off the agony.

He glared at it, but with the pain gone, it was hard to keep his eyes open.

The Birdkin settled down next to him, spreading its wings so that one covered him from leg to toe, while the other curled behind his head to drape across his chest.

Gradually, warmth transmitted itself from one body to another.

Satyendra's glare softened. His eyelids drooped, then sprang open again.

The Birdkin watched him with one eye, the other turned

out to the trees. It began to sing, and though its voice was that of a bird, he knew it, just as he knew the tune. It was his mother's.

The wings holding him were warm, like her arms.

He was safe.

And there, encircled by feathers and song, and a ring of whispering trees, he slept.

Satyendra would not stop crying. Chandni had tried everything she could think of, hugging him, feeding him, soothing him, singing, rocking, she had even considered begging, though pride had so far saved her from that.

The night was coming to an end, and all of them were tired. So far none of them had enjoyed any sleep.

'For suns' sake, shut him up!' bellowed Varg.

'Don't shout,' she retorted. 'You'll only distress him.'

'He's already distressed and so am I. And so is Glider.'

The Dogkin howled in agreement.

'Don't you start,' she warned, and then, as Glider began to howl again: 'No, you will stay quiet.'

They locked eyes for a moment before Glider looked away, putting her head beneath her paws.

Chandni could hear Glider's miserable whimper quite clearly in the sudden peace. Satyendra had finally stopped crying! The elation easily overrode any guilt over giving the Dogkin a hard time.

She laid Satyendra down and settled next to him. There were only a few hours left till dawn and she intended to sleep through them.

Just as her eyes began to close, Satyendra started crying again.

A moment later, Glider joined in.

Chandni squeezed her eyes shut. Perhaps, if she was patient, Satyendra would tire himself out and go to sleep.

'Right,' said Varg, sounding anything but patient. 'That's it! I'm going to kill the little sod!'

'You will not lay so much as a finger on my son.'

Undaunted, Varg clambered into the back of the wagon. 'Oh yeah?'

Chandni sat up, putting herself between the man and Satyendra. 'You threaten a baby when it has been exposed to the horror of the Wild? A baby that you have been ordered to protect. I wonder what Lady Pari would say, if she could see how quickly you forget yourself.'

Varg paused, adding in a more polite tone. 'I wasn't going to literally kill him, just—'

'Just what?'

'Well, you know . . . '

'I most certainly do not know. Please, enlighten me.'

Varg began to retreat from the wagon. 'Nothing. I wasn't going to do nothing. I'm just tired is all.'

'Then I suggest you save your energy and your voice for the foreseeable future. And to be clear, I am speaking literally.' Varg's sudden smile flared the embers of her temper. 'What? Something about this amuses you?'

'I'll be damned. He's gone quiet again.'

It was true, though Satyendra was still very much awake, his dark eyes moving expectantly from Chandni to Varg and back again. When whatever he was hoping for did not come to pass, his face began to crumple and Chandni felt her own copying it.

Please, no more!

She risked a look at Varg, worried that frustration and sleep deprivation would drive him to something stupid. After all, she hardly knew the man. He was clearly a servant of Pari's, though what kind of servant was something of a mystery.

One who is accustomed to danger and being where he should not. One I am sure that is no stranger to violence.

But instead of getting angry, Varg was pulling at his beard. 'Say something horrible.'

'What?' she replied.

'To me. Say something horrible to me.'

'I –' she paused, her mind suddenly blank '– I can't think of anything.'

'You haven't had any trouble before.'

Satyendra opened his mouth and made a little whimper, a miserable singer warming up before the performance.

'Just do it, quick, before he sets Glider off again.'

She had no idea what Varg was babbling about but she decided she didn't care. If he wanted her to list his faults, then she was only too happy to oblige. 'You reek.'

He turned to her, an expression of genuine hurt on his face. 'I do?'

'Yes. I smell you before I see you. It's horrible! As if man-sweat and Dogkin fur had got together and made a baby and rolled it around in the dirt. Your language is disgusting and your manner insulting. You . . . '

'Go on,' he urged, giving a slight nod in Satyendra's direction.

She glanced at her son, just in time to see him smiling. The crying lines had faded from his face, and his eyelids were starting to droop.

'You're not fit to look at us, let alone be near us. It's no wonder Glider doesn't respect you. I doubt anyone does. How could they when you don't respect yourself. You're a walking shambles!'

Satyendra giggled dozily.

Varg winked at her. 'Don't you dare talk to me like that!'

'I'll dare what I want, you disgusting sack of hair!'

'Right, that's it!'

'That is not it, I've only just started. Lady Pari may find it acceptable for you to behave like this but I most certainly do not. Firstly, I expect you to address me properly at all times and to behave with the proper deference. I am a child of the Sapphire and my child or grandchild will be a vessel for the immortal Lord Rochant and as such—'

'It's okay, you can stop now.'

Chandni found herself slightly disappointed. It had been liberating simply to speak her mind without fear of consequence. When she turned back to Satyendra, he was fast asleep, his face a tiny picture of contentment.

'How did you know?' she asked Varg.

'I noticed he quietened down each time you got cross. Seems he likes it when you're angry.'

She frowned at the idea. 'He's never reacted that way before, but then I've never had cause to be angry around him before. I'm not sure I like it. Do you think it's natural for him to behave like that?'

Varg shrugged. 'I don't know and I don't give a Dogkin's shit either, so long as it shuts him up.'

His tone irritated her but Chandni didn't have the stomach for another argument. And anyway, sleep was calling. She settled down, telling herself that a little bit of strange behaviour was nothing to fear given the difficulties of the day. After the Whispercage, it was probably reassuring for him to see his mother being strong. *Yes,* she thought, forcing her fears into something more palatable, *that must be it. He needs to know I can keep him safe.*

CHAPTER SIX

Pari could hear the youngsters muttering to themselves, discussing plans. They sounded worried and close to arguing. They also sounded distracted. She was aware that she should probably take advantage and try to escape.

But she was so comfortable! Whatever fabrics the cart was laden with had accommodated her body's shape perfectly, and she knew that the moment she moved, all of the aches and pains would come flooding back.

Oh Rochant, the things I endure for you.

She tested the cords. The knots were secure but the man who tied them had been in awe of her, unwilling to stay too close for long. As a result there was slack. If she didn't mind a little chafing, she had limited movement of her wrists. *And after all of this, what's a little chafing to add to the list?*

They were keeping their voices low deliberately, but they were young and scared, and she was able to pluck nuggets of information from them as they travelled.

There were only two of them.

They were alone, without support.

They were brother and sister.

The brother, Lan, was the oldest, and he was behind the decision to take her captive. Ami, the sister, was unhappy about it.

Dawn was brightening the horizon, Fortune's Eye bronzing the black clouds.

There's going to be a storm. A bad one.

Pari sighed. There was no point putting it off any longer. 'Lan, can you be a dear and help me to sit up.'

The cart stopped. 'Wot?' he said.

'We need to talk and I'd much rather be able to see your face when we do.'

She heard a few words, hushed, between brother and sister, then Lan spoke again. 'Keep quiet!' Another hiss, from Ami this time, and he added, 'My lady.'

As she did with most instructions, Pari ignored it. 'How did you know who I am?'

'Saw them marks on your shoulder, where your clothes got burnt.'

Before setting out, Pari had taken the precaution of covering the tattoos of her previous lives. Such things identified her far too easily. But whatever the thing of the Wild had spat at her had burned through the body paint she'd used to conceal the marks as surely as it had the clothing on her back.

It would be the shoulder mark that gave me away, she thought bitterly. *A lifecycle I'd much rather forget.*

'Lan? Ami? Are you going to help me up or not?'

The cart stopped and Lan was halfway to climbing up

when he remembered that she was his captive. 'Stop talking,' he demanded.

'My lady,' added Ami in a whisper.

Now they had stopped, it was impossible to ignore the way their stomachs grumbled. Food was shared out, Ami settling next to Pari to feed her some berries and little chunks of sweetdough.

Finally sat up, Pari could enjoy a better view of her surroundings. The Godroad was still empty in both directions, and that was unlikely to change if the weather continued to worsen. 'Where are you from, Ami?'

'Sorn.'

Lan glared up at both of them, but it was too late, a number of things fell into place for Pari all at once. With Lord Rochant between lives, it had been the Sapphire High Lord's responsibility to protect Sorn when the elders called for a hunt but, for reasons unknown to her, Sorn had been abandoned. These two were refugees, either split from their family or, more likely, the sole survivors. 'You came to Lord Rochant's home hoping for sanctuary.'

Ami nodded, and Lan, his shoulders slumping, did the same.

'What happened? Tell me.'

When it was clear that Lan wasn't going to answer, Ami spoke, her eyes on the clouds. 'It had got bad for a while. People had always gone walking, y'know, to the Wild places, but nothing like this. Some even went in the day, just got up from their chores and walked off. Ain't none of them coming back, not ever.

'Elder Jamal asked for tributes, and got them real easy, bloods them, lights the fires and sends them out like always.'

Ami swallowed, memories darkening her eyes. 'The blood and fire brings 'em out, the Wild ones, like it should . . . But . . . '

Lan finished for her. 'But no hunters come! When the Wild ones get done with the tributes, they came for us, bolder than ever.'

Pari waited for a while but neither sibling said anything. 'So you had to flee, I understand. Why come all the way out here? Surely there are other settlements that could have taken you?'

Ami still wasn't looking at her. 'We went to Sagan, along with most of the folk. They took Mama in. She knows some of the safeways in the woods. She was useful. But Lan an' me are carpenters. They got plenty carpenters.'

Pari nodded. 'And so you went to petition Lord Rochant, in his new lifecycle.'

'Mama always said he was fair. 'Cept, he didn't come back like he was supposed to. And everything was wrong at the castle, with people saying stuff about a Tanzanite attack, and some of the guard running off, and nobody knowing what was what.'

'Was that when you became thieves?'

Ami looked like she was about to cry and Lan's eyes had already welled up.

'We ain't thieves,' he protested, 'but we had to eat.'

'I doubt House Sapphire will see it that way.' Pari watched a fat tear track down Lan's cheek. 'But maybe they'll reward you when you turn me in. Let's say that's true. Let's say that House Sapphire elevates you both and you find employment in the High Lord's castle. Do you think you'll be safe?'

They both looked at her then. 'Wot?'

'From me of course. Do you think I won't find a way to destroy you?' She paused to let that sink in. 'It may take decades. It may be that you'll enjoy most of your lives in peace. But know this: even if I was killed I would come back, younger and stronger, and I would find you. While I was between lives, House Tanzanite would investigate. I have a brother and an uncle who love me very much. They know I would never bring harm to Lord Rochant. In time they would learn what had happened.' She paused again. 'What do you think would happen to you then?'

The two looked at the floor.

'Ain't got no choice,' muttered Lan.

'Then let me offer you one. You need a home and a new life. I need help. I am away from my lands, alone, and people are trying to tarnish my good name, the same people that are working against Lord Rochant. Serve me now, and I will bring you under Tanzanite protection. It will be dangerous but if we survive I will see you richly rewarded.'

Ami looked at her brother, hopeful. He was looking at Pari, suspicious. 'How can we trust you?'

'I have little to give you save my word. But I, Lady Pari, Deathless child of the Tanzanite, will protect and guide you, so long as you protect and serve me.'

Ami slid off the cart and took Lan's hand. He gave her a nod and the two knelt before her. 'I swear,' they said together.

'Good,' she replied. 'Now, did you see a cart, like this one only bigger. It was travelling fast, flying no flags.'

'We saw it,' said Lan. 'Came flying past us it did. We was scared they'd come for us but it didn't even slow.'

'That's the one! Would you know it if you saw it again?'

'Reckon.'

'My lady,' added Ami.

'It's all right. We'll be travelling in disguise for a while. Best you get used to *not* calling me that. Now,' she said, slipping off her bonds, and settling in her nest. 'I need to rest while we travel. Keep going as fast as you're able. We'll stop at every settlement and see if we can find news of this cart. It's bound to have caught someone's attention.'

'But,' said Lan, staring at her in shock, 'you was free all the time . . . '

'I wanted you to think I was helpless, and I wanted to know if I could trust you.'

'You're clever,' said Ami, admiringly.

'Ah, my sweet child,' replied Pari, 'you should see me on a good day.'

As the cart started moving again, she thought about what she would do when she got her hands on Dil and whoever was pulling his strings. *Now that will be a good day indeed.*

The servants whirled around him, making the tidy tidier, making artfulness of order, and scrubbing until what was already clean shone like the rising suns. Vasin stood and watched.

He was the eye of calm at the centre of the storm. Except that inside he was anything but calm. He picked up a cushion to squeeze, lest he puncture his palms with his fingernails through clenching his hands so tightly.

Does the High Lord know of our plans? Is he coming here to do to me what he did to mother?

The small dose of Tack he had taken was running out, allowing his nerves to return with a vengeance. He found himself wishing he had something to do, something to distract him. But when Gada had said that he needed help to prepare, what he actually meant was that he needed his younger brother to smarten up and get out of the way.

They had washed him and brushed his eyelids and lips with gold, wrapped his body in bands of silk, then wrapped that in a glittering cloak, clasped with sapphires at the shoulders.

When his family arrived they would be dressed in a similar style, the oddities of their current bodies smoothed over to conceal with artifice the extremes of youth and old age, so they were neither one thing nor the other, timeless. It helped them ignore the shell, and focus on the Deathless spirit dwelling inside.

Vasin had the dubious honour of being the youngest living member of his house. This meant that they had all been present at his birth and had either seen, or had reported, all of the embarrassments of his first life. No matter how many lifecycles, no matter his achievements, there was always a sense that he knew less, was less, than the others. How he hated that!

And how, he realized, he hated them. Just the thought of having to endure so many of his family at the same time made him long to jump from the nearest window. *I live for the honour of my house and yet I have no love for those that rule it. Even Gada's company wearies me.*

There was Rochant of course, he had not witnessed Vasin's childhood as the others had, but he wasn't family, tied to them by crystal rather than blood. *And soon, he won't matter anyway.*

'My lord?'

He blinked at the woman who had materialized in front

of him. She looked familiar and yet he could not place her name. 'What is it?'

'Do you wish the trophy to be on display?'

'Yes.'

She gave a signal and a second servant, gloved, came forward bearing the severed arm of the Corpseman. 'Where would you like it to be displayed? On the wall behind your seat perhaps? Then each time they look upon you, my lord, they will be reminded of your glory. Lord Gada suggested it might look well opposite the main doors, so that it is seen on entry.'

Both ideas had appeal but he shook his head, slapping the table in front of him. 'Put it here. I want them to appreciate its size.' He sat back, pleased. *Let them be close to it and imagine what it must have taken to stand before the Corpseman whole.*

'As you wish, my lord.' She tried to hide her dismay but he saw it anyway.

The armoured limb thunked as its weight connected with the tabletop and both servants winced, making Vasin laugh, though even to him, it sounded nervous.

It had been a long day. Despite the worsening weather, they had made good time, Ami and Lan taking turns to push, so that they rarely had to stop. When they passed a settlement, the drill was simple: Lan would peel off alone to ask after their quarry, while Ami kept the cart moving. So far, the rain had meant they'd met few other travellers on the road, and when they had, the bedraggled souls were in a hurry, heads down, keeping chatter and questions to a happy minimum.

'Will we get fancy food, y'know, after?' asked Ami.

Pari twisted round to answer. Ami's eyes only just cleared the lip of the cart. They looked tired. 'Oh yes. Tanzanite food is the finest there is.'

'You 'ave to say that!' she replied. 'You are a Tanzanite! A Sapphire'd say the same about their food.'

'Ah, but the difference is I'd be telling the truth because unlike most people, I've tried both. Sapphire cooks are excellent, but somewhat lacking in creativity. Lots of nonsense about not overwhelming the flavour of the vegetables. So yes, a cook who works for House Sapphire may do one or two dishes very well, but a Tanzanite cook will do hundreds.'

'Hundreds?'

'Yes. By serving me you'll get to try them all.'

Ami's eyes sparkled at the thought. 'Promise?'

Pari chuckled. 'Yes.' From her vantage point she could make out Lan in the distance, sprinting back after them. 'I don't think much of your brother's running style. Does he usually flick his legs out like that?'

'Yeh. He's always run funny.'

She watched, enthralled by the inefficient motion as the young man drew level with the cart and heaved himself on. He lay on his back, chest pumping up and down, trying to speak. 'Went like . . . before,' he gasped. 'They saw 'em going past . . . plenty fast. Didn't stop for . . . nothing . . . No flags but . . . they reckon they saw . . . uniforms . . . Under the cloaks.'

'House Sapphire uniforms?'

'Yep.'

Pari turned her attention to the way they were going, peering into the hazy horizon. She could make out the lopsided form of Mount Ragged, black against the grey sky.

If they kept going this way they would reach the castle of Lord Vasin Sapphire. Surely the assassins wouldn't want to risk bringing Rochant there? *But then, if they keep him in the cart, they could pass right through and nobody would ever know.*

In a way, it made sense. Any official search for Rochant would start at his castle and go outwards, expanding to include the local settlements and any caves near the Godroad. Nobody would think to look in another Sapphire Lord's castle, and the assassins could move on at their leisure.

But to where? It irked her that she had no idea who was behind the attack and what their goals were. No longer tired, her mind began to work relentlessly, considering what they might be doing to Rochant while she dawdled in their wake. She clung to the fact that they hadn't killed him. It was clear that Dil wanted to, had planned to even. But with Satyendra still alive, they wouldn't dare. Their plan had been to erase him entirely. So long as she could keep the baby safe, Rochant would be too.

But why target him at all? Who would gain? That was what she needed to know. Clearly, it was personal with Dil, but when she'd been hiding in the Rebirthing Chamber, they'd spoken of another, one that would not be pleased with Satyendra's escape. Who would this be?

It had to be one of the Deathless. It had to be. But such an act risked war, threatening an accord that had endured since the end of the Unbroken Age.

Eventually, the floating castle of Lord Vasin Sapphire came into view. In many ways it was a mirror of Rochant's, the same hand behind all of the floating castles of the Deathless. And yet, the architect had made subtle differentiations, giving a distinct character to each one. There was a boldness to Vasin's castle, the towers somewhat thicker, and the rock it sprouted from was blockier. Where the bottom of Rochant's castle tapered down to a narrow point, the underside of Vasin's was a rough flatness, studded with crystal barbs.

Vasin's flag flew from the ramparts, indicating that he was in residence, along with a second, smaller one. *So, he has company, another Sapphire, I see.* She squinted at it, impatiently waiting for them to get close enough to identify the heraldry.

She was so deep in thought that at first she didn't notice the distant shapes approaching along the Godroad on the other side of the castle. There were two dozen of them, like birds, save that they were too big, too perfectly blue, with static wings that scythed the rain, supported by the Godroad's energies.

'Hunters!' exclaimed Lan, sounding boyish in his excitement.

Ami was just as excited. 'Lots and lots!'

'Yes,' agreed Pari. 'Lots and lots. And not just hunters either. See there?' She pointed towards the lead flyer. 'That is Yadavendra, High Lord of the Sapphire. And there–' she pointed to another, skimming low and fast along the surface of the Godroad, the light fragmenting into rainbows between the ground and her wings '– is his daughter, Lady Yadva.'

'I ain't never seen so many flocking at once,' said Lan.

'It's very rare,' agreed Pari, her eyes widening as she caught sight of another entourage behind the first one. 'And that must be Lord Umed.'

'Must be hunting something mighty big,' said Lan.

'Are they hunting Wild ones?' asked Ami.

'Possibly,' replied Pari absently.

'A-are they hunting us?'

'Probably.' She became aware that Ami had stopped pushing the cart. 'But not yet. This isn't a hunting party.' *It's a war party,* she added to herself. 'They're gathering to talk about something important. And urgent too, otherwise the High Lord would have summoned the others to him, rather than travelling here himself.'

Ami bit her lip. 'Should we turn round?'

'No, we go on.'

'But we can't!'

Lan nodded in agreement.

'How can we not?' asked Pari. 'The answers we seek are ahead of us, not behind. Lord Rochant is close and he needs my help. And I need your help. Do this for me and you will be rewarded. Do this for your children if you choose to have any, and they will grow up in my castle, as will their children. The risk involved is for the gain of generations.'

There was a long pause, longer than Pari found comfortable, and then Ami started pushing the cart.

Gada strode into the room. He looked Vasin up and down, satisfied with what he saw, if not impressed. His eyes flicked to the Corpseman's arm, then back to Vasin, cloaked in a frown. 'It is a time for delicacy, brother, not . . . ' He waved at the table. 'This.'

Vasin gritted his teeth, biting back a retort. If he could not remain calm around Gada, he would have no chance when the others arrived. 'You wish me to have it moved?'

'There's no time. The High Lord will be here shortly. I will help where I can but you are host.'

'I know. Any advice?'

Gada's frown lifted with relief. He settled himself at the table, his eyes on the door as he spoke, hushed. 'You must not argue with the High Lord. And I beg you not to criticize or question him by word or reaction. Say nothing unless he asks you.'

'I understand.'

'We must let the fire of his anger wash over us without fuelling it further.'

'Yes, I understand.'

'Remember, humility does not burn, but—'

Vasin's fist came down on the table. 'I said I understand, damn you!'

Gada drew back, his mouth open in outrage, as the sound of marching footsteps began to echo in the outside corridor.

They glared at each other before forcing themselves to turn towards the entranceway, smiles plastered over angry faces.

The doors swung open, allowing his cousin Yadva to enter. Her body was young and powerful, muscles like bricks beneath her tight silks. Bulky, yes, but it was absorbed into her tall Sapphire frame. She was an able hunter, fearless, ruthless, and it was widely known that no tributes survived the hunts that Yadva led.

He stood to clasp her arm, and was surprised to see her smile. 'You put me to shame with your victory, little cousin.'

'Not for long, I'm sure.'

'Depend on that. When Father is finished with us, I want to hear the whole story. All the details.'

Inwardly, he sighed. Yadva would be relentless in her questioning, and she would notice if any of the details did not fit. 'Of course, it's a story I will never tire of telling.'

She clapped him on the shoulder with her other hand. 'Nor will any of us. You've upheld Sapphire honour and heaped some much needed glory on us, too. Make it into a song and I'll sing it at your next rebirth!'

He couldn't help but laugh at that. Strange, was he actually starting to like Yadva? 'Done! I already have the Story-singers working on something, I'll tell them to make it in your range.'

She nodded to him and turned to Gada, her smile vanishing. 'Big cousin.'

'Lady Yadva,' Gada replied. Neither touched the other, and Yadva sat down, her attention moving to the severed arm on the table.

'Damn but I wish Father had sent me on that hunt,' she muttered. 'I've been hearing about the Corpseman since my second cycle. Can I touch it?'

'Of course.'

She ran her fingers over the plates. There was reverence there, but also curiosity. *She's looking for weak spots,* he thought, remembering how he'd done the same when he'd brought it home. There was a slight flexibility in the natural armour, allowing it to move with the arm, minimizing openings and absorbing impacts. How his mother had managed to get in close enough to saw the thing off was beyond him.

For a second time, the doors opened and his Uncle Umed entered. His body was seasoned, somewhere in its sixth decade, and lean, his dark hair grown long and tied high on the back of his head. A thick gold line was tattooed around half of his neck, curving into a claw that touched the bottom of his chin. Uncle Umed's fourth lifecycle had ended in the

Wild and he'd been reluctant to return there ever since, much to Yadva's disgust.

'Lord Vasin, I stand in your hall, Sapphire and bloodkin. May I be welcome? May I be seated?'

'Of course, Lord Umed. You are family, sit, be at peace. My food is yours to share, my walls are yours for shelter, now and forevermore.'

His answering nod was more relieved than anything else and he crossed the room slowly, making Vasin appreciate how far away Uncle Umed's castle was and how fast he must have flown to be here. The two grasped arms, and Vasin felt the tremble in the other man's body, felt the way he leaned against him for support.

When Umed had greeted the others, they sat, an odd silence holding between them. It had been years since they had last been together, and it stirred memories of older, happier times, when his family were at peace. Never to be had again.

Under normal circumstances Vasin would plunge himself in those memories, taking sanctuary there until his family had left again but the words of his mother were loud in his mind: '. . . *you will have to find a way to persuade the High Lord . . . or replace him with another more sympathetic to our cause. Are there any that would support us?'*

He looked at his cousin and his uncle, trying to see beyond the paint, beyond the skin, beyond the bone, to the thoughts underneath. *Are these allies sat in front of me, or enemies to be overcome?*

Their faces were masks and Vasin cursed himself for being absent during his mother's exile. He had no idea how they had reacted to the High Lord's judgement, nothing to guide him in how to approach them now. Gada would know more but he could not see how to question his suspicious brother without raising questions in return.

I was not made for this, he thought, but then hot on its heels another thought came: *Mother thinks I am. She chose me. Not Gada. Me. I have to be worthy of that choice.*

Outside, he could hear a distinctive tapping sound getting closer. *Sky-legs? It can't be.* He frowned, aware that Gada was doing the same. Already certain but unable to believe it, he continued to listen, marking the time between each step and matching it to the bouncing stride of the sprung boots. *But that would mean he was still in his armour. Why come here armoured unless –*

The doors were flung open by gauntleted hands, booming against the walls to reveal Yadavendra, High Lord of House Sapphire. Clad in his crystal skin, he was forced to duck to enter the chamber, his wingtips sparking against the door-frame. In one hand, he held a staff of gold with a gemstone blade and Vasin could not help but watch the tip as it swung back and forth.

Gada had not been exaggerating about the High Lord's mood. His face was ripe with anger, his body radiated it.

They were all on their feet in seconds, even Umed, contrite under his accusing stare. Vasin bowed deeply, then gave up his place at the head of the table, circling round one side as Yadavendra moved around the other. When he stood with the others, he bowed again.

'Sit,' said Yadavendra. It was not permission, it was a command.

Vasin wondered if the chair would be able to accommodate the High Lord's armoured form but he did not get to find out for Yadavendra had no intention of sitting. 'So,' he began, sweeping the head of his staff over their heads. 'We are all here, save for Lord Rochant.'

And Mother, you murderous bastard.

For a moment the High Lord did not speak and Vasin wondered if he'd spoken his thought aloud.

'He will not be joining us, for we have been betrayed. This, I know.'

But how? thought Vasin as the others gave a credible show of surprise. The only way information could reach Yadavendra from Rochant's castle so quickly was via a Heartstone, a perfect crystal broken in two, each half able to communicate with the other. But only emotions could traverse between halves, not facts, and no stone had been found in the Rebirthing Chamber or on Rochant's person. Vasin could see how a Heartstone might alert Yadavendra to there being trouble but no more than that. Was this just the High Lord's paranoia or had he some other means of gathering information?

'The thing I do not know,' continued the High Lord, 'and this vexes beyond imagination, is by whom. Several of our loyal subjects are dead. Lord Rochant's own children, dead. I am told the ceremony of rebirth was a success and yet there is no sign of Lord Rochant himself, not even a corpse.

'Do you hear me? They walked through our defences, past our guards, shedding Sapphire blood as they went, and then walked out again with Lord Rochant's body.' He brought the heel of his staff down so hard the glasses jumped on the table. 'Have you nothing to say? Not one of you?'

Apparently, none of them did.

The High Lord banged his staff a second time. 'This is an

attack at our very heart and we will meet it with full and terrible force, no matter the source.'

There was solemn agreement around the table. Vasin made sure he joined in, all the while feeling the stab of Yadavendra's gaze. *He knows!* thought Vasin. *He knows!* Sweat began to prickle on the back of his neck.

Yadva was first to find her voice. 'Surely someone must have seen something?'

'Many of the guard were killed and the captain has gone missing. The betrayer has covered their tracks well.'

'Do you think another house is behind this, High Lord?' asked Gada.

'I did not come here for your questions,' Yadavendra replied in a near shout, 'I came for answers. Answers! And by the Thrice Blessed Suns you will give them to me or you will know my displeasure!'

Gada slid from his seat and bowed until his forehead touched the floor.

'There will be a grand hunt. The like of which has not been seen in an age. We will search every inch of road, every settlement, every castle, even the Wild if we must! And we will not stop until Lord Rochant has been found and his assailants destroyed.'

A bead of sweat ran down Vasin's back. It was all unravelling. He had to distract the High Lord somehow or it was over. *How is the bastard so well informed? What else does he know that he isn't saying?*

He forced himself to look up and meet the High Lord's eyes. There was only a narrow window of skin visible but it was enough to shock Vasin. Even the heavy gold could not disguise the black marks there, nor the gauntness of his face. The High Lord looked feverish. It suddenly occurred to him that the armour was a feint, a way to scare them from looking too closely, to hide the weakness of the man beneath.

'What is it?' snarled Yadavendra, and he realized he'd been staring, and not in a respectful way.

'You mentioned Lord Rochant's captain, High Lord. I have him.'

He heard Gada's gasp that somehow managed to convey surprise and hurt, but otherwise the room was suddenly very quiet.

'If he is to be believed, the attack came from House Tanzanite.'

The High Lord leant towards him until he filled Vasin's vision. 'Which Tanzanite led the attack?'

'Lady Pari.' There was a narrowing of Yadavendra's eyes but no surprise. 'I was making preparations to travel with the captain as you arrived. She is rumoured to be ill and in her own bed, far from here, while the captain insists she is trapped in Lord Rochant's Rebirthing Chamber. I intend to see which is true.'

Those eyes continued to narrow, becoming slits. 'Very well done, my young Lord Vasin. Yes, we must get to the truth, whatever the cost.'

'Then, do I have your permission to go?'

'No, that is not a job fit for your skills. I will deal with Lady Pari myself.'

Vasin desperately tried to think of a reason to dissuade the High Lord but nothing came to mind. *Please let her body be dead when he arrives. Please!*

'While I go south, Lady Yadva will go east with this guard

captain as my envoy to the Tanzanite. He will lay out our grievances and her edge will cut through their protestations. Either they will produce Lady Pari or they will prove their guilt.' He dismissed Yadva from the room with a glance before returning his full attention to Vasin. 'No, I have need of you in the Ruby lands. They have presumed to summon me. You will go and find out why.' There was a soft clink as his staff tapped against the table's edge. 'And you can take your –' he paused to sneer '– trophy with you. They are easily impressed by such things.'

'Yes, High Lord.'

Finally, he turned his gaze away and Vasin realized he was being ejected from his own audience chamber. There was no time for pride however, he had to reach Dil before Yadva did. As soon as Vasin had cleared the doors and moved out of sight, he began to run.

CHAPTER SEVEN

They stayed as close to the Godroad as they dared, using old paths, overgrown and half reclaimed by the Wild. For the third time, Varg's wagon was stuck.

Fortune's Eye was already above the tree line, gold against the storm-grey sky, while the horizon glowed red with the rising of Vexation and Wrath's Tear.

Chandni leaned out to where Varg was cutting clumps of grass from the wheel. 'We need to hurry.'

'No shit.'

She didn't rise to his use of language but her eyes narrowed, first at Varg, and then at the thickening clouds.

They were on the edge of the forest, the trees rising high on their left. Between those vast trunks were spaces fit to hide all manner of monsters. Chandni fancied that she had already seen a few of them prowling nearby. She hugged her sleeping baby closer.

'How do you know we won't be attacked again?'

'I don't.'

At her sharp intake of breath he held up a hand. 'Hold on now, better save any shouting for when the baby wakes up. I'm taking a gamble but not a bad one. Sagan has just had a successful hunt so, hopefully, the Wild'll be quiet for a while yet. But we know those assassins are looking for you and the baby, which means the Godroad'll be too dangerous. They'll have eyes and ears all over the bloody thing.'

'What about the Whispercage?'

'That was . . . well, the Wild is never completely safe.' Something in her expression made him straighten and soften his voice. 'Hey, don't look like that. We got through it okay. Not many that have been close enough to smell a Whispercage's tit and come back to tell the tale.'

'If,' she began, 'the Whispercage had caught us, what would it have done? Actually, don't tell me, I don't want to know.'

'Look, it's behind us now. Forget it.'

'What if it comes back?' She pointed into the trees. 'What if it's out there now?'

He frowned. 'You seen something?'

'Yes!' Immediately he was turning towards the trees, which had never looked more empty or sedate. 'No. Well, I don't know. I've seen things moving out there.'

'It's a forest. There's always some bugger moving about.'

As he returned to the business of untangling the wheel, dismissive, Chandni felt her temper rise. 'I'm not talking about some little Flykin. They were big, and they're watching us.'

He grunted thoughtfully to himself, and that irritated her too.

'What?'

'I didn't say nothing.'

'But you thought something,' she snapped, hating how ridiculous she was sounding but unable to help it. 'What was it?'

Varg flicked a glance towards the sky. 'You won't like it.'

'Let me be the judge of that.'

'Fine. I'll tell you if you promise not to get pissy.'

She could cheerfully have throttled him in that moment but instead she kept her face a mask of calm and said, 'I promise to be the very picture of serenity.'

'All right. Might be you've got Wildeye.'

'Excuse me?'

'It happens sometimes when people have a rough experience in the Wild. It's like if you look at one of the suns for too long and you get that image that haunts your vision for a bit. Only with you it's not a sun, it's a Whispercage.'

'Are you saying the Whispercage is inside my eye?'

'Maybe.'

'Well,' she said, shuddering, 'thank you for your candour.'

She turned away from Varg to find Glider's white-furred chin resting on the front of the wagon, her unclouded eye tracking Chandni's movement.

'You're not hungry again are you?'

Glider's eyebrows raised in surprise, as if the very idea was an affront. Chandni felt a pang of guilt. The Dogkin seemed to be offering her sympathy.

She leaned out and touched the softness of Glider's ear but experienced no sensation of contact. The feeling still hadn't returned to her right hand. She could see her fingers, tiny next to the great flap of fur, could direct them to scratch in a way that made Glider's eyes close with pleasure, but it was as if she was working a puppet rather than her own limb.

Don't think about it.

But without the distraction of travel, or the imminent threat of attack, she could attend to little else. She nearly woke Satyendra, just to have something to do, but checked that impulse as unworthy.

Carefully, she arranged Satyendra on her lap, and pulled back her sleeve. The cuts she'd made on her wrist and forearm were still raw, the skin raised and angry. More than the injuries themselves, the misalignment of the marks, the messy nature of them upset her. They were proof of her earlier panic.

It wasn't Varg's fault the Whispercage found us. It was mine. She took a moment to think through how much peril her actions had drawn upon them and was overwhelmed by how close she had been to losing everything. She brought Satyendra's hand to her lips and kissed it. *Oh my sweet, darling boy, I have put you through so much and you have been so brave. Truly, you have the heart of a Sapphire.*

She touched the skin around her injuries, unsure if the numbness was spreading or if it was just the scar tissue. The thought that she might have to cut more flesh away, and soon, made her shiver. There would be too much blood, and with them so close to the Wild, something would come, perhaps the Whispercage. She shook her head. It was too dangerous to do anything on the road. Abruptly, she pulled down her sleeve.

Later, when Varg climbed into the wagon, Chandni cleared her throat. 'Before we set off again, I have something to say to you.' He didn't answer, but his face set and his jaw clenched, a man about to weather a storm.

'Oh, Varg, am I really that difficult to be around?'

'No,' he replied, a beat too late to be convincing.

'I know I can be exacting. I've always had high standards and . . . ' She stopped, aware she was in danger of making things worse. 'That isn't what I wanted to say. I wanted to thank you. You've kept us safe and you've been kind.'

'I have?'

'Yes. You have. I didn't see it at first, but I do now. And I see the wisdom in keeping us off the Godroad. If I was alone, I would have used it, and they would have caught me. As it is, I imagine our pursuers will be well ahead, trying to find a trail that doesn't exist.'

He mumbled something, his cheeks going adorably red behind his beard. *Was that a thank you?*

'If we are going to work together, Varg, and I fear that we will have to for a while at least, then it's important that we talk. I like to think I can face most things, providing I have a plan. It seems to me that you have one. I'd like to hear it.'

'I'm taking us to Sagan. I've got a place there we can hide until Pari comes to get us.'

'You live in Sagan?'

'Sometimes. People know me there as a trader. I keep myself to myself so we shouldn't get bothered much.'

'That could work. But what if Satyendra gives us away? A baby crying could raise some awkward questions.'

'I'll say it's mine. They know I got a woman that stays with me sometimes.'

'You have a partner living in Sagan too?'

His laugh was so abrupt that Glider jumped back and started barking at them.

'Suns, no! It's . . . actually I can't say.'

Chandni folded her arms. 'You don't have to. It's obviously Lady Pari.'

He looked as if he was about to deny it but then shrugged. 'Yeah. It's how I smuggle her in and out.'

'That seems like a lot of effort when she's welcome to visit Lord Rochant at her leisure.'

'Well, that's all right for the official visits but sometimes . . . ' he shrugged again.

Chandni did not like the implications of what an unofficial visit might entail. *It is not my place to judge my lord,* she said to herself, aware that she had already come to a conclusion some time ago.

'I think this could work, provided we keep people from visiting. I know my strengths, and pretending to be a villager is not one of them.'

'Pari keeps some paints back there for changing her looks. Might be we could use those.' He gave her a critical appraisal. 'You're right though, it'd take a lot of paint to stop people looking twice at you.'

'Because?'

'Because you got a proper noble face, and your skin is . . . Anyway, we'd best be going.' He snatched up the reins, his eyes very much on the road.

'Why, thank you, Varg.'

She saw him redden again as the wagon began to move forward, and found she was fast becoming fond of the expression.

The path that wound its way up the side of Mount Ragged towards Lord Vasin's castle was in full view of the guards, so while Ami and Lan trudged up its gentle slope, Pari had been forced to take an alternative route on the far side of the mountain.

Unfortunately this meant that the cart, the wonderful, comfortable cart, had to be left behind as well. They'd hidden it off the Godroad at the mountain's base.

It had only taken an hour of walking for all of her aches and pains to return. Several hours had passed since then. She needed a rest. Ami and Lan would be needing a rest too. She worried she was pushing them all too hard.

The rain was easing now, sputtering its last energies in a series of showers, allowing red glimpses of Wrath's Tear through clouds, breaking. Though the wind lashed at her, numbing her fingers and nose, she was sweating heavily by the time she reached the top.

Looking down, she was rewarded by the sight of Ami and Lan waiting below on the last curve of the Godroad before it went on to meet the castle. They had taken off the stolen layers of fine fabric and stood in their own clothes, two scrawny stick figures.

She gave them the signal. To their credit, neither looked in her direction, simply pressing on towards the bridge of chain and wood that connected one of the mountain's lopsided shoulders to the castle's entrance.

Though it was possible, as Pari had just proved, to climb Mount Ragged without being seen, it didn't matter. All visitors had to take the long bridge to get from the mountainside to the castle gates, and there were always at least two pairs of eyes on the bridge at all times.

Pari had thought long and hard about how best to get across but could think of no way that would not catch the guards' attention. If she had her tools and her health, she might have considered climbing the underside of the bridge, but even so, a sharp pair of eyes would notice the bridge behaving oddly and raise an alarm.

She shuffled round to watch Ami and Lan making their way up, Ami making a great show of being in pain as Lan dragged her along, calling for aid.

Two guards came out to meet them, their attitude stand-offish, while Lan took Ami off to a thin patch of ground to the side of the bridge in front of the great walls. They tried to wave Lan back but he threw himself down before them, begging for mercy.

As soon as he had their attention, Pari left her hiding place and stepped onto the bridge. She had to hunch low as she rushed along, keeping her head below the side rail. The odd posture made the muscles in her back threaten to seize but it was far preferable to being seen. Of course, if either guard returned to their post it wouldn't matter how low she crouched, but Pari tried not to think about that.

Just go faster! she urged herself. But by the time she was halfway across, there was no speed left in her legs and she had to content herself with a meaningful shuffle.

She imagined what Rochant would make of it all if he could see her. No doubt he would make some quip about the importance of dignity, softened by a twinkling eye and a half-suppressed smile. Her own smile quickly turned back into a grimace, her breathing, laboured. But she kept going.

'And I said nobody is allowed in. Now go home!' said one of the guards, his words carried to her on the wind.

'But we're from Sorn,' replied Lan. 'Ain't got no home. An' my sister is proper sick. Have mercy.'

'There's nothing I can do. We have strict orders.'

There was a coughing sound and then the second guard, alarmed: 'Was that blood?'

It wasn't blood. Just coloured water that Ami had been holding in her mouth. The girl put a hand to her lips and doubled over, as if trying to hold back the flood.

'What we gonna do?' Lan screamed.

Pari thought she made out a sigh.

'Stay here with them. I'd better speak to the captain about this.'

'Captain'll have your head if you bother her now.'

'I'll worry about her, you worry about them.'

Pari took a deep breath and gathered herself at the end of the bridge. One guard was making his way inside, while the other stood with Lan, his back to her.

She waved to catch Ami's eye and the girl pretended to cough something into her hand, prompting Lan to make a fuss and the guard to mutter nervously to them both.

Pausing only to give an approving nod, Pari crept onwards.

The great doors to the castle were already open, and a carriage was being prepared in the courtyard just inside, a shaggy pack of Dogkin tethered to the front. Though they were too small to pull the carriage individually, this particular breed were tireless in both legs and lungs – their high-pitched barks stabbed at the ear.

Pari would have happily pushed them all off a cliff.

The rest of the courtyard was remarkably empty. She presumed the usual guard had been pulled inside the castle to protect the High Lord and the other Sapphires.

Somewhere within the castle was Lord Rochant. He was close, she could feel it. But, unlike those of her lover's home, the secret ways of this place were a mystery. With the inner castle on alert, and her own name being thrown around as a suspect, she had little hope of getting any further.

I need help. But who to approach? One of the Sapphire here is behind this . . . Vasin? Gada? Umed? Yadva? The High Lord himself? Though Rochant and the High Lord had always been close, she could not help but remember the 'message' tattooed in silver on her lover's body, and wonder. *But why bother to leave a warning if he was going to kidnap him? No. I can't believe the High Lord is behind this.*

But if she approached the High Lord for aid, she would have to admit to breaking his laws, and that would damn both of them. Whilst in the middle of this dilemma she saw a familiar figure hurrying towards the other carriage.

Dil. I'd recognize that poor excuse for facial hair anywhere.

She crouched down by the corner of the wall, wincing as her knees cracked, and pulled her hood further forward. There was only one handler by the carriage, and the Dogkin were keeping her fully occupied. This was her chance!

As Dil reached the door of the carriage, she broke cover. The short space of land between her and Dil seemed to stretch forever.

The handler was wrestling a Dogkin into a harness, cursing under her breath and Pari felt a moment of empathy for the poor woman. There was no empathy for Dil however.

He had opened the door and was throwing some bags inside. Her angle wasn't ideal, but she was fairly sure there was nobody else within.

Nobody to see what I'm about to do to you.

She flexed her fingers against the cold, preparing to strike.

Dil was prodding at one of the bags inside, tucking tassels neatly away.

Only ten feet separated them now.

'Get in!' muttered Dil, pushing at a bag that had wedged itself in the doorway.

Eight feet. She used the carriage to block the handler's view, and approached from Dil's right.

The bag succumbed to Dil's efforts with a thud. 'That's better.'

Six feet. She raised a hand, two fingers extended. *A blow to the throat to stop any unwanted calls for help.*

Four. It would be difficult to move him anywhere without being seen by the handler. Perhaps she would have to incapacitate her as well. At least it would give the woman a brief respite from all the noise.

Suddenly she became aware of running footsteps from the inner gates. 'Captain Dil!' shouted a voice she knew. *Lord Vasin.* Dil jerked upright as if stung, then turned to his left. She moved with him, a shadow of his shadows, using the man's bulk to block her from Vasin's sightline.

'There's been a change of plan,' Vasin said, breathless. He was moving quickly, and would be upon them in seconds.

'My lord?'

Vasin looked over his shoulder towards the inner gates. By the time he looked back, Pari had side-stepped behind the open door, dropped to the ground, and rolled underneath the carriage.

'You will be travelling direct to Tanzanite lands. You will be accompanying Lady Yadva.'

'I don't understand.'

'Your understanding isn't necessary, just your competence.

And mind your tongue on the journey. Lady Yadva might seem aloof but she misses nothing.'

So Vasin and Dil have some kind of history. Interesting. She placed him at the top of her suspects list.

'I will do my best, my lord.'

'Your best?'

She heard Dil's strangled gasp as Vasin grabbed him. 'I have seen your best and found it wanting. You will be perfection itself.'

'Yes, my lord.'

She lost the next thing Vasin said to the low growl of a Dogkin. Pressing her chin to her chest, so that she could look towards the front of the carriage, she found the upside down face of a Dogkin looking back at her. It was an ugly thing even by the standards of its kind, most of the head taken up with a great muzzle, filled with teeth, the nose a small, snub thing perched on the end. Its faded eye was a mere glint of grey, its canine eye a vacant black, no emotional range, just hunger and anger. Pari wasn't sure which she was being subjected to.

Despite this, she put a finger to her lips in silent appeal and was rewarded by the growling being replaced with a surprised whine.

Able to think again, she began to put together the facts. A Dogkin pack like this one was hard to manage but excellent for long-distance travel. The carriage seemed appropriate for noble passengers, but to travel alone was low key for a lady of House Sapphire, suggesting they wanted to draw minimal attention. *Where are you going, Dil? What are you up to?*

'Remember,' said Vasin, sounding further away, 'your mission is to prove guilt, not start a war.'

Ahh, she thought. *It becomes clear. They're coming for me.*

Vasin's boots had splashed some further distance before Dil muttered an answer, something disrespectful, too low to make out but involving sharp objects and rear ends. Then he sighed and began pulling out the bags so recently packed with care.

Pari knew she should do something, but fatigue stole her usual inspiration from her. *This is a task for a younger body.* Despite the danger, her eyes began to feel heavy. *Perhaps, if I rest for a moment, something will come.*

Unfortunately for her, the Dogkin had recovered from its surprise, and was trying to twist round. The harness held it firmly in place, but it barked out an alarm. A second Dogkin head popped into view, and then it started barking along with its pack mate.

'Suns!' shouted Dil. 'What's wrong with them?'

'I don't know,' replied the handler, working her way to the back of the pack. 'But it's coming from here.'

Pari tried a pleading look but it made no difference. They kept on barking until the rest of the Dogkin got the message and joined in. The carriage started to rock back and forth, axles creaking as the excited creatures fought to break out of their shackles and get to her.

As she watched the flex and play of the suspension, Pari's quick eyes identified several key bolts, and she set about loosening them. *May they fall out at a most inconvenient moment.*

Job done, she turned her attention to the Dogkin as they hopped about, stubby tails like raised fingers. Pari narrowed her eyes, pulled out her earring, and waited. *Not yet.*

The handler's attempts to soothe the rear animals seemed to be having the opposite effect.

Not yet.

Pari could see her hand resting on one of their heads. 'I think there's something back here,' she said, leaning down, the tip of her ponytail falling into view.

Now! thought Pari and, with no small amount of venom, jabbed the pin of her earring into the testicles of the nearest Dogkin. It snapped and howled with pain, sinking its teeth into the nearest available target: the handler.

The woman screamed and then everything erupted into chaos, the Dogkin going berserk at all the noise and the smell of blood. For good measure, Pari stabbed the other nearby Dogkin in the testicles too. Dil had arrived on the scene now and was shouting for help while trying to pull the handler free.

Time to go, thought Pari, and forced her weary bones into motion.

More staff were rushing over to help but Dogkin chaos covered her movements as she crawled out from under the carriage. She gave the castle one last look. It pained her to abandon Rochant but it was no good saving him if she wasn't around to enjoy it. She reminded herself that they wouldn't dare kill him so long as baby Satyendra remained safe.

As she made her way back outside, the shouts and barks followed, and she saw the guard from the bridge rushing towards her as if towards his own death.

'Are –' his voice cracked '– we under attack?'

'Yes,' she replied, 'they need you!'

He ran on, weapon drawn and held high, as if charging

into battle. Pari turned her face away, barely able to control the laughter.

Beyond the gates, two pale faces were waiting for her.

'Come on, Ami, Lan. We're leaving.'

'We are?'

'Yes,' Pari replied. 'Now walk behind me, and keep close together. You must do your best to block me from sight, leave as little gap as possible. They'll be back long before we cross the bridge.'

Lan opened his cloak, putting an arm round Ami's shoulder to make a curtain at Pari's back. 'Where we going?'

'Ami and I are going home. It looks like you're going to sample Tanzanite food sooner than I thought.'

'But,' asked Lan, fearful, 'what about me?'

'I'm sorry, Lan, but you can't come with us.'

He looked like he was going to cry. 'What've I done wrong?'

'Nothing. You've been brave and loyal and that is just what is needed here. You see, I have a job for you. One that I cannot do myself that is of the utmost importance.' She wiped her earring on her sleeve and held it out to him. 'You're going to deliver a message.'

The rain began as the village of Sagan came into sight. It thrummed musically on the Godroad, and pattered on the forest canopy. The raindrops bounced, falling faster than the ground could absorb, forming new waterways, tiny and transient.

Chandni retreated into the back of the wagon, cowering with Satyendra under several layers of fabric. Varg and Glider were less fortunate, hair and fur alike plastered down, thick drips collecting on the ends of their noses.

They came to some half-built structures clustering on Sagan's edge, things of mud brick and hay, thrown up hurriedly, haphazardly. Though they had no roofs, scrawny figures gathered inside, some covering their heads, others just standing, frozen, heedless of the needling rain.

Like most settlements, Sagan was built along the Godroad, sturdy houses of old wood gathering as close as they could, forming long, thin rows. Though close proximity to a Godroad did not actually protect the inhabitants from the creatures of the Wild, it did make encounters less likely.

However, crops always failed in the soil near the Godroad, and so a large patch of trees had been cleared to make way for farmland, bravely crossing over the Wild's boundary. Several established fields were visible, each jutting out from the back of a house to use all of the available space, and she could see new ones being cleared, high fences marking out Sagan's new perimeter. Though the forest was held back, Chandni could almost feel the pressure of the Wild trying to return. In fact, several fences were bent inwards by trees, branches curled over the top like fingers, grasping.

Despite the lash of the rain, many people remained outside. They huddled together, a mass of misery, as close to the walls as they could get.

At first, she couldn't understand why they weren't sheltering inside the buildings, but then she got a glimpse of faces peering at her from behind windows, packed in tight, and realized there simply wasn't enough room for everyone.

'There are so many people!' she exclaimed, drawing nearer to the front of the wagon.

'It's got bad,' Varg admitted. 'Sagan's fit to burst. I don't recognize any of the ones outside. Poor bastards must have walked here from Sorn.'

'Do you think they'll have taken your house.'

He shook his head. 'They wouldn't dare.'

Varg's house was set apart from the others, on the border where Sagan met the Wild. It was a small cube of wood, windowless, sitting awkwardly on a slab of rock, supported by stilts on one corner. The front faced the village, while the back looked directly out into the trees. Already, parts of the forest grew stealthily around one side, as if preparing to steal it back into the Wild's embrace.

Another smaller cube sat on top of the main building with a chimney poking from it. This had wooden shutters that were half open. Chandni couldn't help smiling to herself when she saw the smoke coming from the chimney top and the warm light dancing under the door. Clearly someone *had* dared.

'By the thrice shitted suns!' said Varg, pulling the wagon to a stop. 'Stay here. This won't take long.'

She watched in dismay as he leapt from the wagon and splashed up towards the stout door at the front of the house. He wrenched it open, violence in the movement, and she flinched as he slammed it behind him.

'I don't like this,' she murmured and heard an answering grunt.

With a start, she realized that Satyendra had woken up. His dark eyes stared up at her, utterly attentive.

It was hard to be sure over the rain but it sounded as if there was shouting coming from the house.

This isn't right.

Scooping Satyendra up, she slipped from the wagon, to come face to face with Glider.

'Stay here,' she ordered, and started towards the house.

The Dogkin whined but did as she was told.

In the short walk between the wagon and the house, Chandni was soaked to the skin. She pulled back the door and plunged inside, instantly struck by a wash of warm air on her face.

Varg was standing in front of her, hands on hips. On the other side of him, she counted two people hurriedly packing, one of whom was clutching a baby, and there, between the adult's knees, a toddler watched them.

'You can't do this,' she said quietly.

He turned round, expressions of horror and anger warring on his face. 'Stay in the wagon,' he hissed.

'No, listen to me.'

His big hands moved as if to propel her back outside but stopped, impotent, a few inches from her.

'You can't do this. They'll suffer out there. They could die.'

'Lots of people are suffering, but my job is to protect you. No one else.'

'I understand. But these are my people and I have a duty to them.'

'But the risk? They could betray us. What about the risk to your baby and your house?'

'To live without honour is the worst death, one even Lord Rochant couldn't return from. I must do whatever I can, however small, for that is the Sapphire way.'

He looked into her eyes, his horror giving way to dismay, his anger to admiration. 'Fuck.'

She smiled at him. 'I knew you'd understand. Tell them they can stay. Reassure them. No shouting. Say you were shocked at first but now you've had time to think, you've had a change of heart. I'll wait for you in the wagon. We can talk more freely there.'

It was cramped and damp in the back of the wagon, and when Satyendra started to shiver in Chandni's arms, it almost broke her heart.

Varg climbed in to join them, his bulk blocking out most of the weak light. 'It's done,' he muttered.

'Good. We'll have to make our plans quickly. I need to get Satyendra somewhere warm.'

'That's the first thing,' said Varg, wringing water out of his beard. 'Can't call him Satyendra any more. That's no Sagan name, and those assassins'll be asking after it.'

She'd never considered that, but it made sense. The idea of calling her baby by another name appalled, but she swallowed it down. 'Yes. Do you have a name in mind?'

'Something common would be best. How about Kal?'

Awful! she thought. But said yes. This wasn't about whether she liked or disliked a name, it was about what would keep them safe. 'What else?'

'That castle living of yours shows. Nobody down here sees that much sunslight. We'll have to paint you whenever you go outside. And I think you better not go outside unless you have to. I've told them you're sick, that should keep people away for a bit.'

'And what are you going to call me?'

He grimaced. 'Ri.'

'Ri? As in Lady Pari? It's not very subtle!'

'No, but it's easy to remember.'

'Can't we use a different name?'

'Has to be Ri. I've used it in the past.'

She took a deep breath and reminded herself that she was a Sapphire and that, unlike many she could name, a Sapphire was always in control of themselves. 'Very well.'

Satyendra shivered again, making her frown with concern. 'Is there anything else?'

'There's two rooms that are good for sleeping in. Normally Pari would sleep in one and me in the other but that ain't going to work with those four from Sorn living with us. So I'm putting them in one room, so that you, me,' he pointed at Satyendra, 'and little Kal can stay together in the other.'

'I think that's for the best.'

His eyebrows raised in surprise. 'Yeah . . . me too. Good. Reckon it'd be best if you stay in the room. Play up being ill and being shy. Let me do the talking.'

'I'm not used to stepping back and letting others do all the work.'

'It won't be for long. Pari doesn't hang about.' He shuffled closer and began rooting around in the general mess at the back of the wagon. 'Here we go.' In his hand was a small jar of milk-white paste. 'Put some on, then we can get you into the house and out of sight.'

'I think you should do it.'

'Me?'

'There's no mirror here, and it needs to look natural.' She glanced down at her right hand, to check it was still there, and flexed the fingers. 'You do it.'

'All right then. Come a bit closer where the light is.'

She did. The smell of damp man and Dogkin was potent as ever, but she didn't mind it as much as before. *Am I getting used to it already?* she wondered. And then a worse possibility occurred. *Is this what I smell like now?*

Varg was delicate with his applications, the little chunk of sponge somehow ridiculous in his rough fingers. He was so focused that the tip of his tongue peeked out as he worked.

'How did you come to work for Lady Pari?'

'I was born into it. She won my great, great grandmother in a bet.'

'Surely not!'

'Yep. She was so good that a few Deathless fought over being the one to elevate her. In the end it came down to a private bet between Pari and,' he caught himself, 'well, what matters is that she won, and not just one woman either. See, my old gran was pregnant with twins at the time but hadn't told anyone. So Pari takes the mum back to show off at home, and keeps the kids elsewhere.'

'That's horrible!'

'Don't crinkle your face like that.'

'Sorry.' She did her best to keep her face relaxed but couldn't help adding: 'It's still horrible.'

'Clever though. Means the other Deathless don't know about me, and that means Pari can get about without being noticed when she has to.'

'Do you like being Pari's . . . ' she tried to think of what the correct term for Varg would be. 'Servant?'

He looked around the wagon and pulled a face. 'Sometimes.'

They both laughed.

'Well,' he said, dabbing one last time at her nose. 'I think that's as good as it's going to get. Ready to go?'

She looked down at herself. *Ri, I'm Ri now. I'm sick and quiet. I must keep my head down and my mouth closed.*

And this is Kal. Not Satyendra, but Kal. Oh, I hate this already and we haven't even begun.

But when she turned back to Varg, she nodded, committed, and offered her hand.

Vasin rushed through the main doors of his castle, aware that he was attracting strange looks from his staff. It had taken all of his self-control not to kill Dil right there in the courtyard. The man was a thug, guileless. Vasin understood that his family had been cast down by Lord Rochant generations ago, even sympathized a little, but Dil's all-consuming hatred made him unreliable and arrogant. The man had forgotten his proper place.

He'd even had the gall to ask if he could go and hunt down Rochant's grandchild himself. As if he'd trust that job to the fool that let it escape in the first place.

The entrance hall was an open space dominated by the main stairs. Trophies of previous hunts adorned the walls but other than that, they were bare. For the first time he wished there was more clutter, a grand statue or display case, something to hide behind. As it was, he was completely exposed when his cousin Yadva came down the stairs, flanked by her hunters.

He could not muster a smile but managed to meet her gaze as he took her arm. '*Hunt well and thorough.*'

She rolled her eyes. 'It's not much of a hunt is it? Do you think Rochant's captain is telling the truth?'

'I see no reason for him to lie.'

He was distracted by the sound of Dogkin barking outside. Yadva was not. 'And why are you in such a hurry? I thought the meeting was still going on.'

'The High Lord is sending me to the Ruby lands as an envoy.'

'You? Now?'

'You don't agree with his decision?'

She waved back her hunters and took him to one side. 'Father is organizing a grand hunt and yet sends his two best hunters away. Does that make any sense to you?' She did not pause long enough for him to answer, her nostrils flaring: 'Why not let Umed or Gada chatter to the Rubies or go sniffing in Lady Pari's rooms?'

He paused. With all of his own troubles he had not had time to consider the oddity of the High Lord's orders. 'Uncle Umed's body is not ageing well. I doubt a long voyage would suit him.'

'And a vigorous hunt would?'

Vasin spread his hands. 'I'm sure he has his reasons.'

'So am I. That's what bothers me.' She leaned in, dropping her voice. 'We should talk, soon. Just the two of us.'

He caught the look in her eyes, an understanding passing between them. 'Yes. We should.'

'Good.' She gave his arm a final squeeze before striding away. He started up the stairs as she called back to him. 'I haven't forgotten about your story. When I return, I expect all the details!'

He sighed but called back with false cheer, 'You'll get them. And the song too!'

And then she was gone, and Vasin was rushing up the stairs. Though distant, the noise from the courtyard had got worse. *What was going on out there?* He paused at the top, considering whether to go and see for himself but didn't dare waste the time. With Yadva leaving and the rest of his family in close conference, this was his best chance to speak to Yi without being observed.

He made his way down a smaller staircase, passing servant after servant. All were purposeful, attending to the long list of additional jobs that had arrived along with their unexpected guests. *How many eyes have seen me going this way?* he wondered. *And how many are truly loyal?* His life had been so simple before, his worries straightforward. Now he moved in a different world, where suspicion dismantled trust, and inner peace was a faded memory at best.

If Dil, who had grown up in Lord Rochant's care, was capable of betrayal, why not his own staff? He had never paid particular attention to that side of his duties, leaving it to others to manage on his behalf. That would have to change.

Yi met him outside the door that held Rochant. Her face was calm, expressionless, as she bowed. 'You should not be here.'

His stomach tightened. Had he made another mistake? 'I had to come. The High Lord is sending me away. He knows something, I'm sure of it. I don't know how long I'll be gone. Do you think you can keep him hidden?'

'Yes.'

'They may search the castle.'

She looked at him but said nothing.

He felt a growing pressure to be decisive, to give an order, but he wasn't sure what to do. 'How is the prisoner?'

'The same. Do you wish to see?'

Did he? He had no idea. 'Yes.'

Yi opened the door for him and he stepped into the room. Lord Rochant remained bound to the pole, a sack over his head. The sight made Vasin feel sick. He reminded himself that this man shared the blame for his mother's fall, that he was scum, but the words fell flat in his mind, replaced by others, more resonant: *It should not be this way.*

At some point during his reverie, the head within the sack had twitched to face him more directly. 'Silence is a lazy word, don't you think?'

Though the voice was new and youthful, the cadence and intonation were unmistakably Rochant's. Vasin caught himself before he answered. To speak would be to identify himself.

'There are silences of many kinds, and yet we have only one word to describe them all. The silence of a small space is not the same as a large one. Just as it sounds different if one is inside or out. And the silence of the floating castle is different again, though they cannot be considered truly silent. They breathe.' He paused, and there was a glimpse of a smile within the sack, as if Vasin had just conceded a point. 'I know who you are. I know where I am.'

He paused again. 'I am a student of silence, and the things that can be found on its edges. I know, from the way you have started to edge away, that you have lost. But there are many kinds of losing. You still have the power to choose the nature of yours. Come, let us talk. Let us negotiate terms.'

Vasin stepped out of the room and slammed the door shut, pressing his palms against its rough surface. He could imagine Rochant on the other side. Did he truly know or was he bluffing? *He did not say my name. Surely he would have said my name if he had known?*

'Yi, I need that baby found.'

'We are searching.'

'As is my family!' His hands became fists on the door. 'If the search comes here, if they find this place . . . '

He trailed off, unable to say the words aloud, but Yi nodded as if he had. She would kill Lord Rochant to keep his secrets, and herself if she had to.

CHAPTER EIGHT

Chandni stared at the wall in front of her. The wood was warped, dusty, and blackened with age. After a while she could make out patterns in the grain, patterns that drew the eye and held it if studied for too long.

And Chandni had been here for far too long.

There were no windows, the only light in the room coming from the open trapdoor in the ceiling, and a slit cut into the block of stone that formed the heart of the building, where the fire burned, weak in the day, feeble at night.

Chandni knew this for a fact because she had been nowhere else since they arrived, confined like a prisoner with Satyendra. Varg brought her food, and tepid water for cleaning. He also emptied her pot and took away Satyendra's soiled clothes. Her dependence on Varg had soured her mood, leading to a number of comments, regretful, that she intended to apologize for when he returned.

A grumbling drew her attention and she lifted Satyendra from his bed. 'Hello,' she said. She didn't call him by name any more but she couldn't bring herself to call him Kal. It just seemed wrong. 'And how are we today?' *Please be in better spirits than yesterday.*

Sleepy eyes blinked and he stretched in her arms, taut and tiny, before giving her his full attention. Or at least, he gave his full attention to her breast.

Chandni's heart sank as his mouth opened, revealing the little nubs of teeth that were surprisingly sharp. 'All right, but you must try to be gentler today.'

Still open mouthed, he lifted his head, making a desperate little grunt. She knew that crying would soon follow if he wasn't fed, and moved quickly to accommodate him. Her mind drifted as he sucked, wondering what was happening back at the castle. It already seemed like so long ago, as if it were months rather than days that had passed.

We should have heard from Pari by now. Chandni hated waiting on others, especially members of other houses. They were so . . . unreliable. *By the Thrice Blessed Suns, what if she's died? It could be years before her next lifecycle. Years of sitting in this room. I don't think I could bear it.*

Satyendra coughed, spluttering milk all over the two of them. She kept calm and set him upright, patting his back until the gurgle had gone from his breathing.

'Better?' she asked.

Satyendra scowled at her, a study in fury.

'Well, it isn't my fault. You shouldn't be so greedy.'

He began to grizzle, then to demand more feeding. It had been like this since they arrived. Satyendra not taking his milk properly and as a consequence being hungry, and angry, mostly with her.

When she fed him a second time she sang his favourite

song. It was called *One,* and told the story of a Purebird carved in glass that comes to life one day and goes on an adventure to find its family. However, the song no longer seemed to please him. Even when she made the 'swish, swish' noises of the wings at each chorus he regarded her bleakly.

'Is there not the smallest smile for me today?' She stroked his forehead. 'I know, I know. We are in a strange place. And there has been little sleep and little to smile about lately. I don't much feel like smiling either when I look at this drab room. But when I look at you,' she touched him gently on the end of the nose, 'I find that I do have a smile after all. It was just hidden away all this time. Look!' She mustered her best smile. 'Here it is.'

He stared at her, the dark of his eyes cold, and she shivered.

More hours passed. Occasionally she heard the residents of the other room moving about, or talking in low tones. Their children were quiet but she could hear the high voice of the toddler chirping with questions.

Otherwise there was little but the pop of wet wood burning on the fire, and Satyendra's disgruntled murmuring. There was nothing urgent that she needed to do, no immediate demands on her. No excuses.

I've put this off for too long.

She shrugged her shoulder out of her robe and slipped her right arm free. Goosebumps rose on her upper arm only. She turned her wrist upwards and touched each of the cuts there in turn. When she got to the highest one, the one that had hurt to make, she felt nothing.

Chandni pressed harder, being careful not to use her nail

lest she accidentally draw blood. The skin paled under the pressure but it was a visual change only. A horrible certainty grew in her.

The poison is still spreading. Roh only slowed it, she didn't get it all out.

Sliding her thumb up her inner arm, she found sensation again just before the elbow.

Stay calm. Stay. Calm. She inhaled, long and deep, clenching her fists, then relaxed them as she exhaled. *You are a Sapphire,* said the inner voice of her mother, imperious. *You know what must be done.*

There was a knife under the bed. Chandni picked it up and walked to the stone wall that housed the central fire. She slid the blade through the slit and held it there, waiting for the metal to get hot. She tried not to think about what she was going to do, tried to keep her breathing even. When her hand began to tremble, making the knife rattle against the stone, she tried to ignore that too.

When the knife blade was as hot as it was likely to get, she took it out and knelt down, pressing her right arm against the wall and locking it straight. The knife felt awkward in her left hand. She brought it carefully into position so that its edge hovered just below her elbow.

It's the wrong kind of blade, she thought. But then, what other blade was there? It wasn't as if she was in a Cutter-crafter's hall. She had one knife. It was this or nothing.

Questions flew in her mind, borne on anxious wings. *Should I hack or cut? How will I tie off the* . . . Her stomach clenched violently, . . . *stump with one hand? What about the pain? Will I be able to take it? What if I pass out before I'm finished, what then?*

She made a light cut on her arm, an inch clear of the numbness, drawing a thin line of red, a marker for what was to follow. More than anything else, that brought her up short. They were so close to the Wild here that an abundance of fresh blood would be certain to draw something to them. She could face pain, could even, perhaps, face a life without her hand. But what if a Whispercage came again? A memory of its touch, vivid, and the fluttering of rags, of that face beneath the hood, of Satyendra being taken from her . . .

For a moment she was there on the wagon, so sure that she had lost her child. *But I didn't lose him. Satyendra's here. He's right here on the bed.*

She had to turn and check though, force feed her mind evidence to dispel the fear. Satyendra was on the bed where she had left him, watching her, his eyes drawn by the knife in her hand, shaking.

As her gaze followed his, the reality, the stupidity, of what she had been about to do came crashing in, and she cried out, hurling the knife away. It clattered loudly on the floor.

Next door, the voices stopped.

She heard a single set of footsteps cross the room. For a long time they seemed to hover on the threshold. Chandni silently hoped they would not come in. To see another adult in her present state would be too much. The shame alone would destroy her.

When the footsteps returned and the voices started again, she let out a great sigh of relief. *When Varg gets back*, she thought, pulling her robe over her shoulder, *I'll tell him about the assassin's poison.* She had the feeling he would know what to do.

*   *   *

Chandni woke to see a familiar bulk in the darkness. 'You know, for a man that smuggles people for a living, your feet are surprisingly clumpy.'

Varg went over to the slit where the fire crackled and rubbed his hands together. 'Did I wake you?'

'Yes.'

'Ah.'

'You were gone longer than usual. What happened?'

'There's been hunters seen on the Godroad. Apparently, High Lord Sapphire himself has taken wing.'

A little hope sparked in her chest. 'Then I can go home?'

'No.'

'No?'

'We're not going anywhere until I get the word from Pari.'

'Oh don't be ridiculous. You just said yourself that House Sapphire is taking action. We must go to the High Lord immediately. Where is he?'

'Like I said, on the move.'

'You need to be more specific.'

'It's not like they sent me a bloody report is it!' She thought she saw him run a hand through his hair. 'Ah shit. I'm sorry. Maybe we should talk when I've had some sleep.'

'Which direction was he flying?'

'This way, I think. But it's hard to be sure. I hear talk of hunters all over this part of the Godroad.'

'Then we'll go out onto the Godroad and approach the hunters. They will escort us to High Lord Sapphire and all will be well.'

'I can't go along with that.'

'I wasn't asking for your permission, Varg. I was telling you what's going to happen next.'

His silhouette turned towards her, stubborn. 'I don't serve you, I serve Pari, and she told me to keep you safe.'

She was able to keep the anger from her voice but not the sarcasm. 'I suppose you think I'm safer here? In a mouldy box on the edge of the Wild. Oh yes, much better that I stay under your sporadic protection than go to the hunters of High Lord Sapphire. What was I thinking?'

'Weren't so long ago that you were running from the Sapphire.'

'No, I was running from killers pretending to be House Sapphire. There's a difference.'

'An' can you tell it? Cos if you can't we'll be delivering your baby right to 'em.'

'Don't be ridiculous!'

'Keep your voice down,' he hissed. 'You think some of them assassins can't be dressed as hunters?'

'Masquerading as a guard is completely different to masquerading as a hunter.' But was it? Previously she would have said both were impossible, that the Sapphire were above such things, now that certainty had abandoned her.

'Bollocks. It's just getting hold of some clothes. If they're good enough to get into Lord Rochant's bloody castle, I reckon they can manage a few hunter's wings.'

'Please don't tell me I have to stay in this room any longer.'

'Ah . . . '

'Please.'

She heard him scratch the back of his head. 'Did something happen today? They said they heard a scream. Did Kal bite you again?'

'Don't call him that.'

'But—'

'I know the reasoning behind it, I do. But right now I need to hold on to who I am, and who he is.'

Varg came and sat down by the end of the bed. 'Did he bite you though, or was it something else?'

'It was . . . ' She thought about her arm, about the poison. *I should tell him.* 'It was like you said. Another difficult day.'

'I know he can be a bugger but you've got to keep that under control.' He jerked a thumb towards the other room. 'We can't afford to draw any attention to ourselves, and that's the kind of thing that sticks in people's minds.' When she didn't say anything, he went on. 'You said I was, what was it? Clumpy, right? I suppose I am. Thing is, I don't do what I do by being stealthy, I do it by being normal. Someone looks at me, there's nothing to see. Nothing interesting anyway. That's how we have to keep things.'

She wanted to tell him about her arm but the words refused to come. If she told Varg, she would be handing over control somehow. He would insist they cut if off. It would be different if they were home. She could endure anything there. In this place though, she couldn't allow herself to become vulnerable.

He began pulling off his boots. She wasn't bothered any more by the smell, in a strange way, it was comforting. The thought nearly made her burst into tears.

'Varg,' she finally said.

'Yeah?'

'Promise that if anything happens to me, you'll make sure Satyendra gets home.' She put a hand on his arm to stop him answering. 'Not because you have a job or because of Lady Pari's order. Promise you'll do this, for me.'

It was, she knew, a foolish thing to ask and so she was surprised when he covered her hand and whispered that he would.

'Thank you.'

He didn't answer and they sat there, neither willing to move, neither sure what to say.

And then they heard the sound of barking.

'Oh shit!' said Varg, groping around in the dark for the boot he'd just removed. 'That's Glider.'

'Trouble?' she asked.

'She's caught something, and I'm not talking about a Spiderkin.'

Chandni pulled Roh's cloak about her shoulders before reaching for Satyendra. He was awake, but for all his grizzling in the day, he was quiet now, as if he sensed the trouble. Once more, she thanked the suns that he was a true child of the Sapphire.

'What are you doing?' asked Varg.

'Coming with you.'

'Stay here.'

'No. I'm coming with you.'

He clearly wanted to argue the point further but Glider's barking continued, insistent, and his worry about that took precedence. Chandni followed him through the other room, its occupants watching them silently, huddled together. She noted them shrink away from Varg as if expecting abuse and wondered if he had given them cause.

Then he was pushing through the front door, the night air like a slap in the face. Chandni didn't mind, in fact she luxuriated in its hard touch. It was so good to be outside again! The sky was clear, star studded, making ghosts of them as they left the light of the house.

Glider barked a greeting, clearly delighted with herself, then went back to growling at something trapped under her front paws.

'Shut up, for suns' sake,' said Varg. 'You'll have the whole of Sagan on our bloody heads.'

Either Glider hadn't heard him, or she thought the idea appealing. Her barking continued unabated.

'Bloody Dogkin.'

'Let me try,' she said, and Varg stepped back, grateful. 'Hush now, Glider.' She lowered her voice. 'Hush.'

Glider stopped barking.

'Have you caught something?'

The Dogkin wagged her white tail in answer.

'Very good. Can you move so we can see how clever you've been?'

Like a merchant displaying her wares, Glider lifted a paw. Beneath it, mud covered, was a human shoulder. Attached to the shoulder was a very skinny, very scared looking young man.

Varg crouched down next to him, one hand finding the man's collar, the other pressing something sharp against his neck. 'What you doing out here then? Answer me and answer true.'

'Thas Glider in't it?' said the man. 'A-are you Varg?'

'I'm asking the questions. And if you keep moving your hand, I'll open you up.'

The man went very still. 'My pocket. Check my pocket.'

Varg did, producing an earring Chandni knew even by

starlight. He let the young man go, sliding the weapon back into his sleeve. 'All right, this is Glider and I am Varg. Who the fuck are you?'

'Lan, sir. My name is Lan and I serve Lady Pari same as you. She told me to bring you a message.'

'Say nothing more. Not here.'

A few minutes later, the three of them were back in her hated room, Lan nursing a warm drink and several bruises.

'Go on then,' said Varg. 'Spit it out.'

'Lady Pari says you're to wait here till she comes and gets you. She says it's too dangerous to leave yet.'

'When is she coming?' asked Chandni, ignoring the glare Varg gave her.

'She didn't say.'

'You came all this way just to tell us to stay here?'

'She said don't trust the Sapphire.'

'Which one?'

'All of 'em. One's dodgy but she don't know who it is yet.'

Varg went to say something but Chandni was faster. She ignored his frustrated sigh. 'She thinks there's a traitor in House Sapphire?'

'More than one. There's this guard captain who was supposed to be protecting Lord Rochant, but he tried to kill him instead. An' then when he couldn't, he nicked off with him, took him to Lord Vasin's castle. But nobody knows! An' he's telling everyone it was the Tanzanites that did it.'

'You're talking about Captain Dil?'

Lan nodded.

But that was impossible. Dil had grown up in the palace

as she had. They had spoken many times. He had even come to her for help when he'd first been appointed as captain. Could that same awkward, hard working man be a traitor? Had he been hiding his true motives from childhood, or had the rot set in later? If the former were true, decades of foresight would be required, and that would suggest . . . 'Wait, when you said Lady Pari suspects a traitor in House Sapphire, do you mean she suspects a Deathless?'

Lan nodded again. 'It's one of 'em but she don't know which yet so you gotta stay hidden, she said, like a newborn Ratkin before it gets its armour.'

Chandni struggled to digest this new piece of information. Was she to believe that House Sapphire, the greatest of the seven crystal houses, had fallen to infighting? Lord Rochant was the only Deathless not bound by blood to the others, perhaps they were jealous of his special relationship with the Sapphire High Lord.

No, politics was one thing, but to shed the blood of your own people, of innocents like Kareem, Dhruti and Mohit was something else entirely. *And Satyendra,* she reminded herself, *without Pari's intervention, he would be dead too.* The attack had to be driven by more than just ambition. It was against everything they stood for and it damaged the house, threatening the balance between humanity and the Wild. *An act of evil.*

A horrible thought occurred to her. *What if Nidra Un-Sapphire was not alone when she dealt with the Wild? Could more than one Deathless have betrayed them to demons?* She banished it quickly. Nidra had worked alone, she had been told so by Lord Rochant himself. An aberration, he'd said, an infection they had cut away to purify the house.

She returned her attention to Lan. 'And that's everything?'

'Nah, she wants me to take the other earring back, to show I found you true.'

'Tell Lady Pari to hurry,' Chandni blurted. 'Tell her!'

Varg handed over the earring, exchanging an odd look with Lan, and walked over to the door. 'Come on, you know the route back to Pari's?'

'Pretty much, yeh.'

'I'll talk you through it on the way out. You need to go now, while it's still dark.'

Lan didn't take any further encouragement, following the larger man through the house.

This time, Chandni didn't go with them. *Better if I'm not seen. Better if I stay here and stay out of sight.* With Satyendra still quiet in her arms, she crumpled down within herself, and stared at the wall.

How has it come to this? She was questioning the honour of her betters and starting to doubt her house. Such questions used to be unthinkable and now they were part of her everyday life. Not for the first time, she wished Lord Rochant were there to offer guidance and support. But he was not there, and for once, he needed her.

She tried to find a pattern, to trace things back to the beginning, to when they'd lost their way. The attack on Lord Rochant's castle was the most recent problem but far from the first. Before that was Sorn. She remembered the day the request arrived at Lord Rochant's castle for a hunt. She'd been heavily pregnant at the time but had met the delegation anyway and told them that their lord was between lives. *'What will become of us?'* they'd asked, their faces lined with fear and sleepless nights. She had looked them in the eye and told them – with a conviction that now pained her – that High Lord Yadavendra himself would answer the call. After all, that was the way it had always been, since the end of the Unbroken Age.

Her first lie, given in good faith, and all the worse for it.

However, the rot had set in long before that. How far back she could not say for sure, but the first moment she'd really felt it, the first time she had really begun to fear, had been the day of Nidra Un-Sapphire's trial.

It was two years ago, at what used to be Nidra's castle. Chandni had gone there to assist Lord Rochant and to take any final instructions – his body was failing and nobody was sure it would survive the journey home.

She had watched as people came forward to denounce Nidra, telling stories of her odd behaviour. None of it directly proved her guilt, but each tale added to the sense that she must have done wrong. Just a few dared to speak at first, and then more as people saw the way the tide was turning. Nidra's own staff betrayed her, hoping that by damning their mistress they would save themselves.

Though Chandni was sure Lord Rochant would not be taken in, she remembered High Lord Yadavendra's reaction, his nodding along, as if lulled by their lies. He seemed to soak them up like fuel, feeding some dark fire inside. Lord Rochant would whisper in his High Lord's ear, a balm of wisdom, normally soothing, but this time, the balm had no effect, and then Yadavendra was on his feet.

There was a wildness in his eyes, she'd thought, and now, having talked to Varg, she realized it was as if he'd got Wildeye. But instead of seeing Whispercages everywhere, he saw enemies, traitors. That was the moment Chandni began to fear.

Perhaps Nidra's staff felt it too, for they seemed to quiver as one, a herd sensing its own extinction.

'This is a dark age for our house,' began Yadavendra, softly, yet there was something harsh in his voice too, a promise of violence. 'When my predecessor, Samarku Un-Sapphire was found guilty, we gave him back to the Wild and we exiled his line. The rest of his servants were presumed innocent and allowed to continue in service to the house. Many stayed in their former lord's castle, helping the transition for Samarku's replacement, our beloved Lord Rochant.

'Some among you will know that I was not always destined to be High Lord of the Sapphire. Some will remember that my sister, Nidra, was favoured for the role. Samarku wanted her to succeed him. I should have seen it then, the connection between them. I should have acted immediately, but I was blinded by love for my sister. Misplaced love.'

Even though she was nowhere near Yadavendra, Chandni had still flinched away when he raised his staff. 'For my mercy, I apologize to you all. It will not happen again. A sickness must be cut away, completely and utterly, or it will return and spread. We cut away Samarku but it was not enough.' He pointed at Nidra. 'The sickness is still here. I do not know how many my sister infected with her poison. Perhaps all of you now worship the demons of the Wild, perhaps you all remained faithful to me. I don't know, how could I?

'There is only one way to be sure.'

Throughout the trial, Nidra had been dignified, though

she made her disgust plain. Now she begged, asking to be the sole recipient of Yadavendra's madness. If anything, this only made him angrier.

'There will be no more mercy, no more half-measures,' he'd screeched. 'They will be fed to the Wild along with you, my fallen sister. Exile and death for you all!'

She'd thought that was the worst it could get but she'd been wrong. Nidra had been dragged away to face the Bringers of Endless Order while the rest of them had waited, baking under the glare of the three suns.

Distantly, through layers of rock, they could hear her screaming.

Meanwhile, Nidra's people had been penned up in the courtyard and stripped of their possessions, the symbols of office torn from their clothes. They'd seemed to shrink within their rags, like popped blisters, slowly collapsing in on themselves.

They were lessened somehow, and Chandni hadn't realized it at the time, but on that day, the whole house was lessened.

The Bringers of Endless Order had returned, a line of robed figures, black and white and silent. They left a haggard Nidra at Yadavendra's feet and, in his hands, an artifact that Chandni guessed must be a Godpiece. He'd looked at it as if it were alive, before turning disdainfully towards his sister. 'The infection must be cleansed from body and soul.'

Nidra Un-Sapphire was cast out as tradition dictated, but so too were all of her people, every servant, every hunter, young and old, every one was sent with her deep into the Wild, fresh blood running from multiple cuts. None of them would last the night.

Nidra Un-Sapphire's castle was emptied and would be

abandoned, left for the Birdkin and the ghosts, and she'd thought that was the worst it could get, but she'd been wrong.

Even then, Yadavendra was not satisfied. His anger was so intense it seemed to radiate around him, a halo of rage. 'The infection must be cleansed!' he'd said again, and again, sometimes shouting, sometimes murmuring, repeating the words until they lost meaning, were reduced to a kind of animal sound, and Chandni knew something terrible was about to happen. Rochant must have known too, but like her, he could do nothing to stop it.

Tradition dictated that Nidra Un-Sapphire's Godpiece would be given to a new Deathless raised from the ranks of the worthy. But Yadavendra would not have that. 'Infected!' he cried. 'Body and soul!' And with that he threw the Godpiece down and stabbed at it with his crystal-tipped staff. Sparks flew and it skittered across the ground, still whole. His attendants gasped in horror, an unwilling audience, while Yadavendra screamed and gave chase, stabbing the Godpiece, stamping on it, battering it, until, at last, something vital gave out in the structure with a groan and it cracked in two. Yadavendra groaned too, and fell down next to it.

Silence.

Too long.

Everyone staring, not sure what to do. There was no precedent, no tradition to guide them.

It was Lord Rochant who finally took control of the situation, ordering the High Lord taken away and the detritus cleared. Minutes later, the industrious Sapphire had returned things to normal, but Chandni could not forget the image of the High Lord, fallen, and some sacred part of her house broken, forever.

Pari and Ami took turns moving the cart, one sleeping while the other pushed, and the days blurred together in a haze of exhaustion.

She constantly checked the road behind, expecting to see a carriage or hear the Dogkin pack. But of Dil and Lady Yadva there was no sign. True, they'd done all they could to make the most of their lead, travelling through the night, not daring to stop, even if at times she could only manage a pitiful pace. But either Yadva was travelling in a stately manner, highly unlikely given the urgency of the situation, or their carriage had broken down somewhere deliciously problematic.

Many of the Deathless became pragmatic about small setbacks. Measured over the vastness of their lifespans, losing a few hours or a few days meant little. Ultimately, a goal would still be achieved. Indeed, Pari found such wrinkles were often the things that kept life fresh.

Lady Yadva was not that kind of Deathless however, and it made Pari giggle to think about how angry the Sapphire would be and how awful it would be for Dil stuck in close quarters with her.

By the fifth day she found she was not only thinking these things, but picturing them. Her imagined drama playing out before her eyes, colourful, too vivid. So too was her concern over Rochant, when she thought of him.

By the sixth day, she had developed a fever.

From the seventh day onwards, Ami did all the pushing, while Pari stayed bundled up in the cart, cold despite the layers, shivering, sleeping, her eyes unsure what was real and what was not.

In her lucid moments, she knew she had only herself to blame. Her body had reached its limits long ago and she had ignored them, forcing tired bones to keep step with her immortal will until they failed entirely.

The sky passed by overhead, dark, light, dark again, while threads of thought flapped in her skull, incomplete. Sometimes she was aware of water on her lips, or was it blood? There was coughing too, but by the time she had registered such things they had stopped, seemingly having happened hours ago. Had they occurred on a different day? Had they occurred at all?

Her worries for the present summoned memories of the past. She recalled a meeting of the Crystal Dynasties from another lifecycle. It was a traditional get together at the Hall of Seven Doors, to share news and renew bonds, and in this case, make new ones.

A man had come to find her shortly before the welcoming ceremony. In many ways the body he had chosen was unremarkable. It was lean, neat and tall, the hair cropped short to display a golden tattoo of cracks running across one side of the skull. There was a deliberation to his movements that caught her eye however, a sense that every step, and every gesture was made with forethought and planning.

'You must be the new Sapphire,' she said.

'That is correct,' he replied. 'My name is Rochant. Might I have the honour of kissing your hand?'

She had laughed at his boldness. 'Only if I can kiss yours first.'

He held out his hand, a picture of formality, and she kissed it, before holding out her own.

'It is an honour to meet you, Lady Pari.'

'And a most unexpected pleasure to meet you, Lord Rochant.'

'Ah yes, I regret that High Lord Yadavendra could not attend today. He bids me tell you that his love for House Tanzanite remains strong, and that you are always welcome in his lands.' He had placed a strong emphasis on the 'you', somehow making it seem as if the invitation were for her alone.

'Well, such visits are normally the province of my brother, Lord Arkav, but I will be sure to pass on the good wishes.' She leaned closer to him and lowered her voice in mock conspiracy. 'We're both stand-ins today.'

'Then it is only right that we look out for each other.'

She'd smiled, surprised to find herself actually warming to a Sapphire. 'Yes, you watch my back and I'll watch yours.'

How those words have come to shape my life!

The memory slipped away, blurring with others, times she had tried to find him and failed, snippets of their conversations over the years, all jumbled with fever dreams and moments of clarity.

And then one morning, her mind cleared all of a sudden, like shrugging off a cloak when it is no longer needed. She felt cold, and the end of her nose was an icy lump. She was hungry too, and realized she could not remember the last time she'd eaten.

The sky above was dominated by Fortune's Eye, shining bright and gold. On her periphery, she could see tree branches going by, leafless. *I'm moving.*

'Ami, are you there?'

'Yes.'

'Ami!' She sat up and everything spun for a moment, the simple act of changing position bringing with it a wave of fatigue. *Go gently, Pari!*

'Is it you?' asked the girl.

The oddness of the question made Pari turn to get a better look at her. Ami had appeared tired before, but now it was written into the lines of her features, stress, worry, lack of sleep, as if someone had started inking an older face over the younger one.

'Yes. It's me, my dear Ami. I'm here and I'm hungry. Do we have anything to eat?'

They sat on the cart together and shared out the last of the rations. It wasn't enough to stop her stomach rumbling, but it did quieten, allowing her to think about other things, like where she was.

Pari looked about, trying to get a bearing. It took her longer to get over her surprise than it did to recognize the landscape. 'Ami, do you see how the Godroad shines differently here?' The girl looked, nodding as she took in the violet hues that softened the blues from before. 'Do you see that river running alongside it.'

'Yes.'

'And do you see those houses built on the banks, with people fishing from their balconies?'

'I can.'

'That settlement is called Grace. It's known for its dancers and the way they spice their fish eggs.'

'How do you know every place?'

'I don't know all the settlements but I know this one very

well.' She smiled at Ami's confusion, placing a hand on her chest. 'It's mine.' Seeing that Ami remained confused, she added. 'On my land. We're nearly home.'

Ami looked up, her eyes misty with hope. 'We are?'

'We are. However did you know how to get here?'

There was a pause. 'You told me.'

Pari frowned. 'I see. Did I say anything else while I was ill?'

'You said a lot of stuff I didn't get. You shouted sometimes like you was dreaming.' A troubled look crossed her face. 'And there's this one time when you kept saying you was sorry.'

'Did I say what I was sorry about?'

'No but you kept saying "Arky". What's that mean?'

Pari looked up at the sky. She hadn't said Arky. She'd said Arkav, as in her brother. *So much to regret where he is concerned, I'm spoilt for choice.* She continued to watch the clouds as she said, 'I'm sorry, Ami, I don't know what that was about. Probably just a fever dream.'

They'd not gone three paces past the outer edge of Grace when Pari heard the baying of Dogkin. Lady Yadva and Dil had finally caught them up, later than she could have hoped for but not quite late enough. While she was technically on Tanzanite lands, her appearance, coupled with the fact she was not in her castle, would lead to awkward questions. *If only they had held off a few more hours.*

'What we gonna do?' asked Ami.

'Bring me one of the villagers, hurry.'

A woman in her middle years came over, looking wary. As soon as she saw Pari's face, there was a spark of recognition and she started to bow. 'Do not abase yourself, pretend

I am just a traveller.' The woman straightened, attentive. *She's sharp. She senses the opportunity coming. Good.* 'If you help me now, I will make your fortune, by my house and my blood and my good name, I swear it so. But you must be quick. I need two strong people to push my cart to the castle, and I need you to delay the Sapphire carriage that is nearly upon us. Can you do it?'

The woman rubbed her chin. 'You want it to go in the river?'

Oh I like her. I like her very much. 'Yes, that would be perfect. When all this is over, and you see our visitors returning home, come to my castle.'

Two youngsters were found in short order, broad backed and well muscled, and the cart wheels hummed, merry, as they set it skimming along the Godroad.

Ami was sat on top, with Pari tucked under the blankets, out of sight.

And then, as the Godroad began to slope upwards to point towards Pari's castle, they heard an almighty roaring and snapping far behind them, of hungry Dogkin, drowning out the desperate cries of their handler, of a whip cracking uselessly, too little, too late.

And moments later, a splash.

After days of brooding, Chandni stood up. She'd had enough. Of the walls, of the lack of sky, of all of it. House Sapphire was under attack, possibly from itself, its people were suffering, and she had to do something. Anything. Varg must have seen something in her eye for he stood up as well.

'What?'

She lifted her chin to look up at him. 'I'm going to go next door and introduce myself.'

'You're bloody not.'

'If I spend another minute in this room I'm going to kill someone, and as you know, my Satyendra is too important to kill.' She looked to her left, then her right, before returning to him with a withering gaze. 'Which doesn't leave many other options.'

He stood in front of the door. 'Don't make me . . . '

She picked up Satyendra and took a step towards him.

'Don't.' He pulled at his beard, clearly unhappy. 'We can't trust them.'

'They are my people, Varg, not the enemy, and I intend to go and see them. So either you need to make good on your threat or you need to get out of my way.'

She took another step so that her nose was nearly brushing his chest. He was bigger than her, yes. Definitely stronger too, but she was used to command, and he was used to following orders. *And more than that,* she thought, *he is a good man.*

Varg made a strangled, frustrated sound, but he stood aside nonetheless, and Chandni walked through.

The other room in the house was a similar size to the one she'd been trapped in but it was warmer, brighter, enjoying more of the fire's attention. There were four others in the room. A baby, probably close to Satyendra's age but nearly twice the size. A sparky looking toddler, and a worn looking man and woman.

'Hello,' she said, sitting down next to them, and arranging Satyendra on her lap. 'My name is Chandni.' *Not Ri or some other nonsense. I will deal with truth or nothing at all. From* the other room, Varg swore. She pretended not to hear. 'I think it's time you and I had a talk.'

'Are we in trouble?' asked the man. 'Do we have to go?'

'No. No, not at all. But if we're sharing a house, we should get to know each other a little better.' They nodded slowly but said nothing, so Chandni added, 'Shall we start with names?'

Before either of the adults could stop him, the toddler stepped forward with none of the wobble she normally associated with children of his age. 'I'm Dev!' he declared.

'I'm pleased to meet you, Dev. What about you?' she gestured to the man.

'Daddy!' piped Dev, tiny finger pointing.

'Fen,' said the man quietly. He looked thin, veins proud on his arms and neck, but his hands were large, and there was a physical ease to his movements that suggested strength.

'And I'm—'

'Mummy!'

'—Sal,' said the woman. She was bundled up in layers of fabric to keep warm, making her appear larger than she probably was. It looked like she could use a bath and several nights of good sleep. The baby in her arms appeared clean and content however. 'This little one is Min,' she added with a smile.

The next few hours passed quickly, pleasurably, and she learned that the family were refugees from Sorn. While Sagan was able to use their labour, it had no rooms to spare, and so, in desperation, they had broken into Varg's house, only intending to stay for one night.

Most of the conversation was led by her; only Dev dared to ask questions back. *Something has broken these people's spirits,* she thought. And because it was in her nature to cut to the heart of things, she asked them what it was.

Their answer was simple: the Wild. When Sorn's call for aid had been ignored, the denizens of the Wild had not been idle. Before Sorn's elders had made the decision to leave, people had gone missing, and strange creatures had walked through the streets, unchallenged, with blood on their teeth and sacks in their hands, wriggling. The people of Sorn had been abandoned, scarred and broken long before they arrived in Sagan.

They are lost, poor things. Like me. And with that thought, purpose bloomed in her. 'We are all in a place we don't belong,' she said. 'But we are all part of House Sapphire, and we will endure this, together.'

Only Dev seemed uplifted by her words but Chandni wasn't discouraged. She knew that the best way to build trust was through action and shared achievement. Slipping gratefully back into her role of authority, she asked them simple questions to ascertain their skills, and set them tasks accordingly. The same technique was applied to Varg, but his jobs were specifically chosen to get him out of the house. None of the adults went particularly willingly to work, nor in Varg's case, particularly quietly, but they went all the same. *The road to perfection is taken in small steps,* she reminded herself.

Over the following days a gentle transformation began. The fire was banked higher, pushing the cold back to the walls. Clothes were patched and cleaned. Dev was given the role of lookout, and a small drum he could beat if there was trouble. He spent his days standing on a stool in the room upstairs, watching both village and Wild for signs of intruders. He gave Chandni detailed reports of the comings and goings of Sagan's workforce, along with vivid descriptions of anything that moved in the trees. And though he sounded the alarm several times a day, with a high pitched call of 'Killers!' or 'Monsters!' or 'They coming! Aargh!' it was always in earnest.

Everyone slept better, the combination of weary limbs and sense of forward motion keeping the worst of the nightmares at bay. The exception to this was Satyendra, who seemed in a permanent state of disgruntlement. Chandni often watched the other baby, Dev's little brother, Min, with envious eyes. He was so quiet, such a peaceful and undemanding little soul, that most of the time she forgot he was there.

Varg and Fen ventured out each morning, Varg helping the rebuilding efforts, and Fen clearing trees. This was tense work as the trees did not fall quietly, screaming each time an axe bit home. In the evenings they would sit by the fire, sharing news, mainly for Chandni's benefit, and mainly, if she was honest, because she made them.

But often the only sound was the spitting of the fire and the liquid in the pot bubbling.

'Any other news to share?'

'Only bad,' replied Varg. 'The Wild's getting stirred up. Makes it tough on the gatherers.'

'Tough how?' asked Chandni. Satyendra was leaning against her shoulder, restless. She was so used to this now, she barely noticed, stirring the broth that would be their dinner as she waited in vain for the others to elaborate.

'Oh, there's been another fight.'

'What about?'

He shrugged. 'Nothing much.'

'People don't fight about nothing, Varg.'

'This lot do.'

'No, they fight because they're frustrated or because they're scared.' She gave the pot another stir before turning back to him. 'If only I could go and speak to them, I'm sure we could find a solution.'

Varg gave her a warning look. 'You can't save everyone.'

'Not while I'm trapped here, I can't.'

'Ah shit, not this again!'

She was so busy trying to think of a reply and not lose her temper that she didn't notice Satyendra lean over and grab the spoon sticking from the pot. 'I was going to suggest that you spoke to them.'

'Me?'

'Yes. Then you could tell me what their grievances are.'

Varg suddenly had one hand reaching towards her. 'Careful.'

'What?'

'Careful!' he repeated, urgent, horror on his face.

Too late, she realized that he wasn't looking at her directly, his attention was slightly to her left.

Satyendra!

He had managed to take the spoon in both hands and was intent on pulling it to him. As he did so, the pot began to tilt, the boiling broth threatening to pour onto his head.

'No!' she cried, grabbing the edge of the pot and forcing it upright. Satyendra jerked in surprise, spoon slipping from his grip as Chandni swung him around on her hip, putting her body between him and the fire.

Liquid sloshed back and forth in the pot, threatening to spill, but only a few drops were lost, fizzing as they met the flames. When she was sure it was secure, she moved herself and Satyendra away. 'Thank you, Varg. I think,' she added humbly, 'that someone else should stir for a while.'

It was only after she'd checked Satyendra to be absolutely sure he was unhurt that she realized the others were staring at her.

'Is something wrong?'

Varg's face creased with worry. 'That's what I was going to ask you.'

She nodded, thinking she understood. 'I'm fine. A little shocked at how close we came. I really am glad you were paying attention.'

'But, Chandni . . . '

'Yes?'

Varg didn't hold her gaze. He looked so sad, she felt the urge to touch him.

Dev wrinkled his nose. 'What's that smell?'

Chandni inhaled and immediately detected the odour of something burning. 'Our dinner!' she said, torn between the urge to tend to it and to keep Satyendra well away, lest he try for the spoon again.

'It's not dinner,' said Varg. 'It's skin stuck to the side of the pot. Show me your hand, Chandni.'

She realized he was looking at it, and tucked it within the fold of her top. 'It's fine.'

'No it isn't. That's your skin on the pot. Now show me.'

Her shoulders slumped and she held out her arm. She saw rather than felt him take her wrist and turn it over. Three lines were seared white across her hand, one on the finger-tips, one on the top of her palm, and a third on the heel. Around them, the flesh was livid, weeping.

Varg, shaking his head in disbelief, said, 'I know you Sapphire are stoic but . . . fuck.'

'I'm not being stoic. I can't feel it. I can't feel anything from my hand to my elbow on my right side.' She sighed. 'When I was escaping the castle, I was attacked. They poisoned me. We tried to treat it but we only slowed it down. The cook, she told me I'd have to cut away the bits I couldn't feel but . . . everything was so hectic and dangerous at the time. And then later . . . ' She closed her eyes. 'I couldn't.'

'Is that why you were hacking at yourself in the wagon?'

She nodded. 'It's getting worse.'

'You should have bloody told me!'

'I wanted to. I tried.'

'Right,' he said, sounding anything but certain. 'We'll have to go somewhere quiet, as near to the Godroad as we can. And then . . . '

'And then?'

'Then we do what your cook said.'

Dev went over and whispered in his father's ear; after a moment Fen raised his hand as if asking permission to speak. 'Maybe there is another way.' He paused as she and Varg looked at him, like a nervous animal that could bolt at any moment, but Dev held fast to his hand. Fen went on, 'Not far from where we used to live is a tree that fell but did not die. It is an old tree. If you go and feed it, and then put your hand in its roots, it will take the poison away.'

'And there wouldn't need to be any cutting?'

'No.'

'I could keep my hand?'

'Yes.'

She dared to feel a little hope. 'You can take me there?'

'No.' The fear in his voice was palpable. 'But I will tell you how to find it.'

Varg's beard twitched with distaste. 'You're talking about a Hunger Tree?' Fen nodded. 'Then you better tell her what it eats before she gets too excited.'

'What does it eat?'

Fen turned his gaze to the fire. 'Blood. And fingernails.'

The ramifications of what he was saying began to come to her. The tree was a thing of the Wild, and trading with it would stain her honour and soul. If word got back to Lord Rochant, she would be exiled. 'You've used the tree yourself?'

'Not me. My grandmother.'

Chandni didn't answer immediately. It was forbidden to deal with the things of the Wild, and Fen knew it. *Perhaps this is why the High Lord did not send aid to Sorn. Perhaps he was punishing them for breaking our laws.*

But if I am to protect Satyendra, I cannot risk a clumsy amputation, nor can I allow the poison to take me. For his sake, and to ensure the future of my lord, I must do this, and if afterwards I am punished, I will accept that punishment.

Fen was opening himself up to that same risk by confessing knowledge of the Hunger Tree to Chandni. *If nothing else,* she thought bitterly, *I have earned their trust.*

She was going to do it, she realized, and the ease with which the decision was made shocked her. *Is this how it was for Nidra Un-Sapphire? Did she begin with good intentions?*

She had always assumed that there was something wrong with Nidra, an inherent weakness that allowed the Wild to seduce her, but perhaps she once sat, as Chandni did now, believing she acted for the greater good. At her trial, Nidra admitted no guilt. How she'd hated her for that. Yet here she was, afraid, yes, even ashamed, but not guilty.

Satyendra must live, Lord Rochant must return. That is my duty, no matter the cost.

She swallowed down all her misgivings and looked Fen in the eye. 'Tell me where I have to go and what I have to do. Varg and I will leave in the morning.'

CHAPTER NINE

Having seen two Sapphire castles recently, Pari was able to appreciate her own even more than usual. Perhaps the similar nature of the buildings helped to emphasize their differences. Every castle of the Deathless was built long ago upon crystal-laced rock, by the great powers of the Unbroken Age, who then gouged them out of the earth whole, and yet every one of them had a unique character in some way shaped by the nature of the immortal that claimed them.

The Sapphire castles cut hard shapes in the sky, having a bold, almost unfinished edge to them, as if each had been snapped off another, bigger structure. By contrast the aesthetics of Pari's castle drew the eye gently. It was, in her opinion, the work of a more mature architect.

As she drew nearer to the threshold, Pari could feel the tension easing, being absorbed into the walls of the castle, as if it were a great mother, and she its child.

Her majordomo came to meet them at the gates, his face lined with stress. *An unfortunate side effect of working for me,* she mused. His name was Sho, and he had served her all his life. It was Sho she had trusted to cover her absence. His uniform was as crisp as ever, the tanzanite studs still sparkling at his throat. But in the sunslight, she could not help but see how haggard he'd become.

Our time is coming to an end, Sho. But I will come back, again and again, while you will live on only in my memory, and the stories I tell to your grandchildren.

Despite her disguise and the fact she arrived in a Sapphire cart in the company of strangers, Sho still bowed to her as if all were as it should be.

She hauled herself out of the cart, immediately wishing she'd asked for help first.

'My dear Sho, see that the two fine young men pushing our cart are fed and rested before sending them back home.' She paused as Sho waved the men into a nearby receiving room. 'This is Ami. She will be joining the household. I want her given a room, bathed and given new clothes. She is also keen to sample some proper Tanzanite cuisine. For now I want her kept out of sight, the less that others know of her, the better.'

'My lady,' began Sho. From the tone it was clear he was about to embark on a well-meaning but long speech, followed by many pertinent questions. She had time for neither.

'Sho, this cart needs to be disposed of, discreetly and immediately. It was never here.'

'My lady, I must speak with you. It's urgent.'

'And you will. Later. Right now you must do as I've asked. As soon as that's done, prepare for noble guests. I expect company within the hour.'

'Who should I prepare for?'

'Lady Yadva Sapphire and entourage.'

The old man took this in, nodded. 'I will tell the cooks to prepare something mild.'

'No. Have them prepare something spicy. I want her to be uncomfortable. It will help set the mood.'

'I'm not sure if that is wise.'

'I am.' She was uncomfortable herself, all the time, why should Lady Yadva be allowed the advantage of a sense of well being? 'And, Sho, I want you to be here to greet them personally. Hold them for as long as you can. Talk slowly. Walk slowly.' She winked. 'Play up your age.'

A wry look came into his eye. 'I'll do my best.'

She left Sho and Ami to get started, hobbling across the courtyard as fast as she could manage. Servants met her and whisked her to her chambers. Travelling clothes were stripped away and consigned to the fire, while gentle hands helped her to bathe. The water was warm, easing muscles, and taking the weight of weary limbs. Had it not been for the hurried scrubbing she was receiving, Pari would surely have fallen asleep. Dirt fell from her like a chrysalis, crumbling, to reveal a new form beneath. She was barely out of the bath when word came that a group of Sapphire hunters had been spotted making the climb towards her gates.

Clothes were brought, the most ostentatious she owned. A blue-green gown that flowed around her feet, lake-like, so vast that a quartet of servants were required to lift the corners when she moved. Heavy hooped earrings encrusted with stones. Her face was brushed with gold, her nails polished till they shone.

Around her they set out a square of low tables, and decorated them with steaming bowls of rice and meat, aromatic scents bringing the air to life.

A message from Sho informed her that Lady Yadva had arrived.

Pari sat back. All was ready. She was ready. A part of her was actually looking forward to seeing Yadva. After days of scrabbling and hiding and fearing discovery, it was good to be on home ground. Better still to be taking control again.

A sound caught her attention. Not the bellow of Yadva's voice or the sound of a group marching towards her chamber, something softer. She frowned, listened, frowned again. Her body had already placed the sound, identified it as a threat of some kind, even as her mind told her that she knew it.

Just before the figure appeared, the name came to her: Lord Taraka of the Deathless, right hand of High Lord Tanzanite and the holder of whispers.

He approached casually, but she wasn't fooled. It was unlikely that her affectation of warm surprise fooled him either. They'd both known each other far too long.

The body he'd taken in this lifecycle was smaller than his usual preference, and a penchant for loose clothing had given a somewhat square aspect to his usual elegant shape. His steps remained graceful however, soundless save the soft swishing of embroidered trouser cuffs across the tops of bare feet. From his neck several dozen crystals dangled on thin cord, chiming softly.

'Lord Taraka,' she said. 'Be welcome. My roof extends to shelter you, my fire is ready to warm you, my food and drink are yours to share.'

'I hear you and am glad,' he replied, moving around the tables to settle next to her. 'I am also glad to see you up and about. High Lord Tanzanite will be relieved to learn that you are still with us. She had feared you'd slipped between cycles prematurely.'

'As you can see, I am very much alive, though I am touched by the High Lord's concern.'

He put a hand to one of his low hanging crystals, turning it as he spoke. Pari knew that whatever was said here would be captured in the stone, to be picked over at leisure by Taraka and her High Lord. 'There is much love for you within House Tanzanite, so much in fact that no less than three of us have been stirred to action by news of your . . . ' his friendly mask slipped just for a moment, deliberate, to reveal a cold expression '. . . condition.'

'Three?'

'Yes. Myself, High Lord Tanzanite, and your brother. He was most distressed, and we all know how he struggles with bad news.'

What have you done now, dear Arkav?

Pari could feel the conversation slipping away from her. Taraka was leading up to something, and the only thing she could be sure of was that she was in trouble. Her main concern though, was for Arkav. Taraka was right, her brother did struggle, often, and those struggles rarely ended well. 'Where is Lord Arkav?'

'With the High Lord. She feels it best to keep him close.' Something of her dismay must have shown for Taraka leaned across and put a hand on her arm. 'Don't worry. He's safe. No new cuts.'

She gave him a relieved smile, genuine this time, and he gave her a moment before releasing her arm and sitting back. 'He came to us in something of a state, begging an audience with the High Lord. She gave one, of course. Would you like to hear what he said?'

No, she thought, but nodded.

Taraka removed one of his necklaces and placed it on the table between them. Then, with a practised flourish, he tapped it with a golden fingernail, making it chime. The note was soon drowned out by the sound of her brother's voice, tight with worry.

'It's wrong. Wrong! I-I can't . . . You have to do something. Please!'

'Stop.' The High Lord's voice, deep, commanding. *'Breathe.'*

'Yes but—'

'Breathe.'

Pari could actually hear him sucking down air, trying to calm himself. He sounded on edge, vulnerable. The thought of the High Lord seeing him that way, and of what she might do, filled her with dread.

'Now,' said the High Lord's voice from the crystal. *'Begin again. Slower this time.'*

'I went to Pari's. I wanted to see her, but when I got there, they said she was sick and wouldn't let me in. Me! Her brother.'

'What did they say, exactly?'

'They said she was too ill to receive visitors, that she was contagious.' She heard footsteps from within the crystal, rapid, and imagined Arkav striding forward, sudden movement matching his shift in mood. *'But. They. Were. Lying.'*

'You know this?'

'Yes, it was in their words.'

'You swear it?'

'Yes.'

A second flick of Taraka's finger, and the crystal was silent. 'There's more of course. But I think you get the gist. As you can imagine, we all agreed that something needed to be done and so I set off at all speed, arriving here a few days ago, to find,' he spread his hands, 'well, you can imagine my dismay.'

'I can explain,' Pari began but Taraka cut her off with a laugh.

'And I look forward to it. Truly. But let us attend to your guests first. They do not sound inclined to wait.'

She had been focused so completely on the crystal that she had not registered the voices in the corridor. There was no mistaking Yadva now though. The Sapphire was angry, and she felt sympathy for Sho, who did not deserve to be talked to so roughly.

'Enough of this. If I am not brought before your mistress immediately, I will make my displeasure felt.'

'We are nearly there, Lady Yadva, I promise you. It is just around here . . . '

'You said that before. For your sake, it had better be true this time.'

The door was pushed open and Sho, who did not look like he was pretending to be short of breath, said: 'Lady Yadva Sapphire, and Captain Dil of Lord Rochant's castle guard, my lady.'

To her surprise she saw that Yadva's current body was even more bulky than the last one. The muscles bigger, the neck thicker. *She must be breeding them for size.*

They had spared no time coming here, and dark patches of damp showed on her clothes and on Dil's uniform, attesting to their recent dip in the river. Dirt from the road stained their features and coated their boots. Against the gleam of Pari's chamber, the two looked ridiculous.

Pari drank in the moment, savouring every fall of Yadva's expression as she took in the details. *This is almost too good.*

'Lady Yadva of the noble Sapphire,' she said, 'be welcome. My walls are yours, my food, yours to enjoy. Come, sit and join us. You look like you've travelled a long way.' While Yadva recovered from her shock, Pari couldn't help but add: 'And is that Dil I see with you? My, I haven't seen you in, oh it must be years.'

She allowed a pause for Dil to say something but he seemed even more stunned than Yadva. When he realized that the attention of three Deathless was upon him, his cheeks flushed and he executed a bow, as deep as it was awkward.

Pari gestured to a space opposite, forcing Yadva to take it or risk insult. With teeth gritted, the Sapphire crossed the room to join them, her boots squelching with each step.

Taraka looked out of the window, as if the movement of some nearby bird had caught his eye. Pari knew better, however. *He's trying not to laugh.* The thought made her lips twitch. *Don't laugh, Pari. Don't laugh.*

'Please, eat something,' she said, and Yadva started immediately, using the food as an excuse to delay the inevitably awkward conversation. The Sapphire Deathless had expected to find an empty castle and to expose Pari's servants as liars. Now she had been caught, shamed in front of her peers. *And she knows we'll never forget.*

They ate in silence, except for Dil who remained by the door, unable to sit or leave unless invited. Out of the corner of her eye she saw Taraka's shoulders shake with mirth, and she nearly spat out a mouthful of rice. Luckily both of her guests were too intent on the floor and their own problems to notice.

After a while, the spice began to tell, sweat beading on Yadva's forehead.

Pari put her own bowl down. 'It is not like you to leave Sapphire lands, Lady Yadva. I must confess to being curious, what brings you here, and in such a hurry?'

The usually loud voice was replaced with something meeker, almost mumbling. 'I had heard you were . . . sick. I was concerned.'

'So concerned that you came here without sending word ahead? With hunters? So concerned that you came direct to my chambers, without changing? I suppose I should be flattered.'

'I had heard . . . '

'What had you heard, exactly?' asked Taraka, one hand brushing against the jewels at his throat. 'We would love to know more.'

She could almost hear the sounds of Yadva's brain working frantically to dig herself out of the hole. At last she said, 'It appears I was misinformed.' Pari marked the murderous look that was sent in Dil's direction. 'I'd been led to believe that you were in danger.'

'How strange. I'd caught a fever, nothing more dangerous than that. As you can see, this body is getting old, and I spend most of my time in bed these days. The end of a lifecycle is so tiresome, wouldn't you agree?'

'Yes.'

Taraka put a hand on Pari's arm. 'But fear not, Lady Yadva, for we Tanzanite look after our own. When I heard of Lady Pari's illness, I could not help but come to offer my support. Though I confess, my arrival was not nearly as memorable as yours.'

'Please accept my apologies for the intrusion, I will leave you both to continue your business.'

Pari exchanged a look with Taraka. She could see muscles clenching in his jaw. 'I wouldn't dream of it. You must stay, eat with us. It has been too long.'

And Yadva acquiesced. There was nothing else she could do. Pari drew out the meal, enduring her own fatigue to make Yadva squirm for as long as possible. At the end of it, Taraka cleared his throat.

'I trust that you will reassure any other worried members of House Sapphire that Lady Pari is recovering admirably under my care. And should you encounter any further misinformation about her or another member of my house, you will be sure to quell it, yes?'

Yadva's agreement was subdued, but audible.

'Wonderful,' said Taraka, and Pari knew he had captured the exchange for later use.

'Would you like to stay the night?' asked Pari.

'No. That is, I would like that but—' Another glare in Dil's direction, furious enough almost to make her feel sorry for him. Almost. 'There is house business that cannot wait.'

'Then we will wish you a safe journey home, and look forward to seeing you again, in a more traditional manner.'

Yadva stood and bowed, before retreating stiffly from the room. They barely managed to wait until the sound of her sodden boots had reached the corridor before bursting into laughter.

When it had subsided, Taraka wiped his eyes. 'Ah, that

was glorious. The look on her face! Have you ever seen the like?' He chuckled at the memory, smiling to himself, but when he turned to her all friendliness had been put away, his face pleasant but cold. 'Now, where were we? Ah yes, you were about to explain why it is your servants saw fit to lie to a lord of our house, and to tell me exactly, and in detail, where you have really been these past few weeks.'

The cold woke Satyendra up. He was always cold, his small body shivering even while asleep. The only time he wasn't freezing was when the wings came and wrapped him up, then he felt safe and warm.

But often, the wings would go, leaving him alone, leaving him scared. He didn't cry though. Every time the urge came, it was accompanied with a memory of the Whispercage and all noise died in his throat.

Twigs and feathers had been banked around him to form a nest, obscuring him from low-level eyes. He was still vulnerable however, easy prey for any predator that happened to pass by.

He wriggled, restless, his budding teeth chattering together. Some of the nest collapsed.

Time passed.

Eventually, he dozed.

When the Birdkin returned, it brought something dangling in its beak. The Birdkin always returned with something, usually water carried from afar, but this time was different. Instead of drink, a long strip of bloody meat hung down.

Satyendra opened his mouth as wide as it would go, expectant.

With slow care, the Birdkin manoeuvred the offering

directly above Satyendra's open mouth. When it was aligned perfectly, the Birdkin lowered it down just enough for Satyendra to suck on the end.

A gulp of blood went down, and seconds later, knowledge exploded in Satyendra's mind. A single piece of information came first, perfectly formed, like a heavy stone thrown into a lake, rippling.

Crowflies!

It is Crowflies!

Its name is Crowflies!

The taste on his tongue was bitter, alien, and yet he wanted more. He lifted his head slightly, his hands trying to grip the slippery flesh.

Another gulp, and then the meat was torn away, Crowflies hopping back. Something had alarmed it.

Satyendra could hear leaves whispering to one another, passing on the sound of feet crunching quietly on the forest floor. He could see the shape of a person coming through the trees, not a safe shape, not familiar, but not the Red Brothers or the Whispercage either.

Crowflies dropped the meat and jumped into the space between them.

The person shape resolved itself into an old man, his clothes patched and faded to a twilight grey, dark eyes peering out from beneath long, snowy hair. 'What have you got there?' he asked.

Crowflies spread its wings and drew itself up tall, blocking the man from Satyendra's view.

He heard the man come closer but only because the leaves continued to amplify every step. 'What are you up to, demon? Move aside.'

With a screech, Crowflies launched itself forward. There was a flutter of wings, a sharp crack, and then Crowflies was on the ground again, this time on its side.

Then the man's head appeared, blocking out all else.

'Hello there,' he said. 'You don't look like you belong in a nest.' He wiped the blood from around Satyendra's mouth with a rough finger. 'How about you come with me instead, eh?'

When the man scooped up the baby, Crowflies twitched weakly. When he began to stride away, Crowflies cried out: 'Sa-at! Sa-at!'

Another chunk of knowledge landed in the baby's brain, a second piece of certainty that hit with the same force as the first.

Sa-at!

I am Sa-at!

My name is Sa-at!

Sa-at reached out toward the Birdkin but the man was already striding away, plunging them into the tangled trees. Distantly he could hear Crowflies crying, the leaves carrying the faltering noise. 'Sa-at! Sa-at!'

There were a few more screeches, bitter, pathetic, and then nothing, the other sounds of the forest rising to take their place. The man moved hurriedly, always on alert for trouble. His grip on Sa-at was firm, uncomfortable, and each time he turned sharply, or dropped into a crouch, it hurt.

Tears budded at the corners of his eyes but he did not call out, fear of the Whispercage, fear of the brothers, fear of this man, fear, pure and deep, keeping him silent.

While they travelled, the two new thoughts bounced loudly

in his mind. *Its name is Crowflies! My name is Sa-at! Its name is Crowflies! My name is Sa-at!*

Eventually they came to a stop at a large, dead tree. The ground beneath them was blackened and free of roots, the tree itself, hollowed and scorched by some great force. The man made a quick inspection, plucking a lone shoot of green from the black dust and crushing it in his fist, before ducking through a low hole at the base of the trunk.

Sa-at was placed on something soft, and a flame sparked into life nearby, dancing on top of a fat candle that sat on an old human skull. Thick furs decorated the inside of the tree, hundreds of little pelts all stitched together to make a continuous wrap.

The man settled himself with a heavy sigh. 'There. We should be safe now. As safe as anyone can be in this hateful place, anyway.' He gave a little wave, and Sa-at's eyes followed the movement. 'My name is Devdan.' He tapped his chest and said the word again, slowly. 'Dev-dan. I don't know how you got here but I'm going to do my best to keep you alive. Now, let's have a look at you.'

When he reached out to touch Sa-at, the baby flinched, prompting Devdan's white brows to draw down sadly. 'I'm not going to hurt you, I promise.' The candle was moved closer and Sa-at scrunched up his face, turning away. 'Hmm. Well I can see you have all of your ribs. Not all your fingers though. Damn it. Nothing to be done about that.' He spat onto a piece of cloth and began cleaning the blood from Sa-at's hands and face. 'I dread to think what you've been eating. But don't worry, it's all going to get better now. You'll be the third baby I raised here, did you know that? It's true. I'm a survivor. And it looks to me like you are too. Truth be told, it'll be good to have some company.' He tapped the skull, making the candle wobble. 'I talk to old Hollow, but she isn't much for conversation these days.'

Devdan continued to chatter, while Sa-at watched the shadows play on the trunk, flinching whenever they made the wrong shapes. He missed his mother. He missed Crowflies. He missed their touch and their singing.

Fur was wrapped around him, and he was fed something warm, like water but sweeter. His tongue didn't want sweet, it wanted that strange bitter taste again. He drank it anyway, the shivering calming as the cold fled from his fingers, nose and toes.

'Yes,' Devdan murmured, 'you're the third child I've raised here. I'll get it right this time, I'm sure of it.'

CHAPTER TEN

They left at first light, everyone agreeing that to enter the Wild at night was suicide. Varg had managed to find Chandni a pair of boots. They were too big and rubbed at the heels, but she was grateful for them. The route to the Hunger Tree would take them deep into the woods, to places the wagon wouldn't be able to go. Bare feet and ankles would inevitably get cut, and any blood, even a small amount, would be sure to bring trouble.

Though they were leaving the wagon behind, Glider was coming with them, and for that, she was glad. Both she and Varg had been subdued by the knowledge of where they were going and what would happen when they got there, and Glider's enthusiasm was sorely needed. Chandni ran a hand through the Dogkin's snowy fur. 'You'll keep us safe, won't you?'

Glider barked affirmatively, and then proceeded to march alongside her, five paws strutting like a soldier on parade.

'She's showing off,' said Varg.

'She is not!' replied Chandni as Glider turned her snout to the air, offended. 'She's taking pride in her duty. I think you'd do well to follow her example.'

Glider snorted agreement and Varg shrugged his shoulders in mock defeat, before doing an exaggerated march in step with Glider.

The Dogkin seemed to think this was marvellous, barking encouragement and wagging her tail, forcing laughter from them both. Chandni could not help but note the hysterical edge to it.

By the suns, I'm scared! I don't want to do this.

They walked on, any sense of play fading as the trees grew thick around them. Varg pulled out a velvet pouch, and from it, a chunk of tanzanite. He activated it and the stored sunslight was released, glowing, blue and violet, pushing back the shadows. Though not as strong as the suns themselves, she hoped it would ward off the lesser perils of the Wild.

At the sight of it, Satyendra burrowed deeper into her arms, as if disturbed by the glow, and buried his face in her shoulder. They had talked about the insanity of bringing him into the Wild with them but the alternatives were poor. She couldn't leave him with Fen's family, nor could she expect them to protect him from assassins. Bad as it was, in the end, there was only one choice. *My brave little Sapphire,* she thought. *I will not fail you.*

She soon began to doubt her decision though, and could not help but wonder what horrors were lurking just out of sight. The memory of the Whispercage was never far away, its countenance conjured by the twitch of trees on the breeze, and the play of leaf and shadow.

As the morning drew on, the quiet was broken by singing Birdkin and the scurry of small creatures. Shards of sunslight, gold from Fortune's Eye, red and paler red from Vexation and Wrath's Tear, poked through in places. At each one, Varg stopped and held the tanzanite shard underneath until it began to glow again. Chandni doubted the few seconds of exposure would do much to replenish the gem's stores, but said nothing. After a while, her fear subsided into the rhythm of walking, leaving behind only a vague sense of foreboding.

'Over here,' said Varg, pointing towards one of the trees, tall and gnarly. A necklace of skulls hung from its lower branches, all without jaws or upper teeth.

'It looks like the one Fen told us about.'

'Has to be. Means we're going the right way.'

'Do you think we'll be able to get back to Sagan before sunsdown?'

'I reckon. We're making good time. Over halfway there already.'

'And there's the trident,' she said.

Varg nodded, turning his gaze to it. Midway up the tree was a bare branch that splayed into three. No leaves grew on it but Chandni was filled with a certainty that the wood was not dead. 'Follow the third spoke, he said.'

'That way, then,' she added unnecessarily.

'Yep. How's your feet?'

'Blistered but fine.'

He looked down at her boots as if he could see through them, and frowned, worried. 'Should've found a better fit,' he muttered.

'You did the best you could.' She worked the fingers of

her left hand down the back of one heel and probed the sore skin there. 'It's not bleeding.'

'We need to pad them out better.'

'We don't have the time.'

'Sit down. I'll see what I can do.'

'I said no, Varg.' She went to move past but saw that his scowling face was mirrored by Glider's. The Dogkin had turned round, blocking the way on, her unclouded canine eye filled with concern. 'Oh not you as well!'

Glider raised a paw and waved it towards the floor.

'This is ridiculous,' she said, but her irritation was half forced, their sympathy touching. 'Really, I'm fine.'

'And we've got to keep it that way, so sit down and let me take care of you.'

Glider waved her paw again and Chandni gave up. She knew they were right and so she put her pride to one side and sat down. The ground was rough but it felt good to stop.

Varg eased off her boots and, after a swift examination of her feet, and some mutterings about how small they were, began strapping some cloth to them. The air was chill on her toes but his hands were warm, and not at all unpleasant against her skin. She studied his face. It wasn't particularly remarkable but there was something about it that was pleasing. Perhaps it was how easily the blushes showed on his cheeks, or shape of his lips . . .

'Something in my beard?' he said as he worked her left boot back into place.

'What?'

'You were staring at me.'

'No.'

'Yeah, you were.'

'You're mistaken.'

'I bloody wasn't.'

'Actually, I was not staring at you . . . I was thinking.'

'What about?'

She looked away, her cheeks hot. 'Never you mind.' He raised his eyebrows as if she were being unreasonable. She vaguely thought she might be but that didn't make his reaction any less annoying. 'Give me the other boot,' she snapped.

He did so, retreating from her as she hauled it on. Shortly afterwards they were on their way again, maintaining their good pace at the cost of conversation.

Though no roads ran this deep within the Wild, there were pathways. Narrow and winding, made by creatures unknown. According to Fen, the one they were following would lead them directly to the Hunger Tree. In places it was overgrown by fleshy creepers, in others, it had vanished completely, forcing them to search for the rest of the path. This slowed them, and even when they did find the path again, Chandni could not be sure it was the same one.

It was something of a surprise, therefore, when they arrived at the Hunger Tree. The trunk was vast, big enough to carve a tower inside, the bark crinkled like plates of armour. Each of its branches could easily have been a tree in its own right. And yet something, some tremendous force, had toppled it. Chandni didn't like to think about what that had been.

It had not fallen completely, leaning at a severe angle from the ground, its upper half supported by a number of other trees, the great weight spread between their interlinked branches.

Like it was caught by its friends.

Other trees had not been so lucky. Alone, they had fallen, the remains rotting and seething with crawling lifeforms. Sunslight poured through the hole in the canopy and she moved towards it automatically, lifting her face to the sky.

'You ready?' asked Varg.

Chandni thought about the question. She was scared, but she was also determined. When she said yes, she meant it.

'You want me to take Satyendra?'

'Please. And Varg? Stay close.'

He gave a gruff nod as she passed over Satyendra. The baby made no complaints, staring at his surroundings with wonder-wide eyes. *He seems so calm. How can he be so calm when I'm so afraid?* She knew she should be grateful, a crying baby would draw all kinds of trouble on their heads, but it troubled her. After giving him a kiss on the forehead, she turned towards the tree.

Don't stop to think about this, she told herself. *Gather your courage and do it.*

She took three steps towards the Hunger Tree and was about to take another when Glider began to whine. Looking over her shoulder she saw that the Dogkin had held back, afraid.

'Don't worry,' she said, but when she set off again, Glider's whining continued.

Don't worry about Glider. Do it.

A tangle of roots was visible as she got closer, half ripped from the earth. Above them, where they joined the trunk, was a skirt of red petalled flowers. They drew her eye, each one distinct, characterful. Little white crescents grew hard on the stems. Fen had told her that there was one for every person that had fed the Hunger Tree. She wondered which

215

was made by his grandmother. Was it her blood giving colour and shape to a set of those leathery petals?

And what will mine look like, after this is done?

She knelt down, resting her left hand on the trunk, and took a deep breath.

Just put your hand in and keep it there. Simple.

What she was about to do was against the law of her house and she would have to report it when she returned home. There would be consequences. Back at Varg's cottage, it had been easy to accept but now she was here, she could feel her conviction fading. All her life she had strived to be perfect, a role model to her staff and a cherished servant to her lord. After this, she would be remembered as a traitor, weak-willed, self-serving. Worse, a part of her would be given to the Wild, she would be bound to it. It was said that such connections lasted forever. The shame and suffering that would follow would endure long beyond the death of her body.

But what are the alternatives? Should I allow myself to die? Who would look after Satyendra then? Should I trust Varg to cut off my arm and then to hold off whatever is drawn by the blood? No. I will forego happiness and glory, I will sacrifice myself for my house and my child, and I will do so proudly. For I am Sapphire.

She looked down at the fingers of her right hand and straightened them. It was an odd sensation, watching the digits move without feeling any feedback. As if it were not hers but someone else's under her control. Guiding it by sight, she worked her hand between the tangled roots, and into the moist, dark soil beneath.

There was little resistance, and her hand and wrist

disappeared from sight, her elbow brushing against the roots. Apparently, Fen's grandmother had spoken to the tree when she'd gone to it. Chandni considered what she was going to say, fluctuating between feeling nervous and silly. *How do I talk to a tree?* To be informal seemed wrong, it was not as if the tree would answer her. So she fell back on formality. 'Hunger Tree, I am Chandni of House Sapphire, Honoured Mother to a vessel for my deathless lord. There is poison in me, I ask that you take it.' She hesitated on the last words, even though Fen had been insistent. 'And take of me, that what you need.'

Eight words, simple words, and it was done.

She had expected there to be a response of some kind. Not speech, but perhaps an answering rustle or movement. It was only when she turned her gaze to the trunk when she realized there had been one.

All of the red flowers had turned towards her.

She fought down the urge to run away and held her arm in place.

'All right?' asked Varg. He was doing a very poor job of hiding his concern.

'So far,' she replied.

Further off, Glider's whining had graduated to a long, low howl.

She couldn't feel what was happening to her hand, but she did suddenly become aware that there was a force acting on it. A slow but inexorable pull.

She braced her left arm and pulled back, but whatever had her was stronger, and she began to twist forward.

'Varg?'

'Yeah?'

'Could you come here please?' Somehow she was keeping her voice level. *Mother would be proud.*

He was at her side instantly. 'What is it?'

'It's pulling me in.'

'Shit!'

'It's too strong.'

'Suns!'

While Varg put Satyendra down, the tugging on her arm continued and she slid forward until her cheek pressed against the bark. One of Varg's arms looped under her shoulders and held her in place. Between them, they seemed to be able to match the pull but not overcome it.

While they struggled she had the sense of being drained and tried not to think of what the tree was taking from her.

There was pain in her shoulder joint, where the strain was focused, but it felt faraway, and she suddenly became dizzy, as if about to faint.

She was dimly aware of Varg shouting for Glider and had the impression that it wasn't working. 'Glider!' she shouted, aiming for imperious but actually achieving something closer to a shriek. 'Glider, we need you!'

She heard a final panicked whine, then the scrabble of paws. Teeth scraped her back as the Dogkin established a hold on her belt. Varg was swearing, Glider growling, the pain in her shoulder no longer distant, but blazing, immediate, and then she was moving backwards, the three of them sprawling in a heap together.

For a while the sky spun above her, and she was happy to let it. Only when it had stopped and the shock started to fade, did she realize that Varg's arm was still across her chest, and that her head was resting on a Glider-shaped pillow.

'Sorry,' she began, rolling off them.

'It's all right,' mumbled Varg. 'Not like you're heavy.'

'Thank you. Both of you.'

She made a quick fuss of Glider before going to check on Satyendra. To her relief he was fine, too wrapped up in his own world of wriggling to have noticed her problems.

'Did it work?' asked Varg.

She tapped her right hand with her left. There was no sensation there. 'I don't know. This might be my imagination but it feels better. Or lighter. I suppose we just have to wait and see.'

'Has it cut you?'

'No.'

'Let me see.'

She held out her hand and he examined it, scrutinizing one side before turning it over. They exchanged an awkward glance when they saw the missing nails on her middle finger and thumb, leaving the skin beneath smooth and unmarked. The Hunger Tree had taken its due.

'Looks fine,' he said but he didn't let go of her hand. Their eye contact became awkward in a different way.

'Varg,' she began.

'Yeah?'

'I—'

Satyendra's cry of hunger interrupted them, the surprise making her pull her hand free. The eye contact broke. 'I need to tend to him.'

'Yeah.' He squinted up at the suns and frowned. 'And we need to get back while we got the light.'

219

She gathered Satyendra in her arms and they set off. As they reached the edge of the sunslight, she looked over her shoulder to find that the flowers on the Hunger Tree's trunk were looking back. And perhaps it was her imagination, but she was sure that a new one stood with them, its petals vibrant, fresher than the rest.

The Godroad shimmered red beneath Vasin as he flew, and the trees seemed to merge together either side of him in a blur of green. Rather than take a carriage and an entourage, he'd opted to fly the whole way, unsupported, without supplies. It was a reckless decision, committing him to hours and hours of flight.

And it felt wonderful.

At the end of it, he would meet with House Ruby on Yadavendra's behalf. No doubt they would be insulted that his High Lord had not come in person, but he would worry about that when he got there. Such things were problems for the earth not the sky.

The essence currents had been with him the whole way, as if the air itself was sympathetic to his desire to flee, hurling him forward like a bolt of blue lightning.

Wrapped in his second skin of armour, he felt strong again, purposeful, and with each mile he put between himself and the rest of his family, there came a corresponding sense of relief.

His troubles were behind him.

All the intricacies of hiding Lord Rochant, whilst also hunting Chandni and his last descendant, were up to Yi, until his return. He hadn't realized how suffocating it had been, living under his mother's expectations. He wanted to see her restored, of course he did, but the constant lying and scheming, the pressure, it all weighed him down. Each new act took him one step further from the kind of Sapphire he aspired to be. He knew that, in the end, it would be worth it. At least, he hoped he knew. Thoughts of his mother and his honour and the state of the house gave him a headache, and he was glad for the reprieve.

I'm free. If only for a little while.

He intended to savour that freedom.

The arm of the Scuttling Corpseman was strapped to his chest, its weight adding an extra level of challenge to his flight. But rather than struggle with the complication, he revelled in it. For these challenges – balancing weight in the sky, judging and riding currents, portioning out reserves of energy – were simple, honest, and he understood them.

Politics, particularly the tangled ancient mess that passed for it across the Crystal Dynasties, was something else entirely. There were seven houses in all. Four major ones: Sapphire, Jet, Spinel and Tanzanite; and three minor: Ruby, Peridot and Opal. The major houses each had seven Godpieces, and so could empower seven Deathless at any one time, while the minor houses had only three Godpieces each, three Deathless, and much less sway at court. To counter this, they tended to band together in a block, making them more than equal to any single major house. It was not uncommon for a minor house to rely on one of the other houses for aid. As such, their Deathless tended to be more social, more forgiving, and in Vasin's opinion, much easier company.

Either side of the Godroad the ground had become a dark swamp speared through by trees. The settlements running alongside clung to little humps of land and were extended by stilts, and two- and three-storey buildings were common.

People dashed out to the road to watch him as he went by, their forms too small to read. He saluted them anyway.

Another settlement went by, so fast he couldn't see details but something of its shape looked wrong, as if some monstrous mouth had taken a massive bite out of one side of it. This time, nobody came to greet him.

He banked sharply to the left, circling, leaving the currents of the Godroad but with plenty of height and speed to get back. A second pass, lower, slower, gave him a better view. In several places, the wooden walkways had been smashed, the buildings they supported had been dragged into the swamp, a few roof arches still jutting from the surface. He saw people working, using rope and chain to secure their homes to what remained of the stilt platforms, several of which were starting to lean alarmingly. There were others there on watch armed with simple weapons, and among them a couple of Ruby hunters, their wings glinting in the sunlight.

Satisfied that the matter was being attended to, he let his arc complete, his own wings lifting as they re-entered the Godroad's essence flow.

The rest of the flight passed without incident. Whatever the trouble had been, it appeared to be isolated, but Vasin could not shake the image of broken wood from his mind, nor stop his imagination from conjuring the kind of beast responsible.

Beneath him, the trees thinned out, then stopped, leaving a vast swampy lake that spread as far as the eye could see. It was broken only by the Godroad that continued to run, straight and true, along a single ridge of stone, dividing the area in two. Up ahead he could see the floating castle of the Ruby High Lord. With no natural formations to follow, the Godroad simply stopped in the middle of the lake. Pulleys and chains ran from the end of it up to the battlements, ferrying people and goods from land to air in wire cages. From a distance it looked as if the chains formed an anchor, holding the castle in place.

He knew that what he ought to do was glide down to land, present himself to the guards, and wait to be winched up to his Ruby hosts. However, an idea had caught him, a rash and foolish one. The kind that the Story-singers wove into tales.

So instead of slowing and diving, he sped up, aiming not for the end of the Godroad but past it. He saluted the astonished winch operators as he flew overhead, their returning gestures coming long after he'd left them behind.

The water moved faster here, the currents bending to the shape of a giant whirlpool that centred directly beneath the floating castle. If he followed the churning water down to the bottom, he would find a crack in the earth, just like the one under his own castle. And, just like his own, gouts of essence rose from it, constant, their energy holding the Ruby castle in the sky.

There was some interaction between the water and the essence, meaning that instead of gusting straight up, they too swirled, echoing the shape below. Vasin aimed for the edge of the essence draughts, cutting in at an angle.

After travelling along the Godroad, with its strong but constant pull, the sudden shock of the essence current was like iced water to the face. An elemental force grabbed him by the wings, tossing him upwards. He battled the current, riding it, harnessing that energy to fly high and fast. His instincts, honed over many hunts were good, and of all the Deathless he was arguably the best in the air.

After this, there will be no doubt.

Though he had not heard it, a cry had gone out on the battlements at his approach, and faces lined the walls, young, old and in-between, united in common amazement.

Round and round he went, up and up, skirting the sharp edges of the rock and the red crystals that protruded further. The sapphire covering his body sang with energy and the rubies set into the castle sang back, deeper, encouraging.

He was corkscrewing past the castle walls now, aiming for the battlements. The essence currents were weaker here, and he could feel the power ebbing from his wings, the momentum fading rapidly.

Almost there.

A few seconds ago he had felt invincible, unstoppable, but now a sliver of worry reached him, those same instincts that had got him this far telling him that he lacked the angle and the speed to clear the crenellations.

Just a little further.

He could see the inhabitants of the castle clearly now, could hear them cheering him on. A few were singing, though he did not recognize the tune. Those nearest were leaning over the edge, they could see he wasn't going to make it. Hands reached out towards him and he reached up, the tips of his gauntleted fingers over a metre too far away.

The fight between essence and gravity became perfectly balanced and for a second he paused there, one hand raised.

And then he began to fall.

In slow motion, the faces receded, just as a new one appeared. Dark with a stroke of gold across the right eye, she was undoubtedly a Ruby of high birth. She was also jumping off the battlements, diving towards him.

She's not wearing her crystal armour. She's not wearing her wings!

In her right hand she held a spear topped with a crystal barb. She thrust it towards him, and he caught it, his hand sliding down the shaft to catch on the head.

The hands that moments ago had been reaching for him snapped around her ankles, arresting their fall. She grimaced at him, and held out her left hand, which he took, pulling himself towards her with his right.

Above them came a chant, rhythmic, each call accompanied by a pull from the people on the battlements, lifting Vasin another inch. When they reached the top, they stood, and the woman raised her spear.

The cheering was thunderous, a single name, repeated: 'Anuja! Anuja! Anuja!'

Of course, thought Vasin. *This is Lady Anuja, the Ruby High Lord's second daughter.*

She raised her hands, acknowledging their adulation whilst signalling for quiet. 'We welcome Lord Vasin of the noble Sapphire to our domain. He is our honoured guest and friend. And what a flight! Never have I seen the like. It must be recorded. It must be sung of. Do you not agree?'

The crowd roared its approval, and they began to chant his name.

Still high on adrenaline, Vasin grinned wolfishly. It was not the same as being at home but he felt a kinship with these people, a similar thirst for spectacle. As he attended more closely to the crowd, he noted how thinly spread it was for a castle of this size. *I count only two hunters here and very few guards. And where is the Ruby High Lord?*

Anuja held her hands up again, and the cries of 'Vasin!' faded. 'But no matter how brave we are, how skilled or how strong, alone, we will fall. Yes?' A sudden sombreness fell upon the assembled. The response this time was muted, mumbled, and Vasin had the sense Anuja was referring to some other incident. Unable to reach his shoulder, she took his hand and lifted it. 'If Lord Vasin were to fall again, who would be there to catch him?'

There was no hesitation. 'Anuja! Anuja! Anuja!'

'And if I were to fall again, who would catch me?'

'We would! We would!'

'Sapphire and Ruby, Lord and subject, family and friend, we are one! Alone, we are noble. Together, we are unstoppable!'

The cheering was wild now, and Anuja basked in it. It was a strange experience for Vasin. Usually he lost himself in these moments but perhaps it was because of the slight differences between his own people and those of House Ruby, or because he was not leading the exchange, he found himself removed. Yes, these people were elated, ecstatic even, but there was a desperate edge to them.

They need this, he thought. *They need to believe in their own strength too much for it to be true.*

Anuja attended to the sling across his chest. 'I see you bring a trophy with you.'

'Yes.'

'We have many questions.' Some affirmative shouts were

heard, scattered, which she waved away. 'We would hear your answers.' She paused, then added, 'First though, you should rest.'

The crowd made no effort to hide its disappointment.

'Thank you, Lady Anuja. I accept your gifts of shelter, food and hospitality. And I thank you and your people for your quick and sure hands.' He heard a ripple of laughter. 'In return, I offer my word when it is asked for, my spear when it is needed, and my friendship, always.'

Her hand appeared small in his crystal palm. 'Then we are both rich indeed.'

He was led through the crowd and into the castle. An hour later, he was in a small receiving room, fed, bathed, and changed out of his armour. He hated the feeling of having just taken it off, where everything looked too big and he felt vulnerable, weak, diminished.

Anuja came to join him, falling heavily into the chair opposite. 'Do you mind?' she asked, holding up a stick of Nightweed.

Vasin shook his head. 'I could use some.'

She placed the wizened twig in a bowl, lit it, and they both leaned forward to inhale the spiced smoke it produced. It didn't remove the underlying exhaustion, but his eyelids were no longer heavy, his thoughts no longer sluggish.

He looked at Anuja again. He was sure that she'd been taller the last time they'd met. In this lifecycle her body was small but strong looking, the gold on her right eye flashing when she turned her head, like an angry god's. But she didn't seem angry, just tired.

'Why did you do it?'

'The flight?' She nodded. 'I'm sorry about that.'

'Don't be. It's given my people something good to talk about. I just wondered why?'

'I don't know. I didn't really think it through. That was probably the point. Do you ever do things just because you can? Even if they aren't very sensible? Because they aren't very sensible?'

She smiled slightly, her gaze seeming faraway. 'Once or twice. Those are the times I feel most alive.'

'Exactly! Sometimes I . . . just want to feel alive. Is that why you threw yourself off the battlements without any wings?'

'I didn't really think about it. That was probably the point.'

They both laughed and she called for drinks. The richness of the wine smoothed the edge of the Nightweed nicely and Vasin found himself relaxed but alert. Neither spoke for a while, giving themselves over to the sensations.

'The arm you brought. Is it the Scuttling Corpseman's?'

'Yes.'

'Is it dead?'

He thought of his mother, of the fear on her face. 'No, and I have no doubt that it will want revenge.'

'I don't envy you that. Still, the Corpseman's name is known even here. It must have been quite the battle.'

'It was.'

She leaned forward. 'Tell me.'

Here we go. Vasin had told the lie enough times now that it came easily to his lips. He was no Story-singer, but he knew how to hold an audience. But unlike his usual audience, Anuja had questions. Lots of them. Specific, the kind that demanded detailed answers.

'I'm sorry, can we talk about this another time? The journey must be catching up with me.'

Her discontent was communicated in the way she leaned away. 'Of course.' She sipped her drink, making no effort to hide her scrutiny of him. 'Please don't be offended, Lord Vasin, but we were expecting the Sapphire High Lord. Where is he?'

'I was going to ask a similar question about yours.'

There was a flash of gold. 'I asked first.'

'High Lord Yadavendra has matters demanding his attention. He regrets that he cannot come but has sent me in his stead.'

She chewed that over, then looked at him directly. 'Can we be honest with each other?'

'Please.'

She seemed to slump in her chair, the older soul suddenly visible in the young body. 'This is no small matter. It will sit poorly with my mother that he didn't give us priority.'

Vasin found himself slumping too. 'I don't know what to say. Is it something to do with the settlement that had been attacked?'

'Partly. There is a creature in the lake, known as the Toothsack. Generally, it is only a problem for other creatures of the Wild. It's too big to travel inland and it doesn't come near the Godroad. However, one of the tributary rivers, the Whitesnake, flooded recently. Water levels rose and the Toothsack was able to travel. It managed to attack Raften, and you saw the result.'

'I know the Whitesnake, it flows through our lands.'

He became aware she was watching him very carefully. 'The rains have been heavy but not especially so, not enough to explain why a usually tame river would burst its banks. So my mother followed the river, until she found the source of the problem.'

'What was it?'

'A dam. Crudely made, and on your lands.'

'That would place it either in Lord Rochant's or Lord Umed's territory.'

'Lord Rochant's.'

Could I use this somehow? If he had been involved in something like this, the High Lord would have no choice but to punish him. Then it occurred to him that Lord Rochant had only just been reborn and that the other likely culprit was his mother. Would she be willing to sacrifice the Rubies as part of her revenge? He no longer knew the answer.

'Don't worry,' she said, misreading him. 'The way the dam was constructed suggested beyond-human strength, and it is far too haphazard for Lord Rochant's tastes.'

'So your High Lord is not considering Sapphire betrayal?'

Her expression was incredulous. 'Of course not! The idea never even occurred to us. But with Lord Rochant between lives, we needed to ask your High Lord for permission to enter his lands to dismantle it.'

'But when I flew here, I didn't see any signs of flooding.'

'Then . . . I imagine my mother has already been successful.'

It was Vasin's turn to look incredulous. 'Are you? Are you saying the Ruby High Lord has flown into Sapphire lands without permission?'

She sipped her drink guiltily. 'I suppose that depends. If I was to ask for permission on behalf of House Ruby, would you give it?'

'I can't speak for my High Lord.'

'We made the request for an audience in good time. We were clear about the urgency but High Lord Yadavendra did not respond. My mother, my High Lord, had no choice. The last thing any of us want is an incident. Surely you can represent House Sapphire in an emergency?'

Vasin closed his eyes. He could see their position and could see no reason not to support them, but something told him that Yadavendra would see it differently. If he refused to support the Rubies, he'd appear weak, a mere messenger boy, and he'd be leaving them open to disgrace. But if he did support them, he'd be opening himself up to his High Lord's wrath. He looked at Anuja. 'You said you wanted to be honest?' She nodded. 'I trust that what passes between us here will stay private?'

'We're both doing the best we can for our people, Lord Vasin. I trust you. I hope that you trust me.'

'Well, you did just save me from a little death and many lifecycles of ridicule.'

'I did.'

He took a deep breath. 'The truth is, I don't know how my High Lord will react. I've never been that close to my uncle and, well, he's become more . . . ' He tried to think of the right word. *Crazed? Unstable? Violent?* 'Unpredictable. It isn't my place to second guess him. However, he sent me here to represent House Sapphire, and I have to believe that if he knew your situation then he would do the right thing.'

She looked hopeful but had not relaxed. 'Which is?'

'Which is to grant you permission to enter our lands and offer you any assistance necessary.'

Her smile was instant and broad, transforming her face.

231

It was like Fortune's Eye coming out from behind a cloud. 'You honour us. We won't forget it.'

'I'm sure you'd do the same.' They gripped wrists, locked in a moment of mutual respect before flopping back into their seats.

She's just like me, he thought. *Out of her depth and trying not to show it.*

They shared a few drinks in near silence, little fragments of conversation that didn't quite go anywhere.

'Well,' he said at last. 'This Nightweed is excellent, but I'd better retire. It's been a long flight.'

She stood up and walked him to the door. 'Lord Vasin?' He was instantly alert again. Adrenaline responding to something in her voice. 'What did you mean when you said your uncle has become unpredictable?'

He stopped, cursing himself for saying something so stupid. If his poor choice of words got back to the High Lord he would be in serious trouble. 'I didn't mean to suggest there was anything wrong with him.'

'You didn't?' She gave him a knowing look.

'No. I simply meant that . . . That I have found these last years particularly hard. But I believe in my High Lord even if I don't always . . . understand his mind.' He frowned, appalled. That had sounded even worse.

'I probably shouldn't say this, but we're very sorry about what happened to your mother. She was well liked.'

He blinked, surprised. 'Thank you. I know she always thought highly of House Ruby.'

'For whatever it's worth, we never believed the accusations. The Lady Nidra Sapphire we know would not, could not, have sold out to the Wild.' She put a hand on his arm. 'My mother had another reason for calling your High Lord here. She wanted to hold him to account.'

'What?'

'This must stay between us.' She lowered her voice to a whisper. 'To accuse one of his own, to try them, to punish them, that is a Sapphire matter, but there are certain lines that cannot be crossed. We all have a sacred duty to protect our people from the Wild. It is why we are Deathless. When Yadavendra destroyed your mother's Godpiece he not only weakened your house, he diminished its ability to protect this world. That cannot stand.'

'What do you mean?'

'How blunt do I need to be?'

Vasin met her eye. 'No hints, no subtleties. Tell me plainly.'

'It would be better for everyone if House Sapphire could set its own affairs in order.' She looked at him, then sighed. 'We have heard the stories. Yadavendra turning on his own sister with those ridiculous charges, banishing her, breaking her immortal line, destroying her Godpiece. And then Sorn. Why did he not protect his own people?' Vasin had no answer for her and she continued. 'Why did he not answer our urgent calls for help? Why, after repeated urgings, did he send you and not come in person? What was so important that he would forsake us?'

He knew he should defend his High Lord but could find little to say. 'It's not my place to divulge that information.'

'I know you Sapphire enjoy your privacy but we have had contact from Houses Spinel, Opal, and Tanzanite. They are all very concerned with the way the Sapphire have withdrawn from court. It is only a matter of time before the other

Houses take note. All eyes are turning towards you, Lord Vasin.'

'To do what, exactly?'

'Your duty.'

'And if we don't set our own affairs in order?'

'Then my mother will take action. She will convene a council of the High Lords and pass judgement on Yadavendra.'

'There's no way he'd submit to another's judgement.'

'He'll have to. Even a High Lord must submit to his peers.'

'I tell you, he won't.'

'Then there would be war.'

Horrified, he took a step away from her.

'As I said, it would be much better if you could deal with this yourself.'

'I . . . I'll do what I can.'

She took a step after him, closing the distance. 'Know that when you act, you have our support.'

He nodded. Surprise and fatigue numbing him, he stumbled towards his bedchamber. Mother would be pleased. This was exactly what she wanted him to do, to gather allies. Anuja and the Rubies were with him, and by the sound of it, the other Houses weren't far behind. But he did not feel elation, just a dull horror, and the sudden sense of being old. For all of his lifecycles he had been a child up till now. *Would that I could be a child again.*

CHAPTER ELEVEN

It was dark and Sagan was not yet in sight. The last few hours had been hard, fatigue slowing them down. Her encounter with the Hunger Tree had left Chandni feeling empty, but also lighter. Her thoughts often wandered as they travelled, teasing her with memories of easier times in the castle, of good food and comfortable beds.

I miss routines, she thought to herself. She had always been good at planning. Her standards high, her goals manageable. She had only had a few years in her role before Lord Rochant slipped between lives, but he'd made a point of taking her aside on one of his last days.

'Honoured Mother Chandni,' he had said, 'you are the heart of this place. Keep beating strong while I'm away.'

And she had. There was something wonderful in the way the castle operated, the staff performing their individual tasks like a choir of Story-singers, harmonious. They were good at their jobs and she was good at hers and it worked. It felt right.

She missed that feeling.

A stray root tripped her, at least she hoped it was a root. There was only Varg's gemslight to see by, and that was fading fast. The stories said that gemslight held creatures of the Wild at bay.

Is that why we've been unmolested so far?

It was easy to imagine predators lurking just beyond the glow's edge, waiting for the last of the stored sunlight to glimmer and vanish.

Glider's nose nudged the small of her back, urging her forward, and she realized she had fallen behind.

I've lost focus again. I can't think here, nothing makes sense. She held Satyendra close. *If Pari doesn't act soon, I'm going home. I don't care what Varg says. It can't be more dangerous than staying here.*

'All right?' asked Varg, turning back to her. His face looked ghoulish, but then, even Satyendra looked threatening in this light.

'Yes.'

'How's your arm?'

'The same.'

'How's the boots?'

'Fine.'

'Not rubbing?'

'No, Varg. They're fine. If they were rubbing I would have said so.'

He grunted, as if to say: *You wouldn't.*

'I swear to you, they're fine.' She lowered her voice. 'Do you think we're being followed?'

'We're in the Wild at night, course we bloody are! But look,' he held up the light, 'the trees are thinning. I reckon we're nearly back.'

He was right. A few minutes later, she saw starlight, and, another minute after that she was stepping out into the open like a diver coming up from the bottom of a lake. It felt like the pressure lifted from the air and it came into her lungs easier. It even tasted different.

She hugged Satyendra and kissed his forehead. 'We're safe, my darling.'

Varg put the chunk of tanzanite back in its bag, smothering the last of its light, and guided them back towards the house. The bulk of Sagan hunched in the gloom at the other side of the field, fires glinting through windows, and behind it, she could make out the faint glow of the Godroad.

They had just reached the front door when Glider began to growl.

Chandni looked over her shoulder, wondering what had followed them from the Wild.

So foolish to think we were safe! Even if they got to Varg's house, they were not truly safe. *Not unless we slept on the Godroad itself, or,* a miserable part of her mind added, *at home in Lord Rochant's castle.*

But the Dogkin was not watching the forest, she was staring over Chandni's shoulder, nose pointing directly at Varg's house. In the poor light, Glider's human eye was unsettling, as if it might not be clouded at all.

'Ssh,' she said, putting a hand on the Dogkin's neck.

Glider quietened but remained on edge. Chandni turned to warn Varg, but he was already pushing his way through the front door.

Leaving Glider in the shadows, she rushed up the step and into the house. A wave of warm air and the smell of food struck her as she came in, stirring her stomach from its slumber. Fen was stirring the pot while Sal rocked her baby.

Chandni shut the door behind her, surprised by how normal things appeared. She couldn't see anything out of the ordinary, and yet something seemed off.

'Did you?' asked Fen. He didn't need to say what. They all knew what he was referring to.

'It's done,' said Varg.

'Thanks to you, Fen,' Chandni added with a smile. 'Your directions were perfect. We never would have made it without them.' She looked at her right arm, flexing the fingers to check they still worked. 'It's too early to know if the poison has gone but I have hope at least.'

She smiled again but Fen didn't return it. 'Thank you for keeping some food back for us. We're both starving.' Varg made a grunt of agreement, though he hadn't relaxed either.

Why do I feel so tense?

Their baby, Min, was clutching his mother fiercely, his eyes puffy from crying. Unusual but in itself nothing terrible. Despite sitting away from the fire, sweat darkened the fabric under Sal's arms. Chandni assumed that their toddler, Dev, was probably still up in the lookout room. *But why didn't he ring the bell when we came back? He loves ringing it.*

'How are you all? Did anything happen while we were away?'

'No, no,' said Fen, while his eyes said: *yes, yes.*

Satyendra gurgled happily, prompting her to look down, praise on her lips. Since they had lived here, it had become a reflex. She always made a point of giving him a fuss when he was happy, hoping to encourage his jollier self back to the surface.

But, before she could speak, the door to the other room, her bedroom, burst open, and a woman came charging out. She was wearing an old travelling cloak but the needle in her hand was clean, shiny.

Chandni felt, or imagined she felt, a twinge in her right hand, a ghost of an old pain. They had found her again and they had come for her baby.

She saw Varg kick over the cooking pot, spilling boiling water in the assassin's direction. She saw Fen moving with Varg, though whether to help or hinder him, she couldn't tell, and then she was turning, reaching for the front door.

To her surprise it was already opening, letting in the cold night air. A stranger's face appeared in the doorway, and a second needle, glinting in the firelight.

She saw the needle rise up, and for a moment she was back in her lord's kitchens. *But this time there is no Roh to save me.* She flinched back, neither far nor fast enough, but the blow never came, the attacker distracted by a low snarl from behind. Before either of them had a chance to react, Glider's jaws clamped around the stranger's head. There was a scream, muffled, and then a crunch.

The needle dropped to the floor.

Chandni stared as Glider shook the body from side to side. Blood spurted from between her teeth, staining the white fur. When all resistance was gone, the Dogkin flung the body down the front steps and spat out the head, in bits, from her mouth.

There were screams behind her, and the sounds of fighting, but Chandni didn't wait to see what was happening. Using the doorframe for leverage, she hauled herself outside, jumping over the body and the blood. Outside the house, in the middle of the night, she froze.

Where do I go now? What do I do?

Although she knew it was ridiculous, she stood there, clutching Satyendra. She had no plans for this moment, and even if she wasn't tired, improvising had never been her strong point. A part of her mind, the part that spoke with her mother's voice, lambasted her for such a terrible lack of self-control, and while she agreed with every word, she could not think of what to do.

The door banging on its hinges made her look up as Varg emerged at speed with a knife in his hand. 'Run!' he shouted.

'Run where?'

He charged down the step towards her. 'For fuck's sake, just—'

'Watch out for the blood!' she warned.

He dived forward to clear the body Glider had left by the step, falling hard into the dirt at her feet. 'Shit!'

Glider started barking as a cloaked figure appeared in the doorway: she leaned out, squinting as her eyes adjusted to the sudden lack of light. A moment later, Varg's knife appeared in her thigh and she withdrew.

Chandni blinked, then helped Varg get back to his feet. 'Are you hurt?' she asked.

He started moving immediately, pushing her ahead of him. 'Run.'

'What about Fen and the others?'

'Just fucking run!'

Her legs finally got the message and they ran, Glider bounding alongside. 'But where?'

Varg didn't answer and she realized he didn't need to. There was only one place to go. The assassins would find them if they tried to hide in Sagan. She was too recognizable. They would find them if they tried to flee along the Godroad. There was only one place they could go and not be followed.

The Wild.

They were running back into the Wild.

She could hear the sound of things stirring in the dark. She had thought the forest was alive before but clearly it had been asleep. There was a movement in the trees, she was sure of it; shadows, hunched and bestial.

'We can't!' she began but Varg cut her off.

'They're not here for us, they're here for the blood.'

He was right, she realized, and as they plunged into the forest, becoming shadows themselves, the things of the Wild stepped out into the starlight, facing Varg's house, their mouths open.

Pari stared at the ceiling, trying to get the winged figures depicted there to come into focus. She could still identify which was which but the edges blurred, making it hard to see any details. Her eyesight was still working but far from its best.

It was, she reflected miserably, a fair description of her wits as well. *And Taraka knows it, the bastard.*

After Lady Yadva had fled the castle, dragging Dil and the shreds of her dignity with her, Taraka had started asking questions. Difficult questions. Pari still hadn't recovered from her journey, her body worn by travel and ravaged by fever. Putting on a show for Yadva had drained the last of her energy, leaving her weak, unfocused.

And Taraka knew that too, the bastard!

A decent man would have let her sleep first. A decent man would have shown kindness, rather than taking advantage of her state. Perhaps it was a compliment of sorts, that Taraka did not dare give any slack when dealing with her. The thought brought little comfort.

His questions had come thick and fast and she'd struggled to answer them. She couldn't tell him the truth about her and Lord Rochant Sapphire of course. Relationships between Deathless from different bloodlines were forbidden. It was believed such unions would confuse the ritual of rebirth, allowing abominations to slip into the world. If Pari admitted that she was having an affair with a Deathless from another house, they would cast her into the Wild to be forgotten, and give her Godpiece to another. Nor could she admit to being in Lord Rochant's castle during his rebirth ceremony.

So, given the options, she lied, telling Taraka that she had made a discreet visit to one of her settlements to sort out some problems there. However, each of her answers seemed to breed more questions.

'Which settlement was this?' he'd begun.

'Poise, a remote settlement on my northeast border.'

'Why didn't you fly there?'

'Why not fly there?' she'd repeated, as if the question was absurd. 'This body is too old to fly, and I was hardly going to walk there in my armour was I?'

'Then why all this secrecy? Why pretend to be ill?'

'Actually, I was ill. As Sho often tells me, I forget my own limits sometimes.'

Taraka would not be put off. 'You travelled in secret, deliberately. Why?'

'I wanted to see with my own eyes. You know me, I like to be hands-on. If I'd announced a visit I wouldn't have seen the truth.'

He'd raised his eyebrows as she said 'truth'. 'And if I went to Poise now, I would find people that would remember your visit?'

'No, the villagers won't have seen me. I did not announce myself.'

'You didn't? How strange.'

'But that was the point, my dear Lord Taraka: to be unseen. I wanted to know if the reports were true or not. As it happens, they were exaggerated.'

And he'd smiled at her and asked more questions, often variations of his first ones, prodding at times and details. And she'd smiled back and answered them. It was a strange game to play. They both knew she was lying, but without evidence, what was he going to do?

What is he going do? She'd lain awake half the night pondering that question.

It worried Pari that Taraka had been here, in her castle, before she'd got back. He'd had ample time to snoop, talk to her staff, learn things she'd rather he not know . . . She was sure that the Tanzanite High Lord's right hand was fond of her in his own way. She was also sure that if he knew even half of what she had been up to in her last two life-cycles, that he would without hesitation petition for her to be ended.

As she lay there, exhausted but sleepless, she knew that Taraka had been communing with the Tanzanite High Lord, and that, together, they were deciding her fate. Of all the Deathless, he alone had found a way to send coherent messages via a Heartstone, and when Pari wasn't hating him for it, she was trying to work out the trick. It made Taraka indispensable. *And how he knows it.*

Sho's creaky voice sang outside her chambers, asking for permission to enter. She gave it, gauging her servant's mood by the manner of his entrance: hesitant yet resolute.

'I could not help but notice my lady has not eaten breakfast.'

'I'm not hungry.'

'Ah. Mmm,' he said, giving sound but not words to his disapproval.

'Don't start, Sho. I'm not in the mood. Has Lord Taraka risen yet?'

'Yes, my lady. He requested your company but made it clear that he doesn't want to rush you.'

'How considerate of him.' *As if I'd dare keep him waiting. As if I could stand to wait to hear the High Lord's judgement.* 'How is my complexion looking, Sho, any better?'

'It sets off your bruises magnificently, my lady.'

She pulled back the sheet, and climbed out of bed, wincing at how stiff she was. 'And my bruises? How are they?'

'Radiant, my lady.'

'Then we'd best start covering them up. I need to be at my most glorious for Lord Taraka.'

'I have a team assembled outside.'

She paused. 'I'm going to miss you, Sho.'

'And I you, my lady.'

They exchanged a look, long, both nodding gently to the other, years of mutual respect crammed into the gesture. Then he clapped his hands and a stream of servants entered, bearing brushes, paints, silks and scented water.

Two hours later, Pari sat in her audience chamber, resplendent, with Lord Taraka opposite. As he drew out the small talk and called for more wine, Pari tried to read the man. Of all the Deathless, Taraka was one of the most inscrutable, but she had known him a long time. *He looks satisfied. The High Lord must have made a pronouncement.*

As if sensing her scrutiny, Taraka looked up from his cup. 'Did you sleep well?'

'Not as well as I'd like. Sleep always eludes me at the end of a lifecycle.'

'Then, perhaps you need more practice, Lady Pari. I myself slept very well. But then, I always do.'

'Perhaps you would be kind enough to share your secret with me?'

'Perhaps.' He looked away, and she had the sense that he was composing his next sentence carefully. *Here it comes.* 'Have you everything in place for your transition?'

'Yes. My staff have been fully briefed. I'd add that my lands are peaceful, and my hunters vigilant. I do not know who will be assigned to lead the hunts in my absence, but whoever it is will find themselves well supported. The harvest has been gathered and a suitable offering sent to our High Lord. I trust she is satisfied?'

'With the offering, yes. And what are your thoughts on your next vessel?'

'My granddaughter, Rashana. I hear she has performed admirably in her tests and has shown an appetite for investigative thinking.'

Taraka pulled a face of faint sympathy. 'Yes, she shows great promise, but the High Lord feels she is needed to serve the house in other ways.'

'I don't understand.'

'Lord Arkav has become very fond of her and we feel she would be ideally placed to support him during your transition. You know how he struggles when you are between lives.'

'But Rashana is by far the best choice of vessel.'

'Sadly, the High Lord disagrees with your assessment.'

Her voice rose in anger. 'She agreed it when we discussed the matter years ago.'

He gave her a pointed look. 'Then something must have changed.'

Keep calm, Pari. 'Who does the High Lord have in mind? Not her brother, surely!'

'He is a possibility.'

'He most certainly is not! A weak heart that is unlikely to survive the rebirthing ceremony. A habit of not finishing his sentences! I won't have it. Besides, he's too old. Even if I could use him, his skin would only last me a decade or two. It's inefficient.'

Taraka chuckled. 'Fear not, Lady Pari. I only said he was a possibility. Actually, the High Lord has decided on Rashana's daughter, Priti.'

'A child!' Pari retorted. It seemed like only yesterday that the news of her great granddaughter's birth had been announced. She knew she should be trying harder to keep her voice level but fatigue was getting to her. 'The High Lord expects me to live in a child's body?'

'Not at all. We'd groom her until she was of a more suitable age for the ceremony.'

Pari frowned. 'Rashana is perfect. She's ready now. This lifecycle only has a few years left in it, five at most. Priti won't be ready for, what, another decade?'

'It will depend on the girl but my guess would be closer to fifteen years.' He held up a hand to stave off Pari's retort. 'In any case, the High Lord feels a longer span between rebirths will be good for you.'

The wine glass shook in Pari's hand as she fought to keep her rage in check. 'I don't follow how this will be good, Lord Taraka. Please, enlighten me.'

'It will give you time to reflect.'

By that he meant that it would give others time to take advantage of her situation. A longer gap between lives would force her to endure the endless dream they experienced between lives for longer. The one that none remembered clearly, but all feared.

He touched one of the many crystals dangling at his neck, stilling it. 'It will also keep you out of the way until House Sapphire has settled itself. You can't be accused of interfering with their business if you aren't here.' He tapped the crystal, then released it. 'And Priti is a much better match, well worth waiting for. She's sweet, charming, and especially dutiful.'

This is my punishment. A better match, indeed! The girl is nothing like me in temperament. If I can't become more humble and obedient like my wet leaf of a great grandchild, there's a good chance the rebirth won't work. It's devilish. Not to mention the fifteen years of exile. Fifteen years out of house politics! I could happily strangle Taraka and the High Lord with those necklaces.

She took a calming breath. 'Well, I am humbled that our High Lord has given such a great deal of thought to mine and my brother's wellbeing. Please pass on my thanks when you see her.'

'Consider it done, Lady Pari.' He put down his drink and dabbed delicately at his lips. 'It has been a joy to see you, as always, but I must be moving on. This visit, though delightful, has put me behind schedule.'

'Where are you going next?'

'To see our beloved friends in House Ruby. No doubt they have some grand plan they want to discuss. You know, the last time I was there, they were trying to get our hunters training together. Ridiculous creatures! I dread to think what it will be this time.'

She forced herself to smile, as if sharing in the joke. 'It sounds as if a bit of Tanzanite pragmatism is just what they need.'

'I couldn't have put it better myself.' Taraka stood, the crystals jangling together as he did so. 'And what of your own plans?'

'Sedate, you'll be pleased to hear. I intend to bathe, rest, and get everything in order. Oh, and sleeping. Lots and lots of sleeping.'

'Very wise. I'd say we've had more than enough excitement for one lifecycle, wouldn't you?' They said their goodbyes and he was halfway towards the door when he stopped and turned back, an impish grin on his face. 'And thank you for sharing Lady Yadva's humiliation with me. I can still picture her expression.'

They both laughed at the memory.

'Exquisite,' he murmured, bowing one last time to her before leaving the room.

An hour later, Sho came to find her. 'He is gone, my lady.'

'Thank the Thrice Blessed Suns! I trust Ami remains tucked away and secret.'

Sho's face settled into its usual state of concern. 'Yes, my lady.'

'Good, see that it stays that way.'

'You're not planning something . . . rash, are you? It is just that you promised Lord Taraka you wouldn't.'

'Sho, you've been eavesdropping again!'

'Eavesdrop? No, never that.' His mock outrage made her chuckle. 'It is my job to hear everything that happens in the castle, my lady. You yourself taught me that.'

'In that case you'd better shut the door and come closer because I am planning something.'

'Oh no. Does it involve me, my lady?'

She smiled at him. 'Of course it does, Sho. All my best plans do.'

The trees were watching them, Chandni was sure of it. She was also sure that there were things lurking between the trees, and behind the trees, and in the branches.

She was crouched in a small hollow, Varg squeezed in next to her. It was anything but cozy. The hollow wasn't quite big enough to fit them both comfortably, forcing them close. Her nose was jammed into his armpit and a root dug into her hip. It wasn't much better for him; one of her knees was pressing hard into his thigh and he kept muttering something about the position of her elbow.

Somehow, impossibly, Satyendra was asleep, curled contentedly in her arms.

They had run for as long as they dared, following the dying light of Varg's tanzanite, both of them sure that when it went out, the things of the Wild would come. More than once, they had fallen, taking turns to trip or slip. This was what had made them stop in the end: the fear of having an accident and getting cut. Even a small amount of blood spilt this deep in the Wild would spell their doom.

And so they had opted to hide instead, cramming themselves into the earth, Glider squatting over them like a Birdkin mothering her eggs.

'Hey!' Hissed Varg. 'Get your paw off my head.'

Glider made an apologetic whine and shifted, sending a cascade of dirt down to them.

'Varg?' she whispered. 'What's the plan?' She felt him shrug, her face rising and falling with the motion.

'Don't die,' he replied.

'I'm serious. We have no food, no water, no supplies. We need a plan.'

'I reckon that we should be safe for the night so long as we stay down here. There are plenty of feral Dogkin in the Wild so her scent won't bring things after us like ours would.'

'All right. So we wait here until dawn. Good.'

'You call this good?'

'Yes, I do. It's step one of our plan. When it gets light, we can risk travelling. The question is, where do we go?'

'Dunno.'

'What about trying to get back to Lord Rochant's castle?' Varg groaned as she continued. 'If we can get to High Lord Sapphire, we'd be safe.'

'We've been over this, Chand. The assassins would kill us before we got anywhere near him. They know where we are and we know that they can disguise themselves as Sapphire guards. It ain't going to work.'

'I hate to say it but what about trying to get to Tanzanite lands?'

'Too far. And anyway, we'd need to take the Godroad, and there ain't no point doing that unless we find an escort.'

She sighed and he laughed. 'I don't see what's funny, Varg.'

'Sorry. It tickles when you breathe into my armpit.'

'Oh.'

'Nah, I don't think we can get to Pari. If we can survive long enough, might be she'll come to us.'

'But how? Even if we could find a way to survive out here, how would she know where we are?'

'Pari's a Deathless. She's hunted in the Wild since before we were sparkles in our ancestors' balls. If anyone can find us, it's her.'

Chandni took that in, trying not to think too hard about what she could smell. 'I refuse to accept that our plan is simply: sit and wait for Lady Pari.'

'You got a better one?'

'It's not that I don't like the plan, I just don't like our part in it. While Pari is trying to find us, what are we going to do? And don't say: "wait".'

'Ahh . . . Shit, I don't know.'

'Can we make it easier for her to find us?'

'I've been leaving a trail.'

She glared into his armpit, appalled. 'Won't that lead the assassins straight to us?'

'Maybe. But if they're able to follow us in here, we're pretty much fucked anyway.'

'I see. That piece of tanzanite you have, can we use that in some way to signal her?'

'If she's close, yeah.'

So, step one: hide in the Wild. Step two: leave a trail for Pari. 'What about food and shelter?'

251

'I'm not much of a hunter, are you?'

'No.'

'Might be we can forage for this and that.'

She could not help but notice the gloom in Varg's voice.
'Yes, we'll forage for what we need. And I'm sure Glider
will hunt for us too.'

Varg sighed. 'We're fucked.'

'Stop that. Neither of us can afford the luxury of self-
pity. We will forage, Glider will hunt. Now what about
shelter?'

'I dunno, maybe find a bigger hole?'

'That is not acceptable.' She thought about alternatives.
To build a shelter they would need tools – they had none.
Besides, to cut the trees this deep in, and without support,
was madness. 'We have to find somewhere.'

'If there are any decent sized caves or lairs you can bet
your little—'

'Varg, that's enough. I want options from you, packaged
in half-decent language, or silence.'

'Right. Sorry. I was going to say we won't find any lairs
that don't have owners.'

'Then we need some other way to shelter. Do you have
any ideas?'

He didn't reply.

'What about Sorn?'

'What about it?'

'Think about it, Varg, an attack forced the villagers to flee
but that was a while ago now. I bet that if we went there,
we'd find places to rest, and even if the food has been taken
or rotted away, there will be clothes, equipment, things we
need.'

'The fu-sorry – The Wild took that place. Who knows what else we'd find waiting for us?'

'It's no more dangerous than waiting here, is it? At least this way, we'd have a chance.'

'The ones that fled Sorn, they said they saw –' he dropped into such a soft whisper that she had to strain to hear the words '– the Scuttling Corpseman. It was there.'

'*Was* there. Was. Surely it will have killed everyone it could find by now and moved on?'

He grunted, unsure, but she knew he'd do what she wanted. It was just a matter of time. *Step three: go to Sorn for shelter. Step four: survive.*

She allowed herself a tight smile. They might be at the edge of exhaustion in the middle of the Wild but now they had a plan. Things were always better once she had a plan.

CHAPTER TWELVE

They were waiting for Vasin on the Godroad: all of his problems, eagerly slipping back onto his shoulders. Though Vasin dawdled all the way, he soon found home speeding towards him.

He noted more than the usual number of Yadavendra's guards on patrol along the Godroad, no doubt hunting for Lord Rochant, and was forced to wonder how the High Lord had fielded so many so quickly.

It's almost as if he was expecting it . . .

Lady Anuja Ruby's warning rang in his head. If the Sapphire High Lord did not answer for his crimes, there would be war. What if Yadavendra had come to the same conclusion? What if he had taken steps to prepare, and these guards were here to secure the border? Nothing to do with the search for Lord Rochant at all. Perhaps war was to be Yadavendra's answer.

More than ever his decision to withdraw and bury his grief in a haze of Tack smoke seemed like an error. Things had changed so quickly while he wasn't looking, and now he felt like he was struggling to keep up.

His own settlements appeared peaceful when he passed them, save for the search parties moving along the Godroad still searching for Honoured Mother Chandni and her baby. *I only hope that Yi has found them and dealt with them, so I don't have to . . .*

His castle came into view and he noted with relief that only his brother's flag flew, indicating that no other Deathless were in residence. He landed smoothly on top of Mount Ragged, walking the Bridge of Friends and Fools to the castle gates.

No dramatic flights to the battlements this time.

The Gardener-smiths met him in the Chrysalis Chamber and, together, they stripped off his crystal armour, checking each piece for damage before storing it reverently on its rack. Then he bathed and told his staff that he was going to rest after his journey.

In truth, he was hoping that he would find Yi in his chambers but there was no one. He stood for a while, looking at the decorations and trophies, and tried to remember why he had chosen them. A few hangings, the odd gift placed on a shelf. None of it really meant anything to him, and yet, if he got rid of them the room would seem . . .

Soulless. There has been little of me present these last few years and my room reflects that.

He fell into bed, fatigue pushing his worries aside enough to sleep but not enough to sleep well. In the morning, he woke to the red glare of Vexation stabbing through his open window; fresh clothes were ready on his bed and nearby was a servant who appeared to be tidying, his movements hurried.

'Is something wrong?' he asked.

The servant jumped. 'I, no, my lord. It is just that Lord Gada is on his way here and—'

Vasin sat up abruptly. 'Why wasn't I informed?'

'Forgive me, my lord, but I did inform you about an hour ago.'

'I don't remember this.'

'I swear it's true. You didn't answer me, my lord, but you nodded.'

Vasin sighed. It sounded all too plausible. 'Very well. Get the room tidy and get me dressed. Finding me still in bed at this hour might kill Lord Gada, and we couldn't have that, could we?'

'No, my lord.'

He felt very irritable. His brother always had that effect on him. Vasin decided he was going to have to do something about that, if he was to gain Gada's support.

Then a thought began to niggle at the back of his mind, and for once, this irritation had nothing to do with Gada. He turned back to the servant.

'How did you get in here?'

'My lord?' The man pointed to the open arch that led into his chambers. 'I . . . I walked in.'

It was true, there were no physical barriers stopping staff coming in and out. There were societal ones, however. 'Without my permission?'

'I'm sorry, my lord, I didn't want to disturb you.'

'But you already had, apparently, an hour ago. Did you not sing for entrance then, either?'

There was an awkward pause and the servant glanced towards the archway, making Vasin wonder if the man were about to try and run through it. He tried to place the servant's face but couldn't. On its own, this wasn't alarming, lately he'd not paid much attention to his staff.

And if he were an assassin, I would be well on the way to my next lifecycle by now.

'I . . . I'm sorry, my lord.'

Vasin crossed the room in three swift strides, his rigid fingers coming to rest on the servant's throat. 'Tell me, what are you really doing here?'

There was another pause, and Vasin pressed deep, until there was no more give in the man's flesh. 'Tell me.'

'I was searching your possessions.'

'What for?'

'Anything unusual . . . treasures from the Wild, crystals, messages, anything. They didn't specify.'

'Who didn't specify?'

'My lord, I'm finding it hard to breathe!'

'Then you'll answer my questions quickly. Who?'

Perhaps it was an act, but the servant's voice was becoming strained. 'Lord . . . ' He trailed off, prompting Vasin to twist his fingers. The servant squealed in pain.

'Lord who? Answer me, damn you!'

'Lord . . . Gada.'

Vasin pulled back his hand and the servant fell to his knees, gasping. 'You are one of Gada's then?' Still rubbing his neck, the servant nodded. 'And what will you tell Lord Gada when you see him?'

'Nothing, my lord. I will say there was nothing here.'

'Yes, that is exactly what you will say. And from now on, you will watch Lord Gada for me. I will expect a report from you shortly and if I don't learn anything new, I will exact restitution for the insult you have done me. Do you understand?'

'Yes, my lord.'

Vasin made a dismissive gesture and the servant fled the room. Fighting the urge to go after him and kill him, Vasin clenched his fists tight at his sides; it was so tempting to take out his anger on someone, to do something direct and physical.

No, that was the old Vasin. I can't afford to be ruled by my temper any more.

He turned and went to the window, letting the cold air buffet his face. It occurred to him yet again that he was out of touch. He had let others manage the details of his household for him. More precisely, he'd let Gada take care of him for too long, and now anyone in a uniform could walk into his chambers and he'd be none the wiser.

Vasin summoned some of his staff to help him dress, pushing the fact from his mind that he didn't know either of them by name. Gada arrived soon after, smart as ever. Vasin watched as he stepped into the room. *As if he owns it. You don't feel the need to ask for permission either, do you, brother?*

A watercolour smile fluttered across Gada's lips. 'Welcome home.'

Vasin looked at him, really looked, not caring that the behaviour would seem rude. He'd always found Gada annoying, patronizing, even suffocating at times, but he'd never felt threatened by him before. 'What do you want, Gada?'

Gada's nostrils flared, indignant. 'To see if my ungrateful brother is feeling better. You were struggling before the hunt and since then we've barely had a chance to talk.'

'You don't think I can hold it together, do you?'

'I'm sorry my concern is such a burden for you.'

It would have been easy to punch him then. Instead, Vasin turned to the window, letting Gada have his back, and the clouds his outraged glare.

'The truth is,' Gada continued, 'I was worried about you. You've always taken everything to heart more than the rest of us, and things have been fraught of late.'

His brother's feet made soft scuffing sounds on the floor, pacing, the sure sign that a lecture was coming. Vasin pressed his palms against the cool stone. *Don't get angry. Don't argue. Mother needs our help. She chose me for this, not him. I have to be worthy of that choice.*

He took a breath and said the necessary words: 'You're right.'

Gada came to a stop, the lecture dying in his throat. 'Yes, fraught . . . wait, what?'

'I said: "you're right". After Mother's exile, I fell apart. And let's face it, I wasn't exactly together before then. You've always been there for me, picking up the slack, cleaning up my mess, covering for me. I don't deserve you, Gada.' He wondered if that last line was laying it on too thick, but a moment later he felt his brother's hand on his shoulder.

'You know I'm always here for you.'

He reached up and covered Gada's long fingers with his own. 'I know. But nobody was there for you. It must have been hard.'

Gada's hand squeezed once, an involuntary gesture. 'It was.'

'We've never talked about Mother. That's my fault, I know.' He turned to look his brother in the eye. 'What was she like that day, when Yadavendra passed judgement?'

'Are you sure you want to know?'

'I'm sure.'

Gada's hand slipped free. He began to pace again, looking anywhere but into Vasin's eyes. 'She was proud. Defiant.'

'She contested it?'

'No, but neither did she confess. It was strange. Throughout the trial she'd argued and fought them on every detail. You know how she could be.'

'Magnificent.'

'Yes, I suppose, but I was going to say terrifying. I remember thinking how glad I was that I didn't have to deal with her.' He stroked his beard, his eyes focused on the past. 'At the end though, she just accepted the verdict in silence. The strange thing was she'd always known she was going to lose. The High Lord had already made up his mind, she said. She still fought through the trial though, hard enough to convince me of her innocence.'

'Did she convince any of the others?'

Gada laughed, a high sound, mirthless. 'You think they'd tell me? Everyone agrees with the verdict of the High Lord, no matter what they think privately.' A thought seemed to strike him then, and he rushed to the arch, looking both ways down the corridor. When he came back his voice was quieter. 'I can only speak for myself, and I agree with the High Lord, as I do in all things.'

'But you just said you believed Mother!'

'No, I said she was very convincing. That's different to her being right. Besides, Mother is dead. We have to accept that and move on. Our future depends on High Lord Yadavendra now.'

'You really think our mother betrayed us and her people

to consort with the Wild? Because that is what the High Lord decreed.'

Gada looked away. 'I promised Mother I'd look after us. To achieve that I'll believe what I have to.'

'Well I won't! We both know she's innocent. We have to do something!'

'Vasin. Brother. She's dead. Let it go.'

He went to reply but wasn't sure what to say. *Should I tell him the truth? Can he be trusted?* Even if Gada believed him, there was no guarantee he'd agree to help. *He doesn't care about right or wrong, he cares about being on the winning side.* It wasn't easy but Vasin again summoned the words he knew his brother wanted to hear. 'Yes. You're right.'

'Good,' Gada replied, putting a tentative hand on his arm. 'I'm glad you can see it. Now promise me you won't say anything about Mother's trial to the others. As far as they're concerned it's over, a part of our history. If you start asking questions they'll be suspicious, and if word gets back to High Lord Yadavendra . . . ' He began to pace. 'You know he is looking for any excuse to punish us, and ultimately, to replace us. I'm certain he already has people lined up, as does Lord Umed and Lady Yadva. Oh yes, they want to take advantage too, you can count on that. If we're to survive, we need to be beyond reproach.'

'I won't say anything.' *Yet.*

'Good. That's good.' The relief in his face was palpable. 'Now, let us talk about something else. How fare our friends in House Ruby?'

Vasin shrugged. 'They were very glad to see me. They'd have been even happier if our High Lord had deigned to answer their call—'

'Vasin.'

'—Given that they'd asked for him by name—'

'Vasin!'

'—And given the urgency. But judging by the look on your face, you don't want to talk about that either.' Gada's folded arms and pained expression indicated Vasin had backslid into being antagonistic. He forced himself to relax. 'Has the hunt turned up anything while I was away?'

Gada shook his head. 'We went to Lord Rochant's castle. The Rebirthing Chamber was empty. No sign of Lady Pari Tanzanite. And I discovered that not all of the dead guards actually worked at the castle.'

'What do you mean?'

'Two of them were imposters. None of the staff could identify them. In addition, several of the regular guards had been assigned elsewhere. The attack on Lord Rochant was planned from the inside, I'm sure of it.'

Sweat began to prickle on Vasin's skin. 'Do you think they might have been infiltrators from House Tanzanite?'

'It's possible. Something doesn't add up though, and I have the feeling that Captain Dil hasn't told us everything.'

'No?'

'On the night of Lord Rochant's rebirth, I'd have expected him to post all of his veterans inside the castle, rather than out. No, this last minute reassignment seems odd to me. When he and Lady Yadva return, I intend to have a long talk with him. Which reminds me: after the attack, Captain Dil came straight here to you. Why?'

It struck Vasin then that perhaps the whole conversation had been to build up to this point. *Are you investigating me as well? Is that why you were having my things searched, to find evidence?* 'I assume he came because my castle is closest.'

'Do you remember what he said when he arrived?'

'Vaguely.'

Gada's lips twitched downwards. 'Vaguely?'

'Yes, vaguely. Besides, what difference does it make? You already know his news.'

'I do but I'm looking for more details. Something to make sense of the gaps in our picture of that night. Can you remember anything? It doesn't matter how minor.'

'He wasn't very coherent, sorry.'

'I see.'

I hope you don't, thought Vasin. 'Sorry,' he repeated.

'Well, I'd best be getting on.' Gada paused, trying to find the right words. 'I wanted to say what a relief it is to know that we see these matters of family in the same way. I don't know what the others are planning, but we'll survive it if we pull together.'

'I've got your back. Have you got mine?'

Gada summoned his insincere smile once more as he turned to go. 'Always, brother.'

Vasin wandered towards the kitchens. He did his best to appear amiable and bewildered, as if he'd just smoked far too much Tack. This was difficult as what he really felt like doing was charging in and killing everyone he didn't know by sight.

Breakfast was over, and the space resounded to the clink of pots and plates being scraped, cleaned and set out under crystal to bake dry.

Servants did their best not to be alarmed by their lord's

unexpected appearance. He wandered between them, changing direction without warning, generally making as much of a nuisance of himself as he could without actually breaking anything.

He saw a man winding his way towards him, a major-domo, though Vasin did not remember appointing him. *With good reason, I suspect.* He pointed a finger in the rough direction of the man's face, letting it waver a little as if he were unsteady. 'Who are you?'

The man gave a quick bow. 'My name is Vis, my lord.' When Vasin frowned as if confused, he added, with a touch of petulance: 'Your chief of staff.'

'You are? But where is Old Sen?'

'I'm afraid she had to be retired, my lord. Her duties were becoming too much for her.'

'Ah, a shame. I would have liked to have said goodbye.' Vasin looked distant for a moment, in part to maintain his ruse, but mainly so that he did not strangle this man on the spot. *He dares to lie to my face in my own castle!* Sen was the daughter of his previous majordomo, and had followed her mother about the castle as soon as she could walk. She'd been ordering people about with a child's lack of mercy since the age of four. Everyone in the castle knew that Old Sen was a nickname, given in jest. Though Sen was no longer a child, she was hardly past her prime. 'Message,' he added.

'My lord?'

'I want to send her a message.'

'Very good, my lord. I'll have Mal sent to you immediately.'

'Who?'

'Mal, my lord. Do you not remember him? He oversees all of your correspondence.'

Actually Vasin did vaguely remember someone being introduced to him by that name. He'd be hard pressed to pick him from a crowd however. 'Ah yes. Good. Do that. Send him, I mean, so I can send a message.'

'Of course, my lord. Is there anything else I can do?'

'I'm going for a walk. When I get back I'd like something to drink.'

He staggered out, grinding his teeth to keep from shouting. He would find Old Sen, to recruit her again or avenge her, whichever proved necessary. But first he had to see how far the rot had spread.

He spent the day prowling his castle, noting the changes, the little shifts that had accumulated over time to distance him from it. Faces had been noted too, and names. It had been very informative. Some of the families that used to serve him, loyal for generations, had been moved aside by his brother to make way for new staff. All minor reshuffling, all plausible, all reasonable. But together they suggested something he didn't like at all.

Suddenly, the last few years came into a different kind of focus.

When I fell apart over Mother's exile, who looked after me?

Gada.

Though he always complains at my usage, who was it suggested I try some Tack in the first place, to ease my mind?

Gada.

Who was it came and took over my duties?

Gada.

And made sure I knew it, helping, yes, taking responsibility – separating me from the things that gave life meaning.

Gada.

Keeping me in the dark, ripening me for replacement.

Gada.

And when this body dies, will the High Lord bother to bring me back or will someone else take my place?

Perhaps his castle was being prepared for a new Deathless. Someone more amenable to the new order. *Well damn you, brother, and damn Yadavendra, and Rochant too for that matter. I'm not dead yet!*

When the suns had set, Vasin made his way down towards the bowels of his castle, moving slowly and cautiously, unwilling to risk being seen by his own people. The thought depressed him. He loved his people and he'd always assumed they loved him. *Is this what my life is now, suspicion and shadow?*

He arrived in the old, twisted tunnel, and made his way to the door. Lord Rochant would be on the other side, no doubt still hooded and bound. Vasin steadied himself. It was not going to be easy, but if he was going to end this, he would have to face the man inside.

Lord Rochant had boasted that he already knew where he was and who had captured him. He had not volunteered any names though, and Vasin clung to the hope that it was a bluff. Unfastening one of the strips of silk that bound his forearm, he turned it into a neckerchief. Between it, and the sackcloth around Rochant's ears, his voice would be hard to identify.

The door was old but sturdy. It was not locked. Steeling himself, Vasin walked through into the ill-lit space. The rusted pole was still there but nothing else. No Rochant. Not even a sign that he had been there.

Vasin came to an abrupt stop, his mouth suddenly dry. He walked around the pole, checking the darker corners of the room even though they were far too small to conceal a body.

Where is he?

Where is Yi?

He pressed his hands against his chest, trying to keep the panic from spreading. A hundred different scenarios, all bad, played through his mind. *What am I going to do?*

Under the thick canopy of trees, each dawn was slow breaking, gloomy, the forest materializing out of the dark like an army of grey ghosts. What it lacked in beauty, it made up for in joy, for when Chandni could see the trees, she knew they had survived another night in the Wild.

During the day they travelled with care, doing their best to avoid the other denizens of the forest. During the night, they hid in whatever shelter they could find, smearing dirt on their exposed skin to try and hide their scent.

So far, it had worked.

The other part of the plan, the part where they gathered food, had been less successful. *Starvation is such a mundane way for this to end,* she thought.

The cured morsels tucked away in Roh's cloak got them through the first day. After that they'd turned to Glider for help but she refused to leave their side. When Chandni asked her to hunt for them, the Dogkin simply stared, her human eye clouded, her canine one blank.

Neither she nor Varg had much luck foraging either, the handful of nuts and berries they'd found vanishing into their hollow bellies. It was a day since they'd found the stream, and several hours since they'd shared the last drops from Varg's flask.

As a result Chandni was struggling. Her stomach hurt with hunger and her head felt light, as if all her thoughts had leaked away to leave empty space between her ears.

Occasionally, a worry would surface. She knew that as they got weaker they became careless, their trail easier to follow and, if they didn't find food soon, they would be easy prey for any hunter.

And so when she saw the fruit, fresh and plump, each apple as big as Satyendra's skull, she nearly cried out with relief. It was hanging in a cluster from the branch of a nearby tree, well clear of the ground and most predators.

Chandni rushed over, leaning against the tree to reach up with her free hand. The fruit hung tantalizingly close but even on tiptoes she couldn't reach.

'Here,' said Varg. 'I'm taller. Let me have a go.'

She watched as he grunted and strained, but again, he couldn't quite get to them. 'What if you lifted me up?'

He nodded and she placed Satyendra gently on the forest floor. 'Watch him for me, Glider?'

The Dogkin barked agreement and curled herself round the sleeping baby. Chandni allowed herself one grateful stroke of her soft, white head before going back to Varg and the tree.

He boosted her up onto one of the lower branches as if she were weightless.

'Can you get it now?' asked Varg.

'From here I can,' she replied, but when she turned to where she expected the fruit to be, she realized she was mistaken. It was above her still. Steadying herself against the trunk for balance, she stretched up.

'You're nearly there!' called Varg.

The tip of her finger brushed against the nearest apple.

So close. If I can just . . .

The tree moved. Small enough that it could have been caused by her shifting weight or the breeze. One foot slipped from the branch, the other following close behind. Chandni's arms windmilled, wild, as she tried to fight the sudden pull of gravity.

Below her she could hear Varg shouting some useless advice, Glider barking at her and perhaps, just underneath the other sounds, Satyendra, giggling.

She made a frantic grab for the nearest branch, shrieking as it bent away, her numb fingers sliding over it, failing to take hold. Curled leaves, like ears of green, fluttered on their stalks, echoing her cry.

The branch snapped back into place, catching on her hair as she pitched forward. She saw Varg staring up, mouth open, arms out to catch her.

She squeezed her eyes shut, and fell.

There was a thud, soft, then a second one that was accompanied by a single swearword and the sound of Glider's excited barking. On the edge of it, she could just hear her shriek as it was passed from tree to tree, spiralling away.

Somehow she had landed without breaking anything.

'Oh, Varg. I don't know how much more of this I can take.'

His arms, already encircling her, squeezed a little tighter. She realized she was lying on top of him and that she must have knocked him off his feet.

'You were bloody close,' he said. 'We could have another go.'

'I'm not sure. This might sound strange, but I don't trust that tree.'

'Round here, that ain't strange. I don't trust the trees either but we gotta eat, so what can we do?'

She rested her head against his chest. 'Can't we just stay here for a while? You're surprisingly comfortable.'

There was a pause, and when he replied, his voice was husky. 'All right.'

She'd just rest her eyes for a minute. She knew they had to be on their guard and that they needed food. She knew what was at stake, but at that moment, she couldn't bring herself to move.

Except that wasn't quite true. Her left hand had found its way to Varg's face and idled there, exploring the space between beard and cheekbone.

At some point, he began to stroke her hair. Oddly, it did not make her sleepy, quite the opposite in fact. She liked the feel of his hands moving down her back. *I like the feel of him altogether.*

'Varg?'

'Yeah?'

'What are you doing?'

He froze. 'I . . . '

'Don't stop.' His hand began to move again, and her thumb brushed across his cheek to trace the outside of his lips. Somewhere at the back of her mind her mother's voice was railing at her, but she found it much easier to ignore than usual.

She could feel him stirring beneath her. *Already?* she thought. *I've barely touched him.* But Mohit, Satyendra's father, had been the same. She could not help but laugh, the two men were so different in every other way. Sadness followed. She hadn't thought of Mohit since she fled the castle. *Poor Mohit. You weren't the brightest jewel of the house but you didn't deserve to die that way.*

'What?' Varg had stopped stroking her, and he sounded a little hurt.

She lifted her head and pulled herself up so that she could look into his eyes. They were brown, gentle. *Loyal.* With her head tilted forward, her hair curtained off the space around them. 'I was thinking too much.'

He gave her a roguish grin. 'Reckon I could help with that.'

She returned it. 'Yes. I believe you could.'

As she leaned in towards him, she saw that he'd closed his eyes. *Adorable!*

She closed hers too.

Their lips came together.

And then Satyendra began to cry.

Chandni jumped up as if stung, guilt flooding her from head to toe. *After everything that's happened,* said the voice of her mother, back with a vengeance, *you leave Lord Rochant's last surviving vessel on the ground like an unwanted shoe so that you can dally with some hairy Tanzanite rough. Unforgivable.*

She scooped her baby into her arms, kissing his head and murmuring apologies into his hair. Satyendra wasn't interested in either, his hands grabbing for her top.

The trees took up the crying, amplifying it, and Glider began barking nervously.

'What's happening?' she asked.

'Dunno,' said Varg as he hauled himself upright, not quite making eye contact. 'Nothing good.'

'We should go.'

'You gotta shut him up or he'll bring suns' knows what down on us.'

She fed him quickly, wincing when he nipped her. *Please don't draw blood, not here.* To her great relief, he hadn't. When her baby had settled again, they set off, the hanging fruit quickly out of sight but not out of mind.

'How long before we reach Sorn? I thought we'd be there by now.'

Varg shrugged miserably. 'We would be if we were on the Godroad or if we'd travelled close to it on one of the old paths. But we got no cart and we're deeper in than I've been before.'

'How long, Varg?'

'Soon.'

'Today?'

'Yeah . . . I think so.'

He stopped, looking around, looking suspiciously like a man who was lost. 'We've been drifting off course.'

Her heart sank. 'How badly?'

'We're going in the right direction, just angling off, getting deeper in.'

'That can't be good.'

He scratched at his beard. 'Well, it means the assassins are less likely to follow us.'

'Yes, because they don't need to kill Satyendra if we do it for them.' She saw him flinch and realized how tired they both were. 'Sorry. I'm sorry, Varg. I know you're doing your best. Which way do we need to go?' He pointed. 'Lead on then. Hopefully we'll find something to eat at Sorn. A little food and a decent sleep and I'm sure we'll feel much better.'

They travelled on, the sunlight playing on the leaves directly above their heads. Satyendra slept throughout, or sat contentedly in Chandni's arms, and neither she nor Varg felt up to talking, their fading energies going into the placing of one foot in front of the other.

When Glider barked, Chandni's eyes snapped open. She'd nearly fallen asleep on her feet. The Dogkin's tail was wagging, her nose probing the air.

'What is it, Glider?'

Glider gave another bark and raced off into the trees, forcing them to run after her. Not long after she could smell it herself. *I can't believe it. It smells like meat. Cooked meat!*

She couldn't keep up with the others but managed to keep them in sight. Seconds later they came into a clearing dominated by a single tree. A thick haunch of roasted meat hung from a rope slung over one of the branches.

It looked suspiciously like a trap to Chandni. Varg had clearly thought something similar, and was trying to stop Glider going any closer. The Dogkin was not having any of it, however, dragging Varg alongside as easily as she carried Satyendra.

Chandni took a breath. 'Glider,' she said in her most imperious tone, 'stop.'

The Dogkin had the grace to give her a guilty look before she wrapped her jaws around the meat.

There was a twang, and the next moment both Varg and Glider were in the air, upside down, wrapped in a net of thick vines.

'Oh no,' said Chandni as she watched them swing back and forth. 'Varg? Are you hurt?'

'I'm going to kill this fucking animal.'

She came closer and grabbed the edge of the net. The weight of it dragged her with it, but by digging in her heels, she was able to bring it to a stop. 'Are you hurt?'

He looked at her, the patches of face she could see squished against the net a bright scarlet. 'A few bruises. Do you see any blood?'

'No.' Glider still had the meat in her jaws and was chewing with enthusiasm. 'That was very naughty, Glider.'

There was the brief sound of an apologetic whine, and then the chewing continued.

'You shouldn't eat that. It could be poisoned.'

'I hope it is,' muttered Varg. 'Would serve her right, the idiot.'

'You don't mean that.' She turned to Glider. 'He doesn't mean that.'

'Can you get us down?'

'I don't have anything to cut the net but it must be tied to the tree somehow. This trap, it looks like it was made by a person.'

'Or something like a person.'

Chandni remembered that the Whispercage looked a little like a person and decided that she wanted to leave this place as fast as possible. The knot was tucked away further up the tree, and Chandni was just trying to work out how she could get up there without abandoning Satyendra, when she heard Varg hissing for her attention.

'Something's coming, hide!'

She ran to the edge of the clearing only to find herself face to face with another woman. A collection of weather-dyed fabrics masked her true shape but the little bits of skin Chandni could see were wrinkled and worn by the elements.

Long grey hair was coiled on top of her head like a hat. It was hard to tell how old she was exactly, but the lean staff of polished oak was held firmly in her hands.

'Hello—' Chandni began, and the woman's staff flashed out, flicking her legs away. The air whooshed out of Chandni's lungs as she went down on her back. In her effort to protect Satyendra, she fell badly, feeling her left elbow crack hard on the ground.

The end of the staff came to rest against the side of Chandni's head. 'Well?' said the woman, who sounded younger than Chandni expected. 'Talk.'

'Please, we don't mean any trouble. We're just hungry.'

'Must be to trigger my trap.' The old woman used her staff to hook the hair away from Chandni's face. 'You got the skin of one that lives in the sky.'

'Yes.'

'And this baby's a sky baby?'

'Yes.' She pulled Satyendra close. 'He's mine.'

'What you doing down here, sky-born?'

'That's a long story. My name is Chandni, Honoured Mother of House Sapphire. What's yours?'

'Fiya. What's the quick version of the story?'

'We were betrayed, and to protect my son I fled here.'

'Mmm. We know all about betrayal in this place.' The staff moved back to rest at Fiya's feet. 'Come with me, it's not safe to linger.'

Chandni forced her weary body upright again while Fiya walked to the tree. A single prod of her staff released the net, which dumped its contents unceremoniously on the ground.

As Varg and Glider fought to untangle themselves, Fiya

began walking off into the trees. 'Come on, sky-born,' she said, impatient.

'Can my friends come too?'

'So long as they can keep up.'

She helped Glider to free her back paws, and then they hurried after Fiya. Though not far away the old woman was already hard to see, blending against the greys and browns like a ghost.

It was all Chandni could do to keep up.

Eventually, Fiya stopped by a large tree with drooping branches. She stroked it as she passed, in the same way that Chandni would show affection to Glider, and stepped over to the trunk. Now that she was closer, Chandni could see a diagonal gash leading inside it. Fiya paused, bending down to do something, she wasn't sure what it was but it seemed important, ritualistic. Then the old woman was beckoning them to follow her.

Inside, the space was cosy, fur lined. *Warm!* thought Chandni with delight. Some old jars were stacked on the far side, covered in a thick grime that made it impossible to discern their contents. Above, the trunk was hollow but little fingers of sunlight poked through, showing off pockets of purple flowers amid the yellow moss.

'Sit,' said Fiya.

They did, even Glider.

'Got some broth for you. It's cold but it's good.'

'What's in it?' asked Chandni.

'A bit of this and bit of that. It's good, take it. I've only got the one bowl so's you have to share. Got more broth in the pot though.'

The broth had a grainy texture and the little chunks of

meat inside were stringy but Chandni didn't care. She and Varg sped through three bowls' worth with such speed that Fiya's stern expression broke to cackling.

'Told you it was good,' she said. 'Now rest, I'm going to go and make sure nothing followed us back but you have to stay here. All of you,' she added with a stern look at Glider. 'Don't make any loud noise, and don't leave or you won't be able to come back again. Understand?'

They nodded, though Chandni had no idea what Fiya meant.

With her belly full and her body snuggled against Varg and the furs, Chandni fell asleep to the sound of Glider lapping the bowl.

It hadn't taken Vasin long to find the storeroom. Gada had made no secret of putting things there, he'd just moved everything discreetly. *Safe in the knowledge that I was too far gone to notice.* Inside, Vasin found the cured head of a Roachkin, the trophy from his first successful hunt. Next to it were the remains of his original wings. There were flaws in the crystal, stress fractures that had forced him to retire them, but as he ran his fingers over their curving edge, the sapphire hummed softly, conjuring memories.

In his mind he was flying again. He'd been afraid before-hand, he remembered, but the moment he was in the sky, that fear had vanished. He belonged there. More than that, Vasin had felt natural there, as if his soul had flown many times before. It was a surprise for him to learn that not all Deathless had this experience. For some it took many life-cycles of practice before they were able to manage the currents well enough to hunt.

That was the day he'd made his name, he recalled. Being the youngest Sapphire, many slots had already been taken: Yadva was known for her strength, Umed for his grace and patience, Gada for his reliability. Everything he did in his first lifecycle was compared with their achievements, almost always to his detriment. Snippets of disdainful conversations came back to him, and it irked him that after all these years they were still so clear in his mind, when other brighter times had faded away, only salvageable again in the right company. But he flew better than all of them, even Yadva, and none could deny it.

After that day, the family had treated him differently, as if he'd gone from being a favoured pet to an actual person. Those wings had changed him forever.

It had been an indulgence to keep them, usually old suits of crystal skin were returned to the Gardener-smiths, who fed them back to the new crystals to keep the link, but he hadn't been able to let them go.

It struck Vasin that this lifecycle had been something of a failure. It had started well enough, but his mother's trial and subsequent exile had dominated, the trauma precipitating his retreat from public life.

And, if I'm honest, from all life: I sought oblivion, when I should have been seeking answers. If I had been stronger, perhaps I could have helped Mother already.

He realized that one of the reasons he felt so strong in his crystal armour was that it connected him to older parts of himself, to previous lifecycles when he wasn't plagued with doubt. In past days his castle would perform the same function, but many of the things that celebrated his glory had either gone or been moved from prominence, replaced with bland gifts he'd kept out of politeness but rarely displayed.

He was looking at a pair of boots he'd worn in his third lifecycle – *what big feet that body had! Yadva's jokes were so very tiresome* – and was trying to recall why they were significant, when Yi stepped out from behind a set of boxes.

Though poised as ever, Vasin noticed the dark around her eyes and the drawn skin of her face. He checked over his shoulder to make sure no one else was there, but they were alone, this part of the castle rarely used. 'Yi? What happened?'

Her voice was croaky. 'They searched the castle. I had to move Lord Rochant here.'

'He's here?'

She pointed behind the boxes. 'Drugged.'

'What happened to you?'

'Couldn't leave him. Too many unfriendly eyes.'

'I'll get you food and drink.'

She nodded gratitude. 'Nothing big. Nothing obvious. Nothing they can smell.'

'This is a disaster. We need to get him to reveal wherever it is that baby is hidden.' Yi watched him but said nothing, despondent.

Vasin shook his head as if to clear it. 'I'm no match for Lord Rochant but we both know who would be. Do you think you can move him from the castle?'

'Difficult.'

If Yi was saying that then the odds were bad indeed. 'What would you need?'

'Supplies. A distraction. The searches have ended but they'll be watching the entrance.'

Vasin rested a hand on his old wings, letting his eyes follow the contours. *They've always underestimated me. Perhaps I can use that.* Something of his old fire was returning and it felt good. 'Gather your strength, Yi. When you're recovered, I'll get their attention, have no fear of that.'

CHAPTER THIRTEEN

Pari sat on her throne of cushions, trying to rein in her sense of frustration. They had spent a long time propping her up in this fashion and she still wasn't comfortable! The injuries she'd sustained were healing too slowly, and some of them not at all. *This body wants to give up and I can't let it. Not yet.*

In front of her, Ami walked back and forth, her shoes boosted to give her extra height. She was dressed in Pari's clothes, her lips painted gold, her body padded in several places to give it the right shape. *My shape.*

'No, dear Ami. You must be slower and more deliberate, otherwise your youth will spoil the illusion.'

'Got it.'

'And don't speak to anyone but Sho. If a servant comes, you must gesture, like this.' She made a small decisive movement of the hand. 'Or simply use your eyes.' Ami swept her gaze to the left. It reminded Pari of a Birdkin tracking some potential food. 'No. No that won't do. Stay with your hands.'

She bobbed her head.

'And don't nod like that. Just a slight tilt of the head. Slight. Imagine you are balancing a glass of acid on your head. If you spill it, you die.'

'Shall I walk again?'

Pari gestured for her to do so whilst wishing she didn't feel so grumpy all the time. Lord Taraka may have gone, but his visit had left her unsettled. The thought of her brother living with High Lord Tanzanite wasn't helping either.

She was just starting to feel like a drink when Sho arrived with refreshments. At the sound of his voice, Ami retreated behind a nearby screen, a precaution should anyone else be with him. For the moment Ami's presence here was a secret, and it had to remain so if Pari's plan was to be successful.

But Sho was alone, a tray in his trembling hands.

'Ah, Sho, it's as if you read my mind.' She sipped some of the honeyed wine he'd brought, enjoying the feel of the warm mug almost as much as the sweet liquid it contained.

'I have news, my lady. Your young man has returned. I thought it best to keep him out of the castle for now.'

'I agree. Have you spoken to him?'

Sho's face crinkled, unhappy. 'He refused to tell me anything, insisting that his news was for your ears only.'

'He's a good boy.'

'If you say so, my lady.'

They exchanged a look. *Sho's getting grumpy too in his old age. A fine pair we make these days!* 'Find a way to bring him here discreetly.'

She made a gesture to cut off any further grumblings and Sho left.

An hour later, Lan was slipped into the room. Sho had

282

dressed him as a messenger. The boy looked tired but his eyes were bright with excitement. He and Ami hugged each other quickly before the young man rushed forward and proudly displayed the earrings in his hands.

'You found them? Excellent.'

'Yep, the baby an' her mum, an' that Varg, an' their Dogkin. It were a monster! You never said she was so big!'

Pari chuckled. 'Did Glider give you a hard time?'

'Nearly got me head off!'

'It sounds like you've had quite the adventure. Tell me everything.'

'They were in Sagan, like you said. In that house on the edge. They got this family from Sorn living there an' all.'

Pari frowned. 'Go on.'

'Parents and a couple of little 'uns. They want you to come get 'em. Not the family. Varg and the Honoured Mother.'

'What's the situation there?'

'Bad. There are patrols on the roads. Hunters too. And Sagan's packed full of people and there's fights. It don't look good.'

'No, but you've done very good work, Lan.' The young man beamed. 'Sho will give you some decent food and a place to sleep, but don't get too comfortable. You and I will be leaving again soon.'

Strange thoughts occupied Sa-at's dreams. The thing fed to him by the Birdkin had left him feeling like a different person to the one he'd been the day before, his brain could not stop fizzing. For the first time he understood that everything had a name, even him.

Its name is Crowflies!
My name is Sa-at!
Sa-at yawned and flexed his little body, stretching it from
toe tip to fingertip. The skin of his maimed hand tingled
painfully and he pulled it back to his chest with a gasp. This
had happened before, he realized. He had stretched and it
had hurt and then he had forgotten and stretched again.
It is a hand.
It is my hand.
I have a hand!
He decided to have a look at his hand. To his surprise,
two shapes, not one, floated into his eye line.
I have two hands!
This was so exciting, so unexpected, that all he could do
for a while was wriggle and make noises. In doing so, he
lost sight of his hands and forgot why he was excited in the
first place.
A man moved into view, making the candle flicker. Sa-at
could see he was still inside the black tree and that he was
lying on something soft that tickled his feet if he rubbed
them on it.
He rubbed his feet on it.
He giggled.
He rubbed his feet again.
He giggled again.
'I see you like my fur quilt,' said the man.
A word burst into Sa-at's mind: *Devdan.*
He is Devdan.
His name is Devdan!
And then, immediately after, another:
Fur.

This is fur.
It tickles.
Sa-at decided that he liked fur.
'It's good to hear you laugh. Hollow's a good listener but she doesn't say much.'

Sa-at looked up at the sound of Devdan's voice for a moment, then went back to rubbing his feet.

'Good isn't it? Tough to make though.' He held up the end of the fur and pointed to one of the rough squares. 'Every one of these had to be caught, killed and bled. Beast blood doesn't get the same attention as our blood does but it gets enough. When you're older,' he smiled, his yellow teeth stark against the white of his beard, 'much older, I'll teach you the technique. Assuming they let me keep you, that is.'

He held out a hand and Sa-at grabbed it.

Devdan has a hand!
I have a hand!

Without thinking, he tried to put Devdan's finger in his mouth. His gums were itching terribly and he had the irresistible urge to chew on something.

'Hey!' said Devdan, snatching his hand away. 'Got your teeth coming through then, sharp too. Look what you did.' He held his finger in front of Sa-at's eyes, just out of reach. The pale skin had a red patch on one side, with three small indentations, slowly fading away.

'Let me find something more suitable for you to savage.'

Devdan moved out of Sa-at's view but he could still hear the man moving about. Bored, Sa-at had another wriggle, and in doing so, saw something out of the corner of his eye.

It is a hand.

It is my hand.
I have a hand.
I have two hands.

They were not like Devdan's hands. They were smaller and browner. One of them was missing a finger. This made Sa-at sad. A memory came of that finger, of a tongue wrapping round it and teeth, much bigger and pointier than Devdan's, closing on his skin. There was a twinge of pain in his knuckle, remembered.

Very quietly, Sa-at began to snuffle.

'Oh, hey now,' said Devdan, reappearing. 'Don't cry. Here, try this.' He held out a chunk of cured meat. 'Should keep you busy for a while.'

The meat had a salty taste. It was not wet and smooth like his mother's milk nor wet and sour like the thing Crowflies fed him – he wanted more of that! – but chewing it made his gums itch less.

'There you go. That's scale jerky, taken from some of the toughest Lizardkin you're liable to see this side of the Ruby lands. Told you it would help. It's good value too, will probably last longer than either of us.

'I wonder who you are? Doesn't look to me like you were born here. Old Hollow thinks you must have come from one of those floating castles in the sky but I've never heard of any children, let alone tiny ones like you –' he paused to tweak Sa-at's toe '– coming down to our level. Believe it or not, my family used to live in the sky too. Was a long time ago though, back when old Hollow was still alive and a good few years before I was born. I wonder if you were banished too?'

Sa-at continued chewing the meat. It was firm, dry, and

as he worked, drool began to run from the sides of his mouth.

'Well, however you got here, you're special. I'm not surprised that demon was so keen to get its claws into you. The Wild's always hungry for humans, especially babies. But don't worry, I'm going to take extra care this time.' He brought the skull with the mounted candle closer and peered at Sa-at. 'Mmm. Not sure what the demons did to your hand, but at least the injury is healing nicely. Let's hope it stays clean and nothing starts growing on it. Be a shame to have to cut any more of you away.'

The candlelight danced merrily, drawing Sa-at's eye. He let go of the meat with one hand to try and take it, but as he reached out Devdan moved it further away. Sa-at was seized by indignation and he gave a squeal of protest.

'Oh no, this isn't for you. This flame is hot. Dangerous. No touching.'

It is a flame.

It is called a flame.

'See how it melts the wax? You don't want to touch that either. Hot wax will stick to you as well as burn.' He knocked on the skull with his fist. 'Not that old Hollow minds any more. Those of us with skin on our bones like you and me have to be more careful.'

Hollow. Wax. Skin. Bone. The names flew through Sa-at's mind, attaching themselves to objects, forming islands of certainty in a chaotic sea. Suddenly, it was too much. The jerky slipped from his fingers and his eyelids drooped. He felt the need to sleep, to dream, to give his eyes and mind a rest.

Devdan picked him up and started to rock him. It was

not his mother's arms and it was not like being wrapped in the wings. It did not matter, he slept all the same.

Chandni awoke to the sound of Varg arguing quietly but vehemently with Glider. *Not quite yet,* she thought, and allowed herself a moment to enjoy the novelty of being warm. It was getting harder and harder to remember her life in Lord Rochant's castle but there had been a time when every day started in a cosy bed.

Meanwhile, the dispute escalated. Glider's barks grew in volume and Varg started gesturing in a vaguely threatening manner as he spoke. With some reluctance, Chandni sat up.

'What is it?' she asked.

'Glider wants to go out. I've told her she can't but she's not having it.'

'It's not her fault, Varg, she just wants to go to the toilet.'

'How do you know?'

'Call it intuition.' The truth was that now she was fully awake, she needed to go quite urgently herself.

'That Fiya was pretty clear. We can't leave till she gets back. I'm not sure I trust her, but I reckon she knows what she's talking about.'

'I agree. Glider, can you hold on for a while?'

The Dogkin looked at her and whimpered, uncertain.

'I see. Well, please try, for our sake. The space isn't very large and I don't think our host will approve.'

'She won't, trust me,' said Varg. 'I've smelt Glider's mess before.'

Glider put her head on the ground and covered it with her paws.

A little time passed, and Chandni could feel the broth she'd consumed with such abandon pressing to get out. Natural windows in the bark allowed the last of the day's sunlight inside. She used it to examine the space for appropriate nooks or holes. Unfortunately, there weren't any, and the jars looked to be already full, though with what, Chandni could not guess. It would be easy enough to wipe off the layer of grime on the outside and investigate, but the idea of touching them made her feel slightly ill.

'Can we talk about something?' she asked.

'Sure.'

His voice sounded strained, and when she looked at him, she noticed his jaw was set tight. *He's as desperate as the rest of us!* 'Varg, if Fiya doesn't come back soon, what are we going to do?'

'Clench.'

'I'm all for being civilized, as well you know, but this isn't worth dying for. Can you find anything we could use for our . . . indignities?'

'There's the cooking pot.'

Chandni put a hand to her mouth. 'That's disgusting!' Satyendra made a little huffing noise and took on an intense expression that to her horror, Chandni knew well. 'He needs to go too, and he won't wait.'

'Oh shit.'

'Quite.'

They both started searching, more frantically this time. Fiya had few possessions, it seemed, and only one cooking pot. Chandni was just about ready to risk venturing outside the tree when the old woman returned, the sudden appearance of her head at the entrance making them all jump.

'What's this then?' she asked, her voice as hard as her face.

Chandni took a moment to consider how suspicious they all looked, rifling through her things. 'Oh, it's not what you think.'

'Is it not?'

'No. I mean, we're not trying to steal anything.'

Fiya shook her head. 'Would have thought a sky-born would remember the ways of host and guest.'

'I do. That's why we didn't leave.' Satyendra made another huffing noise. Time was running out. 'But we need to go, all of us. Quite urgently in fact.'

'Go where?'

'Anywhere we can relieve ourselves without soiling your home.'

There was a pause, then Fiya's brows shot up. 'Come with me.'

Glider was on her feet and bounding out of the tree so fast that Fiya only just managed to get out of the way. Varg wasn't far behind her, Chandni and her hard working baby close on his heels.

They were led a short distance from the grand tree. By the time Fiya had called them to a stop, Glider had already vanished, done her business, and returned to them, a happy spring in her paws.

'Get your Dogkin to dig a hole. You can all go in that. When you're done, sprinkle the remains with these.' She passed a small drawstring bag to Varg. 'Use plenty. Then cover the hole. I'll be waiting for you outside the tree.'

When Fiya had gone, Glider obliged with a shallow hole; neither of them could stand to wait for a deep one.

'Who's going first?' asked Varg.

'I don't mind. I don't think Satyendra can wait for long but you—'

'Great, thanks!'

She was going to say 'can go after him' but Varg had already straddled the hole. Chandni turned her back, trying not to feel too annoyed. However, Varg's groan of relief was so earnest, she couldn't help but smile.

When she and Satyendra were done, Varg opened the bag he'd been given by Fiya. Inside were dried out leaves, brown and broken into tiny pieces. He tipped the bag at an angle, giving it a generous shake. Glider then covered the hole over.

Chandni kept an eye out while he did this. The usual rustles and chirps of the forest could be heard, but nothing was close. I'm not scared here any more, she realized, and then wondered if that was good or bad.

As promised, Fiya was waiting for them outside the tree.

'Thank you,' said Chandni. 'You know so much about the Wild. Would you be willing to help us learn? I have many questions.'

'I have a few myself,' replied Fiya. 'Tell me more about how you came to be here.'

'Of course.' She wondered how much she should tell this strange old woman but quickly decided she would deal with the situation as she always did, with honesty and dignity. Any other way was beneath a child of the Sapphire. 'Assassins came for my baby, Satyendra, so we fled to Sagan. When they followed us to Sagan, we fled here.'

Fiya glanced at Satyendra, who was far too busy staring at the darkening tree to notice. 'Why were they after him?'

'We still don't fully understand, but enemies of my lord—'

Varg made a cutting gesture with his hand. 'Come on, we might as well tell her the truth.' He looked Fiya straight in the eye. 'The baby is ours, which is a problem given that she's an Honoured Mother. As you can see, I'm no descendant of a Sapphire Deathless.'

Chandni opened her mouth to speak but Varg shot her a glare and she closed it again.

Why is he lying about Satyendra? Surely Fiya will know.

But the old woman just nodded, as if she'd suspected what Varg was saying all along.

'So, found out about you did they?'

'We thought we'd been careful.' He shrugged. 'Guess we weren't.'

'Mmm. Why send assassins though? Why not put you both on trial?'

'They wanted to avoid a scandal.'

'Ah yes,' said Fiya bitterly, 'House Sapphire's secrets have long been protected with blood.'

'And with me and the baby out of the way, they could still pair Chandni with a true Sapphire.'

She hated it when Varg lied. It demeaned them both somehow. She wasn't sure what to do. If she said nothing, she would betray her own principles, but to speak now would betray Varg and it might provoke Fiya. *Lies breed until they fill you, that's what Lord Rochant told me.* The moment for her to say something, to stop this falsehood becoming the bedrock of her relationship with Fiya came and went, and a little of her pride went with it. *What would my lord think of me now?*

Fiya pondered Varg's words for some time. 'Well, you don't

need to worry about sky business no more. They'll soon forget all about you, just like they forgot about us.'

'That was going to be one of my questions,' said Chandni, glad to be able to change the subject. 'How did you come to live here? I was taught that nobody could survive in the Wild.'

'We've been surviving here for generations.'

'We? There are more of you?'

'Oh yes,' said Fiya. 'More than a few strung out through the trees. We live separate, to stop from becoming too much of a lure, but we meet from time to time to share stories and knowledge.'

Varg folded his arms. 'You all got bad history with the Sapphire too?'

'Aye. It's their fault we're here.'

'You were exiled?'

'Not me. I was born and bred in these woods. But my grandparents were sent away when they weren't much older than your baby there.'

'I still don't see how they survived,' said Chandni.

'They learned the ways.'

Varg coughed. 'As simple as that?'

Fiya's bony hand came to land on Varg's arm. 'Nothing simple about it. When my ancestors first came here the Wild reached out every night to take some of them. In the day they scrabbled about, but for all their efforts, they couldn't find any way to make the forest give up its bounty. My ancestors starved and suffered and died. They were dark times. Then, one day, this stranger came, dressed in leaves and mud. Didn't come close, just watched them.

'My ancestors were scared of him, kept their distance.

There was talk about driving him off, even talk about catching him and eating him. They were desperate, see? Fear and their bellies thinking for them.

'Only one voice spoke any sense, and that belonged to my grandmother, Rayen. She said seeing as the stranger was the first thing that hadn't attacked them, that maybe they should go talk to him.

'The others told her that if she wanted to go running towards her death, then they wouldn't stop her. So, the next time the stranger appeared, Rayen did just that.

'For three days, they talked. And for three nights, the Wild didn't take anyone. But while Rayen was away, the others began to doubt. They thought Rayen had been seduced by the stranger. Some said they should act before the stranger's plan could be completed.' Fiya shook her head in disgust.

'On the fourth day, a group of them followed Rayen and set up an ambush.'

There was a pause. Fiya looked to be lost in memories.

'What happened to them?' asked Chandni.

'Nobody knows. None of them that attacked were ever seen again, and that night, Rayen didn't come back to the others. The Wild came though, picking at them one by one. The cold came too, hard winds and harder earth, making food impossible to come by.

'Three nights passed like that, and I know my ancestors thought that was it, but then, the next morning, Rayen came back. The last time they'd seen her she'd had grey hair like mine, but now it was as white as the snow on the canopy, as white as the frost on their faces.' She glanced at Glider. 'As white as the fur of your Dogkin.'

Chandni felt a shiver go down her spine.

'Rayen brought the ways with her. She taught my ances-tors how to treat with the trees, how to make their traps soft, and how to take the blood from a kill without bringing the hungry ones out of the dark. Thing with the ways though, is that there's always a price.

'One day, the stranger came again to watch them. Rayen went to talk to him like she always did but this time, when he left, she went with him. And that was it. Nobody ever saw her again after that. She'd paid the price for them, and they never forgot.' She let go of Varg's arm. 'So no, nothing simple about it.'

She looked from them to the tree and back again. 'Time for you to make a decision.'

'What do you mean?' asked Chandni.

'Can't be having that nonsense every time you need to empty your bladders,' she said. 'I've treated with the roots for you to come and go. Now you need to give a gift.'

Varg gave Chandni an unhappy look. 'What do you mean?' she asked.

'So it can know you. If you want to survive in the Wild you have to give before you can take. I fed and sheltered you out of kindness, but if you're going to stay longer you've got to learn to trade.'

'What would the tree want from us?' asked Chandni, though she had the horrible feeling she already knew.

'Some hair from you both.'

She could have almost cried with relief. *Just a bit of hair! That's not so bad.* But Varg was shaking his head. He leaned in close and lowered his voice, though Chandni was sure Fiya could still hear him.

'Don't do it.'

295

'Why not?'

'You know what they say, once the Wild has a piece of you, you'll never escape.'

'Varg. I've been to the Hunger Tree. If the Wild only needs a piece, then I'm already doomed.'

He looked down. 'I'm sorry, Chand. I didn't . . . '

'It's all right.' She reached out with her right hand to touch him, watching as her fingers brushed his sleeve but not feeling anything. *I wonder if I'll ever get used to that.* 'Really, Varg, it's all right. I knew what I was doing and I've made my peace with it. There's so much Fiya can teach us, and this is Satyendra's best chance to survive. I'll understand if you don't want to take part.'

'Why not leave now, with me? We've made it this far on our own.'

She gave him a sad smile. 'We have.'

'You're going to stay here, aren't you?'

'For a little while, yes. We don't know how long we're going to be here. There's too much riding on Satyendra's shoulders for me to take chances. I need to know how to live in the Wild.'

'We could still try Sorn.'

'We don't know what we'll find in Sorn.' She paused, then added gently, 'We aren't even sure how to get there.'

He looked for a moment as if he were going to argue but then hung his head, defeated. Chandni turned back to Fiya. 'I'm ready.'

The old woman nodded and pulled out a bone-bladed knife. A thick bunch of her hair was separated out, then wound and measured on Fiya's forearm.

Chandni watched wistfully as it was cut off. It was the

first time her hair had been cut. *At least I have plenty left to trade with.*

Fiya took the hair and held it taut above her head, as if displaying it to the tree. She then tied it between a couple of the dangling branches, muttering to herself as she did so.

'Done,' said Fiya.

'No,' said Varg. 'You need to do me as well.'

Mixed feelings rose in Chandni then. Happiness that he was willing to stay, admiration that he would risk his soul for her, and the desire to protect him, to send him away. 'You don't have to, you know? You've done enough.'

'I was told to look after you, and that's what I'm going to do.'

'Lady Pari would understand. It might even be useful if you went back. You could help her to find us.'

He looked pained. 'Maybe I could. But . . . but I can't leave you, Chand, I just can't. It's not about Pari, not any more. It's like you wanted: I said I'd do this for you and I meant it. I still mean it. And if I try and think about walking away, I feel sick. So please, don't ask me to go.'

It took her a moment to get her right hand to grip his sleeve tight enough, but then she pulled him down so that she could kiss him. 'I will never ask you to leave, I promise.'

He was still blushing as he spoke to Fiya. 'All right, do what you have to.'

Fiya came over and tugged at his hair, her lips pressed together in thought. Then she pulled at his beard, hard enough to make him gasp. 'Hold out your hands, make a cup.' Varg did as he was told and, nodding to herself, she began hacking, taking little chunks here and there, until Varg had acquired an untidy pile.

A pinch at a time, Fiya took the hair and pressed it into gaps between the roots, babbling away as she did so, an insensible sing-song that reminded Chandni of the way she talked to Satyendra sometimes.

'Come in,' said Fiya as she ducked through the hole.

When she and Varg went to follow, it felt different somehow, as if a tension she'd been carrying had broken at last. The curtain of branches parted as they approached, making it easier to push through.

Soon, they were all sat together inside the trunk, elbows touching, Glider's bulk filling the gaps between. More food was offered, and gratefully accepted.

There was more Chandni wanted to ask but Fiya had turned away from them, hugging her knees close as if she were a little girl. No, Chandni decided, Fiya had given them enough for one day.

CHAPTER FOURTEEN

His entire staff had assembled in the feast hall, badges bright on their chests. The tables had been pushed to the back to make room for them. Though people were doing their best to hide it, there was a tension in the air. A gathering of the staff could only mean change of some dire kind.

Vasin stepped into the hall. He could taste the fear, sharing some of it himself. They all felt how unusual this was. For the younger staff, this would be their first formal address from him outside of a hunt. How he wished this was a hunt! That was the kind of public speaking he excelled at, full of thrill and spectacle. It woke the blood, as his cousin Yadva was fond of saying.

Well, my blood is certainly awake now.

Elsewhere, Yi would be moving Lord Rochant, smuggling him from the castle to wait at a secret location in the woods. If all went to plan, he would meet them there and take Rochant to his mother who would sort out the mess they had landed in.

And if it does not go to plan, I shall know soon enough.

He held up his hands for attention already given and cleared his throat. 'You are my people. I am your lord. We are one. When I fly out to protect our settlements below, you are the spears at my back, the arms at my side, it is your voice, your love that bears my weight and wings.

'But the truth is I have not flown much of late, nor have I walked the halls as often as I should.'

A few of the staff looked awkward, sensing the apologetic nature of his speech.

'Still, you have carried me. Your service, your loyalty, like a balm for my soul throughout this time of grief and distraction. Now I open my eyes to find that much has changed. Old friends have moved on without my saying goodbye, their work not properly honoured. New faces have appeared –' he paused to make eye contact with those appointed by his brother '– that I must get to know.

'There is much to be done here in the castle and as much that needs doing beyond its walls – we must be cunning if we are to keep ahead of the creatures of the Wild.'

One of the Gardener-smiths could not help but speak out. 'My lord, has there been an attack?'

'Not on us. They know House Sapphire would be quick to answer such a direct assault. No, they attack our fringes, making changes there that impact on other lands, like those of our eternal allies in House Ruby. As I said, we are one. Not just you and I, but all of the Crystal Houses, each of us helps the others.

'We have work to do. While the High Lord searches for Lord Rochant, our lands go unwatched and our enemies are free to act. But above all, while Lord Rochant is missing, we must protect his land as if it were our own. To this end I will be sending skilled people from my settlements to help secure the waterways.

'Leading them will be two of my senior staff, Vis and Mal.'

Mal's eyes went so wide with fear, he wondered if they were about to pop out. However, when Vis bowed, he managed to copy the gesture.

'My lord,' began Vis. 'You honour us. But I am a man of the sky. I know nothing about the woods or the Wild.'

'You protest my order?'

'No, no, I would not dream of such a thing. I fear that we are not worthy of this task you set before us.'

'Fear not, noble Vis. There will be Cutter-crafters and hunters with the necessary skills to navigate and survive the Wild. The problem is scale. There are so many people to manage and coordinate. And I can think of no other I'd rather send to manage such a complicated project, you've done such a fine job organizing my staff.'

He was pleased to see the man flinch before he crumpled into another bow. 'Thank you, my lord.'

'And Mal, your communication skills will be missed, make good use of them out there.'

He held his arms out to the two of them, inviting them close. 'We are one,' he said, embracing Mal and Vis together. Beneath his fingers, their shoulders shook. He squeezed, leaning forward to whisper. 'Tread carefully, my friends, I see you now.'

A gentle push sent them on their way.

Raising his voice, he addressed the room again. 'I have good news. As cover for Vis and Mal, I have asked Old Sen to come out of retirement: she will be performing both their inhouse roles. Not all of you will remember her, but trust me, you soon will.' A few of the longer term staff exchanged grim smiles.

Later, when he had dismissed the staff and returned to his quarters, Gada came to find him. Though there were no creases on his brother's brow or clothing, Vasin could feel his stress. A hunter's smile bloomed.

'Brother, welcome. We have much to discuss.'

Gada's answering smile was weak as ever. 'So I gather.'

After a firm embrace, Vasin offered refreshments which Gada declined. *Nerves always killed his appetite,* thought Vasin.

'You're looking well,' said Gada.

'Yes, I feel better than I have for a long time. More myself.'

'What's this I hear about a foray into the Wild?'

'I'm glad you asked. It would be good if we could combine our efforts on this.'

Vasin outlined his plans to patrol the Whitesnake river, before making sure Gada was up to speed on the mysterious dam-building going on there, in order to talk about building his own dam. 'If anything tries to disrupt the river's flow a second time,' he explained, 'we can control it at the source.'

Gada listened closely, holding his questions to the end. His brother was a good ear when he wanted to be, and while Vasin was absorbed in his talk, it was easy to forget his suspicions, to wish that things between them were, if not warm, easy again.

When he was finished, Gada made a face as if he'd just eaten something mildly disagreeable. 'This is a noble undertaking, brother. Do you not think we should seek the High Lord's permission first?'

'When he came here last, he was bemoaning our lack of initiative. I assumed he'd be pleased.'

Gada raised an eyebrow. 'I do not think it wise for us to make assumptions.'

'That's why I think you should go and explain it to him.'

'Me?'

'Yes, you're better at that sort of thing than I am.' While Gada struggled between wanting to accept the compliment and argue the point, Vasin added: 'You will help though, won't you?'

'Yes, yes, of course. I will have some of my people sent to aid yours. Do you think castle staff are the best suited to go?'

'You heard about that, then?'

'It's been discussed in every corridor, as I'm sure you're aware.' Gada's face softened in what Vasin assumed was supposed to be a patient, kindly manner. 'I don't mean to interfere—'

Oh but I think you do, thought Vasin.

'—but you've always been one for grand gestures. Wouldn't it be better to send one of the hunters to oversee the work? You've asked for my help in this project, so it seems fitting that I bring my expertise to it as well as my resources. Now, in my experience, it is much better to use people in the manner for which they were—'

Vasin held up a fist, uncurling the fingers a beat too late. 'No, I think Vis and Mal are exactly where they should be.'

There was a pause.

Gada took a half step back, a giving of ground, symbolic.

'So be it. Might I ask about your own plans for the immediate future?'

'Playing to my strengths. I'm going hunting.'

'Then I thank you for your hospitality. I'll pack my things and travel to Lord Rochant's castle today to present our plan to the High Lord. For both our sakes I hope that when you return, you have something to present. High Lord Yadavendra's patience is at an end, and I fear we are the ones his anger will fall upon.'

Vasin nodded. 'In that, we are agreed. Go safely, my brother. My doors are ever open to you.'

They embraced a final time. 'As mine are to you. *Hunt well and thorough.*'

Tucked away in tattered clothes, her skin lightened, the gold tattoos hidden from sight, Pari reentered the lands of House Sapphire. Lan was with her. He was pretending to be a trader, she was pretending to be his old grandmother, too far gone to be left alone.

Though the Godroad shimmered as blue here as it ever had, playing beautifully with the gold, red, red of the suns, the people on it had changed.

And not for the better, thought Pari.

They'd joined a caravan, Lan bargaining a place for them on one of the cheaper wagons bringing up the rear. There were no crystal-tipped wheels to be found, the wagon lumbering under the full weight of its cargo. And it was slow. Pari suspected the Dogkin pulling it were even older than her; a trio of mangy creatures, mostly toothless, their faces covered by fringes of grey fur.

Other civilian travellers on the Godroad were scarce;

instead they met with guards in House Sapphire livery. There was variation in them, some groups seeming to Pari more like costumed children or well-dressed bandits, but all of them forced the caravan to stop. Then came a barrage of questions, accompanied by a swift search of the wagons for babies and missing Deathless.

Pari was largely ignored, and if a guard came their way, she let Lan do the talking, feigning deafness rather than waste her energy. After a while she could recite their questions from memory.

There was an aggressiveness to the interactions that Pari took issue with. *They seem so ready to fight. It's as if they* want *a confrontation.*

Eventually they reached Sagan. Even from a distance, the place appeared swollen with people. For all of the sounds of industry and the new homes being built, she could see clots of men and women squatting in the streets, idle, starving.

In order to reach Varg's cottage on the far side of the settlement without being seen, Pari took Lan around Sagan's edge, the young man virtually bent double with the weight of her things. She walked carefully, skirting the Wild, using her staff to test the ground ahead – it was made of Wildwood, a gift from Lord Rochant early in their courtship. It was said to bring good fortune, though they'd both laughed at the idea of a piece of wood having power over her future.

I'll make my own luck, thank you very much.

As they drew closer, Lan began to slow down.

'Are you all right?' Pari asked.

'Yeah, I'm just a bit scared-like.'

'Scared of what?'

'That monster Dogkin.'

She laughed. 'Oh, you mean Glider?'

Lan nodded fearfully, the gesture making him seem very young.

'Don't worry about her. Glider's a stubborn girl but she won't hurt us. Besides, it doesn't look like she's home.'

Varg's wagon was parked outside the house. It appeared undamaged, and the emergency supplies of paint and food were secreted away in their usual hiding place. Everything seemed to be in order, and yet after one look at the house, Pari's heart sank.

'Be on your guard, Lan.'

'Is it proper bad?'

She didn't answer, turning her attention to how little of the building remained visible. The trees had grown since her last visit, their branches covering the side walls completely to curl around the front. Even the smaller cube on the top looked besieged by creepers. 'Oh no.'

Lan looked as if she'd just slapped him across the face. 'It's proper bad, in't it?'

She was nodding even before her eyes came to rest on the front step. 'The Wild has been here.'

'The Wild?' Lan followed her gaze. 'There's blood in the wood!'

'Yes, Lan. There's blood. But it's dried, whatever shed the blood is probably long gone. Stay here, I'm going to have a look inside.'

He set down the heavy pack with extreme care. 'But what if there's somethin' still in there? What if it gets ya?'

'That won't happen. But if it does then I want you to run from this place and keep running until you get back to my castle.'

'Okay.'

Pari crouched down and stared at the bloodstains for a while. Spatters could be found high up on the front wall of the house either side of the doorway. The step was saturated with it.

She straightened and examined the front door. The hinges had come loose at the top, giving it a slight lean. Sections of the frame had been punched clean off, allowing the door to swing both ways. Pari nudged it open with her staff and went inside.

The main room was a shambles. A battered pot lay on its side, the contents spewed out in a fan shaped puddle, dried to a thick crust and peppered with mould. Several sets of clothes had been abandoned here as well, one at her feet, another by the wall, two more in the middle of the room.

All of the clothes were bloodied and torn, as if something had ripped them from their owners. Among them she found Varg's knife, stained with use, and a long needle of the kind she'd encountered in Rochant's castle.

The assassins were here but it looks like they found more than they bargained for. Where are you, Varg? Did your life end here?

It was possible Varg had died in a disguise, but none of the clothes were his, and her instincts were telling her that if he had fallen, it was not in this room.

The second room was largely untouched. Things were a mess, as if someone had quickly searched here, but nothing was broken, and no one had died.

A ladder was set against the wall to allow access to the upper room. Crumpled at the bottom was a sad little pile of clothing and a single diminutive shoe.

Too small even for Honoured Mother Chandni, she thought, though it gave her little cheer.

Something had bled on the upper rungs. Pari took a deep breath, put down her staff, and started to haul herself up.

At the top she froze, her eyes just over the lip. Dappled sunslight shone through the windows highlighting a set of fingers hooked inches from her face. Child sized but too big, too pale, to be Satyendra's, they had been roughly severed just below the middle knuckle. Of the thumb or the rest of the body, there was no sign.

She left the house after that to find Lan shivering by the wagon. 'How many others did you say you found in the house besides Varg, Chandni, and the baby?'

'Four. This couple from Sorn an two little uns.'

'I think Varg and Chandni might still be alive.'

'You do?' Lan didn't sound convinced.

'The question is, where did they go?'

She turned slowly on the spot, looking at the buildings, the field and the trees beyond. 'Where did you go?' she murmured to herself. 'Lan, start working your way out from the house.'

'What am I looking for?'

'Tracks, signs or anything they might have dropped for us to find and follow. If something catches your eye, however trivial, then I want to know about it.'

She stood watch over their pack as Lan began to search. It was a risk, as she had a much better idea of the kind of trail Varg would leave, but Lan had stronger legs and more energy to burn.

He came back with a miserable expression on his face. 'I found this.'

She worried it would be another body part and that this time she would recognize the owner. However, it was too small for that, forcing her to squint and lean forward to identify it. Pinched between Lan's forefinger and thumb was a tuft of white fur.

'Well done!'

'Nah, you don't get it. This was caught on one of the trees. I think they've gone in the Wild.' He shrugged, helpless. 'I'm sorry.'

Pari resisted the urge to slap the boy. 'It's obvious they've gone into the Wild. Much better they be alive in there, than dead here. Now come on, we have to go after them.'

'We can't go in there!' he exclaimed. 'Nobody goes in there! It's death!'

'Calm down, Lan dear. You forget who you're travelling with. That may be death but I am Deathless. In the Wild, I am the hunter.'

'But—'

'And if you say anything about the age of this body, I will prove the lie of it by battering you to death. Well?'

He closed his mouth.

'Much better. Let's move to the far side of the house, in case anyone is watching from Sagan.'

Once there, Pari bid Lan open the pack and unwrap the contents. As the padding fell away, her Tanzanite armour winked up at them. She'd had mixed feelings about bringing it here, for this was all the proof that Lady Yadva or Lord Taraka would need to bury her. But where they were going, it was neither Sapphire nor Tanzanite that she needed to worry about.

At least not for now.

Donning it was a slow process. Despite her earlier rebuttal, she was slowing down, and Lan was a poor replacement for a team of Gardener-smiths. However, both were committed, and piece by piece, they covered her in a second skin of crystal.

She pricked her finger to make the tiniest of cuts, and used the blood to daub the crystal, waking it, before pulling on her gauntlet.

She took a breath, and felt the armour breathe with her, the two movements becoming one as she exhaled. *There. It's done.*

The fears that she'd been holding down began to ease, that sense of completeness that always accompanied the armour giving her strength. It still fit perfectly, taking the strain from her joints, straightening her spine.

On some level, she realized, Lan had forgotten exactly what she was. He remembered now, she could see it in his awe-slack face. She took the coiled whip from his uncertain hands, and checked the barb. It was still sharp, and the cable still stretched and telescoped as well as it ever did.

'Add the supplies from the wagon to our own. I don't want to waste time foraging.'

He leapt to her order, timid as a baby Mousekin. When their things were packed again, he gave a worried look towards the trees. 'What should I do when we're inside?'

'Stay close to me.' She could see he was barely holding it together and considered leaving him behind. But someone needed to carry their food. 'Here,' she said, 'take my staff.'

He accepted it, running a hand over the polished surface.

'It's Wildwood, cut and treated, and given to me by a dear friend. Keep it close and it will bring you good fortune.'

Lan brightened considerably upon hearing this. 'I will.'

It didn't take long for Pari's eyes to pick out another bit of white fur, half buried in the mud, and she set off in pursuit of the rest of it, Lan scurrying after.

Vasin soared through the afternoon sky. He felt good. He felt exultant. Gada had been put in his place, his castle was his own again, and Yi had managed to escape with Lord Rochant without sounding the alarm.

Some way behind him were his hunters, but their orders would soon be sending them elsewhere.

And even if they wanted to, he thought, *they could not hope to catch me!*

Mia, his lead hunter, had appealed to travel with him. 'Should we not be at your side, my lord? How can our spears defend you if we are not together?'

'I travel too far for you to follow. If you and the others came with me, you would not be able to get back.'

'We would all take that risk to protect you.'

'But I am in no danger. Whatever happens, I will return.' In that moment he resolved to take her as a mate when he returned. *I have neglected to have children in this lifecycle for too long.* 'You are irreplaceable, Mia. Should anything happen to me, the responsibility of keeping the hunters disciplined will fall on your shoulders. I trust no other.'

'But I am not the oldest.'

'Nor am I, but we are the best, and on the hunt, that is all that matters.'

And she had said nothing more because it was true.

He banked sharply to the right, circling, showing off his prowess. The formation of hunters, even further back than he'd expected, raised their spears in salute, Mia at their head. He returned the gesture, turned away, and dived sharply towards the carpet of green beneath.

Out of the corner of his eye, he caught a flash of light from within the trees. He felt as much as saw it, and was alarmed, for down there was a hint of crystal, of not-Sapphire.

What was it then? he wondered as the tree tops became distinct, giving him the impression that they were racing towards him rather than the other way around. *Could House Ruby still be here on Sapphire land?*

He could not understand why the Ruby High Lord would be this far south. It just didn't fit, and anyway, that brief sighting had not seemed like a ruby.

The demands of flying took over his thoughts as he pulled out of his dive, skimming above the canopy. Soon, a gap in the trees could be seen, a dark spot amid the green. He rose up, so that his wings were vertical, dragging against the current, coming to a stop just over the hole. With hands raised, he plunged down, feet first, like a dagger into the Wild's heart. His Sky-legs took the impact of his landing, the curved blades bending like a second set of knees.

The sound of his descent echoed through the trees and he could hear the answering sound of movement, of creatures small and large taking action. He smiled to himself.

They're running away.

He walked the rest of the way to avoid attention, and though it was nothing compared to the thrill of taking wing, the way the Sky-legs lengthened his stride and gave energy to every step was enjoyable.

Yi was waiting for him at the rendezvous, hooded and

masked, her skinny frame bulked out with padding under the cloak. At her feet, bound, gagged, and drugged, was Lord Rochant. Vasin had no idea how she had carried him from the road but decided not to ask. Yi's ability to get things done was almost magical, not to mention reassuring.

'Were you seen?' he asked.

She shook her head. 'Were you?'

'Only when I wished to be,' he replied, but the question rankled. This had been the fastest and easiest way to get here, but was it the safest? Would Gada have been able to send people to follow him on the ground? Would Yadavendra?

It is done now, he thought. *Let them come.*

When he wore his crystal skin, his thoughts often turned this way, direct, reckless. There was a sense that he could do anything, face anything. That he was better than this! He'd learned that the relationship between the Deathless and their armour was nuanced, somewhere between rider and steed or parent and child, and he was in control.

He pointed at Lord Rochant with the tip of his spear. 'How long before he wakes?'

'Not long. An hour, maybe two.'

'That should be sufficient.'

'I should warn you, he's been feigning sleep.'

It didn't really matter, out here, whether Rochant were asleep or awake. One handed, he grabbed one of the coils around Rochant's chest and swung him over a shoulder, effortlessly.

'You should go before the suns do.'

'My orders?'

'Return to my castle and watch.'

She bowed, turned and broke into a run, making straight

for the Godroad, while Vasin went in the opposite direction, heading towards the remains of Sorn.

With the extra weight, Vasin couldn't stay in the sky long, but he moved swiftly in a series of bounding glides, swinging Rochant back and forth for balance and momentum.

Nothing barred his path, the forest emptying at his approach, indeed even the trees seemed to back away, the way ahead always open and easy.

Still, he stayed alert for trouble. Alone and on the ground, he was vulnerable. It would not do to be caught out here as his Uncle Umed was. Beneath the dark cloak of the trees, the suns felt far away, almost as if they were in a different sky. He knew the things of the Wild responded to their light, weakened by it in some way, just as they were by the light of the Godroad. It was why nothing twisted flew high in the day.

As the suns set, a little of his bravado went with them. *What if they are not running after all? What if they're waiting?*

With no ambient light to drown it out, the glow of his armour became more prominent, as if a new sun, a sapphire one, were rising to replace the old.

It was rare for hunts to take place at night, and so despite his lifecycles of experience, Vasin had spent little time in the forest after sunset. It shocked him how different it felt. Was it his imagination, or did the trees seem to loom more than they did before?

The way ahead became trickier, tangled bushes threatening to catch at his Sky-legs, and hanging vines his wings. As he came down, taking the energy of his landing and gathering it to spring again, he saw someone in the darkness to his left.

Another leap, another landing, and they were still there, keeping pace.

Not a person, he somehow knew. *A thing.*

Thoughts flew through his mind as he arced into the air again. He could face his pursuer here or press on. If he fought, he'd have Lord Rochant to manage as well as himself. In the mess of a fight, his prisoner might be killed or he might find some way to escape. Vasin couldn't allow either.

If he pushed on, it was not that far to Sorn. Perhaps he could outrun it. Given the choice, he'd much rather fight in a cleared space than in the tangle of the trees.

He had to twist to keep clear of the branches as he came down, their tips shrieking against the inside of his left wing. Also to his left was his pursuer, coming down to land a beat after like a bulky shadow.

When he leapt, it leapt too. Not as high as him but covering similar ground.

From the little he had seen of it he could tell it was large, of at least equivalent size to him in his armour. It was also fast, confident, forcing him forward.

It's acting like a hunter.

Suddenly certain that he was being manoeuvred, Vasin changed tactic. This time, when his Sky-legs touched the ground, he turned towards his pursuer, kicking off at an angle so that their next leaps would intersect.

Mid-air, Lord Rochant dangling from one arm, it was difficult to aim his spear. The creature was already aware of his approach but was unable to do much about it, having already committed itself.

The soft blue glow extended in front of him, giving shape to a dark carapace and horns curving out from the eyesockets

315

of a massive humanoid skull. He saw five limbs. Two legs that bent back at the knee, shiny, black, powerful, and three arms where there should be four, their shape well known, and in that moment he realized his mistake.

The Scuttling Corpseman! screamed his brain. *I'm fighting the Scuttling Corpseman.*

He thrust the spear for its head but it was faster, grabbing the shaft in one hand while grabbing Vasin with the other two. Locked together now, they landed, the Corpseman rising up on its rear legs.

Vasin found his feet no longer touched the ground. As they struggled, the point of his spear wavered but moved no closer to its target.

He'd experienced the disorienting closeness of a thing of the Wild before but never on this scale. The Corpseman smelt of ash and sweet decay, and the sight of it filled Vasin's vision, leaving little room for thought.

But he was Deathless, and some part of him was not cowed. Adjusting the grip on the shaft, Vasin pulled the trigger, and the crystal tip of the spear shot forward on a thin cable, cracking the black shell of the Corpseman's shoulder and burying itself in the meat within.

The monster gave a reflexive lurch and the next thing Vasin knew he was flying backwards, the spear ripped from his grasp. He struck ground a second later, his back first, then his skull.

Before he could get up, before sense could fully return, it was after him, scuttling forward with terrifying speed, his spear still dangling from one shoulder. Ten feet from him, it jumped, arms drawn back to strike.

With nothing else to hand, Vasin raised Lord Rochant like

a shield, putting the bound man between his face and the Corpseman's attack.

He felt the impact of the Corpseman's feet planting either side of him and braced for what was coming.

The moment drew out. Time and again, his heart pounded in his chest, but no attack came. Was it playing with him? Very slowly, he lowered Rochant a fraction, ready to raise him again if need be.

Nothing lurked in the darkness. Even the sense that radiated from the Corpseman was gone. He was alone, save for his prisoner and the whispering trees. As he slowly picked himself up off the ground, it became clear that the Scuttling Corpseman had spared them both, and for the life of him, Vasin could not understand why. *Gone, and my spear with it. Damn. I'll neve see that again.*

It was still dark when Vasin reached the edge of Sorn. He'd approached from the trees, keeping plenty of cover between him and the Godroad, but all seemed quiet. Were it not for the lack of lanterns, it would be possible to imagine the village was merely resting.

For the first time he wondered what had happened to its people. He'd heard many had fled to their neighbour, Sagan, and others had gone to Lord Rochant's castle to beg sanctuary, but he suspected that a large number remained unaccounted for.

Like most of the Sapphire settlements, Sorn hugged both sides of the Godroad, with the most desirable houses nearest, the less desirable ones in the second row, and the farming land spreading out beyond, high-fenced.

There was little left of that perimeter now, great chunks of barrier torn down or smashed, leaving several of the posts standing alone, exclamation marks without a point. The soil of the field was gouged with deep lines, as if heavy weights had been taken from the village, dragged to the forest's edge and beyond.

He came to a stop in the central street that divided this section of houses and called out: 'Mother?'

There was probably a better way to do this, but he couldn't think of it. An ache ran from shoulder blades to tailbone, and his head still felt fuzzy. He needed to stop and rest.

'Mother?' he called again.

A light appeared in one of the houses, the yellow of a torch. Without hesitation, he went to meet it. His mother was waiting in the doorway, and he dropped Rochant in the dirt to scoop her off her feet.

'Sweet one,' she said, 'I did not expect you.'

He laughed bitterly. 'Nothing is as I expect any more, Mother.'

She tapped on his visor and pointed towards the floor. After he had put her down, she gave Rochant's body a nudge with her foot. 'Is this . . . ?'

'Yes.'

The look she gave Vasin was chilling. 'Why is he still alive?'

'I can explain—' he began but she cut him off.

'Not here. Come inside, we'll find a place for this scum,' her foot made a second, more forceful contact with Rochant's body, 'and then you can tell me everything.'

He had to duck and move carefully to manoeuvre his wings through the doorway. There was no door to shut behind him, only a few splinters, but his mother stretched a piece of hide across the opening.

A small fire crackled, barely strong enough to heat the room, a bed of furs laid out next to it. They stashed Rochant next door, his mother tying him to the wall and then attaching a bell to the end of the rope.

Vasin didn't feel the cold in his armour but was sure his mother would. 'Have you lived here, like this, for over a year?'

She came back into the room and sat by the fire, cupping her hands around its meagre flame. 'What else did you expect? A palace hidden in the Wild? Servants?'

He hadn't really thought about it. He'd assumed she was dead. 'I'm sorry.'

'Don't tell me you're sorry. I don't have time for sorry.' She shook her head. 'I don't have time any more. Do you understand, my sweet one? I don't have time.'

Her body was around half a century. Not old but not young either. The golden tattoos that once marked it had been burned off, leaving puffy white scars, the edge of one just visible through a hole in her trouser leg.

Vasin crouched down so that he could lay a hand on her shoulder. 'It's not too late.'

'Tell me of your progress.'

'One of Lord Rochant's descendants eluded your people, a baby. If we can find it, we can end his line.' *How easily I say these things now, and how easily she hears them. Was Mother always this ruthless or has the Wild changed her?*

She clapped her hands together before rubbing them vigorously over the fire. 'What went wrong?'

'What didn't? Nothing worked out as you planned. There was interference on the night of the attack. Another Deathless. I'm told it was Lady Pari of House Tanzanite. She killed some of Yi's team. And then Dil . . . He's not the man you thought he was. When things started to unravel he panicked. With a descendant still alive, he didn't dare kill Rochant, in case he was reborn and could take revenge, so he brought him to my castle.

'The High Lord arrived shortly after. I don't know how the news reached him so fast. It's been all I can do to hide Rochant.'

'Lady Pari, you say? That's a long way for her to go.' Vasin heard her sigh. 'He always was able to win people's hearts.'

'You sound as if you admire him.'

She turned from the fire, her face a set of pale lines. 'I do. I knew him before he was Deathless, before he became my brother's pet. He was a fine man once. Brilliant, in his own way. So yes, I admire him, almost as much as I hate him.'

'I tried to question him, Mother, to find out where the baby is . . . I couldn't do it. I thought that maybe you . . . '

'Yes,' she said.

He eased himself down next to her and pulled off his helmet. They both stared at the circular cracks winding out from the back of it.

I must have hit the ground harder than I realized.

'What happened?'

He lowered his voice. 'The Corpseman. We fought on the outskirts. I wasn't strong enough to take it alone. It had me, Mother, at its mercy, but it didn't kill me. Why?' She didn't answer, and as the fire crackled quietly between them, a nasty thought entered his mind. 'How did you take its arm, Mother? You had no hunters, no wings, no armour. I don't understand how you fought it off, let alone maimed it.'

'Do you doubt my integrity? Do you imagine that I traded a piece of my soul for the Corpseman's arm? Do you think, if I truly was an ally of the Wild, that I would be hiding in this graveyard?'

He held up his hands. 'No, please, I just need you to explain it to me.'

Her eyes went back to the fire. 'It's true I didn't have my armour and I was alone here. Can you imagine what that's like, to be abandoned by your own family?' She saw the way he flinched and her tone softened. 'I wasn't completely forgotten though. Yi managed to smuggle me a weapon before they cast me out. Though Yadavendra had made a show of breaking my spear, he hadn't attended to what happened to the remains. When the spectacle was over, she managed to sneak in and steal the head, fashioning the broken end into a crude handle.'

She produced what looked like a cross between a dagger and a saw. Two feet of sharp crystal, with teeth running down one edge. It looked too big for its hilt, Vasin's mind expecting it to be mounted on a much grander shaft. *Diminished,* he thought sadly.

'There wasn't much of a fight. It was nearly on me by the time I saw it and I knew I couldn't win, so I ran. I wish I could tell you that I had a clever reason,' she waved a hand, 'something about it being territorial and me trying to cross beyond its boundaries, or about moving to fight on better terrain. But the truth is I saw how big it was and I was scared.'

Vasin hadn't even considered that she could be scared. The mother of his memories was always in control, a sharp contrast to the hunched figure of the present.

'I didn't run far,' she continued. 'It came down on me with the speed and precision of our greatest hunters. At the last second, I turned to attack. I knew I'd only have one chance and that I had to make it count. I managed to get my blade into one of its armpits, where the shell is thin and flexible. The Corpseman's own momentum drove it home until I could feel its shell against my knuckles.

'Then it had me by the head with that same arm. I tried to work the knife but most of my vision was covered by its palm and I was in such pain . . . '

It seemed to Vasin that her hands rose unconsciously, to press against her temples.

'But that wasn't the worst of it. You've seen its arm. Do you remember the antennae on its knuckles?'

'Yes.'

'They were moving, probing between its fingers to run over my scalp. I could feel them . . . on my skin . . . and inside . . . I could feel the Corpseman inside my skull. I . . . Oh, my sweet one, I don't have the words. In a way, I'm glad. Perhaps it's better you not truly know.

'I don't recall how long we stood there, but at some point I became aware that the pain had stopped. Its presence was still so strong as to be overwhelming but some part of me was able to think again. I couldn't get its hand from off my head and I was sure that at any moment it would finish me off. Then I realized that my knife was still embedded, my hand pressed against its shell. I began to saw. Carefully at first, and then when it didn't react, desperately.

'It began to make this high-pitched sound and I knew it was in pain. That spurred me on. It was hard work. I was half-blind and so afraid, but I knew this was my only chance.'

She began making a slight back and forth motion with her hand, as if her body were reliving the moment. 'When it came free, there was no blood, just liquid that bubbled thickly in the wound. I still remember the way it steamed in the air. Throughout, it was just standing there, making this terrible noise.' Her shoulders gave a weak shrug. 'When I realized it wasn't going to attack, I picked up its arm and ran.'

Vasin felt his eyes well up with tears. 'I'm sorry,' he said, before wincing.

She straightened, whatever expression her face was wearing fading to something stronger, a secret kept by the fire. 'But no more of that. We have other things to discuss, like what your uncles have been up to, and how your search for allies progresses.'

'House Ruby is preparing to move against Yadavendra, they say that others stand with them. They'll back me, I'm sure of it.'

'Good. What about within House Sapphire?'

'I've not had much luck there. I think Yadva could be won over. I can't speak for Umed.'

Her eyes narrowed. 'My coward of a sibling? He'll go whichever way seems easiest. Yadavendra scares him, so if you want his support, you'll have to scare him more.' She took his arm. 'Win Yadva over. If you have her and Gada, and outside support, Umed will come over to you.'

'Mother, I don't know how to say this but I'm not sure about Gada.'

'What?'

'He's set on winning Yadavendra's favour. He thinks you're dead.'

'My Gada has always been cautious, but have faith, sweet one. When you are in position, tell him the truth and he will stand with you.'

Vasin nodded. It was what he wanted to hear, and yet, for the first time, he found himself questioning his mother's judgement.

'Now,' she said. 'Rest. You need your strength and you need to steel yourself. We are going to face Lord Rochant. It will not be easy.'

He found himself unable to meet her eye. 'What are you going to do?'

'Get the answers we seek. One way or another.'

CHAPTER FIFTEEN

Within the tree, they all had places now, little slices of space where they slept and kept their things. 'Fiya, I've been thinking,' said Chandni from her spot, 'what you said, that your family were once part of House Sapphire. At first I assumed they were connected to Nidra, but they can't be, her banishment was only two years ago. You've lived here your whole life.'

The old woman blinked at her. 'You asking me a question?'

'No. Well, yes. My question is, if you don't mind me asking, which Deathless did your family serve?'

'The Sapphire High Lord, Samarku.'

'Yadavendra's predecessor.' *The one who betrayed us to the Wild.*

Fiya's face soured. 'Don't say that name here.'

'My apologies.' It felt wrong invading Fiya's privacy, but if they were going to stay, Chandni had to know more. 'Could you tell me about Samarku?'

'No.'

'Oh.'

Sensing the change in atmosphere, Glider lifted her head to see what was wrong. Chandni reached out and stroked her until she settled again.

Fiya tutted loudly. 'The faces on you! You'd sour milk. There's others keep the past better than me. You can talk to them if you want.'

'Yes, I'd like that.'

'Well then, you'd better get your things. We've got a long day's walking ahead of us.'

Chandni and Varg exchanged another look.

'I told you,' said Fiya, with the implication that they were either stupid or very, very forgetful, 'we live separate but we meet up from time to time. Next meet is tomorrow. I don't normally go but seeing that you're here I can make an exception.'

'Tomorrow?' asked Varg.

'Yes. I didn't say anything because I wanted time to make my mind up about you first.'

'And have you?'

'Wouldn't be telling you if I hadn't.' Fiya got up and started to put some of the filthy jars in her bag. 'Enough talking. You're worse than Devdan.' She glared at Chandni as she opened her mouth to ask who Devdan was. 'Ask him. When we get there, you can ask him all of your questions. He'll tell you anything you want to know, so long as you don't mind long answers.' As the old woman packed her bag, she continued to mutter to herself. 'Why do people want to talk so much all the time? Tires me out just listening to them.'

Fiya opened up a jar, scooped some muddy paste from it with her fingers, and started smearing it on her face. She bid Chandni do the same.

She and Varg had tried using dirt to cover their scent before, but when she brought the jar to her nose, she could tell this was something else. Mixed scents of crushed leaves, a fiery spice and what she hoped was just very pungent dirt. 'You want me to put this on my face?'

'Your face, hands, neck, and your baby.'

'What about Glider?'

Glider barked derisively and pressed herself against the trunk.

'Don't be ridiculous,' Fiya snapped.

Satyendra allowed himself to be coated without complaint. He even shared a few smiles with her when Varg started moaning. 'I know it smells bad,' she whispered, dabbing a little on Satyendra's chin. 'But if it keeps us safe, I don't care.'

Glider seemed to care, however, keeping as much distance between them as the hollow trunk allowed.

They packed some of the dried fruit and nuts they had left and slipped out of the tree. For someone who didn't like talking, Fiya talked often, stopping to point out particular flowers or to lecture them on the way they walked. 'It's not about being quick,' she said. 'It's about not needing to be. With the right preparations, and a bit of luck, you can move through the trees like a ghost.'

Chandni watched the way the old woman walked, slow, unhurried, she slipped easily under low hanging branches. No brambles caught on her clothes, and when she looked at the path behind, it was only her and Varg's tracks she could see.

'You need to start listening. Get to know the sounds that are natural so you can tell when they stop. The paste I gave you makes us hard to sense but we're not invisible.'

'What do we do if they stop?' asked Varg.

'Move away but don't run, that's like shouting here. You can usually tell which way the trouble is from the way everything else reacts.' She stopped and looked at them. 'But if it's close, then you don't move at all. You hide and wait. Let something else get its attention.'

Chandni digested that as they travelled. Up till now, she'd seen the Wild through a filter of fear, the whole place a jumble of shadows and sharp edges. Travelling with Fiya, it was possible to appreciate the beauty and variation of the place. Whiteleaf flowers as big as her hand, their petals like velvet, that moved whenever they sensed sunslight; Stranglethorn vines lashed between trees, so thick as to bury them; and what she thought were brambles but actually turned out to be baby Hedgekin, rolled up tight while their mother was away.

She edged closer to Varg. 'Aren't they adorable?'

'Nah. Just looks like another thousand ways to get cut and die to me.'

'They are so much more. It all is. Don't you see? We've been scrabbling to survive on the edge of the Wild for as long as I can remember. Only the hunts go deep enough to bring back the plants we need for medicine, face paint, and food dye. Imagine what we could learn here! If we could bring that knowledge back home, it could change the way we live.'

'Keep your voice down.' He gave a wary glance in Fiya's direction. 'She thinks we're exiles like her. Better keep it that way if you want her to stay friendly.'

Chandni nodded. 'Of course, but aren't you a little excited?'

'Getting to the end of the day is enough for me.'

As they walked on, Chandni flexed her right hand,

watching the fingers to remind herself they were there. Since their visit to the Hunger Tree, the poison had stopped spreading through her body. While the numbness hadn't got any worse, stopping halfway along her upper arm, it hadn't got any better either.

I have to prepare myself for the idea that it will never improve.

She had to actively work to stop knocking into things, as if some part of her mind had forgotten that the arm was there. Her main fear was that she would cut herself while travelling and not notice the blood until it was too late. In a way, it was like having a second baby to look after, one that never complained or woke her in the middle of the night.

She noticed that Varg had gone closer to Fiya. 'When this is done,' he said. 'Would we be able to go to Sorn?'

The old woman could not have looked more shocked if his beard had suddenly burst into flame. 'What? No! Why in the name of the Thrice Blessed Suns would you want to go there?'

'We thought there might be supplies, y'know, things we could use.'

'Sorn belongs to the Corpseman now. To go there is death.'

Varg said nothing after that and fell back, the colour gone from his face. Before Fiya had picked them up, they'd been leaving a trail for Lady Pari to follow. Now it seemed that they had unwittingly set a trap for their saviour, one that would send her straight to the Corpseman, and whatever else dwelt in the ruins of Sorn.

Sa-at yawned, his mind stretching along with his body.

I have a yawn!

He wasn't sure which part of him a yawn was yet, but the fact that he had one was very exciting.

Devdan appeared excited too, humming to himself as he gathered various objects Sa-at didn't know and placed them carefully into a bag. 'Big day today!' he exclaimed. 'We're going to go and meet the family. Most of us are old, and even the young ones are full grown now, so they are all going to be fussing all over you.' He gently prodded Sa-at's belly for emphasis.

This initiated his new favourite game. Sa-at pointed at things and Devdan said their names. He started with things he knew:

'Foot,' said Devdan. 'Head. Fingers.' Devdan wiggled his and Sa-at giggled. Sa-at's own finger kept moving. 'Ear. Lips. Nose. How about we try something new today?' The old man pointed to the thick curls of white above his eye. 'Eyebrow.'

Eyebrow.

Its name is eyebrow.

Devdan has an eyebrow!

Devdan pointed at Sa-at's face. 'Eyebrow.'

I have an eyebrow!

'Right, now it's your turn. Foot.'

Sa-at pointed at his foot.

'Very good! Head. Do you know where your head is?'

Sa-at thought for a moment and pointed at Devdan.

'No, that's my head.' He tapped his temple. 'Devdan's head.' He tapped Sa-at's. 'Your head. Now, where's your head?' He smiled when Sa-at got it right and the baby beamed back. 'Good! That's real good. I've gotta say, you're much smarter than the other babies I looked after. Maybe it's being born in the sky that does it.'

They went through the list, finishing with Sa-at finding their eyebrows.

'Well, that's us packed. Are you ready to go outside? Of course you are. You're not going to make any noise when we go are you? Because if you do, I might have to drop you somewhere. Understand? We have to be quiet.'

He wrapped Sa-at in one of the skins before picking him up.

'Now, might be that one of those demons comes after you again but if that happens, don't you worry. I'll keep you safe.' He bent down and scooped some ash from the floor. 'Don't know why, but everything that lives out there is terrified of this. That's why I live in this old blasted trunk. Means I can sleep without having to worry about some demon coming to eat my face off. So, if anything comes to give us trouble, I'll throw some of this at them.

'All right then, you ready? Course you are. You're a born Wildsman, you are.'

They stepped outside, gold shining down through the leaf-less branches. Devdan and Sa-at lifted their heads to the warmth. 'Feel that on your skin? That's Fortune's Eye. The big red sun is called Vexation and the little one, you can hardly see it with the other two so bright, is Wrath's Tear. Might as well soak it up while you can because we won't see much of them from here on in.'

Sa-at stared about him at all the different shapes and colours. His finger hovered in the air, unsure where to point first. A part of his mind was still repeating the names of the suns over and over, while his head wobbled back and forth, trying to see everything at once.

When he finally did start pointing, Devdan whispered in

his ear, a barrage of new information. That, coupled with the gentle rocking motion, soon sent him to sleep.

He dreamed of words and things and songs and wings and Whispercages and mouths and pain and – he woke up. Devdan still held him, the old man's lips smacking occasionally as he worked a piece of scale jerky.

'Welcome back. Think you were having a nightmare, had to shake you out of it cos I couldn't risk you calling out. A baby crying out here, well, that don't bear thinking about. Might be your new teeth playing up. Want something to chew?' He fished out another chunk of scale jerky and Sa-at reached for it and stuffed it into his mouth. 'Yeah, that's it. Thought that was it. I'm a natural with little ones, me.

'We're not far from the meet now. Don't worry if there's no one there. I'm normally the first. It's good though, means we can set the place up and we get to take the best seats. I can't wait to see their faces when they get their first look at you. Yeah,' he said, pausing to chew, 'our first sky-born baby.'

Sa-at looked up at the trees. From high up in the branches, he could see something familiar looking down at him. He pointed at it.

'Hey, hey, what's set you to squirming?'

Sa-at pointed up and Devdan stopped, squinting to try and see. 'Whatever it was, it's gone now. Probably just a bit of sunslight catching a wet leaf. They sparkle sometimes but that's all it was, just a sparkle.'

As Devdan set off again, Sa-at kept pointing.

Crowflies, he thought, delighted. Memories of soft feathers and sour meat rising in his mind. *Its name is Crowflies.*

*   *   *

Pari had followed the trail of white fur, some of it naturally caught on clawed branches, other bits stuffed by hand into bushes. They'd travelled through the night and not been challenged.

'You see, Lan dear, nothing will attack while you're with me.' This was a lie but, like the one concerning the staff she'd given him, it seemed to calm the boy. The truth was more complicated. For all the things her tanzanite armour would repel, there were others it would attract. Her plan hinged on not meeting any of those others.

They'd come across several hiding places that Varg had used to sleep in, and from the indentations in the earth he'd not been alone. *I just hope the baby is still alive or this is all for nothing.* 'We're getting closer,' she told Lan.

'We are?'

'Yes. They rested here, in the hollow under this tree. You see the lines gouged in the dirt?'

Lan nodded.

'They're a symbol. Varg left it for me. I know where they're going. From how roughly its made I also know he made it with something blunt. That means he's unarmed and we need to hurry and find him before something else does.'

She made sure he'd had a good look at the sign, a set of simple lines, crisscrossing, to make an arrow. There would come a day when he might need to use it, if her plans for him came to fruition. That was part of being a Deathless, to prepare for the demands of the future even while attending to the present.

'M-my lady?' Lan stammered as she set off, her Sky-legs carrying her so fast that he had to hurry to keep pace. 'Ain't we going the wrong way?'

'No this is the way, I assure you.'

'But the arrow?' he said, pointing off in the opposite direction. 'It was showing that way.'

'Indeed it was, my observant one. With that being the case, why do you think Varg set the arrow to lie?'

Lan gasped. 'Oh, he's doing that so that if them killers find it, they'll not know where he is.'

'Exactly.'

'Sneaky.'

She winked at him. 'Always.'

They travelled on, the black of night shifting to grey as the suns prepared to rise. The ache in her back and thighs was mitigated by her armour but not entirely banished. This was a concern, as usually only the worst pains could reach a Deathless when fully exalted. *If I feel this bad now, I dread to think what it will be like when the crystal comes off.* She put it from her mind, focusing instead on the size of favour Rochant would owe her when this was done, and what kind of things she might ask him for.

The trail became harder to follow and, after an abrupt change of direction, the tracks seemed to vanish entirely. She came to a stop and considered her options.

'Can we go home?' asked Lan, without much hope.

She ignored the question. 'We could go back to the original trail and assume they'd return to that course, or we could follow this one and hope to pick it up again, but in either case we might get lost and lose them entirely.'

'Has he left any more arrow marks?'

'No.' She looked around. 'Varg hasn't left us anything for a while which, if I'm honest, is not a good sign. But if they were forced to run, there probably wasn't time.

'It doesn't matter. From the direction they were going and the previous marks, I already know their destination. We'll go there directly.'

'Where they goin'?'

'Sorn. It's not far from here.'

They reached the outskirts a few hours later, the light from Fortune's Eye giving a golden glow to the leaves. Lan was puffing at her side, the tough pace and lack of sleep getting to him. Pari didn't dare stop though, in part because she was genuinely afraid for Varg, but equally because she feared she'd not be able to start again.

A savage strength had taken down the fence protecting Sorn's farmland from the Wild's edge. Amidst the broken pieces of wood, Pari found discarded tools and weapons. 'There was a fight here. The people of Sorn mounted a resistance to whatever came for them.' She shook her head. 'Look at this, Lan. A few sharpened pieces of wood and the odd stone-headed spear. Not a piece of crystal to be found. They never had a chance.'

Lan covered his mouth. 'I know that hammer. Belonged to me cousin. She stayed behind when me an Ami left.' Tears budded in his eyes as he stared at the shattered perimeter of his former home. 'Why din't the Sapphire help us?'

'I don't know,' Pari replied. 'But I promise you I'll find out. Lord Rochant would never have stood by when one of his settlements called for aid, and I'm sure this is connected to the attempts on his life. Something is rotten in House Sapphire.'

'We gotta make 'em pay.'

'Yes. Yes we do. The best way to achieve that is to restore Lord Rochant to power. I can only do so much from the outside, and to do even that, I need to find Varg.'

Lan's tears were flowing freely now. She sighed, not having the energy to be patient but not having the heart to force him on. The horrors hinted at here might only be a taste of what they could find further in.

A single teardrop followed the line of Lan's jaw to collect on the bottom of his chin, others followed, the droplet grew, fell, and her eyes tracked it down to the dirt. When she looked up again, there was a new addition to the landscape. It was watching them.

'Lan,' she whispered.

Something in her tone cut through his grief and his eyes snapped up to meet hers. 'Yeah?'

'Very slowly, I want you to get behind me.'

'Wot is it?' he asked, turning to follow her gaze.

'Don't look,' she hissed, and he froze. 'Just do it.'

As Lan edged round behind her, it broke the cover of the trees, scuttling forward on five legs. Easily a match for Glider's size, but black where the Dogkin was white, shiny where it was furred.

Pari let the whip she was carrying uncoil, shaking it out, ready.

The demon before her rose up on its rear legs, and in the sunlight she could see it in all its terrible glory. Three plated arms hung from its body where once there were four, and on its shoulders sat a large human skull. At first she thought that curved horns sprouted from the eyesockets, but with a start she realized they were moving, a pair of feelers straightening until they stabbed towards her. Smaller antennae grew from its knuckles and these too shifted, pointing the same way.

Though Pari hadn't met it before, she had heard the tales of the Story-singers.

336

'Is that . . . ' asked Lan.

'Yes,' replied Pari, not wanting to say its name out loud: *the Scuttling Corpseman*. 'Let us hope it is merely curious.'

They stood facing each other while the Corpseman raised its arms, seeming to probe the air between them.

The hairs prickled on the back of Pari's neck. She could feel the demon as strongly as see it, a sense of strangeness, of something both alive and dead, visceral, almost a taste on her tongue.

It was hard to read. There was no expression to be found in the bone of its face, and the chitinous armour hid the play of its muscles, but Pari somehow knew the attack was coming a moment before its knees flexed backwards.

She bounded forward to get into range and lashed out with her whip, the barb seeking out one of the thick antenna on its head. Impossibly fast, the Corpseman flinched away, avoiding her strike, but the movement had stolen its momentum, giving her a precious second before it could spring for her.

As Pari cracked the whip a second time, keeping the monster at bay, she noticed more details. An old wound where the fourth arm had been that had healed badly, and a fresh one at its shoulder where the shell was cracked.

If a team of hunters were at her side, she would have used them to distract it and then exploit those weak points. As it was, it was taking all of her efforts just to hold the Corpseman back. The barb of her whip sparked off its armoured forearms as it made little hops towards her, closing the distance slowly.

It isn't scared nor is it attacking blindly. It's wearing me down as I would a common animal.

She tried a feint, seeming to aim for its head while she struck out for a knee, yet even as she switched stance, the small antennae on its hands twitched in response, and it leaped.

It's reading me!

Too late, she realized it had been edging her into its range, and now it was in the air, arcing towards her.

There was no time to turn, and she knew that meeting it in close combat was death, so Pari dived forward springing underneath its attack.

They crossed in the air like gymnasts, one going over, one under. The Corpseman's hard fingertips clawed against her wings but failed to take hold, and then she was through, the demon behind her.

Pari landed on her hands and knees, scrabbling to get her Sky-legs beneath her as the Corpseman plunged into the dirt she'd been standing in just seconds ago.

I have to run, she thought. *Loop round and make for the Godroad. It's my only chance.*

She jumped once, then twice, getting her speed up. The third leap took her high enough to trust her wings to the essence currents. They were too weak to climb but if she could maintain her height, she might be able to glide to safety.

Again, she sensed the Corpseman as much as heard it leaping for her, and banked left.

It was the wrong choice.

Black shelled fingers curled around her left wing, locking them together, while a second and third fist struck her. There was the sound of shattering, of crystal screaming, and then Pari was falling from the sky.

Any sense she had left was knocked from her as she hit the ground.

Vasin hovered at the doorway, hugely reluctant to go into the room. His mother was by Rochant's prone and tied body, close enough to touch it, her face trembling with suppressed emotion. He took an involuntary step back, into the cramped living space.

How have I ended up here?

Nothing seemed to make sense any more. They were the Deathless of House Sapphire, proud, noble. They did not belong in this broken hovel! Somehow he had gone from hunter of the Wild and protector of his people, to killer and thief.

Will I have to add torture to my list of crimes before this is over?

He desperately wanted some Tack to calm his nerves, or even some Voidwine, though the dryness of it didn't usually appeal, he'd take anything to get him out of his own thoughts.

His mother waved him over and he had a near over-whelming impulse to run in the other direction. But he didn't run. Instead, he swallowed his misgivings, ducked down and stepped obediently into the room. Sky-legs were perfectly suited for fast pursuit and for maximizing height when jumping. Their potency was a disadvantage in the cramped space however, and he had to press his hands against the beams overhead to keep from bouncing through the roof.

She was standing over Rochant, waiting. It didn't take him long to see what had drawn her attention. In the meat of his shoulder was a red rise of skin, a spot the size of Vasin's thumbnail capped with a tiny scab that was fresh enough to glisten.

Something had recently drawn Rochant's blood. It could only be the Scuttling Corpseman. No small creatures of the Wild would have dared approach him in his crystal armour. A memory of being on his back, Rochant held up as a shield, flashed through his mind. But what if the Corpseman had seen it differently? What if it had seen Rochant as an offering? His blood a trade for their lives.

Rochant coughed, making Vasin bob on his Sky-legs.

'There's no need to creep on my account. I'm awake. I apologize for the quality of my voice, but you see, I haven't had anything to drink. Perhaps one of you could help with that?'

'There'll be no help found here,' said his mother.

Rochant's hood twitched in her direction. 'Wait, I know you. Nidra?'

'Haven't forgotten me then?'

'You know I'm incapable of that.'

She nodded, a strange smile on her face. Vasin wondered if she were about to cry. 'I know,' she whispered, taking his little finger in her hand and bending it backwards.

There was a soft popping sound as it left the joint, masked by Rochant's gasp of pain.

'I have some questions for you,' she said.

At first he thought Rochant was coughing but then he realized the man was giving a ragged laugh. 'Shouldn't you hurt me after I refuse to answer?'

She took the middle finger of his injured hand and began to twist it.

'Wait. Wait!' said Rochant, and Vasin found himself nodding in agreement.

With near infinite slowness she continued the motion until

the finger left its socket. Rochant called out in pain while Vasin simply stood, shocked still.

'My first question is this: where have you hidden the last of your line? The baby.'

It took a while for Rochant to master himself enough to answer. 'If you've dragged me all the way . . . wherever this stagnant hole is, just to ask me that, you're going to be disappointed. I don't know where they took my descendant, I was between lives when it happened.'

'You expect me to believe you hadn't planned for the possibility? I know you.'

'I don't deny it. Yes, I have many plans to protect my line and several of them take account of the possibility that my current body be captured. As such, I am useless to you.

'Now, can we have a conversation without you hurting me?'

His mother didn't reply but neither did she act. Vasin sighed with relief.

'I'm glad you survived, Nidra. I know I shouldn't be but I am. It's admirable. It won't be added to your legend however, you must know that. Your story is over, nothing can change the High Lord's decree. But it isn't too late for your children. I heard Sky-legs a moment ago and I know they weren't yours. Who was it, Gada or Vasin?'

Vasin drew back involuntarily.

His mother remained silent, though there was a rage in her, simmering just beneath the surface.

Shut up! he wanted to shout, as Rochant continued. *Don't you realize you're making it worse for yourself?*

'It has to be Vasin, he always did follow you around like a Dogkin pup.' The hood turned towards him, uncanny, as if it posed no barrier to Rochant's eyes. 'You have broken rules for her, jeopardized your immortality for her, gone against what it means to be Sapphire. Help me now and I will keep this between us. Nidra's destruction need not be yours.'

'You sound very confident given you are in my power,' said his mother.

'These past days I've had little to do but consider my position. I know that you cannot kill me until you have bloodied your hands with all of my children's children, and I know that one still lives. So what are you going to do? Break a few bones? Subject me to some clever agony? It does not matter. Whatever you do to my body, it is temporary. Unlike you, Nidra, I am Deathless. The High Lord cares if I go missing. He will hunt for me, even as far as this. And if he does not find me, there will come a day when that baby has grown to a suitable age, allowing me to return in all my splendour.

'You see, it is a matter of time before I am rescued or reborn.' Despite the tightness of his bonds he managed a slight shrug. 'Keep me here if you wish as you wither and die. It makes no difference. This body is young. It will outlast yours.'

His mother's voice was cold as the south wind. 'Are you finished?'

'Not quite. I have a question for you.' He paused to moisten his dry lips with his tongue. 'Do you really want this to be the way you're remembered? By me? By your son? Isn't this beneath you?'

By way of answer she slapped his dislocated fingers several times, then went to the wall where the boards were being slowly widened by encroaching vegetation. After some consideration she plucked one of the firmer leaves and turned back to them, dark purpose in her eyes.

Vasin could hear Rochant's breath, fast and heavy. It was a match for his own. He'd never been scared of his mother before, not like this.

She carefully straightened Rochant's index finger, holding the tip firmly between finger and thumb, the leaf in her other hand. 'I too have had little to do but consider my position.' She inserted the edge of the leaf under his fingernail. Rochant bucked against his bonds, making the bell on the end of the rope ring out. 'The plant has several names, my favourite is Lady of the Grass. The way the leaves hang reminds me of those long pointed sleeves I used to hate wearing. I've been harvesting it for its poison. A little will numb the skin, a lot will deaden an entire limb. Concentrated, it can stop your heart. Don't worry, I know exactly how much to use. Your heart is safe in my hands. As with most things in the Wild, it isn't personal, the plant just wants to live. As you can imagine, I feel quite an empathy with it.

'I hurt you just now because I wanted you to suffer, but it isn't my strategy for defeating you. This little leaf is. You see, it doesn't just attack the body, it attacks the essence within. Your fingertip will soon stop feeling pain and, after a while, will stop feeling like a part of you at all. There will come a point where you'll struggle to remember it even exists.' She pushed the leaf in a little further but this time, Rochant didn't react. 'You can't see anything because of the blindfold but believe me when I say there is a lot of this plant growing here. Enough to deaden these fine arms, these legs and the cock between them. After that, I will administer

343

some to your lips, your nose, your tongue, your eyes and your ears. Then, in this old and decaying body, I will wait.'

Vasin felt sick. *It sounds as if she's enjoying herself. Who is this woman?*

'You say that what I do here is only temporary but I believe otherwise. A few years with me and you'll barely remember that you have sensory organs and limbs, let alone how to use them. While you fester inside yourself, that baby will be growing into a new vessel, proud and strong. Now imagine trying to align your broken spirit with it.'

Vasin wondered if what his mother was saying was true. He knew a vessel that differed from its intended Deathless limited how fully the soul could return to the world. Was it possible to attack the soul directly, misaligning it from the body to sabotage a rebirth?

'For you, Rochant,' Nidra continued, 'I could hang on for forty years easily, probably more, shaping you like the Gardener-smiths shape our crystals. Yes, it may be that you survive rebirth in some form but it won't be like this one. And don't count on my brother for mercy, either. Yadavendra's care for you will only last as long as your usefulness. Perhaps he'll keep you alive for a lifecycle or two out of pity, if the Bringers of Endless Order don't brand you an abomination, that is.'

Vasin thought back to Dil striking Lord Rochant in his castle and how shocked he'd been. It was nothing compared to this. 'Mother,' he said quietly. 'How is . . . ' he couldn't think of the words to sum up the horror she'd just described. 'How is,' he said again, his voice rising, 'doing any of this going to help in your restoration?'

For a moment she looked angry at his interruption, but

she put it aside. Somehow, that made him more frightened. 'I will withhold the leaf, if Lord Rochant tells us where his last descendant is hidden.'

'But he's already told us he doesn't know where the baby is.'

'He may not know, but he'll be able to guess. His ability to predict and outplan others is renowned.'

Rochant lifted his head. 'Why do you think I'll help you to end my own line?'

'Because if you tell me, I'll see you die quickly. Don't tell me, and I'll turn you into a mockery of everything you aspired to be, the kind of thing the Story-singers use to frighten children.'

This struck Vasin as ironic, for in that moment that was exactly how she appeared to him. A mockery. A monster. But he was no child, not any more. He did not have to sit and listen.

As his mother strode past him out of the room, he looked from her to Rochant and back again, and made his decision.

CHAPTER SIXTEEN

Pari blinked. She was lying awkwardly on hard earth. Her instincts told her she hadn't been elsewhere long, perhaps only seconds. They also told her she was in danger, the fight, the flight, and the fall all still fresh in her mind.

Her intent was to spring up and face the Corpseman, as it would surely be moving to finish her off. Her body had other ideas, behaving like a sleepy Wormkin on a leisurely afternoon.

Come on, Pari, shift yourself!

A turn of her head brought the Corpseman into view, and with it a surge of adrenaline. It had tilted its skull to the sky, the thick antennae drifting back and forth as it felt the air. She wondered briefly if it could sense her at all. *I've assumed it tracks by scent but what if it tracks by sound?*

She paused, half lifted off the ground, held her breath, and waited.

Her theory was swiftly disproved as the Corpseman's

feelers curved round, drawing the skull after, like reins on a Dogkin, until it was facing Lan.

The young man hadn't moved from the spot where she'd left him, fear holding him rigid. He still had her staff, clinging to it as if it might save him.

No, thought Pari. *That will be up to me.* She dragged herself to her feet, scooping up her whip as the Corpseman set off, loping towards Lan with casual ease.

Pari went after it. Her right shoulder dipped as she bounded, sending her staggering at an angle. A desperate glance revealed a jagged stump of tanzanite jutting short and ugly from her left shoulder. The Corpseman had shattered one of her wings, leaving her unbalanced and grounded.

She had not time to consider the ramifications of that, as the distraction had already allowed the Corpseman to close on Lan. With a single swipe of one of its arms it knocked the staff from Lan's hands while the others lifted the young man off the ground, bringing his terrified eyes level with the Corpseman's skull.

'No!' shouted Pari, tilting her body to the left as she charged. The barb on her whip flashed forward, embedding itself in one of the demon's upper arms.

She had a moment's satisfaction when it whirled round, surprised, which quickly gave way to panic as the Corpseman came at her, dragging Lan behind.

Pari was going too fast to stop. She tried to keep low and set her shoulder, hoping that she might get lucky when they collided, but the Corpseman's free hand swept lower still, its palm striking her squarely in the chest. There was a crack, ominous, the armour threatening to break, as Pari came to an abrupt halt.

347

She swayed, gasped, and fell.

Lan still dangled from two of the Corpseman's arms, staring at her, desperate. She willed him to fight, just as she willed her body to start moving again.

Meanwhile the Corpseman returned its focus to Lan, the horn-like antennae ripping the young man's attention away from her as they drifted in to make contact. He squealed, the first sound he'd made, as they probed his squeezed eyelids, and Pari realized that if she was going to do anything, it would have to be now.

But what to do?

She tried a few desperate kicks at the Corpseman's legs, but the blows were weak, and soon she was breathing heavily, painfully, an ache in her chest growing so that it troubled her despite the crystal armour.

It occurred to her that the barb on her whip was still in its upper arm. If she could get a thumb to it, she could press it in, perhaps get the Corpseman to let Lan go.

Come on, Pari, she urged herself.

Get. Up.

Get up!

Slowly, too slowly, she rolled to her left, hauling herself onto one knee. Lan's eyes were open now, the pupils wide, vacant, mirroring each twitch of the antennae. His face had gone slack and peaceful, like a sleepwalker's mask.

Gritting her teeth, Pari dragged one of her Sky-legs underneath her to spring. She'd have been tempted to run while the Corpseman was distracted, save for the fact the idea of her running anywhere in her current state was laughable.

And besides, I gave my word as a Tanzanite that I would look after him.

Those words turned to ash in her mind as the Corpseman shifted its grip, squeezing Lan's ribcage until it cracked, bending inwards. There was no scream, no death cry, just a little air forced out in a wheeze. His vacant eyes became glassy, and then he was dropped, like a toy fallen from favour.

Guilt and sadness rose up in her. *All that untapped potential gone. Such a waste. He had his whole life ahead of him, and I would have made it a good one.*

The Corpseman turned towards her.

'Come on, then,' she said, 'do your worst.' She barely had the strength to stand, let alone fight, but her crystal barb was still in its arm. That was her chance.

She rose as it crossed the distance between them in a single step. There was a pause, as if it was waiting for her to move first. When she didn't, it grabbed her by the throat and pulled her closer.

That's it, she thought, *save me the bother of coming to you.* She could see the antennae roving a few inches from her face. One stretched out towards her eye only to recoil when it tapped against her visor.

Very slowly, she began to reach up towards its arm, the sliver of the barb still visible, glinting in the light of the gold sun.

For a second time, the antennae tried to get through her visor, they were firmer, but the crystal repelled them just as easily, the demon flesh sizzling when it made contact.

You don't like it, do you? Well, you're going to like what I'm about to do to you even less.

She became aware of movement at her throat. The smaller feelers on the Corpseman's knuckles were moving, working their way into the space between her chest plate and helmet. She could feel them probing at the silk around her neck, picking at it, trying to peel it away.

Out of the corner of her eye, she could see her own hand moving into position. *Stay calm, Pari. Don't rush. Let it think it has you.*

The silk went tight at the back of her neck as the feelers forced their way in.

She locked her fingers. The angle of attack was awkward but nothing she hadn't dealt with before.

As something alien made contact with her skin, she made her move . . . And the Corpseman's hand was waiting, snapping around her wrist to lock it tight. With a sinking heart, she realized it had read her again, predicting her attack before it came.

She pit her strength against the demon's, trying to force her hand down, but it was stronger and she was tired, frail, no contest at all.

Only now did she realize how well her crystal skin had insulated her from the Corpseman's aura. It was past her defences now, vile, pungent, seeping into her pores, her blood, her brain.

Pari stopped thinking. It was as if her mind were laid open, exposed for the Corpseman's pleasure.

Then, a memory came, drawn up to the surface in perfect detail. It was night, she was in the floating castle of Lord Rochant Sapphire. They were sitting in his bedchamber together and the atmosphere was electric.

This was one of her favourite memories.

For several years she'd been flirting, testing him to see how far he would go, daring him to go further, and he had paid her back in kind. They both knew the penalty they would face, if discovered. To mix the lineages, over lifecycles, was to create a bloodline where vessels could serve for either immortal, potentially leading to conflict. Worse, if both souls were between lives at the same time, they could be drawn to the same body. The only thing considered more scandalous than two Deathless of the same house getting together, was a union of two Deathless from different houses.

Pari assumed that for such rules to exist, some randy immortals must have experimented in the past, but if such a thing had ever happened, nobody talked about it.

Of course all of this assumed that the immortals involved were too stupid to use contraception, and while Pari could be a slave to her impulses, she was also well prepared for them. There had been months of expectation, careful planning, and then the risk of sneaking inside, all bringing them to that moment.

She'd wanted to have him, there and then, but he'd made her wait, drawing out the transition between loaded conversation and lusty action. They'd talked in soft tones, not needing to whisper but feeling it appropriate.

When he'd undressed her, it was with the utmost care, as if she were made of glass. She'd laughed at the time. 'I can get this off much faster, you know.'

'No,' he'd replied, slowly unwinding the silk from her shoulder. 'I want time to see you as you really are, to take you in.'

She'd been thinking about how much she wanted to take him in, when he'd stopped and said, 'There's gold on your shoulder. I thought it odd that you always kept it covered.'

'It's not a death I'm particularly proud of.'

He ran his hand along the length of her tattoo, the chill of his fingertips making her squirm, then kissed it. 'Will you tell me about it?'

To her surprise, she had. A dull lifecycle ending in a stupid accident where some unsecured crates had fallen on her. The Tanzanite High Lord clearly thought there was some great life lesson in it all, and so had made a point of adding it to Pari's legend.

By the time her tale was done, very little silk remained, and she'd managed to free Rochant from his trousers as well. *At least a part of him is as impatient to get started as I am.*

He'd been making some observation about how mundanity became harder to avoid across lifecycles when she'd lost patience entirely and thrown him on the bed, pinning his lips with her own to stop him talking while she wiggled her hips into position.

They were just getting started when the memory froze, and faded.

She sensed the Corpseman's puzzlement, as if she were a problem to be picked over.

It is studying me. But why? What does it want?

Another memory came, from a much earlier lifecycle. She was in the Hall of Seven Doors, the meeting place of the Crystal Dynasties. The building was rarely used, most Deathless preferring to visit each other in their castles. However, when there were delicate matters to discuss, where guest and host status could interfere with the outcome, or where trust had broken down, the Hall of Seven Doors offered a neutral space under the eye of the Bringers of Endless Order.

Pari had been sent at the last minute, a replacement for her brother, Arkav. It had been the first time one of his black moods had stopped him doing his duty, and her offering to go in his place had mitigated her High Lord's anger somewhat.

Most representatives had already arrived, aside from Houses Spinel and Opal. Both late arrivals were anticipated, the Opal having the longest distance to cover and the Spinel known for keeping others waiting.

To pass the time she'd been looking at the architecture, wondering how the great arches of marble had been moved into place. Her settlements were made of wood and earth, using small bricks and planks, her castle, of crystals shaped and grown that formed a sort of glue for the stone around them. But these were single pieces, massive. Perhaps the whole thing was cut from one great block, but if that were true, why was there not more marble in the area?

Somewhere nearby, no doubt watching their every move, were the Bringers themselves. Pari was glad they stayed hidden, she found the robed figures sinister. There was something distinctly wrong about them. Nothing she could put her finger on, but an instinct, and Pari had already learned to trust those.

Her attention had been drawn by Lady Nidra of House Sapphire. She'd recently sat down and was clearly unhappy about something. A servant was fussing about her sleeves, but whatever they were doing seemed to be making it worse.

A second servant stepped up, taking over. His movements were more assured, and after a few moments Lady Nidra was settled and smiling. As the servant turned to go, Nidra touched his arm, and the two had shared a look.

It was a trivial recollection, she'd not thought about since it happened, but as it froze, she noticed the way the servant walked, the measured steps, the utter control.

It was Rochant! Rochant before he became Deathless!

A third memory. Her brother's first incident. Thankfully, not the incident itself, after he'd calmed: he'd cried while she cleaned him and bandaged him. When others tried to help getting him back to his chambers, she'd insisted no one else touch him. She'd carried him most of the way, Arkav was so weak, she remembered, so unlike himself, she'd not known what to say. She'd tried to communicate her love, her sympathy, through gesture, putting him to bed and tucking him in tight.

The memory froze and she became aware of her surroundings again. The Corpseman no longer held her throat, its arms were under her back, hips and legs. Gently, it was lowering her to the ground.

When its hands moved over her chest, she remembered the way Lan had died, and yet she felt no fear, there was no malice emanating from the demon now, quite the opposite. It pulled at a cracked segment of crystal and the pressure on her chest eased.

She took a few experimental breaths and the Corpseman's hands seemed to rise and fall in time, like coral in the water, bobbing with the waves.

After the third breath, it straightened and began moving back towards the trees. When it reached Lan's body, the Corpseman paused to establish a grip on his ankle, before dragging him away.

Pari turned herself over, noting all the places that hurt badly, aware they'd hurt much worse once the armour came off. She picked up the staff, trying not to think of Lan or the 'good luck' she'd promised him, and used it to lever herself upright. With her Sky-legs on, it seemed more like a walking stick than a staff.

She was about to go into Sorn, wanting nothing more than to find a safe place to sleep for several days, when an instinct stopped her. She found her mind was full of questions.

Why did the Corpseman kill Lan and yet spare me? It seemed almost . . . gentle at the end. And why take his body? What is it going to do with his body?

If she didn't find out, it would plague her for the rest of her lives. She was fairly sure the Corpseman wasn't going to attack her now, something in their relationship had changed.

Something he read in my thoughts.

That led her to more questions. It seemed as if the Corpseman had done the exact thing she aspired to do, to know the mind of an opponent. It had drawn her memories up like pearls from the depths, so clear it was like living them a second time. *But why those memories?* Rochant and Arkav had been on her mind, so perhaps that was not such a surprise. *But why Nidra?* Was it simply the fact that Rochant had been in that memory?

There was more to this, she was sure of it, and so, in half bounds, using her staff for balance, she put her back to Sorn, and followed the Corpseman into the trees.

The tracks led Pari to a steep hill with a trio of scrawny trees jutting from the top, their roots clawing at the sides. Here the tracks ended. She hadn't been able to keep pace with the Corpseman, but was sure it wasn't far away. She stopped and looked for signs, then placed her staff into the last two gouges left by the Corpseman's long toe-less feet. They were deeper than the ones before.

It jumped.

She looked up, judging the distance. If her chest didn't hurt so much, if her wings were intact, she might be able to make it herself.

Ifs aren't worth anything, Pari, she admonished herself. *Now get climbing.*

The hillside was soft, her staff and Sky-legs sliding in a foot and a half before finding purchase. Halfway up she was forced to rest, giving her body over to a tangle of tree roots while she waited for her muscles to stop trembling.

Her ascent so far had left a messy trail, telling the story of her struggle in a succession of overlapping lines and gouges.

No wonder I'm tired. I'm carrying half the hill with me.

As Pari scraped some of the mud from her knees a yellowish glimmer caught her eye. It was buried deep in the hillside, safe from prying eyes. At first she thought it was a square of amber as big as her fist but as she began to excavate, it revealed itself to be far bigger. A darker shape was held inside, trapped and preserved. She kept working, revealing first an arm in the amber, then a shoulder and hints of neck and body. The arm was sleeved, a patched garment of the type favoured in House Sapphire settlements.

I'd wager this poor soul comes from Sorn.

Pari pressed her cheek against the hill so that she could look at its profile. Sure enough, she saw a number of bulges where other bodies could have been packed in. Using her staff, she prodded the nearest one and was rewarded with the thud of something solid. A quick investigation revealed another piece of amber and another body, this time of an old man with only half a head.

She paused to swallow down some bile and blocked in the hole.

The last bit of the climb was less sheer and the roots were thicker and more able to take her weight. At the top she paused to look for tracks and catch her breath. She could see many signs of the Corpseman's passing, old and new, all over the hilltop, like shallow cuts on a well-used chopping board. Of the demon itself however, there was no sign.

Finally her attention came to the tree. From below it looked like a set of silver birches growing close together but was in fact three thick branches splitting off from the same trunk. Curious as that was, it was not the most striking thing about it.

A man appeared to be trapped within the bark. His face and the curve of his belly poked free of the central trunk, the flesh tanned and coarsened by the elements. His arms sprouted from the two side trunks, one on the left and one on the right at mismatched heights, the left roughly in line with the man's shoulder, the right far too high. She saw leaves where fingernails should be, and in places, like the man's right cheek and chin, the skin had flaked away to reveal fresh bark. It was as if the man were growing out of the tree while a second, younger tree grew within him.

The last detail to strike Pari was a faded white line on the one piece of his neck she could see, an old burn with flecks of gold around its edge. *A tattoo! This man had a legend. That means he was Deathless once.*

Only the nose and the lower half of his face were visible,

the eyes and brow still trapped under a visor of bark, but the set of his features changed as she moved, suggesting that on some level he knew of her approach.

'Hello,' she said. 'Do you hear me?'

The man licked his lips, revealing patches of fungus on his tongue. 'Are those sweet words I hear on the wind?'

'They are.'

'Human words from a human mouth?'

'Yes.'

The man sniffed sadly. 'It has been so long. I hear the people as they scurry and chatter but always so far away. Never do they come to talk to me.'

'I'm sorry. Nobody knows you're here.'

'I am forgotten. Fallen and forgotten.'

'My name is Lady Pari Tanzanite and I feel that I know you. Is that true?'

'Ah. Yes. I think I do remember that name. Weren't you the one that was killed by a box?'

Pari sighed. 'Yes that was me.'

'What are you doing here?'

'I'm looking for someone.'

'Were you looking for me?'

'I'm sorry. I didn't even know you were here. I'm still not sure who you are.'

'My name is Samarku.'

She knew that name. 'I thought you were killed in the Battle of Bloodied Backs, Lord Samarku.'

His lips twisted with anger and the branches trembled as if disturbed by a breeze. 'A lie! One of many lies told about me.'

She could hear the edge of madness on his voice, the same

rise of temper that took her brother sometimes. 'The Sapphire are known to keep their business private. Little of your news reaches the Tanzanite lands, and we are always wary of the bits that do.'

'Wise. Very wise.'

'I take it then, that you did not make compact with the things of the Wild?'

'Look at me!' he screeched. 'Would I have asked for this?'

'I ask only out of ignorance. Perhaps the noble Samarku would be kind enough to tell me the truth.'

He sighed then, and the leaves seemed to sigh with him. 'It matters little now. I am undone, my throne taken by that fool, Yadavendra. My castle given to his lackey, Rochant. And my legend smeared forever.

'You want the truth? The truth is that Yadavendra wanted to be High Lord. I was ready to step down and let another take my place.'

'Forgive my interruption, you were ready to die a final time?'

'No, no, I did not seek death, just a rest from the burdens of being High Lord. House Spinel change their High Lord every three lifecycles. It is not such a big thing.'

Pari made no comment. Everyone knew the Spinel were a strange lot.

'He was aware of my plans,' Samarku continued, 'and he also knew that I favoured his sister to be my successor. So he organized a hunt, insisting that all the Lords and Ladies of House Sapphire attended. He said that it would be good for us to fly together one last time under my leadership, when in truth he just wanted to get me out here so he could spring his trap.

'He'd been whispering, you see, spreading rumours that I'd betrayed the honour of the house, that I'd been seduced by the Wild, all to sow the soil for his lies.'

'What happened?'

'The hunt began normally enough. We found the tributes quickly and flew down, forming a protective circle. They had been cut as they are always cut, and they bled well enough, yet nothing of the Wild had come to claim them.

'I had just declared that we would wait when, to my surprise Yadavendra accused me of treachery in front of my hunters, my tributes, and the other Deathless. Naturally, I was outraged and demanded that he take back his words or be prepared to face my wrath.

'He said he would fight me in order to cleanse the house and challenged me to a duel. Can you imagine? I was so furious I could hardly speak. When he raised his weapon in defiance, I was quick to raise mine in response. Little did I realize I had already lost.'

'Lost, lost, lost,' echoed the leaves.

Pari glanced about, restless. She was exposed on the hilltop and in no shape to fight if something came.

'At first, the house stood with me, leaving Yadavendra and his entourage isolated. I was about to give him a chance to surrender when one of his hunters, the one I would later know to be Rochant, shouted in alarm. He was pointing over my shoulder. One by one they turned to see what had struck him so. I did not turn at first, unwilling to put my back on the treacherous Yadavendra, but when I saw the expressions on my hunters' faces, I could not help but turn myself.

'Behind me the trees were alive with creatures, gathered

at my back, facing my enemies, as if to defend me. It seemed the Wild had come after all, but in the guise of my allies. I did not understand. I could not understand. Neither could my family. When I looked to them for support, none of them met my eye.

'Yadavendra's attack appeared heroic, while I seemed like everything he had accused me of. I had little option then but to fight. They didn't expect me to come on so fast.' A nasty smile came to his lips. 'I swear Yadavendra soiled his crystals that day. I would have had him but for Rochant throwing himself in the way. He put a spear in my gut and I cracked his skull.' The smile faded. 'I don't remember much after that, save for the realization that the wound I'd taken must have started bleeding. I'd been so intent on killing Yadavendra that I'd put my back to the Wild, a foolish mistake.

'The next thing I knew, there were hands all over me, clawing to get at the blood they knew was trapped inside my armour. I passed out, but I wasn't destined to be devoured. When I woke, I had a new master, the Scuttling Corpseman. It bound me here, and here I have been ever since.'

'But why?'

'It comes to me sometimes, asks me questions.'

'It talks to you?'

'Not with words, how I wish it used only words. No, it comes for my mind, to sample my many lives. Sometimes I relive things I had quite forgotten. It wants to know how I think, Lady Pari. And sometimes, I get an inkling of how it thinks. There is no hatred there, it is too cold for that. I feel a reserve, a detached curiosity. It is learning from me, learning our ways, but for what purpose I do not know.'

Pari reached out to touch Samarku's cheek. 'Do you want me to end this?'

'Yes,' he whispered. 'But first, I want revenge.'

'I understand. How can I help you?'

'Yadavendra and Rochant, destroy them for me!'

Tread carefully here, Pari. His hatred of Rochant could be used. 'Lord Rochant's line has been attacked and he's gone missing. Were you involved in that?'

'No, but I know where Rochant is. He's in Sorn. I can't reach him there because of the Scuttling Corpseman. But you, you could.'

'Yes, I could. Is his baby there too?'

'I have heard whispers of a baby in the Wild, is it his?'

'Yes, it is last of his line. If you could help me find it, it would give me great power over him. Do you know where it is?'

Glee split the old face wide. 'Don't worry about the baby. I'll deal with that myself.' A horrible feeling stole over Pari as Samarku raised his voice to a shriek, 'My children!'

'Children, children, children,' said the leaves.

'The last child of Rochant is here, a mere baby!' The branches of the tree shook violently.

'Stop!' said Pari.

'Kill it! Wring its neck! Bring the body to me!'

She struck Samarku in the face with her gauntlet, splitting his lip and cracking several teeth. A dark red sap leaked from the cut. As he spluttered, she scooped up a thick slab of mud and stuffed it into his mouth, gagging him.

'Here,' said the leaves, 'a baby.'

'No!' shouted Pari, though her words were whipped away

by the very wind that was empowering and repeating Samarku's words.

'Kill it, kill it, kill it.'

'See that?' asked Fiya.

Chandni nodded. There were nets strung horizontally between a circle of trees standing proud of the others. As she squinted, she could see furs hung there too, brown, grey, and black between the greens of the canopy. A giant quilt of them had been patched together and stretched across another structure to make curving walls. It looked to Chandni as if a giant animal were squatting in the branches. 'Is that a tree house?'

'That's where the meets take place.'

'It looks high,' said Varg. 'How do you get up there?'

Fiya grunted. 'You climb. There's a ladder makes it easier but the first one to arrive has to get up without it.' She gave them both a crooked smile. 'That's why we left late.'

It appeared very still in the trees to Chandni. 'Do you think anyone else is there?'

'Devdan will be there by now. He's always early.' She tutted. 'Never learns. Good for us though.'

'How many of you are there in total?' she asked.

'There's about twenty, all told, though they won't all come today.'

A cold breeze blew against Chandni's back, making the leaves whisper and hiss, and her and Varg shiver. She held Satyendra close. There was a strangeness to the rustlings, as if words were tangled somewhere within the winds.

Fiya stopped, her head tilted to one side, and held up a hand.

'What is it?' asked Varg.

'Sssh!' she hissed.

Three times more, the wind gusted in that strange way. When it had calmed again, Fiya nodded to herself slowly. She turned to Varg but Chandni saw her eyes flick briefly towards Satyendra as she did so. 'I don't like the sound of that,' she said.

'What are you saying?' asked Varg.

'I'm saying we've got to be careful. Should be safe here but that doesn't mean we are. It's always a risk when we gather in one place, and that risk is even greater when there are young involved. The Wild likes flesh that's supple most of all.'

They approached slowly, alert for signs of trouble. As Fiya had said, a ladder was waiting for them. It was made of hair. The strands were a mix of blonde and white, hundreds of them, twined together into slender corkscrews to make the rungs.

The old woman pointed a gnarly thumb at her own chest. 'I'll go first, check it's safe.'

She was just testing her weight on the first rung, when she hissed and froze. 'There! To the left! A Watcher!' She saw Varg and Chandni looking blank. 'There! Where the red berries are growing. Quickly, send your Dogkin to fetch it before the Watcher calls to its hive.'

Glider's ears pricked at the sound of her name and she made a quizzical noise.

'Shit,' said Varg. 'I can't see it.'

Chandni couldn't see anything either but she didn't doubt the sharpness of Fiya's eyes. 'Go, Glider!' she urged. 'Quickly. Get it!'

With a bark, Glider shot forward, racing in the direction Fiya was pointing.

Chandni bit her lip. She wasn't sure what a Watcher was exactly, or what kind of hive Fiya was referring to, but she was sure it would be bad. She took a few steps forward, willing Glider's success, while Fiya shifted the grip on her staff, turning the walking aid into a weapon.

As the Dogkin ploughed into the bushes there was a loud snap, and she disappeared.

'Glider?' asked Varg as he edged forward.

There was a whine from where Glider was but it sounded lower down, as if it was coming from beneath the ground.

'Glider?' said Varg and Chandni together.

The Dogkin's reply was long and self pitying.

They continued to approach the bushes until a hole revealed itself. It was twelve foot deep and wide enough for two people, or one Glider-sized creature, to stand in. Hearing their approach, Glider turned to look up at them, her face a mask of misery.

'Oh no,' said Chandni.

'Oh shit,' said Varg.

Satyendra chose this moment to start laughing.

Chandni stared into the pit, trying to see if another creature were trapped beneath Glider's paws. However there was nothing there. *The Watcher must have run away.* She was just trying to work out the best way of freeing Glider when the Dogkin started barking fiercely.

'All right,' said Varg. 'Shut up and let us think.'

'Something's not right, Varg. She sounds like she isn't happy.'

'Course she isn't, Chand, she's stuck in a hole.'

'No, not sad like that. Like . . . like she's trying to warn us about something.'

Glider continued to bark as she looked up at them.

No, she's looking past us.

She spun round just as Fiya's staff poked Varg between the shoulder blades, sending him face first into the pit. Satyendra gasped at the sight, then threw back his head and roared with laughter.

'Fiya? What are you doing?'

The old woman didn't answer, letting her staff talk for her. Before Chandni could react, it darted forward again, the head knocking against her ankle, sending one foot backwards, out over the edge of the pit.

As she fought for balance, the staff came up under her arm, knocking Satyendra from her grasp. He tumbled awkwardly to the floor between them. Immediately, he stopped laughing and began to scream.

She reached for him but again the staff came, a series of short, sharp prods that forced her back a pace, to where there was no ground, only air.

Her arms windmilled once and, as gravity took her backwards, she saw Fiya was already turning her attention towards Satyendra. Then she fell.

But she did not fall far.

Strong hands caught her shoulders and eased her down. 'You okay?' said Varg. He was standing on Glider's back, a murderous expression on his face.

'I need to get back up.'

He nodded and laced his hands. 'I'll get you up, then you get me out, okay?'

'Okay.'

He boosted her so hard she flew out of the pit, landing on her hands and knees. Satyendra was no longer where he'd fallen but she could still hear him crying. She looked around wildly and caught a glimpse of him stuck over Fiya's shoulder, his little arms reaching out towards her as they vanished into the trees.

'Chand?' called Varg. 'Where are you?'

She turned to look down at them both. 'I'm sorry,' she replied, 'there's no time.'

'What the fuck?'

Glider barked at her in a similar manner.

'I'll come back,' she said, standing up. 'I promise.'

Then she ran. *Fiya can't have gone far. She was walking quickly, not running. Why did she betray us? Why now? What is she doing to my Satyendra?*

For a few minutes, she didn't think, putting all her effort into the chase, trying to look everywhere at once, searching for any signs of the old woman or her baby. She saw nothing. No glimpses of them, no tracks, even the crying seemed further away, the sound shifted by the trees, making it swirl around her, as if a chorus of babies were crying, not just one.

Her mother's voice came into her head, even louder than her pounding heart. *It is not the Sapphire way to run blindly forward like some screeching Lizardkin on heat. A Sapphire thinks first, considers, then acts decisively.*

She came to a stop, the forest around her seemingly empty. *There's no way she could be faster than me.* With a frown, she turned and retraced her steps, forcing herself to go slowly and look for any clues. At first, the only thing she found was another concealed pit that she'd only avoided falling into before by sheer luck. Then, when she'd nearly got back to where Varg and Glider were trapped, she saw it: an old tree with a skirt of brambles growing all over it. Hanging from one of the lower branches was a thread of grey hair. *Fiya's hair.*

Chandni separated out several strands of her own hair, wrapping them round her hand. Without scissors or knife there was little to do but grit her teeth and yank them out, the little spike of pain barely noticed amid the emotions and adrenaline. Taking the ends of the hair in her hands, she held them up to the tree. 'I make this gift to you. Please, let me pass safely.'

She tied the hair to the same branch Fiya had used and then, as an afterthought, kissed the knot.

There was no reaction from the tree, but when she looked again, she saw a gap under the brambles that she was sure wasn't there before.

'Thank you,' she whispered.

On her belly, she crawled underneath, and was rewarded with the sound of crying close by.

Satyendra was on the ground, his mouth a furious circle, the veins on his neck and temple bulging with effort as he displayed his displeasure. Next to him was Fiya, she'd put down her staff and was busy tying a noose to a sturdy looking branch.

Chandni crept forward, being careful not to tread on any dry leaves, though Satyendra was making such a din that she could probably have sung a song and not be heard.

She picked up the staff, testing its weight in her hands, and still Fiya hadn't noticed, her attention fully on the knot. Chandni pulled back the staff, then swung it as hard as she could at Fiya's knees.

There was a snap that reminded Chandni of a dry twig breaking, accompanied by a scream, which did not, and the old woman fell down. Chandni raised the staff again as she walked round into view.

'Why?' she said.

'Because that baby is a vessel for the one that betrayed us all! It must die.' Fiya was moving while she talked, drawing a long dagger from her belt. 'It must die!' she repeated, dragging herself closer to Satyendra with one hand while raising the dagger with the other to strike.

Chandni swung again, smashing the hand and sending the dagger spinning away. 'No,' she said. 'I am a true and loyal servant of the Sapphire and I will do anything – anything! – to protect my son and the future of my lord.'

Fiya had curled up tight with the pain but she still managed to speak. 'It doesn't matter what you do to me. We all know the baby is here. Others will come. They are already on their way.'

'I disagree.' She struck Fiya's other arm, ending any ideas the old woman might have of fighting back. 'I think it does matter what I do to you.' She put down the staff and picked up the dagger. It was a simple looking weapon but the blade was sharp, the bone darkened with long use. Fiya's eyes followed the movement, widening in a pulse of fear.

And she is right to be afraid, thought Chandni.

She took a deep breath and began to speak. 'Powers of the Wild, hear me! My name is Honoured Mother Chandni, servant of the Sapphire Everlasting. I want to bargain.' She pricked Fiya's cheek and raised the dagger high. 'With blood and bone.'

The constant background drone of creature calls and

Birdkin song fell quiet. Satyendra's wailing stopped. Even the wind seemed to hold its breath.

'Don't do this,' said Fiya, her hands pressed desperately to her cheek. 'I beg you.'

Chandni didn't even look at her. 'This blood, for the blood of my son. These bones for the bones of my son. Protect my Satyendra. Keep him alive and safe.'

'You don't know what you're doing,' said Fiya. 'You don't know the ways. Don't you see? They'll take it all from both of us.'

The dagger slashed lightly across Fiya's thigh and Chandni flicked the blood upwards. Another slash, and the blood was flicked down at her feet. Five more cuts she made, one for each of the seven directions.

'Damn you,' said Fiya. 'I will call down such a curse that your little—'

Her words cut off in a gurgle as Chandni dropped to one knee, using all of her weight to bury the dagger in Fiya's throat. *No,* she thought. *There will be no more treachery from you.*

She stood up again, her hands shaking. 'This kill I make for you,' she said aloud. 'This life, for Satyendra's.'

The last of the light left Fiya's eyes and a howl sounded, distant, similar to Glider's but deeper, larger. It was answered shortly after by several others, some of which sounded awfully close. A Dogkin pack, angry and on the prowl.

Chandni grabbed Satyendra and fled. The wind returned, chill as ever, and with it, a wail of distress, a baby's. She knew that cry better than she knew her own voice. *That's my Satyendra!* But when she looked at the baby in her arms, she saw that his face was smooth with contentment, his mouth pressed against her chest.

The Wild is playing tricks on me, she told herself as she made her way back to the pit, and yet no matter how solid Satyendra felt in her arms, nor how often she told herself the crying was fake, she could not banish the feeling of her baby being in trouble and the sense that she was going the wrong way.

Sa-at was crying. Devdan's hands were at his throat, pressing but without conviction. Tears ran down both their faces.

'Guh, I can't,' he said, breaking away.

They were high up in the trees, in a great bowl made of furs and rope. A hole in the roof let smoke out and light in, giving glimpses of nervous clouds skittering by. A brazier hung suspended in the middle of the space, the stones inside glowing a ruddy orange. Devdan had lit it not long after his first attempt to strangle Sa-at. Now the man circled the brazier, pulling at his white hair as he muttered to himself.

'It's not fair. You're a good baby and I was getting everything right this time. Suns, this was supposed to be a good day. Why did you have to be his? Why couldn't you just have been a normal sky-baby?

'I'm sorry I didn't make it quick . . . I just can't do it. Not when your . . . not when I can see your eyes.' He stopped and looked over at Sa-at. 'Please stop crying. It won't change anything. If it were up to me then I'd never harm even the tiniest part of you. But it's not up to me. Do you understand? I don't want to.'

Sa-at did not understand. His neck hurt. He was scared. He continued to cry.

'I'm going to do this myself, before the others get here.' He shook his head. 'Not right for a stranger to do it to you. I just gotta build up some courage and have a think, which is really hard with you bawling. I don't blame you though, it's just it's tricky to do it quick and do it right. Can't use anything sharp. Can't use my hands. But I've got an idea.' He turned and stared at the brazier. 'Won't be long now. I'll make sure there's nothing for the demons to get, after. Least I can do.'

The wind gusted outside, rippling the furs like sails on a ship and setting the ropes to creaking. Devdan stopped to listen. 'Something's not right,' he muttered, then with an apologetic glance in Sa-at's direction, added: 'something else, I mean.'

He took out a pouch and opened the top, taking out a handful of the grey ash he'd collected from his burnt out tree. 'Show yourself. I know you're here.'

A pair of talons hooked round the edge of the hole in the top of the structure, and then a Birdkin's head peered in, with a bone white beak and multifaceted eyes.

Crowflies, thought Sa-at, reaching up to touch it, despite the distance between them being far too great.

'Sa-aat!' cried the Birdkin, dropping through the hole to dive towards them.

'Get back!' shouted Devdan, flinging the ash at it.

Crowflies banked away with a screech, circling above them, before settling again on the edge of the hole in the roof. It held out one of its wings for inspection. Some of the feathers were missing where they had made contact with the ash, others were burning. Crowflies flapped the wing angrily until the flames flickered and died, leaving a thin plume of smoke rising from its wingtip.

'I got plenty more where that came from, demon.'

The two glared at each other while Sa-at took on a new word.

Demon.

It is a demon.

Crowflies is a demon.

The wind gusted a second time, bringing with it another Birdkin. This one landed on the outside of the structure, its silhouette darkening a patch of fur not far from where Sa-at lay. Devdan took a step towards it when a third Birdkin arrived on the opposite side, its hooked talons poking through to wink at them. A fourth arrived, then a fifth, sixth, seventh, then too many to count, slapping against the walls as they landed.

It seemed as if evening had arrived early, the little light that penetrated the stitching around the furs blocked by the numerous feathered bodies.

Then Crowflies spread its wings, they all spread their wings, and night fell.

Only the light of the brazier remained, painting Devdan in a fierce orange glow. He turned on the spot, eyes darting left and right and up and down, his pouch in one hand, some ash in the other.

There was a tearing sound, and then Birdkin began to pour into the room, a shrieking river of liquid black and sharp white, filling the air with wings and noise as they careened around the edges of the space.

Meanwhile, something gathered on the edge of the light near Sa-at, a thing of feathers and the shadows of feathers blurred together, of wings binding to make a shape. Something like a cloak. On something like a human frame.

'Ill met, death flinger,' it said in a voice that seemed to come from the throats of all the Birdkin present.

'But . . . you can't be here,' replied Devdan, though it sounded as much question as statement.

'Oh but . . . ' it paused in mockery, 'I can. A deal has been done, of steel words and bloody deed.' The chorus of Birdkin cawed joyously.

'Begone!' shouted Devdan, casting his ash. It billowed out causing the Birdkin to make alarmed noises. The figure did not move, however.

'What—' It said.

'Whaaaat?' chorused the Birdkin.

'—Is this?'

Devdan reached into his pouch, throwing more of the ash. 'Begone!' he said again.

'No. I am called and I am come. It is you that will be gone, not I. Be pained. Be flayed. Be food.'

It waved a wing-like arm and a wind knocked Devdan backwards until he fell against the brazier. He called out, dropping the pouch before slumping to his hands and knees.

Sa-at caught a glimpse of him there, before his cries and body were smothered by wings and beaks, brief flashes of white in the darkness.

Then the figure had moved between them, bending down to peer at Sa-at. Like Crowflies its eyes were multifaceted but larger, and it seemed that each tiny surface moved, as if a living thing in its own right. 'I am Murderkind, a prince of this place.'

Murderkind.

It is Murderkind.

Its name is Murderkind!

'Yes, little seed. Very good, very quick. Remember my name, remember me. I promise I will remember you.' It leaned down to touch its forehead to Sa-at's. 'Be alive. Be safe. Be friend.'

There was a flurry of wing beats, and Murderkind was gone. The Birdkin left soon after, scattering through the many holes, allowing the day to return.

Sa-at squeezed his eyes against the sudden glare, then a wing moved protectively between him and the sunlight.

'Sa-aat!' said Crowflies, hopping forward.

Sa-at smiled.

A long piece of meat hung from the Birdkin's beak, fresh and bloody. Sa-at reached for it eagerly and began to suck.

CHAPTER SEVENTEEN

The suns had begun their descent when Chandni got back to the pit. She could still hear the Dogkin howling to each other, and had the sense that they were on the move. Even though she had only been gone for a few minutes, it felt much longer.

Varg was sitting on the ground, feet dangling in the pit, his broad shoulders slumped. Though he'd managed to free himself, Glider's sad whine still emanated from inside.

He turned as she approached, his face cracking with relief. Mud streaked his cheeks, chest, and thighs, and was caked in his nails. She'd worried he'd be resentful for being abandoned but there was no sign of it as he pulled her into a tight embrace.

'I promised I'd come back.' He made a grunt of acknowledgement and she added, 'I'm sorry.'

When they parted his arm seemed reluctant to leave her, settling against her hip, keeping her close. 'You found him then.'

'Yes,' she said, planting a kiss on Satyendra's forehead. 'What about Fiya?'

'We don't need to worry about her any more.'

He nodded, his eyes going to the bloodstains on her hands, then widening in horror. 'Are you hurt? Is it bad?' He spun around as if expecting to see a demon in every tree. 'Shit. We have to go, now.'

She looked away, unable to meet his eyes. 'It's not mine. It's Fiya's. The Wild has already taken what it wants from her.' The stains on her hands were old, as if they'd been there for hours rather than minutes. 'I'm fine, really. No cuts, just bruises. You?'

'Same.'

A silence grew between them, full of unspoken questions and feelings, that Chandni quickly found unbearable.

'I'm so confused, Varg. She seemed genuine. Why take us in, feed us and teach us, if she planned to kill us all along?'

'Dunno, but I reckon we can worry about that later. We need a plan and a place to go before all the suns set.'

'Yes,' she replied, looking over her shoulder. 'Fiya said that others would be coming for us, for Satyendra specifically. I doubt we have long.'

She realized how quickly she'd adjusted to living inside Fiya's tree and how safe it had felt. They couldn't go back there now. While it was likely the tree would still accept them, it would be the first place Fiya's family would look.

The illusion that she was growing used to the Wild, the feeling that she could cope here, even make a temporary life here, vanished, leaving behind a more familiar sense of dread.

'I've had enough of this place,' said Varg. 'I say we go back to our original plan and make for Sorn.'

Chandni nodded. 'Fiya was too scared to go there, perhaps her family will be too.'

'And that's where Pari will go to find us.'

She still wasn't convinced Pari was coming for them but kept her doubts to herself. 'What about the Corpseman?'

'I'm hoping it'll be long gone by now.'

We're pinning so much on luck, but what choice do we have? She decided to focus on something more practical instead. 'How will we get there? I'd struggle to remember the route back to Fiya's tree, let alone the Godroad or Sorn.'

Varg made an unconvincing attempt at looking confident. 'I got a rough idea.'

There was a polite bark from the pit, prompting them both to look over. 'Don't worry,' she said, 'we'll find a way to get you out.'

Varg frowned. 'Yeah.'

In the end they tied Varg's jacket to Chandni's cloak and dragged Glider out while the Dogkin did her best to scrabble up the side. It was slow, messy, and despite them telling her to be quiet, Glider made so much noise that Chandni could only hope that Fiya's family were either deaf or several miles away.

By the time the Dogkin was out of the pit and on her feet, the colour was leeching from the trees, gold and reds giving way to grey, and Satyendra was fast asleep.

Chadni and Varg sagged against each other, catching their breath. She barely noticed his smell now, nor the fact that his hand was sweaty as it brushed hers.

And I must reek of far worse things than sweat! It's a wonder he doesn't run screaming into the forest.

'Ready to go?' he asked.

'Not really. I'm exhausted.'

Varg nodded agreement.

She leant into him, letting his chest take the weight of her head. 'What a strange life this is. I feel like I've lived here for years instead of days.'

'Yeah.' He began to stroke her hair and she tucked a hand inside the back of his trousers to warm her cold fingers.

'Varg, do you think we'll survive?'

'Dunno. Hope so.'

'Yes.'

'Hang on, there's something in your hair.'

She went very still. 'Is it alive?'

'Nah. At least, not any more.'

A hundred visions played through her mind, of Spiderkin corpses, Flykin husks and, impossibly, some piece of Fiya. 'Tell me what it is!'

'It's a feather. A big black one. Here, I got it.'

Her head jerked back as he pulled. 'Ow!'

'Sorry, I can't get it out. Must be caught somewhere.'

Another round of howls echoed from nearby. The closest one hadn't moved but the others were louder, a few coming from behind them, a few more from their left. She had the horrible feeling they were being flanked. 'Actually, I think I am ready to go now, Varg.'

'Yeah. Me too.' He let go and started walking. 'Sorn is this way.'

Glider sniffed, unimpressed, and pointed her nose in a different direction. 'Are you sure it's not that way?' she asked.

He paused, pulling at his beard thoughtfully as he looked from one to the other.

'How about you?' she asked Glider.

Glider gave an authoritative bark and padded off into the trees. Chandni followed her, leaving Varg to sigh and do the same.

Vasin stepped out onto the streets of Sorn. It was getting dark and conventional wisdom told him that this was the time to stay indoors. However, he'd decided that he'd much rather face all the horrors of the Wild than spend a moment longer in a room with his mother.

Thankfully she'd left Lord Rochant alone since her initial attempts to loosen his tongue and, to his amazement, had already drifted off into what appeared to be a pleasant and easy sleep. He knew that when she woke, she would start on Lord Rochant again, and then he would stop her. Somehow.

This is not going to end well, he thought, and took a sip of honeywine from his flask. The sweetness was welcome though it failed to completely mask the bad taste in his mouth.

In the distance, he could hear the sound of wild Dogkin calling to each other, coordinating as he would with his hunters, and was glad that they were too far away for him to be the prey.

Soon, he would have to return to his castle. If Mia and the others hadn't heard from him by morning, there was a good chance they'd begin a search or even worse, tell the High Lord. He'd hoped his mother would prove equal to Lord Rochant, then they could end this part of the plan.

And yet she had proved more than his equal. He didn't doubt that she would break Rochant, and soon.

It was painful to remember how she had been in the days

of his first lifecycle. It was from her he'd learned that there was a relationship between the Deathless and their winged armour. *'The sapphire armour supports you, empowers you. A wise Deathless draws strength when needed but never, ever lets themselves be drawn.'*

'I don't understand.'

'Power is a tool. The hand should direct the tool, never the other way around.'

He'd nodded, then frowned. *'I'm sorry, Mother. I still don't understand.'*

'You will.'

He did. And she had totally forgotten.

I just don't know what will be left of any of us when she's done.

He wondered if he were being a fool to cling to his ideal of being a Sapphire. Certainly High Lord Yadavendra did not match it, neither did his Uncle Umed, nor Yadva or Gada. *Nor even my mother any more.* And if he took a good hard look at himself, he knew he was little better.

Cowards and bullies and lost souls, all following the lead of a madman.

Though it was a poor substitute for his usual drugs, Vasin took another sip of the wine. The right thing to do would be to take Lord Rochant back with him tomorrow and end this charade. A little voice in his mind reminded him that Rochant had suggested there might be a way out for himself as well, if he took action now, though any deal would doubtless leave him at the other Deathless's mercy. Was that a price worth paying to be free of worry?

Would he ever be free of worry again?

His musings were interrupted by a glow in the darkness,

a blue-violet shimmer moving closer in measured short bounds. *Sky-legs? Here?* He wondered, going closer for a better look. Glowing as he was, the thought of hiding seemed ridiculous. *Let's just get it over with.*

Long before he saw the armour, he'd recognized the aura as House Tanzanite. The flash of crystal he'd seen in the Wild as he'd flown here came back to him. *I should have known they were coming here,* he thought as he pulled his helmet on. *I should have warned Mother.*

He could see them more clearly now as they moved in bouncing strides towards him. *Lady Pari Tanzanite. Of course it is.* She was using a wooden staff to walk with and one of her wings was missing. There were cracks in her chest plate too. Despite her sociable manner, he'd always suspected Pari to be far more dangerous than she appeared. Perhaps it was the ease by which she conducted herself, a kind of sureness that seemed part of her very being.

'Lord Vasin,' she called, coming to a stop and inclining her head.

He gave a slight bow, feeling the protest from his back and shoulders, still sore from his encounter with the Corpseman. 'Lady Pari of the Tanzanite Everlasting.'

In many ways, this was the worst of all possible outcomes, and yet the terror he'd felt at discovery had melted away. Apart from the staff, she was unarmed, and she appeared to need it to stay upright. Her body was old, not to mention tired and quite possibly injured. He would be faster than her, and without a wing she couldn't take to the air, giving him all kinds of interesting attack options.

'Well,' she said, breaking the quiet that was stretching between them. 'This is awkward.'

'These are House Sapphire lands. You shouldn't be here.'

'Really, my dear? Is that your gambit? To be precise, these are Lord Rochant's lands, which I already have permission to cross, and I wager that if we took a look around we'd find all sorts of things that shouldn't be here.'

'You won't be coming any closer.'

She sighed in a way that made him feel as if he was the one being unreasonable. 'As a matter of fact I will. The only question is what you're going to do about it.'

In the dark, his fists glowed, starlike, as he raised them. 'I think you already know my answer.'

'Yes, but I always hold out the hope that life will surprise me.'

She took another half bound forward, using the staff to steady herself. One more of those and she would be on him. He readied himself, feeling his body shift automatically into a combat stance.

He watched as her knees bent slightly, and copied her. She flicked upright, and he jumped back in response. By the time he realized it was a feint, he'd sailed back through the air five feet. With a snarl he gathered himself to spring, im-agining the arc he'd take to come down on her with maximum force.

'Actually,' she said, holding up a hand. 'Can we take a moment first?'

He wobbled awkwardly as he checked his momentum, his fists hovering, uncertain. 'What?'

'Before we fight. Can we take a moment? I see a bench over there that I'd really like to try. Is that all right? I've done a lot of travelling lately and my legs really aren't up to fighting right now.'

'But—'

'If we fight now, it will be awful, like two Slugkin trying to mate. Can you imagine! Let me catch my breath and we can kill each other in a more dignified fashion.'

'I . . . ' he trailed off.

Pari seemed to take his confusion for permission and hopped her way over to the bench where she lowered herself down. It was too low to tuck Sky-legs under, so she stuck them out in front.

'Ahh. That is so much better I can't even tell you. Perhaps I will commission a new tale for the Story-singers; the woes of my toes!'

'Are you making a joke?'

'I might be. People outside House Sapphire have been known to do that on occasion.' The exaggerated wink she gave him was so ridiculous, so cheeky, that he couldn't help but smile.

'Would you like a drink before we fight, Lady Pari?'

'I rather think I would. Would you like to share this seat with me before I beat you to a pulp, Lord Vasin?'

They looked at each other for a moment and then, despite everything, burst out laughing. For a while it was all they could do, and soon both of them were holding their sides.

'Truly, that was a gift, Lady Pari. Thank you.' He sat carefully, making sure his wing did not catch her shoulder. Armoured as they were, the bench was snug, but neither of them complained as they passed the honeywine between them.

Pari held up the bottle to her glowing arm to check how much was left and drank before passing it back to him. 'I must say, I'm surprised to find you here. This doesn't really seem your style.'

'Tell me about it.' He took a long, deep swig from the bottle.

'I have a question for you, Lord Vasin. What are you planning to do if you win?'

'*If* I win? Have you looked at yourself lately?'

She looked at the helmet sitting in his lap. The back of it no longer glowed properly, black lines spiderwebbing out from where his head had impacted with the ground. 'I could say the same to you.'

'I encountered the Corpseman on the way here. It wasn't pretty.'

'Happens to the best of us.'

'You too?'

'Yes. It wasn't pretty either.'

He raised the bottle. 'I'll drink to that.'

And they did, several times.

'Actually,' said Pari. 'I'm glad I ran into you because it means I can clear something up that's been bothering me. You see, I was surprised to run into the Corpseman at all, given that you supposedly defeated it already.'

Vasin cursed to himself. Why was he talking so freely with a Deathless from another house? Had he learnt nothing? His mother would be livid if she knew. A few half hearted excuses presented themselves in his mind but he let them go.

'The stories are exaggerated. It's maimed, not dead.'

'That's interesting.'

'What is?'

'You said, "it's maimed" rather than "I maimed it".'

Damn but she's sharp. It belatedly occurred to him that perhaps she hadn't been drinking as deeply as she appeared to be, and that maybe, he was slightly drunk.

Pari chuckled. 'No denials, my dear?'

He groaned inwardly. What was he going to do, even if he won, string her up next to Rochant? At best, that presented a temporary solution. Her old body wasn't going to last long, and there was nothing he could do to stop Pari's rebirth.

'What do you want?'

Pari smiled. 'Not a fight. How about I tell you how I see the situation and we go from there?'

'Fine,' he replied, taking another swig before remembering he'd meant to stop drinking.

'I suspect you have Lord Rochant hidden here in Sorn. I intend to take him somewhere safe. I also suspect that your intentions are the opposite. I know that a Sapphire Deathless is trying to wipe out Lord Rochant's line, though the exact reason escapes me. How am I doing so far?'

'Well enough.'

'Now, your being here tonight suggests that you are that Deathless, and yet your behaviour speaks of either the most horrendous underestimation of my abilities, or there being more to this than meets the eye.'

'It's certainly complicated.'

'Is it? I'd assumed you were either seeking revenge for your mother or you had plans to elevate a new Deathless in Rochant's seat. Though given what I know of your house, I'd have thought Lord Rochant would be the last man you could afford to lose.'

He sighed. 'I haven't lost him, he's in there.' He gestured towards the house. 'It's true what you say, though, the Sapphire are a mess. I'm a mess and I don't know what to believe any more. You want to take Lord Rochant home, go ahead, I won't stop you.'

Her lips quirked in surprise, and then she slowly got up. 'I suspect that's the best offer I'm going to get. Very well, Lord Vasin, though if you'd permit me one more question, I'd be grateful.'

'At this stage I don't see that it will make things worse.'

'That's the spirit. Why are you being so accommodating? A moment ago you were prepared to beat me to death, now you're all but rolling over and displaying your belly.'

Vasin sucked the last drops from the bottle. 'I've found my limits, Lady Pari. I thought by doing this I could restore the past, but the more I've done, the more I've changed, and not for the better.' He looked at her. 'What's the point in winning if we destroy ourselves in the process? There's no gain replacing one broken wheel with another. No, I'd rather let it go than travel any further down this path. Maybe it will result in my death, but at least I can still die a Sapphire.'

'If it makes you feel any better, that is the most Sapphire thing I've ever heard anyone say. I won't make any promises but I'll put in a good word to Lord Rochant. It seems to me that House Sapphire needs you both.'

He tried to smile but had the horrible feeling he'd just done a rather poor impression of Gada. 'He's in the side room to the left as you enter, but I'd advise you go quietly so you don't wake Mother.'

Pari took a step back, a look of genuine surprise on her face. 'Nidra is in there? Alive?'

'Yes. Even the Corpseman couldn't kill her.'

'Ah, she was the one who took its arm, not you!'

'It showed her mercy, spared her life, and that was her reply.' He looked into the depths of the bottle. 'It would be best for both you and Lord Rochant if you were gone when she wakes up.'

Pari walked towards the house, leaving Vasin on the bench. She wasn't worried about putting her back to him, there being no hint of threat in his manner. *Besides,* she thought, *I'm in no state to stop him if he changes his mind. Better to at least keep my dignity.*

Though it felt like she'd come off the victor in their exchange, she'd been troubled by it. There was a hidden history to House Sapphire that seemed directly tied to the attack on Lord Rochant. Between Samarku Un-Sapphire's account, and the things Vasin had told her, she'd put together many pieces of the puzzle, but something was missing.

The disappointment of not finding Varg here with the baby was mitigated by the news that Lord Rochant himself was inside. She feared for her servant's life, perhaps Vasin had already killed Varg, before this change of heart. She hoped not, now that Lan was dead she needed Varg more than ever if she were to get home intact.

Nidra. The name kept floating through her thoughts, niggling. Clearly, she had been involved in this move against Rochant, no doubt using Vasin as her agent. *Revenge then. Lord Rochant played his part in her exile, now she is getting him back. I'd probably do the same in her shoes. This must be the first step in some larger scheme against Yadavendra.*

She pushed the door open quietly, mindful of Vasin's warning. It wouldn't do to face Nidra in her current state. Luckily, the woman still slept soundly, her furs wrapped tight around her to ward off the cold.

Sky-legs were not made for stealth but Pari took her time,

testing the floorboards with her staff to find the quietest route. Soon she had turned left, passing into the second room.

Lord Rochant was revealed in the light of her armour, his beautiful new face hooded and his clothes dirty. Two of his fingers jutted at wild angles from their sockets, and his arms were tied in a position designed for discomfort, his head hanging down, awkward.

Her heart leapt at the sight of him, alive, even as she shuddered at the obvious signs of torture. *What twisted things these Sapphire are.* She stored her outrage for another time. When they were away from here and recovered, revenge would be taken accordingly.

She also noted a small bell tied to his ropes.

My first priority.

As she grabbed the clapper and tore it out, Rochant spoke, his voice calm but made rough by a dry throat. 'Back for more?'

'Always,' she whispered, putting a finger to his lips before pulling off his hood.

Instantly, he became alert. 'I was beginning to think you'd never arrive.'

'Oh, it was quite the adventure, but I always get there in the end.'

'A story I'd love to hear once you've got me out of this place.'

She glanced over her shoulder. All seemed quiet in the other room, yet her hands paused at the knots by his wrists, held there by instinct. Samarku's story and Nidra's seemed connected somehow through the Corpseman and High Lord Yadavendra. She had the suspicion that Rochant knew the details. 'Seeing as I have you here at my mercy, how about you answer some questions before I free you?'

The half-lit expression on his face was priceless. 'That's low, Pari, even for you.'

'What can you do? I'm a devil.'

'Yes, a very kissable devil.'

She rewarded the compliment with a hungrier kiss than she'd intended. *It seems this old body isn't as dead as I thought it was.* 'You know, my dear, being tied up suits you. Perhaps I should keep you this way.'

'I'm not going to dignify that. If you have questions, ask them. If not, untie me.'

'You wouldn't be taking that tone if you'd known what I've had to endure in order to find you.'

He glanced at his bound wrists and dislocated fingers. 'Please forgive my lack of sympathy.'

'You'll never guess who I came across in the woods on the way here.' He waited patiently for her to continue. 'The Scuttling Corpseman. It hunted me down just outside of Sorn. Killed a young man I'd become rather fond of and then nearly did the same to me.'

'Are you all right?'

'You know me,' she said with a light shrug, 'I'm a survivor. But as you can see, I'm not at my best. It had me, Rochant, and yet it let me go. Why do you think that it did that?'

'I have no idea.'

'Indulge me, have a guess.'

'Maybe it was playing with you.'

'I wondered that myself, but that didn't match the way it treated me at the end. It was careful, gentle in its own way. It even tried to undo some of the damage it had caused.'

'Perhaps it was charmed by you. I don't know. Can you untie me now, please?'

'Whatever the reason, it's astounding, isn't it?'

'Yes, yes, astounding. Fabulous!' he said, that famous reserve starting to slip.

'And yet you don't seem surprised.'

His features hardened. 'Is this a rescue or an interrogation?'

She wasn't sure where this was going. It certainly wasn't how she'd imagined it, but something in her couldn't stop. An urge was taking her thoughts in this way and she had to see it through. 'Interestingly, I'm not the only one to have been spared by the Corpseman. It once spared Nidra as well, I know that for a fact.

'Yet I can understand why the Corpseman might show kindness to Nidra, after all, she was accused of making a deal with the Wild. Perhaps they're kindred spirits. But me? I am Deathless, I am the enemy, the hunter. It doesn't make any sense.' She paused for a moment to study him, searching for some sign as to whether she was getting close to the truth. However, Rochant gave nothing away, studying her with equal intensity.

'But,' she continued, 'what if Nidra hadn't made a deal with the Wild at all? What if someone else had? Someone who loved her so much that any protections he gained would extend to her as well.'

'What are you talking about?'

She waved him to silence. 'You know, when I saw the Bringers tattoo you in the Rebirthing Chamber, I thought the silver marks on your cock were a warning to keep away from me. But it wasn't about us at all, was it? The High Lord had found out about your affair with Nidra.'

He sighed. 'I admit we were lovers once, a long time ago, before I was Deathless. Before you.'

'Then why add it to your legend now?'

'Because,' said a voice from behind them, 'Yadavendra didn't know about it until my trial, when he tortured the information out of me.'

Pari turned to see Nidra standing there, a simple but nevertheless lethal looking spear held in her hand. Despite her weatherworn clothes and unpainted face, she still carried herself like a Deathless. Unlike Vasin, there seemed no room in her manner for doubt, and unlike Rochant, she had full use of her limbs.

Oh dear, thought Pari, but she kept the dismay inside, raising her bravado like a shield. 'Ah, Lady Nidra. I must say you're looking in rude health for a dead woman.'

'No need for titles or pleasantries any more.'

'I suppose not, though I'd still make a case for the pleasantries.'

The point of Nidra's spear aligned itself with the deepest crack in Pari's chest plate. 'You aren't taking him anywhere.'

'Forgive my asking, but what ended your relationship?'

'His ascension of course. When he became a Deathless, I ended our affair. He begged me not to, but he was mortal then, he didn't understand.'

'I still don't,' whispered Rochant.

It seemed to Pari that someone who adhered to the rules so rigidly, who overruled their heart to do the right thing, was the last person to betray their house, but she had to know. 'I'm sorry to ask this, but have you ever made a deal with the Wild? Have you ever consorted with them in any way, by accident or design?'

Even before the angry retort left Nidra's lips, Pari knew, in her bones, that the woman had done no such thing.

'Ask me that again and the next thing you'll see will be the Bringers of Endless Order at your next rebirth.'

'As I thought,' Pari continued, 'which rather begs the question of who did make the deal.' She took a moment to shift into a more comfortable position, letting the staff take its share of her weight. 'I believe you, Nidra, just as I believed Samarku, your disgraced High Lord, when he denied it.'

Both Nidra and Rochant seemed caught out by that fact, allowing her to talk without interruption. 'The same trick, the slander that he was dealing with the Wild, was played on him. It saw him and his retinue exiled and scrubbed from the histories.

'Two people benefited from this; Yadavendra, who became the new High Lord of the Sapphire, and Rochant, who became Deathless in reward for his service.'

Nidra was nodding to herself. 'Poor Samarku, he has been here all this time?'

'Yes.'

'But how? His body must be ancient.'

'It is, and I fear no longer retrievable.' An image of the tree growing from the man growing from the tree rose unbidden and she shivered. 'He's part of the Wild now, but let us turn to those we can affect. It seems to me that either Rochant or Yadavendra made a pact with the Wild. We all know how Yadavendra gained from Samarku's fall. And Samarku told me that he had you in mind to succeed him as High Lord, not your brother. So it seems clear to me that Yadavendra could be behind this. He has motive.'

She turned to Rochant, who was staying mysteriously

393

quiet. 'However, there are other factors. If the deal was done with the Corpseman, and I think there is compelling evidence that it was, then I could understand why Yadavendra might wish it to protect his sister, but not why it might protect me. We barely know each other. But you love me enough, don't you, Rochant?'

'You know I do.'

'Just as you love Nidra.'

She wanted to stop here, not to say what was in her mind. 'It was you, wasn't it? You treated with the Wild to destroy Samarku, elevating yourself and Yadavendra. And then, when he wanted Nidra gone, you did it again.'

He said nothing, his gaze going to the floor.

Pari felt the satisfaction of having got it right, but also a great sadness. A part of her had been hoping to be proved wrong. She sighed, suddenly feeling her age in her soul as deeply as in her joints. 'Ah, I have been such a fool.' She turned the staff between her hands a couple of times. 'I should have seen that there was only one Deathless in House Sapphire who would not be bound by its codes, who would be clever enough and daring enough to do something like this.'

Rochant looked up at her, a fire in his eyes. 'Pari, you and I both know the rules weren't meant for us.'

'But the Wild, Rochant. Your actions betrayed the very heart of what we are. We are Deathless! We are supposed to protect against the Wild.' She shook her head, reeling as the truth of what Rochant had done hit home. 'Samarku's people, Nidra's people, the people of Sorn, all of that suffering and death! Why did you do it? Why? What were you thinking?'

'Release me, and I'll explain. The world is bigger than either of us dared imagine.' That smile touched his lips, the kind that came when he talked about his passions, the one that made him boyish and charming.

She could still see Nidra's spear, ready to move if she did. She looked at Rochant, feeling the pull of his gaze, holding it for as long as she dared before shaking her head and turning to Nidra. 'Don't worry, dear, there'll be no need to shed any of my blood today. Lord Vasin has reached his limits and it seems that I have reached mine.' She took a deep breath to steady herself. 'Now, how about you and I go next door and discuss what we're going to do about this sorry mess.'

With effort, she straightened and began to leave the room, Nidra backing away ahead of her, keeping her in sight, keeping that spear head ready.

'Don't do this,' Rochant urged. 'I love you.'

I love you too, she thought. But she didn't say it. *I will never give voice to those words again.*

They went to the far side of the house. A glance revealed that Vasin remained outside on the bench where she'd left him. Pari leant against the wall, and Nidra took up a position between her and the doorway. Neither spoke immediately.

I suppose I will have to be the one to start this. 'What do you think would happen if we took the news of Rochant's betrayal to High Lord Yadavendra?'

'He could be in on it, and even if he isn't,' Nidra shook her head 'my brother loves Rochant. He wouldn't believe us. My word and Vasin's are suspect, and yours would anger him, seeing as this is Sapphire business.'

Pari refrained from pointing out that such a catastrophic

failing within a house was really everyone's business. 'Do you have any proof?'

'No, but give me time and I might be able to get some out of him.'

Pari found she didn't want to think about that. 'I've put my immortality at risk coming here, Nidra, and so has your son. We need to think about how we secure our future, and how we might restore yours.'

'My brother won't stop until he has Rochant back.'

'Then let's give him back.'

Nidra's eyes narrowed. 'What?'

'Not him,' replied Pari, pointing towards the other room. 'The last of his line. If Vasin brought Yadavendra the baby, along with proof of Rochant's death, then your son becomes the hero and the search will be ended. But don't get too excited, I don't think we should actually kill Rochant, I think you should keep him here.'

'Why?'

'Think about it. What will happen when the baby comes of age?'

'Well, my brother would have it go through the ceremony of rebirth and . . . ' she nearly dropped the spear head, her eyes widening with realization. ' . . . it would fail because Rochant's soul would still be here. The Bringers would test the vessel, find it wanting and declare it to be an abomination. Then we could kill Rochant at our leisure.' She reached over and put a hand on Pari's gauntlet. 'Oh Lady Pari, I have underestimated you.'

Pari smiled. 'Many have.'

'But where is the baby? Neither my son nor my brother could find it.'

'Don't worry, I'll find it.' *If it's still alive.* 'The hard part will be restoring you. For that we need a new High Lord of the Sapphire, and I can think of none better than your son. I'd say he has about twenty years to get into position to strike, depending on how long High Lord Yadavendra feels he can manage without Rochant.'

'You overestimate my brother's patience, Lady Pari. We'll be lucky if he waits fifteen.'

'Then you'd best make your preparations quickly.'

'We've already been taking steps in that direction.'

'For whatever it's worth, I'll do what I can to see he has the Tanzanite's support.'

'That is worth a great deal to me. But why? Why go out of your way to help us?'

Pari sighed. 'Because it feels like the right thing to do. I can't help Samarku, but I can help you.'

'And how do I know you won't betray us?'

She'd been expecting this question to come up sooner or later. 'The way I see it, Lord Vasin and I know enough to destroy each other if any of this came to light. We have no choice but to trust in our mutual desire to live. Besides, this is bigger than you, me, or your son. This concerns the fate of House Sapphire and all the Crystal Dynasties. If Yadavendra isn't brought to heel, we'll turn our gaze inward, fighting each other instead of the Wild.'

Nidra set down her weapon. 'Then, Lady Pari, from this moment, consider us bound. I swear that if you help me now, I will never forget. My spear will find your enemies, my wings will bear your burdens, and my halls will ring with songs of your glory, for now and evermore.'

Pari held out her hand and Nidra took it, the two clasping

wrists. And then, because it felt right, and because she was tired, Pari leant forward, till their foreheads touched.

When they parted, Pari examined Nidra closely. Her body was still strong, but weathered, at least five decades worth of wear on the skin. 'Do you think you can hang on for fifteen years?'

Nidra laughed. 'Watch me.'

I like her, thought Pari. 'I wish we had spoken properly sooner.'

'Time enough for regrets when I am Deathless again,' replied Nidra, plucking the spear from the wall. 'Now let's go and find my son. There are plans to be made, and work to do.'

CHAPTER EIGHTEEN

The howls of the pack had become more regular, more urgent, seeming to Chandni almost like communication. *Or orders being given.*

Without needing to say anything, they all sped up, from slow walk all the way to near jog. It was difficult managing any kind of pace in the dark, especially while carrying Satyendra. She had hold of a patch of Glider's fur in her free hand, letting the Dogkin guide her.

And still the pack drew closer, flashing eyes now visible between the trees at their back, and other howls to the left and right. *If we don't do something soon, they'll overtake us and box us in.*

She could see them now, like white ghosts on the edge of her vision, each a match in size for Glider, but leaner, wilder, hungrier.

Varg unveiled his chunk of tanzanite, holding it high. As the aura of violet-blue brushed against the nearest Dogkin, there was a unified howl, and the startled pack recoiled to the safety of the shadows. Though the illumination was comforting, its glow was often snagged on its way to the ground by leaf and branch, making shadows that jumped, confusing.

They stumbled on as best they could, slowing to a more measured pace. 'Not far to Sorn now,' said Varg.

'Will the light hold them off?'

'I bloody hope so.'

'How long before we get there?'

'I dunno, maybe an hour.'

'And how long before the light fades?'

'Longer, at least two or three hours.'

'Good.'

They continued in silence for a while, the pack stalking them at a distance. Chandni was unable to keep her eyes from the edge of the light, certain that the radius of its protection was already shrinking.

She was pinning her hopes on getting to Sorn but it occurred to her that it was no longer a place of safety. The Wild had taken it. What if they got there and the Dogkin followed them in? Or worse, what if they encountered the Corpseman?

Because they were working so hard on not falling over, and because the pack was no longer announcing itself, they nearly walked straight into the two Dogkin blocking their path.

Glider came to an abrupt halt, pulling Chandni to a stop next to her, Varg carrying on another pace before realizing the danger. She felt as much as heard Glider's growl as two sets of sharp teeth gleamed where they touched the violet-blue light ahead.

The Deathless

'Keep eye contact,' whispered Varg. 'Whatever you do, don't look scared.'

Chandni thought that Varg could do with taking his own advice on the fear front. If they couldn't smell it on him, they'd certainly hear it in his voice. Nevertheless, she did what he said, falling back on her lifetime of training, composing her features, drawing on every ounce of her Sapphire pride.

Keeping eye contact was more difficult. *Which one of these monsters should I look at?* Now that they had stopped, she could see they were surrounded, the rest of the pack closing the circle around them – to look at one meant turning her back to another.

She decided that it was better to attend to one or two of the Dogkin than none, and focused on those in front of her, straining her senses for any sign of the others making a move.

But none did. She had the horrible sense that they were waiting for something, even if it was just for Varg's light to fail.

'Do you think we should try walking forward?' she asked. 'They might make way for us.'

Varg licked his lips as if about to speak but didn't answer straight away.

'Well?' she prompted.

'Wait. Let's just hold a bit.'

'I think that's what they're doing, waiting on us. We should take the initiative while we can.'

The crystal in Varg's hand started to hum, softly at first, then louder. As it trembled, the light around them shook, and then, on the edge of it, Chandni saw a Dogkin approaching. It was no larger than the others and yet it seemed larger, drawing her gaze to it effortlessly. Like the rest of the pack, its fur was white and sleek, and she had a sense of it being old, for it moved with a deliberate step. Unlike the others, this one had only four legs and a single tail, but what caught Chandni's attention most of all was its eyes. Like all Dogkin, it had mismatched eyes, one human, and one canine. Unlike them however, the human eye was a clear blue, unclouded, and when she met it, she felt a shiver deep in her soul.

Suddenly, vividly, the memory of having despatched Fiya came into Chandni's mind. For a second it was as if she were there, and then it passed, leaving her staring at a snarling face.

Before the leader of the pack could move, Glider shrugged off Chandni's grip and surged forward to meet it, growling low. The other Dogkin tensed but did not spring, their collective attention going from Varg and Chandni to the confrontation.

In that moment, she felt a great love for Glider. *She has such courage, such devotion. In her own way she is as loyal and true as any of the great heroes in Sapphire history. Does she see us as her pack, I wonder, or as her masters, or even as friends?*

The two Dogkin faced off, each growling at the other, but neither moved to strike. Chandni saw them like duellists before a match and was sure that the winner of this psychological battle would also win the physical one.

'Chand,' said Varg, with a hint of desperation. 'I can't hold on.'

'What do you mean?'

'The tanzanite. It's shaking so much I can feel it digging through my hand wraps and into the skin. If it cuts me out here I'm finished.'

'Then put it down.'

'If I do that, it'll go out.'

Chandni looked at the pack. She was no longer sure that it was the crystal holding the other Dogkin at bay anyway. 'Put it down, Varg.'

He bent and placed the tanzanite at his feet. Immediately, the humming began to ease, and its aura faded. Chandni took Varg's hand. It was down to Glider now.

In the last of the gemslight, they watched as the two Dogkin continued to growl at each other, making tiny shuffles left, then right, each moving to check the other, but neither quite committing themselves to full combat. And then, to Chandni's horror, she saw there was to be no combat, that the contest between them had already happened. The growling simply stopped, as did the movements, and Glider dipped her head. The older Dogkin padded forward, opened her jaws wide, and slowly, carefully, bit down on Glider's skull. Instantly, Glider's legs and body went limp.

Chandni wanted to cry out, to express her sadness, to let Glider know in her last moments that someone cared, but she feared doing so might break the spell and bring the rest of the pack down on them. *Poor Glider, you were so good to us. You didn't deserve to die like this.* She thought about the family back in Sagan, who had been killed by the assassins, of the guards slaughtered at Lord Rochant's castle, of her poor Mohit. So many had suffered that Satyendra might live. *Was it all for nothing? Will my sacrifice be for nothing too?*

The pack leader lowered Glider's head towards the floor until her body flopped sideways into the dirt, motionless. The leader stood straight again, raised her head skywards, and howled, long and deep. The other Dogkin howled with her, shaking the trees with their dirge. To Chandni it felt like it went on forever. When at last they were done, their heads came down as one, all of their mismatched eyes fixed on the humans.

'Varg,' Chandni whispered.

'Yeah?'

'I think it's time to pick up the tanzanite again.'

'Right.'

As Varg started to crouch, the Dogkin snarled, and as he reached out for the crystal, they charged forward. A violet-blue glow briefly flared into life, and then went out again, as one of the pack knocked into Varg, sending him spinning to the ground.

Chandni held Satyendra close, straining her eyes to see where the crystal had landed. Before she could find it, one Dogkin was snapping at her front, another at her back. She twisted and jumped away, hearing fabric tear and come loose. Varg was calling for her, the Dogkin were barking, and yet Satyendra stayed quiet and small, squeezing his little body as close to hers as he could.

Then, from above, something burst through the canopy, and her world exploded into light, sharp, clear and blue, the kind of light that made her spirits soar with relief.

Lord Vasin Sapphire came down on the nearest Dogkin like a comet, his gauntleted fists striking its body so hard that she heard bones snap. As she and the rest of the pack gaped, astounded, he was landing in a crouch, his Sky-legs bending, gathering energy, and then he was leaping up again, taking another Dogkin by the throat and lifting it. The action seemed foolhardy, the monster at least as big as him, but somehow, impossibly, he lifted it with ease, hurling it backwards to spin into a nearby tree.

By the time she registered the sound of impact, Lord Vasin was in the air once more, twisting, diving to come down on another hapless Dogkin. Yelps and snarls sounded around her, and she could see that in each place he touched them, their fur had burnt away, leaving black handprints on muzzles and necks.

When he landed a third time the pack fled, and it occurred to her that she hadn't seen their leader since his arrival. Varg was struggling to get up, and Chandni went to help, though only enough to get him to one knee. Once he was steady, she joined him, bowing her head in deference to the glowing Deathless.

Her blood sang as he turned towards them. 'When I saw your light shining through the Wild I came at once. You are Honoured Mother Chandni?'

'Yes, my lord.'

'And the babe in your arms carries the blood of Mohit, child of Rochant, lord of the Sapphire Everlasting?'

She tried to ignore the way Satyendra was whimpering in her arms. 'Yes, my lord.'

The sound of his hands clapping together were like the chiming of bells. 'Then we have cause to celebrate. I imagine you have quite the story to tell, when you are suitably rested, of course.'

She tried to keep the sadness from her voice. 'That we do, my lord.'

'Good. My people are hungry for stories of our glory and I tire of telling mine. I assume this man is Varg.'

'I am,' said Varg.

'Come then, Lady Pari awaits you in Sorn, and I must return the Honoured Mother and her child to their rightful place in the sky.'

'My lord,' asked Chandni, 'might I beg a moment?'

'What for?'

'To check on Glider, a beast that belongs to Lady Pari. She has helped keep us safe all this time. Without her, it would have been our corpses that you'd have found just now.'

'All right, but be quick. There are other things lurking in the dark.'

She nodded her thanks before helping Varg to stand. He made a grunt as he came upright.

'Are you hurt?'

In the light of Vasin's armour she saw his eyes twinkle. 'Just bruises.'

She smiled and they went over to where Glider lay.

'Well I'll be . . . ' murmured Varg. 'She's still breathing.'

One side of the Dogkin's face was swollen, with blood congealing around two puncture wounds, one above her eyebrow, the other under her jaw. *Not human blood,* thought Chandni, though she still found herself checking over her shoulder. While the demons may not come running for Dogkin blood, there were plenty of regular predators that might. The Dogkin's left eye was swollen shut, a puffy egg in a fur nest, but her right one regarded them weakly.

'Glider!' said Chandni, crouching down to stroke a paw. 'Do you think you can stand? Please try. We can't stay here and I can't bear to leave you behind.'

The Dogkin slowly rose, her head swaying slightly from side to side, like a giant drunkard.

'Good girl! I knew you could do it. It's not far to Sorn, we'll be safe there. If you just go a little further I'll get you more of that sausage you like.'

Glider's lips smacked together and she stared at Chandni with her canine eye.

'I don't have any now but I'll get you some, I promise. Now come along, we have to go.'

She and Varg led Glider over to where Vasin was waiting. As soon as he saw them approach, he turned and strode away, his easy pace deceptively fast.

While they hurried after him, Varg's hand crept into Chandni's. Though she couldn't feel the contact, she urged her fingers to curl round his.

'I think this is it.'

'What do you mean?' she asked.

'Pari will have work for me, she always does, and that Lord Vasin just said he was going to take you away.'

'Take me home, you mean.'

'Yeah, but I won't be coming with you.'

'No.'

They were both quiet a while. She found she did not want Varg to go, and certainly not so quickly. *I've become used to having him around. Could I ask for him to stay with me?* She dismissed the idea almost immediately. They'd never trust a servant from another house, particularly one with Varg's background. Besides, it was clear that House Tanzanite needed him, and his skills would be wasted in Lord Rochant's castle. *And I'll be dead. When Lord Vasin hears I have dealt with the Wild, not once, but twice, he will have me ended.*

I'm not even good enough for exile. When she thought about the reality, really thought about it, she knew it wouldn't work.

But then he said: 'I'm going to ask Pari to let me go. When I've finished this job, whatever it is, I'm going to come back for you.'

She replied: 'Good.' And she meant it.

Pari lay in the back of Varg's wagon, trying to think about the future, trying in fact to think about anything other than the way her body felt. Now that Lord Vasin was taking Rochant's grandchild back to house Sapphire and its High Lord, she hoped things would calm down.

As soon as her armour had come off, and she'd come down from that elevated state, the injuries inflicted by the Corpseman coupled with the cost of yet another ill-advised adventure nearly reduced her to tears.

When she thought about the risks she had taken, and what she had endured for Rochant, only to find out he was a traitor and a monster, well, she had cried about that several times. *I have displeased my High Lord, made an enemy of Lady Yadva Sapphire, nearly caused great embarrassment to myself and my house, and for what?*

She sighed, doing her best to ignore the rattling that accompanied the movement of air in her lungs. *At least I know the truth now. If not for this debacle, I would have been connected to Rochant when he was found out, and then no amount of charm would spare me from High Lord Tanzanite's wrath.*

The brief burst of positivity was soon drowned out again.

How did I not see it sooner? I pride myself on my ability to read people and he played me like a child in her first lifecycle. And curse it all, I had feelings for the man. He excited me in a way that I haven't been excited in a long time.

Of course, she knew that in truth he hadn't played her on every front. She believed him when he said he loved her. *A twisted love, but powerful, like a drug. I enjoyed it so much that I didn't think to question the rest.* She swore she wouldn't make that mistake again.

The wagon had slowed down, and she could hear Varg swearing at Glider. After it became unbearable, about two minutes later, Pari unwrapped herself and crawled up to the front. She regretted leaving her warm cocoon the moment she did so, then regretted it all over again when her joints began shrieking.

'What's going on?' she demanded.

'It's Glider. She's not up to it.'

'Neither am I but we do what we must.'

'Yeah, what are you doing out here? You should be resting.'

'There is no resting when Glider is like this. Ridiculous animal!'

Glider had not been herself since the Dogkin bit her, though physically, she was fine. One of her eyes was still gummed shut but it wasn't as if she used that one to see. However, despite her ears being perfectly intact, she was sluggish to respond to commands, and had the tendency to drift off or even stop if not attended to constantly.

The two of them took turns to order the Dogkin to hurry up, leading to a rather enjoyable game of trying to come up with the most outrageous curse. Swearing had always come naturally to Varg, and she was quite impressed with his efforts. In the end however, her extra lifecycles of travel, coupled with the fact that he remained shockable, enabled her to carry the day.

'You know,' Pari said once Glider had picked up the pace again. 'We might have to get a new Dogkin.'

Varg looked genuinely upset. 'Don't say that! She's just hurt is all, she'll soon pick up. And anyway, she'd never forgive me if anything happened to Glider.'

Pari looked at Varg. His attention was on the Godroad, and he seemed oblivious to what he'd just said. Her eyes narrowed. 'She? You are referring to Honoured Mother Chandni, I presume?'

A sudden burst of colour suffused his face. 'Yeah.'

'Tell me, Varg, what would a brood mother of another house have to do with the animals I keep, and the decisions I make regarding their future?'

'Nothing,' he muttered.

'Exactly. If Glider keeps up a good pace for the rest of the journey and refrains from making such an awful racket when I'm trying to sleep at night, then I'll keep her on. If not, she's going. Understood?'

'Yeah.'

'Good.'

He'd been tense since they'd left Sorn, and not, she suspected because House Sapphire had patrols on the Godroad.

Varg awkwardly cleared his throat.

Ah, here it comes.

'Pari?'

'Yes, Varg?'

'When I've got you over the border and back to your castle . . . '

'Yes?'

'I was wondering . . . '

'Yes?'

'Well . . . '

'Do get to the point. I'll be between lives before you finish at this rate.'

He cleared his throat a second time. 'If you'd let me go.' When she didn't reply immediately, he added: 'I can take Glider with me if you like.'

'Let you go? You know that isn't how it works.'

'Yeah, but—'

'It's out of the question. I have need of you.' She saw the stubborn set of his jaw and sighed. 'Do your duties well, and I'll make sure you're sent back to Lord Rochant's castle from time to time. That's what you want, isn't it? To see her.'

'What duties? You're not going to travel again are you?'

'Not in this lifecycle, no. I intend to spend what little time I have left in this body either sitting, sleeping, or indulging. But as I am doing that, my dear Varg, the world will still be turning. While my weary bones rest, and after, while my soul drifts, you will need to act in my stead.'

'Is something up?'

'Something is always up. Now, after you have smuggled me back inside the castle you will be required to travel to Lord Taraka's domain. Discreetly.'

'You want your name kept out of it?'

'Precisely. You will be there as an independent trader. Lord Taraka and his people are always horribly well informed, so you'll need a new name and a change of appearance.' He grunted in understanding. 'Once there, you will find a way to get to Priti and ingratiate yourself.'

411

'Which one is that?'

She slapped him lightly on the arm, 'Rashana's daughter of course, my great granddaughter. The High Lord has decreed that Priti is to be my next vessel.'

'Oh, right.' Varg looked uncomfortable. It was rare for a Deathless to discuss such things outside of family and very specific staff. 'Is she in danger?'

'Only of being too dull.'

'Eh?'

'Your job is to get close to her. I don't care how long it takes, well actually I do, but I don't want you to rush. Whatever happens, Taraka must never suspect my hand.

'After you've made contact with Priti and won her trust, I want you to teach her things, the kind of things her other tutors won't.' She gave Varg a sufficiently naughty grin to make him fix his eyes on the road again. 'Give her a taste for adventure.'

'And then what?'

'That's it. They're trying to limit her world, and I need you to show her some of its forbidden delights, but here's the tricky bit: you have to do it all in secret, and you have to make sure she keeps it secret too.'

'Why?'

'Taraka of course, he wouldn't like it.'

'I mean why do it at all? What's the point?'

'That's not for you to worry about.'

He made an unhappy noise but said no more.

She ordered him stop the wagon so that he could repackage her comfortably in the back. Then, as they set off, she settled in with her thoughts.

Taraka and my High Lord think they have cowed me with

their strategy. They seek to bend me to their will, make me malleable. They think they will force me to become obedient in order to match my soul with Priti's body and survive my rebirth. But I will not plane off the edges of myself to fit into a shape of their choosing. No, I will take Priti and mould her to my image, and then I will wait, and plan, and take whatever steps I need to to protect Arkav and myself in the future.

Yes, she thought. *That's more like it, Pari.*

Spend less time thinking about what I've lost, and focus on what I've gained and what needs to be done.

Rochant may be lost to me, but I have new allies in House Sapphire now, Nidra and Lord Vasin. Secrets and fear of mutual destruction bind us, a much more enduring bond than love can ever be. If I can help Vasin take House Sapphire and restore Nidra to their ranks, I'm certain they'll help me in return. No matter how dark my plans turn.

Those plans were just starting to take a pleasing shape in her mind when Varg's voice cut across her thoughts.

'If I do this for you, then after, I want to be with Chandni.'

'If? If you do this?'

He carried on as if she hadn't spoken. 'I don't care if it's part of some mission, I just want to be with her. It's not much to ask.'

'You are mine, Varg. I raised you, taught you, clothed you. You owe your very life to me.'

'Yeah, I know. But what you're asking . . . I'll be giving you my best years.'

'I already told you that I would allow you to visit.'

'I want to live with her.'

'In the castle? Oh yes,' she said, unable to stop the sarcasm, 'you'd fit right in there!' She couldn't see his face but the way his shoulders slumped was almost too much. *Oh dear. Poor, poor Varg.* 'You've really fallen for her, haven't you?'

'Yeah.'

'Well, I suppose I could let you go, it might be useful having some eyes and ears in the Sapphire lands. Though I should warn you, you may find her different when she's back at court with her stuffy friends.'

'What do you mean?'

'I mean that your relationship with her was forged in peril. It was scary and dangerous and I've no doubt you were an excellent guardian. How strange and exciting you must have seemed to her. But how will that relationship survive when she has guards, staff, a whole castle at her disposal? Think about it. She won't need you any more, and you won't fit in there.'

'She isn't like that.'

'I'm sure you know her better than I do.'

'Piss off.'

'Does that mean you've changed your mind?'

'No. Swear you'll find a way.'

'So be it. I, Lady Pari of the Tanzanite Everlasting, swear that when you have discharged your duty and I have returned, that I will see you placed within House Sapphire in a manner suitable to both of our needs. Happy?'

'And promise you won't kill Glider.'

'Fine, but I'll still kick her if she asks for it.'

He chuckled. 'All right.'

'Are you satisfied now?'

'Yeah.' He twisted round to face her. 'I mean, thank you. This is . . . '

'I can see.'

'Yeah,' he smiled at her, shy, and turned back.

Pari closed her eyes and smiled a very different smile of her own. She'd been planning to send him to spy on the Sapphire anyway.

Everything is falling into place. I may have misplayed this hand, but I'll more than make up for it with the next one. The thought of her brother, alone with her High Lord, remained a worry however. *Be strong, my dear Arkav, hold on. When I return, I'll come for you.*

Lord Vasin had escorted Chandni out of Sorn, the Dogkin's sad whine following them through the woods. She tried to tell herself it was because she'd failed to deliver on her promise of more sausage, but deep down she knew it was more than that. *Glider didn't want me to go. I didn't want to go either.*

Everything had gone smoothly until they'd reached the Godroad. Soon after they had broken the cover of the trees, a fleet of Lord Vasin's hunters had dropped from the sky around them. Orders were promptly given, and it was not long after that she was helped into a swiftly procured carriage, the original owners not in sight.

With trusted hunters driving and surrounding the carriage, and Lord Vasin himself gliding ahead of them, they pulled onto the Godroad to return to Lord Rochant's floating castle.

That was when Satyendra began to scream.

As with most babies, Satyendra had a whole spectrum of crying, and Chandni liked to think she was reasonably good at telling the difference between the noise he made when bored, to the one he made when frustrated, or when he was scared. This wasn't like any of those. This was pain, mixed with a pure animal fear.

When she picked him up and put his head on her shoulder, he bucked and kicked, his legs lashing out with surprising force. Chandni rocked him close, soothed with her voice, but it was as if he couldn't hear her.

Someone had, however, for there was a knock at the window, followed by the appearance of the lead hunter. Chandni recalled her name: Mia. She was young to hold the post, suggesting either a great deal of talent or backing from someone powerful.

'Honoured Mother? Is everything all right in there?'

'Yes,' Chandni replied, narrowly avoiding Satyendra's fist as it flew past her nose.

Mia pressed her ear against the glass. 'What was that?' Between the door and the screaming, it was clear she couldn't hear a word.

'Yes!' Chandni shouted. She hated raising her voice. It was so undignified.

'What?'

Before she could reply, Satyendra flailed again, bashing her cheek. It took her a couple of tries to get a grip on his arm but she managed it. His screaming became even more frenzied, and she worried she'd accidentally hurt him. *Am I squeezing too tight? I don't understand.*

As she struggled to hold him still she noticed something odd about the skin on the back of his hand. It seemed to be bubbling, like water boiling in slow motion, rising then settling again and again. Each time, it seemed to lose some of its colour, going from brown to white, until it became translucent, displaying muscles that swam, like creatures beneath the surface of a lake.

Dread hooked itself inside her. She did not want to know any more. She did not want to lift him from her shoulder so that she could see his face.

But that is what she did.

No.

The skull was visible through the skin, the teeth through the lips, and these seemed far too long, the gums reduced to pale shadows at their roots.

No, no, no.

Within the dissolving thickness of the flesh, he seemed a small and wiry thing, his arms gangly sticks, too long for the body, fingernails turning into vicious claws. The eyes rocked wild in their sockets, devoid of colour, the pupils tiny dots that seemed to float there amidst the threads of veins.

Such was her horror that she didn't realize the carriage had stopped. She was gripped by an unthinkable conviction: *This cannot be my son.*

Mia opening the door made her shriek as she put her back to the hunter, tucking Satyendra's hand into his wrap, pressing his head into her chest.

'Honoured Mother! Honoured Mother! Are you all right?'

'Yes, yes, you startled me, but I'm fine.'

There was a pause as Mia tried to surreptitiously glance over Chandni's shoulder. 'What about him?'

'He's been through a lot.' She could feel Satyendra's muffled screams against her chest and his knobbly chin, pressing so hard it was sure to leave a bruise.

Another bruise, she thought, and then immediately thought of Varg. *Oh if only he were here.*

'Is he . . . having a fit? He's very loud.'

Mia didn't have the guile to hide her disapproval. For a horrible moment, Chandni thought she had seen something of Satyendra's flesh peeking from the cover. But no, the reaction wasn't extreme enough for that. *She probably wonders how this noisy baby can possibly grow up to be a suitable vessel for Lord Rochant.* However, it was one thing to make judgements, it was another to let them show on your face. 'It is not your place to comment, hunter. My Satyendra has faced assassins and monsters and things you would not, and could not, understand. He has remained stoic throughout, a credit to the house. If he wants to cry now, in the privacy of this carriage, then he has more than earned the right.'

The young woman's nostrils flared with anger but she took a breath and then apologized. Chandni accepted it with a slight nod.

'And I'd thank you to close the door and get this carriage moving again. We must not keep Lord Vasin waiting.'

Mia seemed to agree with that fast enough, for seconds later the door had been shut, her face gone from the window, and the soft hum of the crystal-tipped wheels skimming over the Godroad became audible under Satyendra's cries.

Not knowing what to do and not wanting to see any more, Chandni squeezed her eyes shut and clung to Satyendra. *We have come through so much together, surely we will find a way through this fresh torment.*

She wrestled with the unmotherly sense that she was holding a thing and that her son was somewhere else, wrestled with it and crushed it. *There are many other explanations. If my Satyendra has become infected, it would*

418

make sense that the Godroad would burn it out, like a body does the fever.

An image of that face, that bloodless face, hung in her mind's eye. She screwed her eyes shut tighter, shaking her head.

No. He is not a monster. He is my son and he needs me. No one can see him like this.

She began to plan, considering which servants were best to ask for, and which should be sent away at all costs. She had planned to confess her crimes to Lord Vasin as soon as they arrived but that was no longer an option. *Satyendra needs me still. Only I understand the situation. Only I can protect him.* And if Lord Vasin judged her poorly for not confiding in him sooner, so be it.

When the carriage left the Godroad to bump its way across the Bridge of Friends and Fools, Satyendra simply stopped, his screams dying in his throat and his head falling limp. The change was so sudden that she put a hand on his chest to check his heart was still beating.

In the sudden peace, with his body warm against hers, she found her own head becoming heavy.

She dozed, dipping in and out of sleep as the carriage wheels jolted up and down, until they'd left the bridge, passed through the main gates and come to a stop in the courtyard. It wasn't far from where she'd first met Varg, barefoot, bandaged, and on the run. That felt like a lifetime ago.

Then, as now, she hid Satyendra under her cloak, the one gifted by the cook, Roh. *Ah, I must make sure Lord Rochant hears of her service and is properly rewarded. As soon as Lord Vasin is finished with me, I will go and see her, to say thank you and return her cloak.*

The door opened again and she climbed out to find Lord Vasin towering over her. She could see cracks in the crystal of his wings, but they were still beautiful, their curves caressed by the sunlight.

'Honoured Mother, may I?' he said, holding out his hands.

With horror, she realized that he wanted to take her baby. The question was a courtesy, one that she could not refuse. But if Lord Vasin were to see Satyendra in his current state . . .

'Do not fear,' Vasin added. 'I will be gentle with him.'

'I do not fear you, my lord. But what of the assassins?'

'Ah, of course. It must be difficult coming back here after everything that happened. I assure you, the assassins are dead. They will not trouble you nor your baby again, you have my word.'

Incredibly, she found herself thinking about Varg. *What was it he'd said? That Lady Pari suspected a traitor among the Sapphire Deathless? Some hand behind the attacks.* She'd dismissed it as nonsense at the time but what if an enemy of Lord Rochant remained, hidden?

'Will you be staying to protect us, my lord?'

Vasin turned his head away, his face unreadable beneath the helmet. 'That will be up to the High Lord. But we'll find out soon enough, he's waiting inside.'

'High Lord Yadavendra is here already?'

Vasin turned back to look at her, a firmness in his gaze. 'Yes, and he's expecting us.' He opened his hands again. 'May I?'

It was the second time he'd asked. If he had to ask a third then she'd likely be punished for irreverence. If she'd felt it might save Satyendra, then she would have endured it. But she had been raised a Sapphire, and when a Deathless asked you something, there was only one response to make.

'Of course, my lord.'

She opened her cloak, bowed her head, and held up her baby.

Vasin looked at the baby being passed up to him. It was tiny, no doubt taking after its mother. *Such a fuss over this fragile little object.* It hung loose in her hands like a sack, the limbs dangling, a thread of slobber swinging gently from its chin. He automatically committed the image to memory. On the rare occasions he got to see vessels in undignified positions, he always made sure to remember, so that he could call them to mind when his family were being intimidating. It was a petty kind of revenge, for of course, the family had all presided over him in his first lifecycle, and never tired of dredging up stories of bladder failure or when he'd fallen on his face, or when he'd—

He gritted his teeth and pushed the memories aside. It didn't matter anyway, for this baby would never become the vessel for Lord Rochant. This baby would grow up, go through the rebirthing ceremony, be tested, failed, judged and destroyed. Then his mother would kill Lord Rochant's last remaining body. Given that, whether the baby slobbered or not today was irrelevant.

It shook slightly in the Honoured Mother's hands and he considered letting her keep it. However, the image of him striding into the main receiving chamber and presenting his prize to the High Lord was too attractive to pass up. *But will this sad excuse for a baby diminish the moment?*

Vasin could see two different ways to showcase his victory. He could go direct to the High Lord, caked in the grime of his adventures and show strength. Of course, it was not the done thing to attend an audience wearing one's crystal skin, but had not the High Lord himself stamped on that tradition? This way, he could face Yadavendra on equal footing.

The alternative was to bathe, dress appropriately, and paint a picture for the ages of himself as the model Sapphire. If he was going to take Yadavendra's place one day, it might be better to honour every tradition to the letter, to show the house that he represented a return to stability. Becoming High Lord was a long game, and he only had a decade or two to make it happen. *Moreover, Mother's life depends on my success. I cannot afford a single misstep, especially at key moments like this.*

But what was better to display? Power or respectability?

He decided to take the baby and examine it before he made his decision, and noted that the Honoured Mother was glancing up at him in what seemed like barely concealed terror. No doubt she was reliving the night of the attack.

'You are safe here,' he murmured, lifting it from her.

Some element of the travel or exposure to the Wild had disagreed with it. It's eyes were puffy from crying, and it had a speckled rash all over, red spots dusting the brown skin. At the touch of his gauntleted hands, it began to stir, unhappy, and he passed it back hurriedly.

I cannot present it in this state, he thought, wincing as he imagined the scene. *Behold Lord Vasin, they will say, as he tracks mud across the halls, proudly carrying an ugly, wailing drool sack. No, I will not give my enemies or their Story-singers such a gift.*

'Prepare yourself, Honoured Mother, and your child for an audience with the High Lord,' he snapped. 'Do what you can about his appearance.'

She looked at her baby and choked back a sob of relief. To his surprise he realized she was not embarrassed by the state of it, but delighted with what she saw.

'Of course, my lord,' she replied. 'If it please you, I will hand pick some of our best to attend you and your hunters, ones whose discretion can be relied upon.'

'It does.' He gestured for Mia to join them. 'Go with the Honoured Mother. See to it she has whatever she needs, and keep her presence here secret for as long as you can. If possible, I want to make our good news a surprise.'

He sent word that he needed an immediate audience with High Lord Yadavendra but did not give details. *Let him be the one to worry for a change.*

The Gardener-smiths ceremonially removed his armour, one piece at a time, placing it on a temporary stand in another room, sealed and separate, to stop it bonding with any of the crystals growing in Rochant's Chrysalis Chamber.

The aches in his back and neck returned, as sudden as they were vengeful, and he was grateful for the bath and the massage that followed.

Afterwards, they dried him, painted him, and wrapped him in silk. Considering how little of his own things were here, Honoured Mother Chandni had done an impressive job of finding cuts of cloth that he favoured. *How did she know?* he wondered as he inspected himself, and wished his own staff were as savvy.

Naturally, the High Lord had taken residence in Lord Rochant's throne room. When he, Mia, Chandni, and the baby arrived, the doors remained shut, a stern-faced guard informing them that they would be permitted entrance shortly.

He's making us wait. The petty bastard is trying to score a point, but it doesn't matter, I've already won this day, and if he doesn't know it yet, he soon will.

It was incredible the difference an hour had made to her baby. Cleaned, wrapped in bright colours, and sleeping peacefully in her arms, it was virtually unrecognizable from the lumpy eyesore he remembered. He had no idea if they had treated its rash with oils or simply painted over it, and he didn't care, the effect was all that mattered.

When the doors finally opened, he flashed a grin at Mia, who met it with one of her own, reminding him that there was equally pleasurable business to attend to afterwards.

It was tempting to carry the baby in himself, but the potential for it crying and spoiling his moment soured the idea. *I must always think of Mother. No unnecessary risks.*

He turned to Mia and Chandni. 'Wait here until I call you.'

The layout of the room was such that visitors had a long walk to the throne, giving Rochant, or whoever sat in it, plenty of time to scrutinize supplicants. Yadavendra was there, his armoured form shocking in the space. *Does he ever take it off?* Vasin had always been told that there were dangers to staying in an exalted state for too long, not to mention practical difficulties.

It seemed the rest of his family were there too, making a loose half circle between him and Yadavendra. Yadva, Umed, even Gada, all of them dressed in their finery. He felt like he'd interrupted a secret meeting of the house. One that nobody had seen fit to tell him about.

A flicker of worry crossed his heart but he marshalled himself. Whatever they may or may not be planning, nothing would deny his triumph. *In fact,* he told himself, *it is good that they are all here to witness me.*

'My High Lord,' he said, bowing, 'my family, I bring news—'

'Wait,' replied Yadavendra, cutting him off. 'We were just hearing of Lady Yadva's exploits. Go on, daughter, I'm sure Lord Vasin will want to hear this.'

Yadva inclined her head, and Vasin was struck again by her size. She was the only one in the room not dwarfed by the High Lord, and she was out of armour, a close fitting layer of silks hugging her musculature, with an open robe, sleeveless, flowing over the top. 'After a thorough investigation I can reveal that the Deathless of House Tanzanite remain our true and eternal allies. The rumours that Lady Pari was here are just that, rumours. I saw her at her home with my own eyes. She's stuck in a crusty old corpse that can barely muster a walk, let alone break into this castle and kill our best.

'But,' she said, the word punctuated by a loud smack as she slammed her fist into her palm. 'I do not come back empty handed.' She paused to look at each of them in turn, her eyes reaching Vasin's as she added: 'In fact, I know exactly who orchestrated the treacherous attack on Lord Rochant and the reasons behind it.'

She left a dramatic pause, the kind of theatrical trick used by the most crass of the Story-singers, and yet she had the room. Vasin's throat was suddenly dry. If she revealed him as the traitor here and now, the fact that he had returned Rochant's blood relative would count for nothing.

They will destroy me in this very room.

Even if he ran, he wasn't sure he could outpace Yadva, and even if he could, Yadavendra would be on him in two sky strides, his gemstone blade in Vasin's guts on the third.

'I had plenty of time to think on my travels,' Yadva continued. 'And it struck me that I had gone all that way on the word of one man: Captain Dil. I questioned him, and when it became clear that he was trying to hide things from me,' her fist raised into the air, like the head of a hammer, 'I questioned harder.'

If she broke Dil then he would have told her about me. They will know about Mother! He glanced about, trying to keep his movements small. *I must find a way out of here. I must escape. I must warn her they are coming.*

He did not dare edge backwards, not with the way Yadva was watching him. When he made his move, and it would have to be soon, he would need to be decisive. Out of the corner of his eye he could see a balcony. If he could reach it, he could throw himself off the end. He might live out the day but it would mean true death. They would condemn him and the High Lord would forbid his rebirth, giving his Godpiece to another. Or worse, the High Lord might order his rebirth purely so that they could punish him.

Death! Every path before me ends in death and pain!

As he fretted, Yadva went on with her address. 'It turns out that Dil's ancestry is murky indeed. When his great grandfather was but a child, his family served the fallen one, Samarku. But unlike the others, he escaped banishment into the Wild and was adopted by well-meaning fools. Instead of accepting his good fortune, the vile man nursed his bitterness, passing it to his children, who passed it to theirs, who dutifully infected Dil with it.

'But no more. I have cleansed this sickness, and his lies will fester no more in the next generation, for he has no children.' She raised her fist again. 'Any more.'

Vasin fought to keep the panic from his face. What Yadva had said was only half true. Perhaps Dil's great grandfather had been attached to Samarku but the man had lived most of his life in happy ignorance. It was his mother, Nidra, who had made contact with Dil in secret and poisoned his mind with stories of his family's betrayal. Vasin wondered if he dared to believe his luck. If Dil had held out and protected Vasin's honour, then he and his mother were safe. The investigation would end.

'Forgive me, Lady Yadva,' said Umed. 'But are we to believe that all of this subterfuge and death was the work of one ordinary man?' His uncle looked tired and like he'd much rather be sitting down. The tattoo on his neck gleamed with sweat, and his voice quavered. Vasin thought it was cruel for Yadavendra to force him to stand in his condition.

'Actually, Uncle,' interrupted Gada, 'in a way, it was not the work of one man. It was the work of several, over generations. I think there is something almost Deathless about it all.'

'Exactly,' said Yadva, and he knew her well enough to know that it irked her not to be dominating the conversation. 'But in the end, he was no match for the real thing.'

'So a man is dead,' said Yadavendra, pacing before the throne in long ponderous strides. 'It means nothing. Where is our immortal friend? Where is Lord Rochant?'

Vasin waited as Yadavendra's glare cowed the room, each head bowing as the tip of his staff stabbed towards them, accusing.

But Vasin did not bow. His gaze met the sparkling tip of Yadavendra's staff, unflinching, before rising to lock eyes with the man himself. 'My apologies for being late to this gathering, my High Lord. I have just returned from a hunt.' He only dared risk a short pause, lest he be interrupted. 'A most successful hunt.'

'I will be the judge of its success, not you,' came the cutting reply, and yet the tip of Yadavendra's staff wavered.

I see it. Surely they all see it.

'I regret to inform the house that Lord Rochant's current lifecycle is over. I found the remains of his body in the woods.'

Yadavendra moaned and staggered back as if struck.

'However,' he added quickly, 'there is still hope.'

'There is?' asked Yadavendra, his voice smaller than usual, lost.

Vasin smiled, and then bowed as he signalled Mia. 'May I present Honoured Mother Chandni and her child; Satyendra, of the blood Sapphire, son of Mohit, son of Lord Rochant.'

There was such sweetness in that moment that he wished he could encase them all in ice, so that he could savour it forever. Umed was nodding proudly, Yadva had punched the air, even Gada's smile was halfway to warm. And Yadavendra's reaction was the most striking of all: tears ran from blood-shot eyes as he leapt to where Chandni stood. 'You are sure this is he?'

Chandni and Vasin assured him that it was.

Yadavendra swept the child from her, one handed, holding it above his head like a trophy. 'He is returned to us! Lord Vasin, you have excelled yourself this day. It will not be forgotten.'

The baby began to squirm in the High Lord's crystal grip, and he saw Chandni start to reach out before checking the impulse.

'And so, the wretched traitor and his assassins have been broken by my daughter, and this seed, that will grow to house Lord Rochant, our truest friend, has been returned to us by my nephew.'

The baby began to cry, *quite urgently,* Vasin thought, *as if it were in pain.* Yadavendra's eyes twitched in irritation. 'Truly this is a great day for the Sapphire.' He gave back the baby with more care than Vasin expected, leaning down to whisper in Chandni's ear, before straightening to add: 'You will all stay here tonight. We must feast.'

Vasin moved carefully down the corridor to his assigned room. The feast had been good, every sip of every drink, every bit of smoke inhaled, every mouthful of every dish, sublime. *Truly, victory over my family is the best sauce.*

When he reached the doorway, he paused, even his dulled senses sharp enough to detect that someone else was inside. A lusty smile tugged at his lips. He'd hoped that would be the case.

'Well met, my huntress,' he began, then stopped. For it was not Mia sitting on his bed, but a form twice as big and many times more threatening: Yadva.

'I am hardly yours to claim, little cousin,' she replied.

She seemed far too alert, and yet he remembered her drinking as heartily as ever. 'Cousin? To what do I owe the honour?'

'We need to talk.'

He suppressed the urge to yawn, it really had been an excellent feast. 'Now?'

She nodded, a predatory look in her eye. 'Now.'

'Is this about the story of how I fought the Corpseman? I'll tell you if you want, but you'll get a much better version if you wait till morning.'

'This isn't about the past. This is about the future.'

'Mine? Yours?'

'Yes, and House Sapphire's.'

He rubbed at his face, remembering too late that it was painted and he'd probably made an ugly streaking mess of it. 'Go on.'

'I enjoyed torturing Dil, did I mention that? He didn't resist much at all. There are Ratkin with more loyalty and Wormkin with more spine. My father was right to call him a wretch.' Her lip curled in distaste. 'I'd barely touched him and he was spilling his secrets, or rather, yours.'

Strangely, the tension that had been digging into his shoulders eased, and instead of saying something clever, or launching into a denial, he began sizing up the distance between them, and how lucky he'd need to be to survive close combat with her.

Yadva shook her head, and gave a throaty chuckle. 'You had us all fooled, you tricky bastard. Leading us to believe you were strung out on drugs and grief, when all the while you were planning a coup.'

She thinks I was behind this? Does she know about Mother or did Dil sacrifice me to protect her?

'But you know what, cousin?' Yadva continued. 'I was pleased when I found out. I thought you'd lost your spark but you were hiding it all these years, lulling us before the strike.'

'Why didn't you tell them at the meeting?'

'Because I like you. And because I agree with you.'

He couldn't help but look surprised at that. 'You agree with me?'

'Yes. My father is not the man he was, and without Rochant to prop him up, he'll fall much more easily. Delaying Rochant's resurrection another generation was a masterstroke. By the time that baby grows up, there will be little left of my father, but then, I'm sure that was your intention all along.'

Vasin managed not to laugh at that. *If you only knew what a blundering mess I have made of everything.* 'Well,' he said, 'you have me at a disadvantage. You seem to know all of my plans while I know none of yours.'

'Mine are much simpler. When the time is right, when my father makes another grand mistake, or when his sanity gets so bad that even cowards like Umed and Gada feel the need for action, you are going to denounce the High Lord.'

He tried to take this in. 'If I do that, Yadavendra will destroy me.'

'Oh if you did it now, he would, and we would stand back and watch while it happened. But I can see the path he is on, just as you can. A few years from now, maybe a decade, maybe more, but soon, he won't be able to stand against you. We'll need to get the others on side for things to go smoothly. It wouldn't do for House Sapphire to embarrass itself again. You work on your brother, and I'll manage Uncle Umed.'

'What about Rochant?'

'He's a realist. If he sees the house turning against my father, he'll follow. And if he doesn't, well,' she clenched her fists, making the knuckles crack, 'he'll be in his last body, weakened after his extended absence.'

'And if I succeed, then what?'

'Then, cousin, you are going to back me,' her palm slapped hard against her chest for emphasis, 'to succeed him as the new High Lord.'

He gave up all pretence of composure and gaped at her.

'Notice that I did not make it a question. You owe me.' She stabbed at him with a finger. 'I could have destroyed you today, yet I chose not to. But if I changed my mind . . . ' She didn't need to finish the sentence. Being Yadva, she did anyway. '. . . They'll send you to your last death, be certain of it.'

Vasin sighed. At a stroke, Yadva had ruined his plans. If he did what she asked, then his mother's fate would be in her hands, not his own. But what was the alternative? He sighed again.

'I'll do what you ask.'

'I know,' she replied, standing and clapping a heavy hand on his shoulder. 'You're mine now.'

He watched her gloating swagger as she left, and wondered how he was possibly going to salvage the wreck his life had become. One thing Vasin was sure of however: he hated his family just as much as ever.

An urge to find some Tack rose so strongly that he'd taken several steps to meeting it, taking out the locked box containing the last of his stash and opening it, before he realized what he was doing and stopped himself.

There is no time for distractions any more, he reflected, *every year that passes is one closer to Mother's final breath. I must be what she thinks I can be: her saviour. Yadva will help me remove Yadavendra, and I have until then to find a way to remove or control her.*

432

He picked up a little of the Tack, rolling it between his fingers.

But would it matter if I had this one night to relax? My plans will take years to put in motion and decades to complete. Surely one night won't make a difference?

He thought of his mother out in that shack with Lord Rochant and sighed. One night could make all the difference.

With a shudder, Vasin closed the box.

Acknowledgements

Although this is a new series, most of the people involved have remained the same, which is exactly how I like it. There's an odd thing about our culture where we tend to make a fuss when people do something well for us the first time, but don't make anywhere near as much fuss when people consistently do things well for us, year after year. So without further ado, let's make some fuss!

Four books, a novella, and a short story later, and I'm still having my work made better by my editor, the fabulous Natasha Bardon. Sometimes it's the ending, sometimes it's the beginning, but it's always relevant. I already have suspicions about what she'll want me to change on book 2. We shall see . . .

As ever, big thanks to cover wizard Jaime Jones. His work has not only made my books look lovely, but my house too. And of course, Dom Forbes, for making all the design elements hang together so nicely. Then there's Joy Chamberlain, my copy editor, who endures my terrible crimes against

435

language so you don't have to. Also, a special mention to Jack Renninson (a new person!) for providing an extra level of edits. I hope he appreciates the changes I made after his suggestions, and forgives the ones I didn't.

Thanks to Jen Williams for another year of advice giving and rant enduring. I am so glad I listened to her about that extra read-through!

What to say about my agent, Juliet Mushens, that I've not already said? I guess that's the point here. She's still just as amazing as ever. Always knows how to reassure me, always there when I need her, takes no shit, gets things done. She's the best. I look forward to repeating these things for years to come. Thanks, Juliet!

This book was difficult for me for a number of reasons. It's the first in a new series and a significant shift in tone from what I've written before. I wanted to challenge myself and do something different, yet better, whilst retaining everything I liked about my previous work (I have since learned that such a thing is impossible). As such, I've been a bit squiffy at various points along the way, and, if I'm honest, a touch on the needy side. So a warm and hearty thanks to my wife of awesome (+5), Emma, for being there throughout this book's genesis, and for being patient. I couldn't do it without her.

And finally, a word of thanks to you, dear reader. You are the essence beneath my wings.